Richard ~~~~~~ ~~~~~~ ~~~ 1947. He grew up in Ca~~~~~ ~~~ took a BA in English Literature from Willamette University, Oregon, and an MA from Loyola University, Los Angeles. He worked as a schoolteacher, a librarian, a mystery magazine editor and a report writer for a law firm before becoming a full-time writer. His novel FLESH was named Best Horror Novel of 1988 by *Science Fiction Chronicle* and also shortlisted for the prestigious Bram Stoker Award, as were FUNLAND and his short story collection, A GOOD, SECRET PLACE. Richard Laymon wrote many acclaimed works of horror and suspense, including THE STAKE, SAVAGE, AFTER MIDNIGHT and the three novels in the Beast House Chronicles: THE CELLAR, THE BEAST HOUSE and THE MIDNIGHT TOUR. He died in February 2001.

For up-to-date cyberspace news of Richard Laymon's books, contact Richard Laymon Kills! at: http://rlk.cjb.net

'An uncanny grasp of just what makes characters work . . . readers turn the pages so fast they leave burn marks on the paper' *Horrorstruck*

'If you've missed Laymon you've missed a treat' *Stephen King*

'A brilliant writer' *Sunday Express*

'Once again, Laymon offers unexpected, well-rounded characters blown about in a narrative that moves like the wind' *Publishers Weekly*

'Laymon's biggest strength is that he is able to provide lighthearted fun and disturb at the same time' *Fear*

The Beast House

Richard Laymon

headline

First published in 1986
by New English Library

First published in this new edition in 1994
by HEADLINE BOOK PUBLISHING

A HEADLINE FEATURE paperback

20 19 18 17 16 15 14 13 12 11

ISBN 0 7472 4781 1

Typeset by Keyboard Services, Luton, Beds

Printed and bound in Great Britain by
Clays Ltd, St Ives plc

HEADLINE BOOK PUBLISHING
A division of Hodder Headline PLC
338 Euston Road
London NW1 3BH

March 31, 1979

Mr Gorman Hardy, author
Baylor and Jones Publishing Co
1226 Ave. of the Americas
New York, NY 10020

Dear Mr Hardy,

I am writing to you because I have just read your book, <u>Horror at Black River Falls</u>, which I know was a best seller and must have made you a fortune. As the book is supposed to be a true story, I am wondering whether or not you might want to write a story I know of. It is also a true story. It is even more horrible than what you wrote in your other book. Let me tell you, it makes my hair stand up just thinking about it, and I don't scare so easy.

It is about a haunted house in the town where I live, except the house isn't literally haunted if you mean ghosts. It is haunted by some kind of a <u>thing</u> that's slaughtered maybe fifteen or more people over the past hundred years. I mean slaughtered. It makes mincemeat out of them.

I think it would make a terrific book for you to write.

If this sounds interesting to you, please let me know right away as I'll find someone else otherwise. I happen to think this is right up your alley. You can call it <u>Horror at Malcasa Point</u>, which is where I live and where the house is that the monster lives in, which is known as Beast House. Maybe you have heard of it.

Here is where I come in. Last Summer, I got my hands on this really ancient diary that was written in 1903 by Lilly Thorn. I work at my parents' motel, and found the diary under mysterious circumstances in one of the rooms I was cleaning. Nobody knows I have it. (Except now you know. You must promise to keep this a secret, as I would be in deep sh trouble if words of it got to certain people. I mean seriously. We are talking here about my life.)

Anyhow, this diary I found is <u>hot stuff</u>. Lilly Thorn, the woman that wrote it, was the very first person ever to live in Beast House, and she goes into all kinds of details about where the monster came from, and what it's like, and everything. I mean _everything_. If you can believe this, she even had sexual intercourse with it. I don't mean once, but constantly like she was obsessed. It's steamy stuff, as you can see from the xerox of the page I'll attach. The diary also goes into the first murders and let me tell you, this sure is not the way they tell it on the tour!

So if you are interested in another best seller, I think you should let me know and maybe we can split the take.

Sincerely,

Janice Crogan

Janice Crogan
The Welcome Inn
Malcasa Point, CA 95405

PS This thing here makes your ghost in Black River Falls look like a sissy.

From Diary I Found

He moved behind me. His claws pierced my back, forcing me to my knees. I felt the slippery warmth of his flesh press down on me, and I knew with certainty what he was about. The thought of it appalled me to the heart and yet I was somehow thrilled by the touch of him, and strangely eager.

He mounted me from behind, a manner as unusual for humans as it is customary among many lower animals. At the first touch of his organ, fear wrenched my vitals, not for the safety of my flesh but for my everlasting soul. And yet I allowed him to continue. I know, now, that no power of mine could have prevented him from having his will with me. I made no attempt to resist, however. On the contrary, I welcomed his entry. I hungered for it as if I somehow presaged its magnificence.

Oh Lord, how he plundered me! How his claws tore my flesh! How his teeth bore into me! How his prodigious organ battered my tender womb. How brutal he was in his savagery, how gentle in his heart.

I knew, as we lay spent on the earthen cellar floor,

PS See what I mean?

GORMAN HARDY
PO Box 253
Cambridge, Mass. 03138

June 3, 1979

Miss Janice Crogan
The Welcome Inn
Malcasa Point, CA 95405

Dear Janice,

I must begin by offering an apology for the lengthy delay in answering. Unfortunately, my publisher was rather slow in forwarding your letter of March 31.

Since the publication of *Horror at Black River Falls*, I have been bombarded by fan letters, not a few of which offered ideas guaranteed to inspire another blockbuster. Most such suggestions, of course, were utter tripe. Yours, however, did arouse my curiosity.

Unfortunately, my preliminary research has turned up very little about 'Beast House'. I was able to determine, through various traveler's guides of California, only that such a place does exist in the town of Malcasa Point, that several murders allegedly took place there, and that guided tours of the house are available. While this information is rather paltry, it does substantiate several of the claims made in your letter.

I found myself most intrigued by the photocopy you enclosed of the diary page. If the diary proves to be authentic and if it contains sufficient material along the lines you suggest, it might very well provide a launching pad for a study of 'Beast House'.

Naturally, I must read the diary in its entirety before making any commitment. Enclosed find my check in the amount of twenty dollars to cover copying and mailing expenses.

Very truly

Gorman Hardy

Gorman Hardy

June 11, 1979

Gorman Hardy
PO Box 253
Cambridge, Mass. 03138

Dear Mr Hardy,
   Enclosed is your check for twenty dollars. I am really glad
you are interested and I am sure your not trying to pull
something, but no way am I going to send you the whole
diary because where does that leave me? Maybe I am
paranoid, but I need to have an agreement about my split
before you can see any more diary. I think fifty-fifty would be
fair, as its all my idea and you can't do anything without the
diary.

       Sincerely,

Janice Crogan

       Janice Crogan

GORMAN HARDY
PO Box 253
Cambridge, Mass. 03138

June 16, 1979

Miss Janice Crogan
The Welcome Inn
Malcasa Point, CA 95405

Dear Janice,

Naturally, I am disappointed by your response concerning the diary. I do, however, understand your reluctance to place trust in a total stranger. As a professional writer for nearly twenty years, I have frequently been 'stabbed in the back', not only by strangers but by those I deemed friends. One can never be too cautious.

While I do not feel that the situation, at this time, warrants an agreement of any kind, I want to assure you that I remain interested in pursuing the project.

During the last weekend in August, I will be addressing a convention of the National Library Association in San Francisco. If you are agreeable to the arrangement, I will visit Malcasa Point following the convention, prepared to discuss terms with you, read the diary, and embark on such research as will be necessary to get the project under way.

Very truly,

Gorman Hardy

Gorman Hardy

1

'What you need,' Nora said, 'is a good fucking.'

'I see.'

'Look around you, take your pick. You're the best-looking gal here.'

Tyler didn't look. Instead, she took a sip of her Baileys.

'I'm serious,' Nora said.

'You're plastered.'

'Plastered but lucid, hon. You need a good fucking. You've been pissin' and moanin' ever since we got to San Francisco. Shit, if you didn't want to come to the convention, you should've stayed home.'

'I didn't know it'd be this bad,' Tyler said.

'What'd you expect, Ringling Brothers? These things are always a drag. What do you want from a bunch of librarians?'

'It's not that.'

'What is it?'

'The city.'

'What's wrong with the city? It's gorgeous.'

'I know.'

'You pissed 'cause the cable cars aren't running?'

'Sure,' Tyler said. She tried to smile, but couldn't.

'Come on, what's wrong? Cough it up.'

'I just feel rotten, that's all.'

'Rotten how?'

'Rotten lonely.' Tyler lowered her gaze from Nora's shadowy face. She stared at the candle in front of her. Its flame streaked and blurred as tears came to her eyes. She backhanded the tears away, and took a drink of her Irish cream. 'It's this damn city,' she said. 'Being here again. I thought I'd be okay, but ... everywhere I go, everywhere I look, they're all places I've been with him.'

'A guy.'

Tyler nodded. 'He even brought me up here once to see the revolving bar. We had margaritas. Then we walked down to North Beach and went to the City Lights and that second-hand bookstore across the alley I showed you yesterday.'

'When was all this?'

'About five years ago. I was a senior at San Francisco State. Dan – that was his name – Dan Jenson. He lived in Mill Valley, over in Marin. I met him on the Dipsey Trail.'

Nora made a face. 'The Dipsey Trail?'

'It goes from Mill Valley, up into the hills around Mount Tam, and finally ends up at Stinson Beach. Anyway, that's where we met. I was hiking it with my roommate, and he was running it to get in shape for the annual race ...'

'And it was love at first sight?'

'He knocked me on my can,' Tyler said. The memory of it forced a smile. 'I gave him hell for running me down. Not exactly love at first sight. That came later – five, six minutes later.'

'Was it onesided?'

'I think he loved me, too.'

'So what went ... oh no.' Nora suddenly looked stricken with pity. 'He died?'

'Hardly. I was accepted for graduate school at UCLA and he had a job in Mill Valley. I wouldn't give up grad school, he wouldn't give up his job. Simple as that.'

'Jesus, I don't believe it. You just threw each other away like that?'

'We both wanted our careers. I told him he could be a cop anywhere, but ... he was very stubborn. So was I.'

'That was the end of it?'

'I wrote him a letter. He never ... The way he looked at it, the whole mess was my fault. I was supposed to drop everything and marry him.'

'Oh Christ, he actually *proposed* to you?'

'He actually did.'

'Brother.'

'And you know what else?'

'What?'

'I'm twenty-six, I've got a job half the people at this convention would kill to get, and I'm thinking I made the biggest mistake of my life when I left Dan.'

'This just occurred to you?'

'It occurred to me a long time ago. I just figured, you know, I'd meet someone else.'

'And you haven't.'

'Nobody I love.'

'What're you gonna do about it?'

'What *can* I do? I made my choice five years ago. I just have to live with it.'

'Not necessarily.'

'Yeah. There's always the Golden Gate. Conveniently located.'

'Don't even joke about that,' Nora said.

'I really feel ... oh shit,' she muttered as she started weeping again. 'I really feel ... sometimes ... like I threw my life away.'

'Hey, hey.' Nora reached across the table and took her hand. 'It's not the end of the world. What I was gonna suggest – you feel so strongly about this, why not give him another shot? We're how far from Mill Valley? Not very far, are we?'

Tyler shrugged and sniffed. 'I don't know, half an hour.'

'So drive over tomorrow and look him up.'

'I can't do that.'

'Why the hell not?'

'It's been *five years*! He's probably already married ... He might not even live there anymore.'

'If that job was so important he let you slip out of his fingers, he'll be there.'

'I can't, Nora.'

'Why not take a shot? What've you got to lose? For all you know ...'

'No.' The thought of it made her sick with dread.

'If you need some moral support, I'll come with you.'

Tyler said, 'We have to drive back tomorrow.'

'What for? We've got two more glorious weeks of summer vacation before the rat race starts. What's so important you have to get home? 'Fraid your house-plants'll croak? Let's drive over to Marin, first thing in the morning, and try to find this Dan of yours. If it doesn't work out, what've we lost? An hour or so? We can still make it to LA by dark.'

'I don't know. I want to think about it.'

'What's to think about? Go for it.'

'I don't know.' Tyler finished her Baileys. She rubbed her face. 'I ... feel so confused. I'm going back to my room. Are you gonna stay here?'

Nora nodded. 'Night's young. I'll leave the connecting door unlocked. Wake me up at first light, okay?'

'First light? Sure thing.'

In her room on the sixth floor, Tyler flopped onto the bed. The ceiling seemed to be revolving slowly like the bar she'd just left.

She'd had too many drinks.

How many? Let's see. Three vodka tonics at the cocktail party before the banquet. God knows how much wine with dinner. Three or four glassfuls, maybe. Then two snifters of Baileys Irish Cream in the bar with Nora. No wonder the ceiling wouldn't stand still.

No wonder she'd blabbed.

If she'd been sober, she would've kept all that about Dan to herself. Nothing like a few drinks to loosen the tongue, make you say things you wish you hadn't.

Let Nora put down a few more, maybe she won't remember and they can drive on back tomorrow the way they'd planned.

Fat chance.

I can always tell her no. Put my foot down.

Her legs were hanging off the side of the bed. Her feet, resting on the floor, felt cramped. With an effort, she lifted one across her knee and pulled the shoe off. She sat up to take off the other, then remained motionless while a wave of dizziness passed.

5

At least she didn't feel nauseated. Just a little tipsy.

Tipsy's the word for it, all right, she thought, and let herself tip over. She drew her legs up and lay on her side, a bent arm cushioning her head.

What'll I do?

Stir your bones and take some aspirin and a few glasses of water or you'll really feel like hell in the morning.

The morning. God, the morning. What'll I do?

Tell Nora no. No, no, Nora, I don't want to go.

Why not?

Because, damn it, it would hurt too much to see him again – even to try. He'll have a wife, and she could've been me. You don't know he's married. He might be single and lonely. He might still want you.

Sure thing.

Why did I open my mouth to Nora? Because I drank too much. And if I fall asleep like this, I'll be sorry. Rolling onto her back, she drew up the skirt of her sheath dress. She raised a leg, and started to unfasten a stocking from her garter belt.

Dan hated pantyhose. To please him, she'd stopped wearing the things. She'd never gone back to them.

She'd never gone back to smoking pot, either.

And she still wore her hair short, the way he liked it. Makes you look like Peter Pan, he'd said. Peter Pan's a boy, she'd reminded him, and added that perhaps the hairstyle appealed to his latent homosexuality. Oh yeah? he'd said. Come here and we'll see if I'm a fag.

Big macho cop.

God, she missed him.

She pulled the garter belt out from under her. She

slipped her panties down, and kicked them off. Then she stretched, enjoying the feel of the cool bedspread against her buttocks and legs. She could doze off right now, so easily. With a deep sigh, she sat up. She struggled with the zipper at the back of her dress, pulled the dress over her head, and removed her bra. She climbed off the bed and started to gather her clothes.

While she'd kept her hair the same, stayed away from pantyhose and pot, changed very little about herself since leaving Dan, there was one major difference. She'd been chubby, then. In her first term at UCLA, she'd dropped fifteen pounds. As if she'd left her appetite with Dan. Though the appetite had eventually returned, she'd had no trouble keeping the weight off.

She took her nightgown from the suitcase, but didn't put it on. She stepped in front of the mirror. Her eyes looked a little funny. That was the booze. She drew a forefinger over her cheekbone. For all Dan knew, she didn't have cheekbones. Or a waist. Or hip-bones.

She grinned at the Tyler Moran he'd never seen.

He'll go ape, she thought.

Her heart started thudding, for she suddenly realized she would be making that trip tomorrow. No matter the pain, no matter the outcome. If she didn't, she would always wonder about Dan, about the second chance thrown away, and she would never stop regretting it.

Her racing heart made her head throb.

She put the nightgown on. In the bathroom, she took three aspirin and drank three full tumblers of cold water.

Then she went to bed.

She lay in the darkness, remembering the look and feel and voice of Dan Jenson, wondering how he might have changed, worrying about what she might find tomorrow in Mill Valley, hoping.

Tyler smiled the next morning when she saw the Mill Valley bus depot through her windshield. 'That used to be the best place for paperbacks in the whole town,' she said. 'Wish I had a buck for every hour I spent in there.'

'How're the nerves?' Nora asked, grinning at her from the passenger seat.

'Holding out. But just barely.' She wiped her sweaty hands on the legs of her corduroys. The nerves, in fact, were not good. Her heart was beating fast, her mouth was dry, and the armpits of her blouse felt sodden.

'A quaint little burg,' Nora said.

'It used to be quainter.' She drove slowly along Throckmorton, past brightly painted shops. The road curved. To the left was a wooded area. 'Here's where the old mill used to be. The Dipsey Trail starts over there.'

'The famous Dipsey Trail.'

She turned right onto a sideroad, and stopped at the curb.

'This it?'

'This is it,' Tyler said. She took a deep breath and let it out slowly. 'It's that apartment house across the street.' Ducking, Nora looked out of the window. 'Rustic,' she said.

'Quaint and rustic.'

'Can you hack it?'

'We came this far,' Tyler told her, and tried very hard to smile.

8

'Do you want me to wait here?'

'Are you kidding?'

They climbed from the car. While Tyler waited, Nora took her sweater off and tossed it on her seat. 'Won't be needing that,' she said. She stepped around the rear of the car. She was wearing short culottes and tennis shoes, and without the sweater it was plain that she wore no bra. The powder blue T-shirt clung to her breasts. Her nipples made the fabric jut as if fingers were pushing it out. Tyler wished Nora had kept the sweater on, and she had second thoughts about her friend coming along.

What if Dan...? No, that's ridiculous.

He probably doesn't even live here anymore.

They crossed the street and climbed a slanted walkway toward the weathered wood-frame apartment house. Nora's breasts jiggled slightly with each step.

Dan won't notice. *Of course he will.*

Even dressed modestly, Nora drew men like iron filings to a magnet. Her size must be part of it. She was five eleven barefoot. She dwarfed most other women, Tyler included. She was slender, but not at all gawky. Though her face was a bit too long, her teeth too prominent, her chin not quite prominent enough for real beauty, her blue eyes had an intensity that made the imperfections less noticeable. And there was something erotic about her wide mouth, her full lips.

Nora radiated sexuality. Not only men noticed it. So did women, and many seemed to resent it.

Tyler was not very happy about it herself, as they stepped into the shadowed entryway.

Don't worry, she told herself. I'm the one Dan loved.

Besides, Nora won't try anything. She's my best friend. She knows how I feel.

Yeah. Outclassed.

Forget it.

Tyler stepped close to the panel of mailboxes. 'He was in number four,' she said.

The name, embossed on a strip of red plastic above the mail slot, was B. Lawrence. They checked the other labels. 'No Jenson,' Nora said. 'You sure you've got the right building?'

'Positive.' She felt a tug of disappointment, but it was mixed with relief. Her voice sounded shaky as she said, 'I knew it'd be a waste of time.'

Nora squeezed her shoulder. She looked determined. 'It's not over yet, hon. You're with Nora Branson, ace reference librarian. What I don't know, I find out. Just a matter of research. First we check on B. Lawrence, then the manager. If they don't pan out, there's the telephone directory. If that doesn't work, we'll pay a visit to the local constabulary. If Dan's not with them anymore, they'll probably know where he went. He'll have friends in the department, not to mention a personnel file that'll tell where they sent his references.'

'Maybe we should just forget it.'

'No way. This is your life we're talking about. You obviously love the guy. One way or another, we're gonna find him for you. Where's number four?'

Tyler sighed. 'Upstairs.'

She followed Nora up the wooden stairway to a balcony that stretched the length of the building front. They stopped at the first door to the right. Five years ago, it had been stained wood. Since then, someone had applied bright, lime green paint. The trim was orange. A wind-chime of clay pipes, suspended just above the door, clinked softly in the breeze.

Tyler knew that Dan didn't live here anymore, but her heart thudded wildly when Nora rang the doorbell. She took deep breaths, trying to calm herself.

The door opened. A short, chubby woman in a *muumuu* and curlers smiled out at them. 'Greetings,' she said. 'What can I do for you?'

Before Tyler could answer, Nora said, 'We're looking for Dan Jenson. Apparently he used to live here.'

'Righto. Steely Dan the cop. My old bud. You friends of his?'

Nora darted a thumb at Tyler. 'They're old buds.'

'Ah ha!' Nodding, she studied Tyler with one eye half shut, and shook a forefinger at her. 'I *knew* it, knew I'd seen your face. Knew it the minute I looked at you. You're the girl in the picture. That eight by five he kept over the fireplace. Sure. That *was* you, wasn't it?'

Tyler shrugged. She didn't know the picture, but Dan had always been snapping photos of her. He liked to catch her unaware – for the 'natural look', as he called it. He'd even taken a shot, once, as she stepped out of the shower. She blushed at the memory. Obviously, that hadn't been the picture he'd blown up for the mantel.

'The girl he called Tippy, am I right?'

Tyler nodded.

'Tippy?' Nora asked.

'Short for Tippecanoe,' she explained. 'Tippecanoe and Tyler, too.'

'That's Dan. Always one for the nicknames. I was always Barbie Doll. I lived down in number one, back when he was here. He used to have me up for pizza. Oh, he made luscious pizza.'

'My recipe,' Tyler muttered. She felt an ache like homesickness. 'I showed him how to make it.'

'Oh, I'm drooling at the thought of it. How I miss his pizza.'

'I could send you the recipe.'

'Would you?' She snatched Tyler's hand and squeezed it. 'You're such a dear. It's no wonder at all Dan was that stuck on you. He'll be tickled to death to see you again. You will be . . .?'

'Then you know where he is?' Nora asked.

'Why, sure.'

Tyler's heart lurched.

'He left here . . . oh, better than two years ago. I moved right in. My old apartment was so cramped, it was like living in a closet. This is two bedrooms, you know. Gives me some space to spread out. A girl needs her elbow room.'

'Is Dan still in Mill Valley?' Nora persisted.

'Oh no. He took a job on the force up at Malcasa Point. Said he wanted to get out of the Bay Area, though I can't imagine why. You know Malcasa? No? Let me tell you, it's the sticks. I can't feature *any*one living there. But different strokes, am I right? Not even a decent restaurant, much less a movie theater. I doubt there's a shopping mall within fifty miles. When I say sticks, I mean sticks. But that's what he wanted and that's what he got.'

'Malcasa Point?' Nora asked.

'Hang on a sec, I'll get the address.' As she stepped over to a lamp table, she kept talking over her shoulder.

'I'll admit, now, I haven't heard from him in a year or better. Got a card from him last Christmas – no, that was two Christmases ago, not long after he moved. Seemed to like it fine up there.' She took an address book from the lamp-table drawer, and came back. 'I sent him a postcard from Naples this past December. Spent the holidays there. Oh, a marvelous city, Naples.' She flipped through the pages of her book. 'Ah, here we be. Jenson, Dan. Ten Seaside Lane, Malcasa Point.'

Tyler's hand trembled badly as she scribbled the information on a notepad. 'Why don't you give me your name? Is it Lawrence?'

'Righto. Barbara Lawrence. That's Barbara with three a's, not like Streisand. Can you imagine, Bar-bra? Sounds like a steel brassière, am I right?'

'When Dan wrote to you,' Nora said, 'did he say anything about being married?'

'Not a word. Single, far as I know.' She winked at Tyler. 'Now you will send me that recipe, won't you?'

'Absolutely.'

'How far is this Malcasa Point?' Nora asked.

'Oh, you can make it in, I'd say, maybe three hours. That's if you don't dawdle. You go straight up the Coast Highway, on a good piece past Bodega. You have a map?'

'In the car.'

'Well, you can't miss it. Now, make sure you give Dan regards from Barbie Doll.'

'We'll do that,' Tyler assured her.

'And for the love of Mike, whatever you do up there, don't miss the Beast House tour. Tacky tacky. You'll love it. It's a scream.'

13

2

After five minutes on the narrow, twisting Coast Highway with its cliff only yards away and the ocean far below, Tyler fastened her seatbelt.

'Might be better off without it,' Nora told her.

'You're right.' She opened the buckle. 'It'd hinder my leap.'

'I'm just glad we're on the inside lane.'

'We won't be, coming back.'

'Let's take an inland route.' Nora picked up the map and studied it for two or three minutes. 'Maybe take 128 over to 101.'

'Whatever,' Tyler said. 'We can worry about it when the times comes.'

'I think we'd better plan on spending the night in Malcasa. It'll be mid-afternoon by the time we get there.'

'Let's just play it by ear.'

'Wonder what it's got in the way of motels.' She opened the glove compartment and pulled out the Automobile Club tour guide for California and Nevada. 'Let's see here. We already know there're no decent restaurants, much less a movie theater.' She flipped through the pages. 'Here we go. Los Gatos, Madera,

15

Mommoth Lakes. Whoops, no Malcasa Point. Maybe we won't spend the night.'

'Every town has a motel. There must be at least one.'

'I hope so. Nothing Triple-A-approved, though. Maybe a fleabag or two. Let's see what the little burg's got in the way of attractions.' She turned toward the front of the book. 'Malcasa, Malcasa,' she mumbled as she searched. 'Ah-ha! It's actually here, can you believe it? Malcasa Point, altitude thirty-four feet. Such height! Hope I don't get nosebleeds. Only one entry for the place. Beast House. Not to be confused with *Animal House*.' She chuckled at her little joke, then began to read aloud from the guide book. "Beast House, 10 Front Street. Claimed to be the scene of several grisly murders, this Victorian relic was built in 1902 by the widow of the notorious outlaw, Lyle Thorn. Featured are displays of the murder scenes with lifelike wax figures depicting the victims. Tours daily ten till four; closed holidays. Adults four dollars, under twelve, two dollars." Maybe we can take it in while we're there.'

'Barbie Doll thought highly of it,' Tyler said.

'Right. Tacky tacky.'

In the rearview mirror, Tyler saw a Porsche closing in fast. She held her breath as it swung out and roared alongside. It shot by. It swerved back into the lane, missing their front bumper by inches, just in time to avoid a head-on with an approaching station wagon.

'Asshole,' Nora muttered. 'Porsches, VW bugs, and pickup trucks. Gotta watch out for 'em. They've all got maniacs behind the wheel.'

'Not to mention the big rigs,' Tyler said. 'At least there's none of them along here. Nothing like an eighteen-wheeler tailgating you.'

'They're murder. Somebody ought to build a truckers museum and fill it with wax figures depicting their victims.'

'Call it Peterbilt House.'

They stopped for lunch at a restaurant overlooking the water of Bodega Bay. Nora drank Dos Equiis with her plate of fried clams. Tyler, nervous about the twisting road ahead, had a glass of Pepsi with her cheeseburger.

'Look familiar?' she asked, nodding at the expanse of glinting water beyond the window.

'Should it?' Nora asked.

'Remember *The Birds?*'

'The film?'

She nodded, and bit into her burger. Juice dribbled down her chin. She mopped it off with a napkin. 'Yeah,' she said. 'Way across there? That peninsula's where Rod Taylor lived.'

'No kidding?'

'Remember? Tippi Hedren took a motorboat across to it, and that bird divebombed her?'

'Sure. So that's where it happened. I'll be damned. I saw that film three or four times.'

'The schoolhouse is around here someplace, I think.'

'How about the Bates Motel?'

'Wrong movie.'

'That's probably up at Malcasa Point. The one Triple A won't approve.'

'Actually, it's at Universal Studios.'

'I know that, dimbo. Just making a little joke.'

On the way out of Bodega, they drove past a small, wood-frame schoolhouse. 'Bet that's the one they used,' Tyler said.

'Where's the jungle gym?'

Tyler shrugged.

'They probably had to junk the thing after all those birds crapped on it.'

They left Bodega behind. In a short while, Nora was asleep, slumped down in her seat with her knees against the dashboard, her head tilted sideways, her mouth drooping open. Tyler felt a little groggy herself. She lowered her window to catch the fresh ocean breeze on her face.

Thoughts of Dan filled her mind, memories of their times together. She could hardly believe that in just a couple more hours she might actually be seeing him again.

He'd kept a photo of her above the fireplace. He wouldn't have done that unless he still cared. And he'd talked to Barbie Doll about her.

Barbie Doll. What an awful nickname.

He used to invite her up for pizza. Had they...?

Tyler felt a tightness inside.

Not Barbie Doll. Why not? Because she's a good ten years older than Dan, and fat? I wasn't exactly svelte and it didn't bother him. At least he never complained.

And so what if Dan did have something going with Barbie? Why not?

Hell, they were probably just friends.

Five years. Face it, he's been with plenty of women since me. Some of it must've been serious.

She wiped her sweaty hands on the legs of her corduroys.

What's the good of thinking about it?

But she couldn't stop. With a sick feeling of despair, she wondered how many women he'd taken to bed. Who were they? Did some remind him of her, and make him miss her? Maybe he never thought about her at all anymore, her image erased by a new love.

Stop this!

At least he's not married. Or he wasn't as of two Christmases ago. Or he had been married by then, but didn't mention it in his card to Barbie. Anything was possible. He might even have moved again. Might've left Malcasa. Wouldn't that be . . .

She was shocked from her thoughts as she rounded a curve and faced a green pickup truck. It was just ahead passing an RV, speeding straight at her. She hit the horn and brakes.

Nora lurched awake. 'Holy shit!'

Tyler swung wide to make room, her right-hand tires spraying up dirt and gravel on the road's shoulder.

The driver of the pickup smirked and saluted the brim of his cowboy hat as he shot past.

Nora gave him the finger. 'Asshole!' she yelled.

Tyler steered her car back onto the road.

'Christ,' Nora gasped. She clutched her chest as if to keep her heart from jumping out. 'Fuckin' redneck scum-butt!'

Tyler took a deep breath. Her own heart was sledging. Her legs felt hot and weak.

'Fucker woulda killed us,' Nora said. 'What'd I tell you? Pickup trucks! Put a bastard in a pickup, he thinks he's King Shit.'

Moments later, a green pickup appeared in the rearview mirror. Tyler groaned. 'He's coming back.'

'You're kidding.' Nora looked over her shoulder. 'Oh, shit.'

'Maybe it's not him.'

'It's him. Oh, shit. Guess I shouldn't have flipped him the bird.'

The truck bore down on them. Then it was tailgating, speeding along no more than a yard from their rear bumper, its horn blasting. Nora faced forward and shrank down in her seat. She made a sick-looking smile at Tyler. 'What do you think, is he pissed or horny?'

'I don't want to find out,' Tyler said. She searched the area ahead. For as far as she could see, the two-lane strip of road was bordered by brown, desolate hills and a slope dropping away to the shoreline. No gas stations where she might stop for help. No shops or cafés. No dwellings of any kind.

'Where's the highway patrol when you need it?' Nora muttered.

'Where's civilization when you need it?'

Tyler eased down on the gas pedal. The pickup fell away as the speedometer needle climbed from fifty-five to sixty to sixty-five. Then she was pushing seventy. She was on a straightaway, but she could see a bad curve in the distance – maybe a mile ahead. And the pickup was gaining fast.

'No way,' she muttered. She took her foot off the accelerator. Their speed dropped quickly. She gazed at the rearview, trying to fight her growing panic as the truck raced closer. It didn't seem to be slowing. She braced herself for the impact. At the last instant, the pickup swung into the southbound lane and pulled alongside. Its horn blared like someone screaming into Tyler's ears. Instead of passing, it kept even. The road ahead was clear, at least for now. She half expected the pickup to swerve and bump her, sending the little Omni careening into the hillside. Her foot hit the brake pedal. The pickup shot by, cut in front, and slowed. She mashed the brake. With a glance at the rearview mirror, she saw a Mustang bearing down fast. She was doing twenty, then fifteen, the pickup blocking her way.

'Oh, Christ!' she cried. She pulled onto the bumpy shoulder and stopped. The pickup swung over. The Mustang to the rear crossed the center line and sped past. The pickup backed up until it almost touched the Omni's front bumper.

With a trembling hand, Tyler cranked her window. She elbowed the lock button. Through the rear window of the pickup's cab, she watched the man take off his cowboy hat.

'You wouldn't happen to have a gun handy?' Nora asked.

'Oh, sure.'

'I didn't think so.'

The man scooted across the front seat. He opened the passenger door and climbed down. He didn't look at them. He scowled at the ground as he ambled closer.

He was a big man, maybe thirty years old, with eyes that seemed too small for his massive face, and thick bulging lips. His jaw looked broader than his forehead.

'Fucking Neanderthal,' Nora muttered.

He suddenly looked up. His tiny eyes flicked from Nora to Tyler. His lips curled into a grin. He raised his middle finger and twisted his hand slowly as if screwing it in. Tyler pressed her knees together.

'Pig,' Nora said.

Using his middle finger, he gestured for them to come out.

Nora leaned close to the windshield. 'Not on your life, shithead!' she yelled.

'For Christsake!' Tyler gasped.

Smirking, the man snapped off the Omni's radio antenna. He swung it like a riding crop. Tyler flinched as it lashed the windshield.

'Shove it up your ass!' Nora yelled.

Tyler punched her shoulder. 'Stop that! It's bad enough! Christ, don't antagonize him.'

He struck the windshield again. Tyler rammed the shift to reverse and sped backward, the car bouncing over the rough ground of the shoulder. She wanted to swing out onto the road, but a huge camper van was rushing in from the rear. Steering away to avoid it, she felt the car tip. She hit the brakes. The RV roared past, close enough to make the Omni shudder with its buffeting wind. She shifted to first, stepped on the gas pedal and let out the clutch. She heard a rear tire spin. But the car didn't move.

The man, jogging toward them, stopped to pick up a rock the size of a softball.

Nora shoved her door open. She leaned out and glanced back and shut the door and locked it. 'We're hanging over the ditch,' she reported.

'Oh, great.'

'That rock, he can bash his way in.'

'I know, I know!'

The man hurried closer, rock in one hand, antenna in the other.

Tyler tried again to make the car move.

'Look,' Nora said, 'he'll just demolish a window and get in anyway.' She opened her door again.

'Don't!'

She climbed out and stepped toward the front of the car.

'Nora!'

She leaned back, rump against the hood, and folded her arms across her chest. The man stopped jogging. One side of his mouth twisted up. He tossed the rock away, shifted the antenna to his right hand, and walked slowly toward her, switching the air.

With a groan, Tyler turned off the engine. She set the emergency brake and got out. Her legs felt rubbery as she walked to the front of the car. She rested against the hood, shoulder to shoulder with Nora.

About four feet away, the man stopped. His gaze roamed slowly down Nora's body, then slid over to Tyler. She felt cold and sick inside. She tried not to squirm.

Nora said, 'Like what you see, liver-lips?'

With a snarl, he whipped the antenna. It whistled by their faces.

'I'm shaking,' Nora said.

He pointed the antenna at a cluster of bushes beyond the ditch. 'Get going,' he said.

'It can talk,' Nora said.

'Move!'

'What've you got in mind?'

'Gonna fuck your asses.'

'No fooling. With what?'

He lashed her shoulder. She flinched and gritted her teeth. 'I'm gonna take you down, buddy,' she muttered, and lunged at the man. He rammed a knee into her belly, doubling her, and flung her sideways. As she tumbled into the ditch, Tyler drove a fist at the man's face. She felt his nose smash under her knuckles. He blinked and shook his head. Blood gushed from his nostrils. Snarling, he clutched Tyler's throat and shoved her backward. The front of the car collapsed her legs. He slammed her down on the hood. His other hand tore at her blouse. Blood spilled onto her face. She punched the side of his head. She kicked, but he was between her legs, leaning down on her, mashing her against the hood. Blinking his blood out of her eyes, she saw his fist rise like a hammer about to strike. Then he looked over his shoulder. He thrust himself off her and whirled around. Raising her head, Tyler saw his pickup racing toward them.

'Hey!' the man yelled.

Tyler sat up, slid forward, and got her feet on the ground as the truck skidded to a stop. She glanced to the side. Nora was scurrying up out of the ditch, hair in her eyes.

The truck's passenger door flew open. A lean man in white pants and a polo shirt jumped down. He nodded to someone inside. The truck rolled forward. It veered to the right. The other door swung open. A man leaped out, windmilling as he caught his balance.

'No!' the big man roared as his pickup nosed down the slope of the ditch. It stopped abruptly with a crunch of metal, a tinkling shatter of headlights. The man covered his ears. He fell to his knees as Nora, coming up behind him, lashed his back with the antenna.

Now that the truck was out of the way, Tyler saw a blue Mustang parked a distance up the road.

Nora tossed the antenna aside. She nodded at the pair of strangers who were standing just in front of the cowering man. 'Are you ladies all right?' asked the one in the polo shirt. He looked from Nora to Tyler.

Tyler pulled her blouse shut, and nodded.

'Too bad about the truck,' said the one who had crashed it, shaking his head and sounding extremely sincere as he stared at the man. He was shorter than his friend, with a crewcut and a chubby boyish face. His neck was thick. His T-shirt was stretched taut over his broad shoulders and bulging chest. The brass buckle of his belt read Colt. He wore blue jeans that looked brand new. Their cuffs were rolled up about three inches. He wore scuffed cowboy boots with pointed toes. Tyler figured he must be gay. That would mean his friend was, too.

The friend squatted down, bringing his face close to the kneeling man. 'Now here's the plan,' he said in a calm voice. 'You get to your feet and apologize to the ladies. You pay them for the antenna. Then you go back to your pickup and stay there.'

'What if I don't?' he muttered.

The man patted his shoulder. Gently, he said, 'I'll let Jack rip your face off.'

They stood up. The big man turned to Nora and Tyler.

He kept his head down. He rubbed a sleeve across his mouth to wipe the blood away. He made gasping, sobbing sounds as he reached into a rear pocket and took out his wallet. He pulled out a ten-dollar bill and held it out to Tyler with a shaking, red-stained hand. Jack leaned in close, and eyed the bill. 'Cheap bastard,' he said. He snatched away the wallet. He plucked out a twenty, took the ten from the man, and gave them both to Tyler. Then he handed the wallet back.

'Now apologize,' said the lean one.

'Sorry,' he murmured without looking up.

'It's quite all right,' Nora said. She took a step toward him, arms stiff at her sides, and shot a fist into his groin. His breath exploded out. He dropped to the ground clutching himself, and Nora slammed a knee into his bleeding nose. The blow knocked him backward. The lean man hopped out of his way. The blocky one named Jack grinned at Nora and began to clap.

3

'Nora Branson.' She offered her hand to the muscle-bound man.

'Jack Wyatt,' he said, shaking it.

'Tyler Moran,' Tyler said, and shook hands with the lean one.

'Abe Clanton.'

'Names like a couple of gunslingers,' Nora said, shaking with Abe as Tyler squeezed Jack's hand. She was surprised by his gentle grip.

'Yup,' Jack said. 'We're mean *hombres*.'

Looking past Abe, Tyler saw the big man stagger down the side of the ditch and climb into his pickup.

'I guess this was our lucky day,' Nora said.

'We saw him force you off the road,' Abe explained. 'We were right behind you.'

'Good thing. That was great of you guys to stop. A lot of people would've kept on going.'

'Yes,' Tyler said. 'We sure appreciate it.'

Abe nodded slightly. He looked into her eyes with a steady, probing gaze. It made her nervous. She wanted to look away, but couldn't. 'Did he hurt you?'

Tyler shook her head. 'Not much.'

'That's *his* blood, I hope.'

27

'I think so.'

'Look,' Nora said, 'you guys are heading north? Why don't we all stop somewhere, we'll buy you a drink?'

The suggestion made Tyler's pulse quicken. She glanced down at her torn, bloody blouse. 'I can't go in anywhere like this.'

'So change,' Nora said.

'I guess I could.'

'How about it, fellas?'

'Fine by me,' Abe said.

Jack rubbed his hands together. 'All *right*.'

'Why don't you follow us?' Nora asked. 'First decent place we spot, we'll pull in.'

'It's a deal.'

'Whoops,' Nora said. 'One second. We're stuck here.' She nodded toward the rear of the car.

'Gotcha,' Jack said.

Abe leaned over the driver's seat. He released the emergency brake. He gripped the steering wheel and open door, and pushed while Jack shoved the rear end. The little Omni rolled away from the ditch. Abe reset the brake. 'Okay,' he said. 'We'll wait up ahead for you.'

'See you in a bit,' Nora said.

As the men started toward their car, Tyler knelt on the passenger seat and took a plastic container of Wet Ones from the glove compartment. She crawled out. Plucking one of the moist towels from the pack, she scrubbed her face. The paper came away smeared brown-red. 'Did I get it?'

'Most of it.'

'God.' She gave the pack to Nora.

They went to the rear of the car. While she opened the

hatchback and unfastened her suitcase, Nora cleaned herself. Her arms were dirty and grass-stained and scraped from her fall into the ditch. The knee she'd driven into the man's face was smudged with his blood.

Tyler waited for a car to pass, then took off her blouse. She stuffed it into a corner of the trunk. 'Damn,' she muttered, seeing the blood spots on her white bra. Well, she couldn't change into a clean one – not here by the road. Her skin, too, was stained as if sunburnt in splotches. Taking a towelette from Nora, she cleaned most of it off her shoulders and chest and belly. She turned to Nora. 'Is that it?'

'Under your chin.'

'God.' She rubbed.

'That's got it. Shit, he bled like a stuck pig.'

'Pig is right,' Tyler said. She made sure her hands were clean, then took a fresh yellow blouse from her suitcase and put it on.

'How am I?' Nora asked, turning round.

Tyler brushed some dirt and bits of weed from the back of Nora's T-shirt. 'Okay,' she said.

She shut the suitcase and hatchback. They hurried to the front and climbed in. A van sped by. Then the lane was clear. She pulled out and glanced at the pickup as they passed it. The cab was low in the ditch, blocked from view by the tailgate. She was glad she couldn't see the man inside.

'Asshole's gonna need a tow truck,' Nora said. 'Not to mention a new set of nuts.' She waved at the Mustang as they drew alongside it.

Abe nodded. He was at the wheel. He pulled out behind them.

'Not bad, huh?' Nora asked. 'An escort.'

Tyler picked up speed. The blue Mustang kept pace, staying several car lengths back.

Nora rubbed her shoulder.

'Hurt?'

'Not like the knee in the guts, the bastard.'

'You got him pretty good.'

'We both did. Scares me, though. If Jack and Abe hadn't come along, he would've had our asses on a plate.'

'Yeah, probably.'

'That Jack's a hunk, isn't he?'

'He must lift weights,' Tyler said.

'You suppose they're gay?'

'They're nice guys, regardless.'

'Yeah. Well, there's nice and there's *nice*.'

'I don't think they're gay. I mean, I sort of wondered at first . . .'

'Yeah. But that Abe sure looked you over.'

Tyler felt heat rise to her skin.

'Still, two guys travelling together.'

'*We're* travelling together.'

'Right!' She snorted. 'They're probably wondering right now if we're a pair of dykes. Ha ha.' She rubbed her belly. 'How about that Abe? I wouldn't kick him out of bed, either. Did you hear how he talked to that bastard? "Now here's the plan. First you apologize . . ." Sounded like Dirty Harry, didn't he? More to that guy than meets the eye, I tell you that much right now.'

'What do you mean?'

'He's a way you don't get in ballet school. Hard eyes. They *both* had hard eyes, did you notice that? Except when old Abe was checking you out. Then they got very

30

soft.' She chuckled. 'And maybe someplace else got *un*soft, if you know what I mean.'

'Nora.'

'You're right. I don't think they're fags. God, I hope not.'

'I don't see what difference it makes,' Tyler said. 'It's not like we'll be dating the guys. We're just gonna buy them drinks, right? We'll probably never see them again.'

'You never know, hon. You just never know.'

4

'Wonderful! Fabulous! Swing over, Brian, get some shots. Too good to be true, wouldn't you say? *Beast House*. What do you think?'

'Nice,' Brian said.

'Nice? It looks positively dripping with evil.'

The Mercedes moved slowly past the small, roadside shack that appeared to be a ticket booth. On its wall, a sign weathered to the dirty gray of the driftwood read BEAST HOUSE in crimson block letters that dripped as if recently painted with blood. Looking over his shoulder, Gorman Hardy saw a girl inside the booth's open window, a blonde of fourteen or fifteen. She held an open paperback on the counter shelf.

Gorman, who had celebrated his fifty-sixth birthday by hurling an empty bottle of Chivas Regal into his mirror to destroy the fat, gray-haired man looking back at him, still had eyes sharp enough to spot his own book covers at a hundred paces. The book in the girl's hands was not *Horror at Black River Falls*.

Several cars were parked along the walkway fronting the grounds. Brian eased into a space between a Datsun and a grimy station wagon with a tail end like a family album of stickers. Glancing over the array of red hearts,

Gorman gathered that the clan had loved Hearst Castle, the Sequoia National Park, Muir Woods and the Winchester Mystery House. It had left its heart in San Francisco, and it wanted the world to know that one nuclear bomb could ruin the entire day. That one, he thought, should sport a bleeding heart. A Beast House bumper sticker, if such were available, might very well add a dripping valentine to the collection.

'You getting out?' Brian asked.

'I'll wait here. Try to keep a low profile.'

'Just a tourist with a Nikon,' he said, and climbed out.

As the door thumped shut, Gorman opened the glove compartment. He took out his Panasonic microcassette recorder. Holding it near his lap, out of sight in case someone might be watching, he said, 'Preliminary observations on Beast House, August 1979.' He turned and stared out the open car window as he spoke.

'The house, set back about fifty yards from the main street of Malcasa Point, is surrounded by a seven-foot fence of wrought-iron bars, each bar tipped with a lethal point to keep intruders out, or perhaps to keep the beast inside.' He smiled. 'Good one. Use that.' In ominous tones, he repeated, 'Perhaps to keep the beast inside.

'The only access appears to be through an opening behind the ticket booth, where a lithe teenaged girl is engaged, even now, in reading my previous book, *Horror at Black River Falls*.' Why not? he thought.

'In contrast to the lush green of the wooded hills that rise up beyond the fence, the grounds of Beast House appear singularly flat and dreary. No trees or flowers bloom inside the fence, and even the grass is mottled with brown patches as if the earth itself has been poisoned by the evil contagion of the house.'

Now we're cooking, he thought. Lay it on, lay it on!

'Though the day is cloudless and bright, a sense of insufferable gloom chills my heart as I gaze at the bleak building.' He nodded. Not bad. Rather Poe-ish. 'The Victorian structure seems a monument to things long dead. Its windows, like malevolent eyes, leer out at the quiet afternoon as if seeking a victim.' Nonsense, of course. The windows were simply windows. From the rather rundown appearance of the house, Gorman was surprised that none was broken. The owners, obviously, were taking some care of the place. The lawn could use more water, and the weathered wooden siding could use a good coat of paint. Such improvements, however, would take away from the aura of deterioration they probably wished to cultivate.

'Especially unnerving,' he continued, 'are the small, attic windows that look out from three gables along the steeply slanting roof, draped in shadow from eaves like brooding eyelids. Peering up at them, wondering what might lurk inside, I feel a chill creep up my spine. If I don't look away soon, I know that a dim, ghastly face will appear at one of the windows.' Such eloquence, he thought – such nonsense. But he suddenly found himself staring at the farthest attic window. A chill had indeed crept up his spine. The skin at the back of his neck felt tight and tingly. *If I don't look away soon . . .*

He lowered his eyes to the gray metal recorder. He

listened to its quiet, reassuring hum for a few moments, then looked again toward the house, taking care to avoid the high window.

'At the far end of the roof,' he said, 'is a tower. It has a cone-shaped top. A widow's peak ... no, a witch's cap, that's what it's called. There are windows under...' He switched off the recorder.

Twisting around, he eased his head out the car window and looked back. Brian wasn't in sight. He pulled in his head, turned the other way, and spotted the younger man through the rear window. Camera to his eye, Brian was standing on the other side of the road directly across from the ticket booth. Gorman reached to the steering wheel. He gave the horn a quick beep. Brian lowered the camera, nodded, and returned to the car. Instead of opening his door, he ducked and peered in at Gorman.

'Are you about finished?'

'Any time. I got some sweet ones. Found out they're running another tour in forty-five minutes.'

The news didn't please Gorman; it gave him a chilly, liquid feeling in the bowels. 'Not today,' he said. 'I'd prefer to wait until we've talked to the girl.'

'Fine by me,' Brian said, and climbed in. 'The motel's just a couple of miles up.' He swung out from behind the station wagon. 'The gal said it's on the right, we can't miss it.'

'The girl in the ticket booth?'

'She's the one. Name's Sandy. Very cooperative.'

'Have you ever met a young woman who wasn't?'

'Very few,' Brian answered. A smile creased his lean

cheeks, and he gave Gorman a sample of the sincere, penetrating gaze that made him such a hit with the ladies.

'Watch where you're driving,' Gorman said, unable to keep the bitterness out of his voice. After four years of almost daily contact with Brian, he still found himself, at times, seething with envy. The thick blond hair, the pale blue eyes, the flawless skin and trim young body seemed to mock Gorman, make him look by comparison like an aged and overweight bulldog. It hardly seemed fair.

'Wonder what they do for kicks in this burg,' Brian said.

'Our friend Janice will provide you with some distractions.'

'Hope she's not a dog.'

'Dog or not, you'll abide by the game plan.'

'Sure, sure.'

After a few blocks of souvenir shops, cafés, sporting-goods stores, bars and gas stations, they reached the far end of town. The road curved into a forest. Gorman looked back, wondering if they'd somehow passed the Welcome Inn.

'Don't worry,' Brian said. 'We didn't miss it.'

'Sandy told you we couldn't.'

'Should be just ahead.'

And it was.

On the right, looking cool in the shade of pines, stood the Welcome Inn's Carriage House, a quaint-looking restaurant with bright white siding and green trim, an antique buggy adorning its lawn. A walkway led from the entrance to an auto court where a dozen bungalows surrounded a parking area. Except for two cars, the lot was deserted.

'Looks like they're not full up,' Brian observed.

'Very astute,' Gorman said.

Just beyond the entrance to the court, the road flared out for parking in front of the office. Brian slowed and swung over. He pulled up close to the front porch. 'Want to wait in the car?' he asked.

'I hardly think that would be appropriate.'

'Thought you might want to make notes.'

While Gorman put his recorder into the glove compartment, Brian twisted the rearview mirror and patted down the sides of his windblown hair. Then they both climbed from the car. They mounted the wooden steps to the porch. Gorman pulled open the screen door and entered first.

With light pouring in from the door and windows, the office seemed bright and cheerful. He saw no one, but through the half-open door behind the registration desk he heard the voices and music of a television. Stepping up to the desk, he tapped the plunger of a call bell. He turned around. Brian had wandered over to a rack of travel brochures.

'If there's a Beast House, grab a few.'

Brian nodded without looking back.

Gorman scanned the calico curtains, the pine paneling of the walls, the glossy green and yellow body of a fish mounted above the entry, the couch resting beneath one of the windows, its tweedy green fabric faded from the sunlight. A few magazines were neatly stacked on an end table.

Hanging on the far wall was an enormous map

labeled MALCASA POINT AND ITS ENVIRONS, VACATION PARADISE with oversized cartoon characters enjoying the various activities: a little man surf-fishing; a family sunbathing and swimming at a beach; a boat offshore full of cheery anglers one of whom had managed to hook a scuba diver. The diver had exclamation points trapped inside his air bubbles. Back on land, the map depicted an array of hikers and campers in the wooded hills, a man in waders fly-fishing in a stream, rafters riding the rapids. At the center of the map loomed the Welcome Inn, shown in detail and larger than the entire town of Malcasa Point. Gorman's eyes followed the main road downward to a drawing of Beast House. Over its roof hovered a white apparition twice the size of the house. In spite of fangs and claws, the creature bore a marked resemblance to Casper the Friendly Ghost. The word 'BOOO!' was scrawled across its belly.

'Sorry to keep you waiting.'

Turning, Gorman smiled at the girl. 'Quite all right,' he said.

She pushed the door to the living quarters shut. The latch clacked into place. She glanced toward Brian, then fixed her eyes on Gorman. 'Mr Hardy,' she said.

'Janice?'

Her head bobbed a bit.

She was not a dog, which must please Brian. Nor did she appear to be underage, a possibility which had worried Gorman. From the correspondence, he had assumed her to be a teenager but had never pinpointed her age. He guessed, now, that she must be eighteen or close to it.

39

She was slim and attractive, with golden bangs brushing her forehead, hair flowing down the sides of her face to her shoulders. The white of her bra showed through the thin white cotton of a T-shirt that read Welcome to The Welcome Inn.

Brian, he thought, must be quite pleased indeed.

The girl glanced over her shoulder as if to reassure herself that the door was firmly shut. Then she looked again at Brian, who was staring at her. In his hand were a few brochures.

'He's with me,' Gorman explained.

He came forward as if summoned.

'Janice, I want you to meet Brian Blake – my research assistant, photographer, chauffeur.'

He reached over the counter. Janice, her face puzzled and wary, shook the offered hand. From the letters, she must have assumed Gorman would come alone. Was she wondering if this man's presence would affect her share?

In rich, sincere tones, Brian said, 'Pleased to meet you, Janice.' He kept his hold on her hand. 'Very pleased.'

A blush tinted her cheeks. Her mouth opened as if to speak, but no words came out. Suddenly, her eyes widened. 'Bri ... *the* Brian Blake?' she blurted. Her stunned expression brought a smile from Gorman. She looked as if she were gawking at a movie star, awestruck and a little frightened. 'My God,' she muttered.

'Nothing to be afraid of,' Brian said. 'I left the spook back in Wisconsin.'

'God, I don't believe this.'

Brian relinquished her hand. It dropped, limp, to the counter. She continued to stare at him.

'As you may remember,' Gorman said, 'Mr Blake and I worked very closely together on *Horror*. He not only recounted the tragedy during our tape sessions, he also was responsible for the photographs used in the book. I've kept him on as an associate ever since. He's really an invaluable asset.'

Janice nodded. She still looked a trifle dazed. 'Must've been awful for you,' she said, her eyes fixed on Brian's.

'It's like Nietzsche says.'

'Huh?'

'What doesn't kill us makes us stronger.'

'Yeah. Yeah, I guess so.'

'Besides, it was a long time ago. I suppose I'll never be over it completely, but ... I'm coping.'

'Well...'

'This,' Gorman interrupted, 'is probably not the ideal place to talk.' He nodded toward the closed door behind which, he assumed, her parents were busy with other matters. 'Why don't you check us in to our rooms? Then we'll make arrangements to meet later, after we've had a chance to rest up from the drive.'

'Good idea,' she said. She made a shaky smile and licked her lips. 'Will you be together or...'

'Separate rooms,' Brian told her.

'Very good.' She snapped a pair of guest registration cards down on the counter. 'Would you each fill out one of these?' she said in a firm, practiced voice. Obviously embarrassed by her earlier loss of composure, she was trying to appear businesslike. This delighted Gorman. From the tone of her letters, he'd been prepared to face a rather tough, cynical bitch, an operator. Now, he realized she wouldn't be the obstacle he had feared. The toughness was no more than a thin shell, easily cracked.

He finished filling in his card.

'All our units,' Janice said, 'are equipped with queen-sized double beds, color TV, and complimentary coffee.'

'Magic fingers?' Brian asked.

A slight frown drew her brows together. She studied him as if trying to figure something out, then seemed to give up. With a shake of her head, she told him, 'I'm afraid not.'

'Well, shit.'

A grin split her face.

'I could just shit, couldn't you, Gorman?'

Now she was softly laughing.

Brian gave her a pitiful look. 'I can't sleep without Magic Fingers.'

'Aw, poor boy.' One of her hands lifted as if to pat him on the head. She caught herself, and lowered the hand behind the counter. 'You'll just have to suffer,' she said. She smiled at Gorman. 'Is he always this way?'

'Just around beautiful women.'

Her face went red as if magically sunburned. 'Anyway.' She took a deep breath. 'How long do you expect to be staying with us?'

'I believe two nights should be sufficient, don't you?'

'Depends, I guess. What're you planning on?'

'Why don't we discuss that in the privacy of our rooms?'

'Yeah, that'd be better.' She glanced at Brian, and quickly looked away. She picked up the two registration cards. 'Will this be cash or charge?'

'Do you take Visa?'

'Yes, we do.'

Gorman used his card to pay for both rooms. After he signed the receipt, Janice turned over the card to compare signatures. 'I'm no imposter, young lady.'

'Huh? Oh. Just force of habit. I know you're Gorman Hardy.'

'The paperback edition didn't have a photo.'

'I saw you on the *Today* show.'

'Ah. Am I even more handsome in person?'

'Oh yes. A lot more handsome.'

'Why, thank you. You have an endearing quality about you, Janice.'

She shrugged, muttered thanks, and reached under the counter. She came up with two keys, each attached to a tab of green plastic. 'I'll put you in five and six. They're together with a connecting door.' She swung an arm out behind her. 'Just drive through, they're the third duplex on the left. The ice machine's just outside the office here, and there's a soft-drink vending machine beside it.'

Gorman nodded. Leaning against the desk, he asked in a quiet voice, 'When would you be able to join us?'

'I can usually get away. Mom'll be over at the restaurant most of the time, and Dad's pretty loose. I just tell him I want to go out, and he takes over the office.'

'Excellent. Now, as I understand it, they know absolutely nothing about our purpose here.'

'Right. Nobody knows but me.'

'It's imperative that we keep it that way. At least for the present,' he added.

'I'm not gonna tell anyone,' Janice said. 'Are you kidding? It's my neck.'

Brian peered closely at her neck. She met his eyes, blushed and looked back at Gorman.

'Would one of our rooms be a convenient meeting place?' he asked.

'Sure. Good as any. I'll bring in some clean towels, just in case, but nobody's even gonna notice me.'

'Very good. Say room six, then, in an hour?'

'I'll be there.'

'And bring the diary along.'

5

'*Voilà!*' Nora blurted, startling Tyler. She jabbed a finger against the windshield.

Just ahead, on the left, was a white-painted adobe restaurant with a red tile roof. The sign in front, hanging from a miniature lighthouse, read Lighthouse Inn.

Tyler checked the rearview. The Mustang was a hundred yards back. She signaled for a turn. A moment later, the Mustang's turn light began to flash. She swung across the road, into the paved parking lot.

Nora leaned over, twisted the mirror and studied her reflection. She started brushing her hair. Tyler pulled into a space and stopped the car. She waited for Nora to finish, then turned the mirror toward herself. Her blonde hair was slightly mussed, but she thought it looked all right. She checked her face for blood. She couldn't see any.

The Mustang eased in beside them. Tyler grabbed her handbag off the back seat, and climbed out. The ocean breeze felt cool and good. It tossed her hair. It flipped open the bottom of her untucked blouse as she stepped around the car, exposing her tanned belly to Abe's stare.

She had neglected to fasten the last button. She closed it now, and Abe lifted his gaze to her face.

Not hard eyes, she thought. But probing, maybe a little amused.

'Bet you're surprised we found a place,' Nora said.

'I was beginning to wonder.'

'Boondocks, USA.'

Jack hurried ahead and pulled open the dark wood door. He held it while the others stepped into the dimly lighted foyer. A blonde girl in a turtleneck and kilts came forward, clutching menus to her chest. Abe told her that they'd come in for cocktails, and she led them through a nearly deserted dining room to a table by the windows. Abe pulled out a chair for Tyler. Jack did the same for Nora. 'A waitress will be by for your orders,' the girl said, and left them.

'Nice joint,' Jack said.

'We picked it special,' Nora told him.

'Come here often?' Abe asked, raising an eyebrow at Tyler.

'Whenever we're in the neighborhood.'

'We're from LA,' Nora said. 'How about you?'

'Here and there,' Jack said.

'These are a couple of very evasive guys,' Nora said.

'What are you, bank robbers?'

Jack grinned. 'Now there's a thought, huh, Abe?'

'I guess you might say we're itinerants.'

'Farm workers? What do you hear from Caesar Chavez?'

Jack laughed. It was more of a giggle, high-pitched and quiet, an odd sound to come from such a powerfully built man but, Tyler thought, somewhat appropriate to his baby face.

A waitress came. Nora ordered a vodka martini, Tyler a margarita. Abe asked for a Dos Equiis, was told there was no Mexican beer in stock, and settled for a Michelob. Jack ordered the same.

'So,' Nora said, 'you're not on the lam?'

Smiling slightly, Abe shook his head. 'Actually, we just got ourselves mustered out of the Marine Corps.'

'Ah-ha! Leathernecks.' She grinned at Tyler 'What'd I tell you? Tough guys.'

'You just got out?' Tyler asked.

'We've been civilians since Monday.'

'In since '67,' Jack added.

'Holy shit. That's what, twelve years?'

'We liked it,' Jack said.

'But not enough to re-up again,' Abe added.

Jack wrinkled his nose, shook his head. 'Gets to be a drag when you haven't got a shooting war.'

'Are you kidding?' Nora asked.

'Not that we particularly enjoy combat,' Abe said.

'Speak for yourself,' Jack told him.

'But the peacetime corps is a lot of dull routine, and after the last fiasco we're not going to see any real commitment of ground forces for some time. Not much point being a soldier without a war. So we thought we'd get out and see how the other half lives.'

'What'll you do?' Tyler asked.

'As little as possible,' Jack smiled.

'Right now, we're busy playing tourist. Left Camp Pendleton on Monday, took the Hearst Castle tour at San Simeon, came up through Monterey and Big Sur, stayed a few days in San Francisco. Just seeing the sights.'

'Hanging loose,' Jack said.

The waitress brought the drinks.

'To fortunate encounters,' Nora toasted.

'Hear, hear,' Jack said.

'And thanks for helping us,' Tyler said.

Abe smiled. 'Our pleasure.'

They drank. After a few swallows, Jack sighed loudly.

'Ah,' he said. 'That do hit the spot.'

'You ladies are from Los Angeles,' Abe said. 'What brings you up here?'

'Just...' Tyler started.

Nora broke in. 'We're hunting up one of Tyler's old flames.'

Why did she have to say that? Tyler felt herself blushing. 'Well, we were in the area anyway for a conference in San Francisco. We just thought we'd look him up, see how he's doing.'

Abe looked at her. Was that disappointment in his eyes? Or just interest, curiosity?

Tyler shrugged. 'We used to be ... very good friends. I haven't seen him in five years.'

'Hoping to rekindle things?'

She stared down at her margarita. 'Something like that, I guess.'

'He's supposed to be living up in Malcasa Point,' Nora said. 'That's about an hour more up the road. We'll be spending the night there.'

'Now there's a coincidence,' Jack said. 'So are we.'

Abe looked at his friend and raised his eyebrows.

'Remember in the car? Not half an hour ago. I say,

48

"How about stopping the night at that Malcasa Point?"
And you say, "Sounds good to me."'

'That's right,' Abe said.

'Maybe we'll run into you gals up there.'

It was Abe's turn to stare at his drink. He turned the
bottle slowly, looking down its neck.

'Who knows?' Jack continued, grinning broadly. 'It's a
small world.'

'And a very small town,' Nora added.

'If we just should happen, somehow, to run into you
gals, maybe we might buy you dinner.'

'Maybe they'd rather we didn't,' Abe said.

Tyler scooted down in her seat. 'I don't know,' she
muttered. 'I might ... have other plans. I mean, if I find
Dan.'

'If she finds Dan,' Nora said, 'I'll be all alone in a
strange town with nothing to do.'

'We'll take care of that,' Jack told her.

Nora squeezed his thick forearm. 'You've got a deal.
Look, why don't you guys follow us up so you won't get
lost, and we'll have us a fancy Marine escort if we run
into more weirdos?'

'You bet,' Jack said.

6

Brian, sitting on the edge of a bed, saw Janice stride past the front of the rented Mercedes. She saw him watching through the window, and smiled. She had changed into a sleeveless yellow sundress, sashed at the waist, its breeze-blown skirt pressed to her thighs. She carried a stack of white towels. From the crook of her elbow hung a tote bag. 'Here she comes,' he said, and took a sip of his martini.

Gorman rushed to open the door. With a slight bow, he said, *'Entrez.'*

Janice stepped in. Balanced on one foot, she used the sole of a white sneaker to push the door shut behind her. Gorman lifted the towels from her arms. He set them on the dressing table, and smiled at her like a gracious host. 'Pull up a bed, my dear.'

'Thanks,' she said in a thin voice. She sounded very nervous. She gave Brian a quick, tight-lipped smile, and sat on a corner of the other bed, her knees pointed away from him. After lowering her bag to the floor, she sat up straight and rigid. She smoothed the skirt against her thighs. She licked her lips. 'Is ... are the rooms okay?' she asked, glancing from Brian to Gorman.

51

'They're charming,' Gorman said. 'Would you care for a cocktail?'

She nodded, her bangs stirring against her forehead. 'Sure, okay.'

'Should we card her?' Brian asked.

She let out a quiet, uneasy laugh. 'I confess. I'm only eighteen.'

'Close enough,' Brian said. 'Just don't tell on us.'

This time her laughter was not so strained. She turned her head to watch Gorman pour two fingers of martini into one of the motel tumblers. He set down the glass shaker, skewered an olive with a cutlass toothpick, and plopped it into her drink. He handed the glass to Janice, freshened Brian's drink and his own, then swung out a chair and sat facing her. He raised his glass to eye level. 'Let me propose a toast. To Beast House, our partnership, and our imminent prosperity.'

They clinked the rims of their glasses, and drank. Janice took a small sip. She grimaced and smiled, then tried another sip and nodded as if this one was an improvement.

'Too much vermouth?' Gorman asked.

'No, it's fine. Just fine.'

'Now shall we, as they say, talk turkey?'

'Fine.'

'I've given much thought to your proposal of a fifty-fifty split and while it does seem rather steep, there would, as you pointed out, be no book without your cooperation. It is, after all, your idea. And you *are* the one, after all, in possession of the diary. Therefore, I've concluded that your request is reasonable.'

Her eyebrows lifted, disappearing under the curtain of bangs. 'That means you'll go for it?'

'That means I'll go for it.'

'Great.'

'Brian?'

Brian set aside his drink and snapped open the latches of an attaché case beside him on the bed. He raised the top, removed a manila file folder, and slipped out two neatly typed papers. He handed both sheets to Janice.

'I took the liberty,' Gorman explained, 'of writing up an agreement. It spells out, basically, that I'll be sole owner of the copyright, that you'll be free of any liability in connection with the proposed work, and that you'll receive a fifty percent share of the proceeds from any and all sales. It also stipulates that your participation in the project shall be kept secret. I added that for your benefit, since you seemed to believe you might be in some danger if your involvement became known.'

Nodding, she read the top sheet. When she finished, she slipped the other one over it.

'They're identical,' Gorman said.

She scanned it. 'Well, they look fine to me.'

Leaning forward, Gorman held out his gold-plated Cross pen. 'If you'll sign and date both copies . . .'

She pressed the papers against her thigh, and scribbled her signature and the day's date at the bottom of each contract. Both had already been signed by Gorman Hardy two weeks ago.

'One's for you and one's for us,' Brian said. She handed one of the sheets to him. She returned the pen to Gorman. She folded her copy into thirds, and slipped it into her tote. Reaching down beside a folded sweater, she pulled out a thin, leatherbound volume. A brass lock-plate was set into its front cover, but the latch hung loose by the strap on the back.

'The diary?' Gorman asked.

'It's all yours.' She gave it to him, and took a hefty swallow of martini.

Gorman opened the book to its first page. '"My Diary",' he read aloud, '"Being a True Account of My Life and Most Private Affairs, Volume twelve, in the year of our Lord 1903. Elizabeth Mason Thom." Fabulous,' he muttered, and riffled through the pages.

'It's pretty boring stuff till you get into April,' Janice said. 'Then she gets into it pretty hot and heavy with the family doctor. Around May eighteenth is when she starts with the beast. She called it Xanadu.'

'Xanadu? As in *Kubla Khan*? "In Xanadu did Kubla Khan a stately pleasure dome decree, where Alph the sacred river ran through caverns measureless to man – down to the sunless sea."'

'I guess,' Janice said. 'That's what she called him, anyway. Xanadu. It gets pretty far out, the diary, and I would've figured she made it up, you know, but it pretty much explains what's behind the killings in Beast House. I mean, those murders really happened, no question.'

'Mmhmm.' Gorman opened the diary at random, and began to read. '"His warm breath on my face smelled of the earth and wild, uninhabited forests. He lay his hands upon my shoulders. Claws bit into me. I stood before the creature, helpless with fear and wonder, as he split the fabric of my nightgown."'

Brian whistled softly.

Janice glanced at him, and made a slightly lopsided smile. The drink, he figured, was getting to her.

'"When I was bare,"' Gorman continued, '"he muzzled my body like a dog. He licked my breasts. He sniffed me, even my private areas, which he probed with his snout."'

Janice eased her knees closer together.

'Well,' Gorman said, shutting the book, 'it appears that this little memoir does, indeed, live up to your reports. How exactly did it come into your possession?'

'Like I said in my letter, I found it in one of the rooms here.'

'Could you be more specific?'

She drained her martini, and nodded.

'Refill?' Gorman asked.

'Sure, okay,' She opened her eyes wide as if to test how well the lids were still working. Gorman took her glass, poured in an inch of the clear liquid, and handed it back to her. She took a small drink. 'Anyway . . .'

'Would you mind if I record you?'

A puzzled look crossed her face. 'Aren't I not supposed to be in the book?'

'That's true. None of what you say need find its way into the work, but we'll be on safer ground with a statement regarding the manuscript's origin. You may not be aware of it, but there were accusations regarding the veracity of our previous book.'

'Huh?'

'*Horror at Black River Falls*,' Brian told her. 'Some people accused us of making up the whole damn story.'

Janice frowned. 'No, you didn't do that. Did you?'

'No way,' Brian said. 'But we didn't have much proof to back up our claims. That's why we want to tape what you say. Then, if somebody gets on our case, we've actually got a recorded statement to prove the conversation happened.'

'Ah.' She nodded. 'I see. Okay.'

Gorman lifted his small recorder off the dresser top. He switched it on. 'The following is a statement by Janice Crogan of Malcasa Point, California, in which she explains how she came into possession of the diary of Elizabeth Thorn.' Leaning forward, he placed the device on the bedspread by her hip.

'Okay,' she said. 'I'm Janice Crogan. My folks own the Welcome Inn here in Malcasa, and I help them with it. I found the diary in room nine, one day last summer. In June. Late June. We haven't got any maids here. Dad says that's the kind of overhead that kills you. Me and my mom – my mom and I – we do all the cleaning. That's how I found the diary. It was under one of the beds. In room nine. Did I already say that? Anyway, it was in nine. One of the guests must've lost it there.'

'Do you have any idea who that might have been?' Gorman asked.

She shook her head. Her left cheek bulged out as she pushed it with her tongue. She frowned at her drink and took another sip. 'Could've been under there a while. I don't know. But there was a woman and her kid in nine a couple days before. That was when ... uh ... this guy...'

Suddenly, Janice's face crumpled. Her eyes squeezed shut and her mouth twisted into a parody of a smile as tears spilled down her cheeks. Sobbing loudly, she pressed one hand across her eyes. Her other hand shook, sloshing her drink up the walls of her glass.

Brian took the glass from her. She hunched over, burying her face in both hands. He sat down beside her and wrapped an arm around her quaking back. 'Hey, it's all right,' he said in a soothing voice. 'It's all right, Janice.' He squeezed her shoulder.

'I'm sorry,' she blurted between sobs. 'You must...'

'Shhh.' Gently, he stroked her hair. He caressed her back. It bounced under his hand, but he liked the warm feel of her skin through the fabric.

Slowly, she regained control of herself.

Gorman gave her a Kleenex. She blotted her wet cheeks, wiped her eyes, blew her nose. Then she sat up straight and took a deep breath that sounded shaky as she let it out.

'Better?' Brian asked.

'Better.' She sniffed. She shook her head as if ashamed of her behavior. 'I'm sorry. I . . . I thought I was over it. Guess I'm not, huh?' She made a feeble smile. 'See ... This guy I was telling you about, he ... *God*.'

Brian's hand slowly roamed her back. 'It's all right,' he said.

'I caught him trying to break into one of the cabins,' she said quickly, as if to get it over with. 'He had this girl with him, a little kid named Joni. He'd killed her parents and kidnapped her, and – God, the awful things he did to her! We found out all about it later. But this guy, his name was Roy, he grabbed me and he tied us both up in one of the rooms and ... messed with us. Raped us.'

'How awful,' Gorman said.

'Yeah. He ... he was a ... so horrible.' She shut her mouth tightly, jaw muscles bunching, and took a hissing breath through her nose. 'Anyway, that was two days before I found the diary. I don't know if it has anything to do with it. Joni got loose, and ran off, and the guy took off after her. That was the last I ever saw of him. He just vanished, and so did four of our guests. All five of them ...' She shrugged. 'Like they fell off the face of the earth.'

She lifted her glass off the floor, and took a sip. 'Something else strange, too. These people – they were in nine and twelve – they left all their luggage and stuff behind. A car, too. That stuff was still around that night. But when morning came, everything was gone. Except the diary, which I found the day after. Whether they left it or not, I haven't got the slightest idea. It could've been under that bed for days, a week, no telling how long. Anyway, that's about all there is on how I found the diary.'

'And you didn't tell anyone about finding it?' Gorman asked.

'No. I was alone in the room. Vacuuming. I looked inside the thing, and knew right away it had to do with Beast House. I recognized the woman's name – Thorn. She's the one that built the place, and her kids and sister were the first victims. She wound up in a nut-house someplace. I knew all of this from the tour. I used to go on the tour all the time. Not that I enjoyed it much, but I mean it's kind of a major attraction around here so whenever we had visitors from out of town – like relatives and stuff – it's a place we always took them to. So I was pretty familiar with the story you get on the

tour and my eyes nearly fell out when I read the diary.
Anyway, I hid it in my room and read the whole thing
later on. It gave me a pretty good scare.'

'Why is that?' Gorman asked.

'Read it, you'll find out. I mean, I knew *some*one had
murdered all those people, but I figured it was . . . I don't
know what, but not a monster, for Godsake. I figured
that was all bullshit till I read the diary. Then also I got
a little nervous about just having the thing. If certain
people found out . . .'

'Which people?'

'Well, like Maggie Kutch. She's the old bag that owns
the place. Beast House. You'll see her if you take the
tour. And there's this slime, Wick Hapson. He's like her
flunky. He's the one sells the tickets.'

'A young lady,' Gorman said, 'was in the ticket booth
when we stopped there earlier this afternoon.'

Janice shrugged. 'I don't know who she'd be. I've been
trying to keep my distance from the place. I mean, you
can't help going by it sometimes, but I haven't been on
the tour since I read the diary. And I don't intend to,
either. Maybe they hired some kid. I wouldn't know.'

'After reading the diary, what did you do?'

'Nothing. I kept it hidden. I thought a lot about
throwing it away. It made me nervous just having it
around. But then I got to thinking it might be valuable.
When I read your book last March, that's when I
realized there might be a book in it. That's when I
decided to write you a letter.'

Leaning forward, Gorman picked up the recorder. 'Is
there anything else you'd like to add?'

'That's about all, I think.'

He switched it off.

Janice drank the remains of her martini. She set the empty glass on the bedspread. 'What now?' she asked.

'Now,' Gorman said, 'I shall read the diary. Tomorrow, we'll take the tour. Would you care to join us?'

'I don't think so. I don't know. Maybe. I'll think about it.'

7

Pacific Coast Highway had curved inland soon after they left the Lighthouse Inn. Now they were passing through an area of wooded hills. The briny, fresh smell of the ocean was gone, replaced by a sweet scent of pine. The blue Mustang vanished as they rounded a bend. Tyler eased off the gas until it reappeared in the rearview mirror.

'There,' Nora said.

A sign reading MALCASA POINT, 3 MI, pointed at a sideroad to the left. Tyler slowed and signaled the turn, and swung sharply across the empty lane.

'Wait for 'em,' Nora said.

She slowed to a crawl until the Mustang made the turn, then picked up speed again. The road curved along a shadowy hillside, sloping gradually downward. Not far ahead, a squirrel scampered over the pavement, bushy tail up like a question mark. Tyler touched the brake. The squirrel finished its crossing in plenty of time.

As the hill to the left fell away, she glimpsed the ocean through the trees along its crest. The breeze coming in her window suddenly turned slightly cool and smelled again of the sea.

'Almost there,' Nora said.

Tyler's stomach lurched. Almost there. Her hands were slippery on the wheel. She rubbed them, one at a time, on the legs of her corduroys. 'Let's find a place to stay before hunting Dan up,' she said.

Nora agreed.

At the foot of the hill, the road curved to the right. A sign by the ditch read WELCOME TO MALCASA POINT. POP. 400. DRIVE WITH CARE. Tyler took a deep breath. Her lungs seemed to tremble.

She gazed ahead. The road led flat and straight through the center of town. The town ahead was small, no more than a few blocks long, with shops lining both sides of the street before the road turned in the distance and vanished into the woods.

'The sticks, all right,' Nora said. 'I hope it does have a motel. And I hope *that* isn't it,' she added, looking to the right.

Tyler glanced that way. Through the bars of a wrought-iron fence beside the road, she saw a two-story Victorian house with weathered sides, bay windows, a peaked tower.

Nora said, 'Here, we thought the Bates house was at Universal Studios.'

'Maybe they moved it.'

'Gee, should we stop for the tour?'

'That's just what I'd like to do,' Tyler said, and kept on driving. The Mustang stayed a short distance behind them as they moved through town.

Nora, leaning toward the windshield, studied the road-side businesses. 'Where's the Holiday Inn?' she asked. 'Where's the Howard Johnson, the Hyatt?'

'There's gotta be some kind of motel.'

'I sure don't see one. Maybe you'd better pull in at this gas station and we'll ask.'

'We can use a fill-up anyway,' Tyler said. She signaled well in advance, then swung over and eased the car up beside the row of full service pumps. Killing the engine, she looked over her shoulder. The Mustang stopped at the self-service island, and Abe climbed out. He nodded a greeting, then turned away to open his gas tank.

Tyler pulled her hood release as a lean, sour-looking man stepped around the front of her car. He crouched by her window. The name patch on his shirt read Bix. He peered inside as if sizing them both up, and one side of his mouth stretched over. 'Ladies,' he said.

'Hi. Fill it up with unleaded, please.'

He gave the window sill a pat, then ambled around to the other side.

'Guess I'll make a pit stop,' Nora said. 'Go while the going's good.' She left the car, eased past the pumps, and headed for the station building.

Tyler climbed out. She stretched, feeling good as her muscles strained. The breeze off the ocean smelled fresh. Mixed with the subtle aroma of pines was a faint, pungent odor of gasoline. The breeze chilled the sweaty back of her blouse. Reaching around, she plucked the clinging fabric away from her skin.

Abe was watching the pump as he filled his tank.

She turned to Bix as he approached.

'Check under the hood for you?' he asked.

'Please.'

He nodded. His eyes strayed to her breasts and paused there for a moment before shifting away. Then he stepped past her. He bent over the hood and felt under its lip for the catch.

Tyler glanced down to make sure her blouse was buttoned. It was. 'Is there a place to stay around here?' she asked.

'A motel, like?'

'Yes.'

He licked his lower lip. He stared at her breasts as if the answer were written there. 'Only one,' he finally said. 'That'd be the Welcome Inn, about half a mile up the road, on your right.'

'Thank you,' she said.

He raised the hood. Tyler was glad to be hidden from his view. She considered asking the location of Seaside Lane, but wanted as little as possible to do with him. She could find Dan's place without the help of this lech.

Abe was still bent over the rear of his Mustang, pumping in gas. She walked over to him. He looked at her and smiled. 'What's up?' he asked.

'The guy says there's a motel about half a mile up the road.'

'I was starting to wonder if we'd find one.'

'Apparently there is only one. The Welcome Inn.'

'Clever.'

'He says it's on the right.'

'Fine. We'll follow you in.' The feed clicked off. He pulled the spout out of his tank and stepped backward, holding it away from himself so gasoline wouldn't drip onto his Nikes. He hung up the nozzle. Then he sniffed his fingers. He caught Tyler grinning. 'Stinky,' he said.

She laughed. 'We've got some Wet Ones in the car.'

'Thanks,' he said. 'I'm a big boy. I can live with it.' He screwed the gas cap on.

'Oil's half a quart low,' Bix said, coming up behind her.

'Thanks,' she said. 'See you later,' she told Abe, and returned to her car. Watching from the window, she saw him pay cash. He pushed the wallet into his rear pocket. It made a small bulge. The other pocket apparently empty, curved smoothly over his right buttock.

The passenger door swung open. 'Hi ho,' Nora said, climbing in.

'Everything come out all right?' Tyler asked.

'Right as rain. Did you ask Clyde about a motel?'

'Bix. Yeah. Dead ahead.'

'Terrific.'

Tyler found her credit card as Bix approached.

'Eleven-fifty,' he said.

She gave him the card. He left with it. 'What a turkey,' she said.

'Yeah?'

'Like this.' She leered at Nora's breasts, wiggling her eyebrows and running her tongue across her lips.

'Ask him for a date. Definitely.'

'Right.'

A moment later, he stepped in front of the car. He jotted down the license plate number and came back to Tyler's window. She took the plastic clipboard from him, and started to sign the receipt.

'You with those guys?' he asked.

Tyler didn't answer.

'They're our Secret Service escort,' Nora said.

'Yeah? Who you trying to shit?'

Tyler plucked her card from its slot.

'You don't recognize Amy Carter when you see her?'
She ripped off the top copy of the receipt.

'Well, now,' Nora went on. 'I guess you wouldn't. She's incognito.'

Tyler handed out the clipboard. Bix yanked it from her hand. He crouched and stared in at Nora. 'You're a real laugh.'

Tyler started the engine. She released the emergency brake and shifted to first.

'Wi—...'

She popped the clutch. The car lurched forward.

'I didn't catch that!' Nora yelled, turning in her seat.

'I did,' Tyler said.

'What did he call me?'

'A wise-ass cunt,' Tyler said, and pulled onto the road.

'Did he?'

'Please. Don't flip him the bird. He knows where we'll be staying.'

'Ah. Well, all right. Coward.'

'That's me.'

'Seaside?' repeated the pleasant, bald man behind the registration desk. 'Did you come in by way of town?'

'Yes,' Tyler said.

'What there was of it,' Nora added.

The man chuckled. So did Jack Wyatt, who was waiting behind them with Abe.

'Well,' the man said, 'you want to head back through what there is of town. Just this side of the monster palace, you'll see a dirt road on your right.'

'Just this side of Beast House?' Tyler asked.

'Yep. The monster palace. The road's called Beach Lane. It'll take you to the beach parking, but you don't want to go that far. Just about a hundred yards in, you'll come to Seaside. That'll be to your right. Doesn't go to the left.'

'Thank you,' Tyler said.

'Where's the best place for dinner?' Nora asked.

'You're there. Right next door. The Carriage House. Of course I'm partial as I run the place. But you can't do better. Fine steaks and seafood and ambience at moderate prices.' He checked his wristwatch. His arm, unlike his head, was matted with hair. 'If you're after something to cut the thirst, our Happy Hour's just started. Two drinks for the price of one, and free hors d'oeuvres. Runs till six.'

'Hey, all right!' Nora said. She turned around. 'Maybe see you guys there. Say in an hour or so?'

'I'll be there,' Jack assured her.

Abe nodded. He met Tyler's eyes. 'Are you going off now to look up your friend?'

'Yeah, I guess so.'

'Good hunting,' he said.

'Thanks.'

He frowned at his shoes, then looked again into her eyes. 'That offer for dinner's still open. Have him join us.'

'Right,' she said. 'He and his wife.'

'The eternal pessimist,' Nora said.

'Anyway, good luck.'

'I'll need it.'

Abe and Jack stayed in the office to check in. Nora

67

followed Tyler outside. 'You sure you still want to find Dan?' she asked.

'What does that mean?'

'Looks to me like our friend Abe is more than a little interested in you.'

Tyler trotted down the porch stairs and got into the car. Nora climbed into the passenger side. 'He's gorgeous,' she added.

'I hardly know him.'

'Ah, but admit it, he makes your little heart go pitty-pat.'

'You're imagining things,' Tyler said, and started the engine. She headed for the courtyard entrance. 'You don't have to come along. If you'd rather stay here and clean up, or...'

'Do I smell?' Nora sniffed her armpits.

'I don't want to keep you from the Happy Hour.'

'No sweat,' she said. 'Hey. Ritzy clientele.'

'Yeah.' Tyler drove slowly past the gray Mercedes, and pulled to a stop in front of the next duplex over. 'Really,' she said, 'you don't need to come.'

'You telling me I'm not wanted?'

'No. I just thought you might prefer to stay behind, that's all. The way you were trying to talk me out of it.'

'I was only pointing out there's no law you have to go looking for Dan. It's obvious you're nervous about it, and it's also obvious you've got eyes for Abe.'

'I don't have "eyes" for anyone,' she protested.

'Uh-huh. Sure.'

'Come on, let's get our stuff in the rooms.'

A few minutes later, after throwing her suitcase onto

one of the beds, washing up, putting on fresh lipstick and brushing her hair, she stepped to the connecting door. 'Ready,' she called.

'Meet you at the car,' Nora answered.

She left her room. Abe's Mustang was parked in front of a bungalow just across the courtyard.

As she stepped around the front of her Omni, Nora's door opened. Tyler watched her friend hop down the steps, breasts jiggling inside her T-shirt. For just a moment, she felt threatened and wary.

A faint scent of perfume entered the car with Nora. 'Loins all girded?'

'My loins are fine,' Tyler said.

'You okay?'

'Just a little nervous.'

'Let's went, Queeksdraw.'

Rounding a bend, they left the wooded hills behind. The service station appeared just ahead.

'Pull in,' Nora said. 'I want to give Clyde a piece of my mind.'

'Bix.' Tyler glanced to the left, saw the man crouching to check the air in a Honda's tire, and pressed harder on the accelerator.

'Wonder if he's related to the asshole we met on the road. You oughta see the welt that sucker raised on me with that aerial.'

'Must have hurt.'

'He'll think twice before he pulls that kind of shit again.' A few minutes later, Nora said, 'Better slow down, here comes the monster palace.'

Tyler glanced ahead at the old house. Its windows,

catching the late afternoon sunlight, looked plated with
gold.

'This might be it.'

She took her foot off the gas pedal. As the car lost
speed, she swept her eyes along the roadside to the
right. Just past a five-and-ten was a vacant, wooded lot.
The trees stopped at a dirt road. She flicked the arm of
her turn signal.

'That's it,' Nora confirmed. 'Beach Lane.'

Tyler eased down on the brake, and swung onto the
narrow, rutted road.

'Your Dan believes in roughing it.'

'So it seems.' The area to the right, where his house
must be, was thick and shadowy with trees. By
comparison, the rolling, weed-choked field to the left
looked bare. Off in that direction stood a two-story
house of red brick, alone except for a separate garage.

'That's unusual,' Nora said.

'What?'

'How many actual brick houses do you ever see in
California?'

'Maybe it was built by eas—...'

'I'll be damned. Look at that. No windows.'

Tyler looked again. Sure enough, the only visible wall
was an unbroken expanse of brick. 'Maybe on the other
sides...'

'Guess they're not very view-conscious.'

Tyler laughed.

Nora shook her head and faced the windshield. 'Ah,
here comes Seaside.'

Tyler stopped by a row of mailboxes lined up along a
raised shelf. The gray metal hoods were labeled two,

four, eight, and ten. She rolled past them, and peered down the narrow lane. 'Maybe we'd better walk,' she said. 'Can't be too far.'

'You don't want to block traffic,' Nora said, flashing a smile.

'God forbid.'

Tyler drove past the entrance to Seaside. Not far ahead, the road widened into a parking area. She stopped against a log. A wedge of ocean glinting sunlight showed through a break in the low hills ahead. A footpath curved along one of the slopes.

'Nuts,' Nora said. 'We should've brought our suits.'

They climbed from the car. A stiff breeze tugged at Tyler's hair, molded her blouse to her body. When she turned away from the ocean, it pushed at her back as if urging her to rush.

Nora met her behind the car. She was slipping her arms into the sleeves of her red sweater. Her face was wrapped with tendrils of blowing hair. As they walked along, she buttoned the sweater.

Thank you, wind, Tyler thought.

They hurried to Seaside. There, the trees shielded them from the wind but also kept out the sunlight. They walked in silence through the deep shadows.

Tyler shivered – partly from the chill, mostly from the knowledge that she might, in minutes, be face to face with Dan Jenson. What were the chances, after five years, that he would welcome her, that they could pick up where they left off? Slim, she thought. Minuscule. But she had come this far. There was no turning back. She clenched her teeth to stop her jaw from shaking.

From a cottage on the left, a dog began to yap. A gaunt

man appeared behind the screen door. Nora raised a hand in greeting. The man stood motionless, a dim shape through the screen, staring out at them.

'Charming,' Nora muttered. 'Let's hear some "Dueling Banjos."'

They passed a clapboard shack with boarded windows, then came upon a wheelless bus propped up on cinder blocks. They paused to stare at the mural painted on its side: a ghost ship with tattered sails becalmed on a glaring sea. A human skeleton clung to the helm. A giant albatross floated before the ship, an arrow in its breast. Above the bus's door hung a sign carved in driftwood: CAPTAIN FRANK.

'Interesting neighbors your Dan has,' Nora said.

They continued down the gloomy road to its end, where a path led toward a small, green-painted cottage with a screened porch.

'That must be it,' Nora said.

Tyler's heart pounded hard. 'I don't see a car anywhere.'

'Maybe he's not home yet.'

They walked down the path. Tyler followed Nora up the porch steps. Nora knocked on the door, then pulled it open. Except for a swing suspended from its ceiling, the porch was empty. That seemed odd to Tyler. Similar cottages she'd known as a child while vacationing with her parents always had porches cluttered with gear: fishing rods, a tackle box and minnow bucket, a fishnet, an old Coleman lantern, a refrigerator well stocked with soda and beer, hooks on the walls draped with rain slickers and beach towels. There was none of that.

'No doorbell,' Nora whispered. 'I'll let you do the

knocking.' She stepped away from the door and sat on the swing. Its chains creaked and groaned as she pushed it into motion.

Tyler rapped lightly on the door. She waited, then struck harder. 'I don't think he's home.'

'It's only about four thirty,' Nora said from the swing.

Tyler cupped her hands to a glass pane in the door, and peered inside. She could see no more than the kitchen. 'Maybe Barbie Doll gave us the wrong address,' she said.

'I doubt it. She was flaky, but not stupid.'

'Well, nobody's home.'

'Shall we wait, or try again some other time?'

Tyler shrugged. Though disappointed, she also felt relieved; her eagerness to meet Dan was mixed with such anxiety that she was almost glad they had failed. 'It might be a long wait,' she said. 'Cops have weird hours. He could've just started a shift, or something.'

'Then you want to leave?'

'We don't want to keep you from the Happy Hour.'

'I'm perfectly willing to wait.'

'No, let's go.'

They left the porch and walked up the path to the dirt road.

'Maybe,' Nora said, 'we can check a phone directory when we get back, make sure we do have the right address. You might even give him a ring, unless you're intent on making a surprise appearance.'

'Yeah, that's an idea.' A phone call, she thought, would be much easier on the nerves. That way, at least, she might find out how he stood. They could arrange to meet, regardless. Even if he was married or engaged or there was some other reason not to renew their relationship, she still would like to see him again.

'Ahoy there!' a man called.

Seated on a lawn chair atop the strangely painted bus, a beer can raised in greeting, was a white-bearded man. He wore a ragged straw hat, a Hawaiian shirt, and plaid Bermuda shorts.

'Captain Frank?' Nora asked.

'At your service, mateys.'

'We're looking for Dan Jenson,' Tyler called up to him. 'He lives at the end of the road?'

'Not anymore.' Captain Frank chuckled softly. 'No indeed.'

'He moved?'

'You might say that.'

'Do you know where we can find him?'

'Can't find him anywhere tonight. Try tomorrow, if you're of a mind.'

'Where?'

He tilted the beer can to his mouth, then crumpled it and tossed it down. It landed on the layer of pine needles beside his bus. 'Oh, Dan's not far off. No, indeed. Just down the road a spell. Can't miss it. A place called Beast House.'

'He *lives* there?' Tyler asked.

'I wouldn't say that, not exactly. Go on by in the morning. Tell him Captain Frank sent you, and give Danny boy my regards.' He waved them away.

'Thanks,' Tyler called.

They started walking.

'He must work as a guard there,' Nora said.

'Yeah. I suppose. But he must live someplace.'

Nora shrugged. 'You can ask him all about it tomorrow.'

'I guess this means we'll have to take the tour.'

'You'll love it. Tacky tacky.'

'I can't wait,' she muttered.

'Let's get back to the inn and get tanked.'

8

Tyler pulled to a stop in front of their bungalow at the Welcome Inn. 'It'll take me a while to get cleaned up and changed,' she said. 'You can go on ahead to the restaurant, if you'd like.'

'Fine,' Nora said. 'Meet you there.'

They climbed from the car.

Alone in her room, Tyler checked a drawer of the night stand between the beds. She found a Gideon Bible and a telephone book. She looked up Jenson, Daniel in the directory. The address listed after his name was 10 Seaside Lane.

According to Captain Frank, he didn't live there now. Not anymore. No indeed.

She flipped the directory shut. The date on its cover was February 1978, making the book more than a year and a half old.

She considered dialing information.

Maybe later. Right now, she had neither the energy nor the desire. She sat motionless on the edge of the bed, the phone book resting on her thigh, and stared into space. She felt weary. Her mind seemed out of focus. In the pit of her stomach was a tiny knot of fear.

She wished that she was home in her own apartment, her life untouched by Barbie Doll, the horrible man on the highway, the leering Bix, the man who stared out like a specter from his cottage on Seaside, or Captain Frank on top of his grimly painted bus. *Give Danny boy my regards.*

And then she thought, *Why not leave in the morning? First thing.* As Nora pointed out, *there's no law you have to go looking for Dan.*

Just get in the car, tomorrow, and bid farewell to all this. Tyler suddenly felt better, as if realizing she could leave had lifted an oppressive weight from her spirits. The knot of fear in her stomach loosened. She *could* leave. Nobody would force her to seek out Dan. Nobody would force her to take the Beast House tour.

If I don't want to, she thought, *I won't.*

She put away the telephone directory, pulled the curtains across the windows, and took off her clothes. Inspecting her bra in the dim light, she doubted she could ever remove the bloodstains entirely. Even if she succeeded, she would never forget this was the bra she had worn when the man attacked her. It would always be a reminder. So she took it into the bathroom and dropped it into the waste basket.

Standing by the road, she had cleaned most of the blood from her skin. But she hadn't taken off her bra. Some blood had soaked through it, leaving faint rust-colored blotches on her breasts.

In the shower, she lathered her body with a thin bar of motel soap and used a washcloth to scrub her face and neck, her shoulders, her arms, her breasts – every inch of skin that had been touched by the man or his blood.

She rinsed. She turned her back to the spray and looked down. Her breasts were tawny to the tan line, then creamy white to the darker flesh of her nipples. No trace of the blood stains remained. Nevertheless, she soaped the washcloth and scoured herself once more before leaving the tub.

The bath towel was threadbare and half the size of her towels at home. After drying herself, she wrapped it around her waist and left the steamy bathroom. She turned on a lamp. The towel pulled loose as she sat down at the dressing table. She left it draping her lap and brushed her hair. Only the fringes at her neck were damp from the shower. With the short length, she had no trouble fixing her hair up enough to look presentable.

Leaning against the table's edge, she studied her face in the mirror. Her eyes needed help. Definitely. They looked haggard and slightly dazed. With a conceal stick from her makeup bag, she covered the smudges under each eye. She darkened her feathery lashes with mascara, then brushed her lids with light blue shadow. A vast improvement.

As she put on lipstick, she wondered why she hadn't bothered to do all this before driving out to look for Dan. Well, she'd been in a hurry. And nervous. Maybe it was something else, though. Maybe it was simply that she thought he wouldn't mind her scruffy appearance. Or maybe, deep down, she had somehow known she wouldn't find him.

She got up from the table. Its edge had left a crease like a long red scar just below her rib cage. She rubbed it as she carried the towel into the bathroom.

She had already decided what to wear. Though she would have preferred slacks because of the chill outside, she'd made up her mind to wear a skirt instead. Rummaging through her suitcase, she took out what she needed. She stepped into fresh panties, hooked her garter belt around her hips, and sat on the bed to put on her nylons. She'd selected a blue tweed skirt. It wasn't very summery but then, neither was the weather. Not at night, anyway. With the skirt on, she slipped into a wispy bra. Its silken feel made her nipples rigid. She drew a white cashmere sweater down over her head. It wasn't thick enough to hide the jut of her nipples completely, but her only other white bra was in the bathroom waste basket. A black one might show through the sweater.

'What the hell,' she muttered.

With Nora at the same table, who would be looking at her anyway?

Abe, that's who.

She felt a rather pleasant, nervous tremor. It stayed with her as she stepped into her heels, put a few necessities into a clutch purse – including her room key – and approached the connecting door.

'Nora?' she called. 'Left yet?'

'Five minutes ago,' came the answering voice, followed by a guffaw. 'Want to come through? My side's already open.'

Tyler pulled open her door. The room was a twin of her own. Nora was seated at the dressing table, changing her earrings. 'I'm just about set,' she said. She had on the same green gown she had worn to last night's banquet. With her low neckline and spaghetti straps, she looked considerably more formal than Tyler.

'Going to a prom?' Tyler asked.

Nora eyed her, grinning. 'My, don't *you* look preppy. Going to a frat dance?'

'Call me Muffin.'

'I just figured I might as well give the boys something to look at.'

'Where's Jack going to pin your corsage?'

'To my boobie, darling.' Finished with her earrings, she took a white, cable-knit shawl off the bed, wrapped it around her shoulders, and picked up a purse that matched her gown. 'Shall we be off?'

Outside, the breeze was mild. The sun felt much warmer than Tyler had expected. It hung above the distant tree-tops, blazing into her eyes. She lowered her head and watched her shoes move over the courtyard's asphalt. 'What time is it?' she asked.

'About five thirty. The tail end of the Happy Hour.'

'I hope Abe and Jack are the patient type.'

'We're well worth waiting for.'

'Right.' She hesitated. 'I've been thinking.'

'What?'

'I'm not sure about all this business ... looking for Dan, digging up the past. Maybe it'd be better to call it off.'

'Getting the jitters?'

'I've had the jitters all along. But nothing's been going right, you know? It's almost as if I'm not meant to find him.'

'Meant? That's a cop-out.'

'And if I do find him, and if he's not married or

81

something, who's to say we're still ... I don't know, the same people? I know I'm not. He's probably changed, too.'

'No harm in giving it a shot.'

'Isn't there? I don't know.'

Nora frowned at her, looking concerned. 'What *is* it?'

'I just ... it didn't seem like such a bad idea, last night. But after everything today ...' She shook her head. 'I have this kind of sick feeling about it.'

'Just nerves.'

'No, it's more than that. I have this feeling that if I do find Dan, I'm going to be very sorry. I'm going to wish I hadn't.'

They crossed the entry drive to a shaded walkway.

'It has been one hell of a day,' Nora agreed. 'I can't blame you for feeling a bit down. But maybe you'll feel different in the morning.'

'Maybe,' Tyler said.

Nora pulled open one of the double doors, and they entered the restaurant. The hostess's desk, with a gooseneck lamp shining down on the reservation list, was deserted. No one was seated in the dining area to the right, but the tables were set. A woman in an ankle-length dress was bent over one, lighting the chimney candle of its centrepiece. From the left came the sounds of quiet conversation and clinking glass.

They stepped past the desk, past the partition behind it, and entered the cocktail lounge. Several people were seated at the bar: a lone man joking with the bartender, a middle-aged redhead with her hand on the thigh of the man beside her, a husky gray-haired man sitting with a blond fellow. Tyler turned her eyes to the tables. She spotted Abe and Jack in a corner booth, and Jack waved. 'They're over...'

'That's Gorman Hardy,' Nora said. She was leaning sideways as if to get a better look at someone down the bar.

'The one with the other guy?'

'That "other guy" is Brian Blake.'

Tyler could only see the back of the older man, but the blond one was talking, head turned enough to show the side of his face. 'You might be right,' she said.

'Of course I'm right. Let's go over and say hi.'

'Must we?'

'He's not such an asshole.'

'I never said he was.'

'Effete, arrogant, and slimy – same difference. Come on, don't abandon me.'

'What the hell.'

Nora waved at Abe and Jack, then lifted a forefinger to signal they would be over in a minute. Tyler, smiling toward Abe, shrugged and shook her head like an unwilling accomplice. She followed Nora down the bar.

The younger man looked over his shoulder as they approached. He was indeed Brian Blake, whose ghastly experiences had been the subject of Hardy's bestseller. He didn't appear to recognize either Tyler or Nora, but then, his eyes had barely settled on their faces before sliding down to check out the rest. Apparently pleased by what he found, he bestowed a smile.

Hardy swiveled himself sideways. 'Ladies?'

'Mr Hardy,' Nora said. 'We met you at the NLA.'

For just an instant, he looked wary. He covered it

quickly with a smile. 'Oh, yes. Certainly.' His gaze shifted from Nora to Tyler. 'We spoke briefly at the cocktail party, I believe.'

'I didn't have the pleasure,' Blake said.

'I'm Nora Branson. This is Tyler Morgan.'

'Pleased to meet you,' he said, and shook hands with both of them. 'I didn't attend the party, but I suppose you caught my talk.'

'It was fascinating,' Nora said. 'Horrifying.'

'Thank you.'

'You almost made a believer out of me.'

He looked amused. 'Almost?'

'I don't think I'll ever quite believe in ghosties till one goes bump into me.'

'*Touché*,' said Hardy. He laughed and picked up his martini. 'I suppose you were also skeptical of the book. You did read the book?'

'I don't know anyone who hasn't.'

'Neither do I, my dear, neither do I.'

'Could we buy you ladies a drink?' Blake asked.

'No, thank you,' Tyler said. 'We're with some others. In fact, we shouldn't keep them waiting.'

Nora snapped her fingers. 'You're the Mercedes, I'll bet. We're neighbors.'

'In that case, perhaps we'll be seeing you again.'

'Are you just passing through, or ...' Her eyes suddenly widened. 'You're here for Beast House! You're going to do a book on it. That's the "secret project" you referred to at the party.'

'Oh, no,' Hardy said. 'Not at all. We're on our way up to Portland for another speaking engagement.'

'We do plan to take a look at the place,' Blake added.

'Of course. We could hardly pass through this area without stopping in for the famous Beast House tour.'

'When'll you be doing it – tomorrow?'

'First thing in the morning,' Blake said.

Nora grinned. 'Maybe we'll see you there.'

Tyler's stomach tightened. 'We'd better get going,' she said.

'Yeah, we'd better.'

'Our loss,' Blake said, and winked at Nora. *Winked*.

'*Ciao*,' Hardy said.

Tyler winced. 'Bye,' she said.

'See you later,' said Nora.

Finally, they were heading for the corner booth. 'Isn't that incredible!' Nora said in a hushed voice.

'Brian Blake?'

'Him, too. No, I mean that they're gonna be doing Beast House.'

'They aren't.'

'That's what he said, but that doesn't make it true. They just don't want word getting out, or some damn rip-off artist will beat them to the punch with a Beast House book.'

'Maybe.'

'Maybe? I'd bet on it. And we can be there when they take the tour. It'll be like being part of literary history. *We were there when Gorman Hardy first stepped inside Beast House!*'

'*You* were there.'

'Aw, you'll . . .'

'Sorry we kept you waiting,' Tyler interrupted.

'No problem,' Abe said, rising to his feet. He had changed into gray slacks and a blue blazer. He wore no tie. His yellow shirt was open at the throat. 'Did you run into some friends?'

'Not friends,' Tyler said. She slipped into the booth and sat down beside him.

Nora sat across the table. She patted Jack's forearm through the sleeve of his flashy plaid sport jacket. 'Those two at the bar,' she explained, 'are Gorman Hardy and Brian Blake.'

'Brian Blake?' Jack asked. He looked at Nora with the eagerness of an enthralled child. 'Sure. The middle-weight contender out of Pittsburg.'

'No,' Abe said. 'That's Byron Blake.'

'Well, who's this guy?'

Abe signaled to the barmaid. As she approached, Nora said, 'Do you know that book, *Horror at Black River Falls?*'

'Saw the show.' He looked at Abe. 'They ran it at the post last month. That haunted house flick where blood came out of the faucets and the gal ended up opening her wrists.'

'I saw it,' Abe said. He didn't sound impressed.

The barmaid arrived. After they gave their orders, she cleared off the table and left.

Leaning forward, Jack peered at Nora. 'This Blake, he's the pretty one? I don't remember him in the movie. Who'd he play?'

'He wasn't in the movie,' Nora told him. She spoke cheerfully, without any hint of reproach. 'It was about him. It was his house in real life, and his wife's the one who committed suicide.'

'Bullshit,' Jack said.

'What's bullshit?'

'It never happened. Who are they trying to kid? Okay, maybe the guy's wife pulled the plug on herself, but ghosts? Blood spurting out of the faucets? All those dirty words showing up on the walls? An ax flying at the guy? All that stuff really happened? No way.'

'You could ask him,' Nora suggested.

'Do *you* believe it?'

'I don't know. I've heard him talk on the subject, and he sure sounded convincing.'

'Nobody sounds more convincing than a guy with a good con.'

'The other fellow,' Abe said. 'He's actually Gorman Hardy, the author?'

'He is,' Tyler said.

'I've read some of his books. Including his ghost story.'

'Did you believe it?'

'I didn't disbelieve it.'

Jack's face contorted. 'For Chistsake, Abe.'

'More things in heaven and earth, Horatio...'

'Ghosts?'

'Remember Denny Stevens?'

'Not Denny Stevens again. You were hallucinating.'

'The whole platoon was hallucinating?'

'Mass hysteria.'

Abe arched an eyebrow at Jack, then glanced from Nora to Tyler. His hands were folded on the table. He looked down at them. 'Stevens was on point. This was in the jungle near the Vu Gia River, back in '67. He stepped on an anti-personnel mine. When we got to him, his right leg was gone. He was already dead from loss of blood. The femoral artery...' He shook his head. 'A couple of hours later, we came to a village. According to

87

our intelligence, the VC had cleared out. The village was supposed to be safe, right? We stayed on our toes, just in case, but we didn't expect trouble. We were about fifty yards from the first huts when Denny Stevens came walking out from behind one. He came walking right toward us, just as if he had both legs.'

'Which he did,' Jack added.

'He was carrying his right leg. Had a hand under the boot, the thigh propped against his shoulder.'

'God Almighty,' Nora muttered.

'We were all ... slightly stunned. We just stood there, gazing at Stevens. He used his free hand to wave us off, then he kind of melted into a puddle and vanished. We took cover as if every one of us knew for a fact that he'd come back to warn us. Just about then, all hell broke loose. We got chopped up pretty good, but it would've been a wipe-out except for Stevens.'

'You'll have to forgive Abe,' Jack said. 'He's usually not insane.'

'Every survivor of that firefight will tell you the same story.'

'You oughta tell that guy Hardy about it,' Jack said. 'Maybe he'll put you in a book.'

The barmaid came with a tray of drinks. There were two of each. She distributed them, and Abe paid. 'I'll be right back with more hors d'oeuvres,' she said and took away the tray.

Abe twisted his fingers around the lip of a Dos Equiis to clean it and raised the bottle. 'Which is why,' he said, 'I don't disbelieve Hardy's book. But I don't necessarily believe it.'

'Nora thinks he's in town to write about Beast House.'

'He denies it, of course,' Nora said. 'But I'm onto him. I'm gonna be there tomorrow when he goes on the tour. Even if I have to go alone.'

'Want company?' Jack asked.

'You betcha.'

Abe looked at Tyler. 'Did you have any luck finding your old friend?'

'No. Well, we went to his place, but he doesn't live there anymore.'

'We found out he works at Beast House,' Nora said. 'Hey, maybe if we play our cards right he can get us in free.'

'I don't know,' Tyler said.

'Butterflies,' Nora explained.

9

Alone in his room, Brian Blake picked up the telephone and dialed the office. A man answered, but he was prepared for that. 'I'm sorry to bother you, but I don't seem to have an ice bucket.'

'I'll send one right over to you.'

'Appreciate it,' he said and hung up.

He went to the connecting doors and opened his side. Gorman, rereading the diary, looked up at him.

'She's on the way,' Brian said. 'I hope.'

'Excellent. Enjoy yourself, but handle her carefully. We certainly don't wish to alienate her.'

'Trust me.'

'Do I have a choice?'

Laughing, Brian shut the door. He removed a tan jacket from his suitcase, and slipped his arms into the sleeves. He was fastening the buttons when he heard a gentle knock. 'Room service?' he called.

'Your ice bucket.' Janice's voice. Brian smiled.

He opened the door.

'I filled it for you,' she said.

'Thank you.' He took the plastic container. 'Come on in for a minute.'

She stepped inside, and looked around the room as if

91

expecting to find Gorman. She had changed into blue jeans and a powder blue sweatshirt.

'How are you feeling?' Brian asked as he shut the door.

'You mean the gin? I'm okay now, but I sure conked out. I almost missed supper.'

He belted his jacket. 'How about an adventure?'

She looked intrigued. 'What do you mean?'

'Gorman asked me to check on something. You want to come along?'

'Where to?'

'I won't tell.'

'Do we walk or ride?'

'Ride, then walk.'

'How long'll it take?'

'An hour or so. It all depends.'

'On what?'

'Whether we get lucky.'

'It sounds so mysterious.'

'You game?'

She shrugged one shoulder. 'I got nothing better to do. I'll tell Dad I'm going for a walk.'

'Will he buy that?'

'Sure. I take a lot of walks. Just pull off the road and wait for me.'

Brian gave her a head start, then took his camera out to the Mercedes. He drove slowly through the courtyard, turned toward town, and stopped along the roadside. There was no traffic. He killed the headlights. Looking back, he saw Janice leave the motel office and trot down the porch stairs. She walked quickly with a bounce in her step as if eager to run. As she crossed the road, Brian flipped a switch to unlock the passenger door.

'All set,' she said, climbing in. As she swung the door shut, Brian noticed a pleasant, faint scent.

He smiled. He hadn't noticed this aroma in the room. Had she actually taken time to put on cologne for their 'adventure'?

'*Now* will you say where we're going?' she asked.

He put on his headlights and eased onto the road. 'Beast House,' he said. He watched her mouth fall open.

'Not me. At night? You're out of your tree.'

He laughed.

'You are kidding, right?'

'Right. Half kidding.'

'Only half?'

'We'll stay outside the fence. What I want to do is go around behind the place and scout around.'

'What for?'

'The hole.'

'The *beast* hole? For Godsake, what for?'

'To see if it's there.'

'Oh, man, I'm not sure about this.'

'Do you want me to take you back?'

She sighed. 'You weren't kidding about an adventure, were you?'

'Should be fun, huh?'

'Jesus.'

'Chances are, we won't find the thing anyway. If it exists at all, it's probably well hidden. It may have even collapsed by now. But if we *do* find it, you know what that means?'

'I guess it means the diary's not a fake.'

Rounding a bend, they left the dark stretch of road

behind. The main street of town was lighted with lamp-posts.

'It might also mean,' Brian said, 'that we would have access to the house.'

'Now I know you're crazy.'

He slid his gaze down her slim body. 'You might be just about the right size...'

'No way, José.'

Brian laughed. 'Actually, I only want to locate the hole and get some shots of it. The tunnel to the house is probably blocked by now, anyway. Unless the beast still uses it.'

'You just had to say that, didn't you? You're having a great old time.'

'Wonderful.'

She laughed softly as she stared out the windshield. Then she looked at him. 'I guess you must've read the diary, huh? What did you think?'

'That Thorn gal either had a very active fantasy life, or she ran into something a bit odd in her cellar.'

'A bit odd?'

'More than a bit.'

'I'll say.'

'It's too bad she didn't describe the thing in more detail.'

'As far as I'm concerned, she described more than enough.' Janice pressed her knees together. 'Look, there's the Kutch house.' She nodded to the right.

Brian glanced at the brick house set back a distance from the road.

'See anything funny about it?'

'No.'

'No windows. That's where Maggie lives. The one who owns Beast House? They say she built it without windows to keep the creature out.'

'Seems excessive,' Brian said. Turning his head, he watched Beast House as he drove slowly by. Its windows caught the moonlight. Its dull gray walls were smudged with shadows. 'Must be pleasant in there at night.'

'It's bad enough in daylight. Are you sure that wouldn't be a better time to go looking for this hole?'

'We don't want to attract attention.'

'The thing's nocturnal, you know.'

'Worried?'

'I just think you'd have a better chance finding the hole in daylight.'

'Well, it's worth a try.'

'How come Mr Hardy didn't come along?'

'He's chicken.'

'Smart man.'

'I'll protect you,' Brian said, and patted her knee.

'Gee, thanks.'

He steered around a bend, and the distant lights of Malcasa's main street vanished from the rearview mirror. The road curved upward through wooded hills. He drove farther than he wanted, looking for a shoulder wide enough to accommodate the Mercedes. When he found one, he turned out and killed the headlights.

'Oh, man,' Janice muttered.

'What?'

'It's dark.'

'All the better for sneaking around, my dear.' He

slung the camera strap around his neck and climbed out. While Janice scooted across the seat, he opened the back door. He lifted a blanket and flashlight off the floor.

'What's the blanket for?' Janice whispered.

'In case we want to make out.'

She looked at him. She said nothing.

They started across the road, Janice staying close to his side. 'Actually,' he said, 'it's in case we do find the hole. I'll want to get some shots of it, and we can use the blanket to shield the flashes.'

'Clever.'

'Disappointed?'

'Oh, sure.'

They walked along the edge of the road, heading down the slope toward town. Janice's cowboy boots sounded loud on the pavement. When the wind rushed through the trees, it seemed to Brian like the noise of an approaching car. He often looked over his shoulder.

'Nervous?' Janice asked.

'I don't want to get run over.'

'Fat chance of that.'

'You get careful,' he said, 'after you've had a close one.'

'Did you . . .?' she suddenly turned her face to him. 'My God, that's right. I forgot about that. Must've been pretty hairy.'

'You see your own car speeding at you without anyone at the wheel – yeah, I'd say it's pretty hairy.'

'Awful,' she said. 'God, you've been through a lot. I don't know how you stood it.'

He shook his head slowly. 'I came very close . . . to

taking Martha's way out. When I found her in the tub, and all that blood...'

Janice patted his forearm, gave it a gentle squeeze.

'Well,' he said, 'it was a long time ago.'

'You must still miss her.'

'Not a day goes by when I don't ... Hey, let's not get maudlin here and spoil the fun.'

'Fun?'

'I'm all right. Honest.'

She let go of his arm, and nodded. Her face was a dim blur in the darkness. Brian brushed her chin with his forefinger. 'Let's find that hole,' he whispered.

Near the bottom of the road, with the corner of the Beast House fence in sight, they crossed a shallow ditch and started along the slope. Brian led the way through the underbrush, ducking beneath low branches, climbing or descending to bypass trees and thickets, always staying roughly parallel to the fence. When he came to a cluster of rock, he climbed onto it and found a smooth surface. He sat down to rest. Janice settled down beside him. He put a hand on her back. 'How you doing?'

'Okay.'

With no trees blocking the view, Brian could see the rear corner of the fence not far below. The lawn of Beast House was pale with moonlight. Just in back of the house stood a small enclosure of latticework. 'The famous gazebo,' he said, 'where Elizabeth and Dr Ross had their "blissful delights".'

'Guess so,' Janice said. 'Do you really think we're gonna find that hole?'

'Should be over there,' he answered, pointing toward

the hillside directly behind the house. 'Just outside the fence.'

'It could be anywhere.'

'Elizabeth wrote that the tunnel came out just beyond the property line.'

'But I don't remember she said in which direction. It might've been along the back, or it might've been along this side. For all we know, we already passed it.'

Brian grinned. 'Or it might be *right behind us!*'

'Creep,' she muttered, and nudged him with her elbow. He struck back, tickling her side. She squirmed and yelped.

'Shhh. It'll hear you.'

She clamped her arm down, pinning Brian's hand against her side. 'Gotcha,' she said. 'No more tickling, okay?'

'I promise.' He slipped his hand free. 'Why don't you wait here and relax a minute? I'll be right back.'

'Not a chance. Where you go, I go.'

'Fine with me. Pick a tree.'

'Oh. In that case. Stay close, though, okay?'

He climbed over the top of the outcropping. After only a few steps, he turned around. The back of Janice's head was a shaggy silhouette in the darkness. 'Don't peek,' he warned.

'I won't.'

He unzipped his pants and relieved himself. Then he climbed over to Janice. 'Ready to go?' he asked

'All set.'

He picked up his flashlight, tucked the folded blanket under one arm, and led the way down the rocks. The hillside slanted down to a shallow ravine, then curved as if to follow the line of the fence. Though there were few trees here to give them cover, Brian felt certain that they couldn't be spotted from the distant road. Only someone looking out a rear window of Beast House would be able to see them crossing the slope.

The windows were all dark.

He waited for Janice. 'Anyone in there at night?'

'I doubt it.'

'Just the beast, huh?'

'Very funny.' She didn't sound amused. 'As a matter of fact, they say it wanders the house at night.'

'Looking for Elizabeth?'

'Looking for victims.'

'Let's hope it stays away from the windows.'

Janice lagged behind, staring at the house, then hurried to catch up. 'Maybe we ought to get out of here,' she whispered.

'We haven't even started searching for the hole.'

'C'mon, what are the chances we'll find it? You said yourself that we probably wouldn't.'

'What're you so worried about?'

'I'm not worried, I'm scared shitless.'

'What for?'

She waved toward the house. 'It can *see* us.'

Turning to Janice, he shook his head. He let the blanket and flashlight fall to the ground, and put his hands on her shoulders. He could feel her trembling. 'There's nothing to be afraid of,' he said.

'I'm sorry. Really. But . . .'

'That business with Elizabeth was more than seventy years ago,' he said in a calm, soothing voice. 'Even if the stuff in her diary is true, which I strongly doubt, that creature would be ancient by now. Decrepit. Probably dead. At any rate, nobody's been killed since that kid almost thirty years ago.'

'What do you mean? It killed three people last summer.'

Brian frowned. 'There's nothing about that in the travel brochure.'

'Well, it's outdated.' She glanced at the house. 'They were killed up there, in a corridor on the second floor.'

'The police must've investigated.'

'Sure, but they couldn't come up with an answer. They don't think the beast had anything to do with it – at least that's what they say. They said it must've been a nut.'

'They're probably right.'

'They just *said* that. They can't admit there's some kind of a goddamn monster in the house.'

'There is no monster, Janice. I mean, that's nonsense.'

'No, it's not. You read the diary.'

'Thorn was crazy.'

Janice stared up at him. She smiled slightly. 'If she was crazy, what the hell are we doing out here looking for the goddam hole?'

Brian let out a quick laugh. *'Touché,'* he said.

'Let's leave.'

'Gorman thinks there might be a hole. He's more gullible than me.'

'Let him come and look for it.'

'What'll I tell him?'

'Just say we couldn't find it.'

'That would be fibbing.'

She glanced to each side. 'I don't see the hole. Do you see the hole?'

Brian laughed. 'You're really something, Janice.'

'Am I?' She put her hands on his sides, and stared into his eyes. 'What kind of something?'

'Later. We've got to get out of here, remember?'

'No. Come on, you started it.'

'You're funny,' he said. 'And crafty. And cute.'

'Cute? Hamsters are cute.'

'Okay, how about beautiful?'

She tilted her head. 'That's nice. Now we can leave.' But her hands didn't leave Brian's sides.

He eased her close and she pressed herself tightly against him, arms wrapping his back, mouth opening, sucking in his tongue. She squirmed and moaned in his embrace.

Brian slid his hands under the back of her sweatshirt. Caressing her, he pictured himself gloating as he described it all to Gorman. *Nothing to it, really. I just worked on her emotions, played on her fears till she needed some reassuring, gave a comforting pat here and there, a little wit to break the tension. Worked on her sympathy by leading into some sad talk about my poor departed Martha. Tried to keep a sexual undertone going, joked that I'd brought the blanket for making out, even took a leak out there so she'd have to think about my dick. Stayed close enough so she could hear the piss splatter.*

Masterful job, Gorman would say.

He unhooked the back of Janice's bra. She didn't object. On the contrary, she stepped back enough to make a space between their bodies so Brian could lift

101

the cups away and caress her breasts. Her nipples felt like rubber posts. She arched her back as he thumbed them.

'Shouldn't we leave?' he asked.

Her mouth hung open, but she didn't speak. She shook her head wildly from side to side, making her hair fly.

He slid the sweatshirt up above her breasts, crouched, and used his tongue. Her trembling fingers pushed through his hair, urged his mouth hard against her breast.

Actually, Gorman, it was a cinch. She was as hot to trot as they come.

No, he shouldn't admit that. Let Gorman think he's a superstud.

Which, of course, I am.

As he sucked first on one breast, then on the other, his hands plied her firm rump through the seat of her jeans.

I took it slow, he would say. Didn't want to spook her.

He brought a hand to the front. The crotch of her jeans felt warm and moist. He pressed against it, feeling the jut of her mons through the heavy fabric. She writhed on his rubbing fingers as if she wanted them in.

Straightening up, he pulled her sweatshirt over her head. The bra came off with it. He caressed her bare neck and shoulders as she feverishly unfastened his jacket and shirt. When they were open, she squeezed herself against him. Her breasts, slicked with Brian's saliva, felt cool at first, then warm. Her hands went to his shoulders. They pulled the shirt and jacket down his arms. The chilly night air made him flinch, but her hand took his mind off the cold as it pushed inside his pants and curled around his erection.

'Let's put the blanket down,' she whispered, her fingers gliding. 'That's what you brought it for.'

'It is?'

Grinning, she gave his scrotum a gentle squeeze. Then she took out her hand. They spread the blanket nearby. It was puffy from the weeds beneath it. She walked on the blanket, her moonlit breasts jiggling as she stomped it down.

Lying on her back, she crossed each leg to pull off her boots and socks. She opened her jeans, lifted her buttocks off the blanket long enough to tug the pants out from under her, and raised her feet. 'Give me a hand?'

Brian gripped the cuffs and slid the jeans off her legs. The panties were around her thighs, very white below the dark triangle of her pubic thatch. Crouching beside her, Brian drew the flimsy garment down to her ankles and off.

While he shed the rest of his own clothes, he watched Janice squirm slowly, caressing herself. She had her knees up, her heels dug in to keep her from sliding down the gradual slope.

Her legs spread wide for him when he knelt. He kissed her inner thighs, nibbled and licked, easing lower until his mouth found her wet center. She jerked as his tongue darted. 'God, Brian,' she murmured. He pushed his tongue deep into her hugging warmth. She thrust against him, moaning.

Then he moved up her body. His tongue flicked into her navel while his hands glided up cool skin to her breasts. He squeezed and massaged them. Then he let them go and braced himself above Janice and kissed each breast and eased higher until he met her mouth.

As she sucked his tongue into her mouth, Brian slid his penis into her.

Mission accomplished, he thought.

Half accomplished, but the rest would be easy after this. Just get her into his room tomorrow night for round two and keep her busy. Talk her into showering with him so Gorman would have a chance to snatch her key. Gorman would have the tough part, sneaking into her place to find the contract and exchange it for the phoney that gave her nothing. Brian's part would be a cinch. And fun.

Better than this.

In spite of the blanket, the ground was brutal on his knees. But he kept at it, kept driving into Janice. She was going wild, thrashing around and shoving up to meet his thrusts and tugging his buttocks to force him deeper.

She would drool at the chance for an all-night fucking session.

Why don't you sneak over after your folks are asleep?

She would absolutely drool. At both ends.

She was gasping under him, eyes squeezed shut, head jerking from side to side. A few more good thrusts...

Something cold and slippery smashed down on Brian's back. His knees shot out from under him. He slammed flat against Janice. Her breath blasted against his face.

Brian thought, *Who in hell...?*

Then the teeth clamped his neck.

10

Tyler took Abe's hand as they left the Carriage House
'That was a delicious dinner. Thank you.'

'My pleasure.'

'So,' Jack said, 'should we try that place?'

'The Last Chance sounds like a dive,' Nora said

'We could look for someplace else,' Abe offered.

'The waitress seemed to think it's fine,' Tyler said.

'Hell, I love dives.'

'Nora's an expert on dives.'

'Especially the triple back somersault.'

Jack nudged her with an elbow. Giggling, she stumbled sideways toward the hedge. Jack grabbed her, and she wrapped an arm around his back.

'Anyhow,' she said, 'I am inappropriately attired for a dive of any ilk and must therefore retire to my boudoir for a change of habiliment.'

'She wants out of her prom dress,' Tyler translated.

'Need a hand?' Jack asked.

Nora swatted his rump.

'I'll want to get a jacket,' Tyler said.

They agreed to meet at Abe's car in five minutes, and left the men. Tyler entered the room after Nora. Even as she shut the door, Nora's gown swirled to the floor.

'Aren't they great?' she asked. Stepping out of it, she staggered and dropped onto the bed, her breasts bouncing.

'Are you all right?' Tyler asked.

'Fine and dandy.' Flopping backwards, she smiled at the ceiling. Her pubic hair was matted flat by her pantyhose.

'You aren't going to pass out on us, are you?'

Nora rolled her eyes. 'Hardly. I'm fine. Are you fine?'

'I'm fine.'

'So am I.' With a sigh, she sat up and started to pull her shoes off.

Tyler went through the connecting doors and slipped into her windbreaker. She brushed her hair and put on fresh lipstick. When she returned to Nora's room, her friend was on the mattress, legs hoisted in the air as she pulled on a pair of white jeans. The pantyhose lay on the floor. 'So what do you think?'

'About what?' Tyler asked.

'My lily-white ass. *Abe*. Honest Abe.'

'I like him.'

She raised her bare rump and pulled up the jeans. 'Like him a lot?'

'Very much.'

Nora sat up. She started to put on socks and loafers. 'So, gonna fuck him?'

'For godsake.'

'Take your mind off Dan.'

'Sure. Let's have a foursome.'

'I could go for that.'

'You've got sex on the brain.'

'And proud of it.' Laughing, Nora stood and slipped

106

into a plaid shirt. She buttoned it only halfway up, and tucked it into her jeans. 'If I were you,' she said, 'I'd go for it.'

'I know you would.'

'You only go around once.'

'My life is not a beer commercial.'

With a laugh, Nora zipped her fly. 'Let's went, Queeksdraw.'

'Jacket?'

'And hide my considerable charms? Bite thy tongue, wench.'

They went outside. Abe and Jack were waiting in the Mustang. Leaning across the seat, Abe opened the door. Nora climbed in back with Jack.

'You look good in your dive habiliments,' Jack told her.

'I look better without 'em.'

'Bet you do.'

Tyler slid onto the bucket seat and pulled her door shut.

'No funny stuff back there,' Abe said as he started the car.

'Far be it from us,' Nora said with a giggle.

'Are you sure you two are librarians?' he asked.

'Nora's a librarian. I'm a media specialist. That's their five-dollar term for a school librarian.'

'*I'm* a school librarian,' Nora protested.

'Don't look like one,' Jack said.

'She's college,' Tyler said. 'I'm high school. They don't fool around that much with projectors and . . .'

'Just when I'm horny,' Nora said.

Though there were no other cars in sight, Abe

signaled his right-hand turn before swinging onto the road. The headlights bore pale tunnels into the darkness. 'If this place turns out too sleazy,' he said, 'we can always try somewhere else.'

'Let's hear it for sleaze!' Nora called out. She and Jack clapped and whistled.

'Do we want to be seen with these two?' Abe asked, smiling at Tyler.

'I think we're stuck with them.'

'He's trying to pull the wool over Tyler's eyes,' Jack whispered loudly. 'Point of fact, Abe's an animal. Tell you the time he pissed on Colonel Lockridge? Jesus jumping Christ.'

'Jack!'

'You ... urinated on a colonel?' Tyler asked.

'Just on his legs. He had it coming.'

'Right in the fuckin' officers' club.'

'In the restroom?'

'Right in the fuckin' officers' club,' Jack repeated, louder. 'After that, they called him "Whizzin' Abe".' Abe, laughing softly, shook his head. 'It was a long time ago. My manners have improved.'

'Two years ago.'

'You're asking for it, Jack.'

'What did this Lockridge do?' Tyler asked.

'Changed his pants,' Jack answered.

'No, I mean...'

'He'd insulted a friend,' Abe explained.

'Remind me never to insult your friends.'

'You've nothing to fear.'

'Whizzin' Abe is a gentleman with the ladies,' Jack said. 'Usually. Though I do remember that time...'

'And here we are,' Abe said. 'The Last Chance Bar.'

The sign, just ahead, lit up the darkness with red neon letters. An upper corner sported the outline of a tipping cocktail glass. 'What do you want to bet,' Nora said, 'the other side says First Chance Bar?'

As if to satisfy her curiosity, Abe drove past the sign before turning onto the gravel lot.

'It does, it does!' Nora blurted. Someone back there slapped someone's bare skin.

The tires crunched over gravel as Abe drove along behind several parked cars. The building, a squat adobe box, had neon beer signs in both its front windows. Tyler heard muffled sounds of music from inside: Waylon Jennings singing 'Luckenbach, Texas'. Abe pulled to a stop beside a pickup truck, and they climbed out.

He took Tyler's hand. The music stopped as they entered the bar. Through the noise of voices and laughter came the jingle of a pinball machine, the clack of pool balls. The warm air was thick with swirling ribbons of smoke. As they made their way toward a table, Tyler saw a few heads turn to inspect them. One of the faces, ruddy and white-bearded, belonged to Captain Frank. He stared at her, one eye squinted almost shut. She nodded a greeting. A corner of his mouth pulled crooked, and he turned back to the bar.

'Know him?' Abe asked.

'We ran into him when we were looking for Dan.'

Abe pulled out a chair for her. She sat at the table, her back to the wall, and saw Captain Frank glance over his shoulder. Then Nora blocked her view of the man.

A barmaid came. As she cleared away a couple of beer mugs and mopped some wet rings and puddles off the table, Nora eyed her costume: cowboy boots, blue denim short-shorts, and a blouse in the pattern of a red bandanna. The blouse was knotted in front, leaving her midriff bare. 'What'll it be, folks?'

'I like your outfit,' Nora said.

'Do you? It's my own creation. Gives the fellas something to look at.' She winked at Abe. ''Course, Charlie says it's shameless.' She laughed. '"Struttin' your wares like a floozy." He goes on and on, but we bought us a brand new twenty-nine-inch Sony TV from my tips, and I don't hear him squawk about that, do I?'

'Men are just weird,' Nora pronounced.

'Can't live with 'em, can't live without 'em. You folks on vacation?'

Nora nodded.

'Well, that's real good. Hope you're having a ball. Now, what can I fetch you?'

They discussed it for a moment, then Abe ordered two pitchers of beer.

'I'll be right along with 'em, and I'll bring along a nice bowl of popcorn to keep you wanting more.'

When she was gone, Nora said, 'I wonder if they've got any openings.'

'You just want to strut your wares,' Tyler told her.

With a prolonged stare at Nora's cleavage, Jack said, 'She's already at it.'

'Get in there!' yelled a man at the pool table. 'All *right*!'

From the juke-box at the far end of the room came the voice of Tom T. Hall singing 'I Like Beer'.

'Reminds me of Le Du's joint in Saigon,' Jack said, looking across at Abe.

'Does at that,' Abe said. 'Le Du was a great lover of the old West,' he explained. 'Found himself a pair of woolie chaps somewhere, and he wore them no matter how hot it was in that bar of his. He had a ten-gallon hat that must've been nine gallons bigger than his head.'

'Was he a half-pint?' Tyler asked.

Abe laughed. 'That, and then some.'

'He got what he had coming,' Jack said, grinning mysteriously.

'Oh, no.' Nora wrinkled her nose. 'Was he a sympathizer?'

'Yup,' Abe said. 'A sympathizer with Hoppy, Gene and Roy.'

'Don't forget Randolph Scott. That was his favorite.'

'Last we heard, Le Du's the proprietor of the Hole in the Wall saloon in Waco, Texas.'

'Hope he's improved his costume,' Jack added as the barmaid approached with a laden tray.

She set out the pitchers, the frosty mugs, and a bowl of popcorn. When Abe reached for his wallet, she said, 'It's already been taken care of. Compliments of Captain Frank.'

Abe looked perplexed. 'Who?'

'The fella over there.' She nodded toward the bar. Captain Frank had swiveled around on his stool to face them. 'Said the girls are old mateys.'

'Did he?' Nora asked. 'That's sweet. Why don't we ask him to join us?'

Tyler felt a tightening in her stomach.

'That okay with you guys? He's probably lonely.'

Shaking her head, the barmaid walked away.

'It's all right with me,' Abe said.

'Long as he doesn't try to move in on us,' Jack added. 'Can't have that.'

'I'll go get him.' Nora stood, and made her way toward the bar.

'Who *is* this guy?' Abe asked.

'Captain Frank,' Tyler said. 'Just an old guy who fancies himself a seaman.'

Abe frowned. 'What's wrong?'

'Nothing, I guess. I just find him a little ... strange. You ought to see his bus.'

'If he makes you nervous...'

'Too late, now.'

Nora, holding onto the old man's arm, was steering him toward the table. He drank from a half-empty mug as he walked. He had on the same faded Hawaiian shirt and Bermuda shorts he'd been wearing that afternoon. His scrawny legs looked out of place beneath his massive torso. He moved with a list.

When they neared the table, Nora found an empty chair for him, and placed it next to Abe. ''Preciate it, mate,' he told her, and sat down.

Nora made introductions.

As Abe filled the man's mug from one of the pitchers, everyone thanked him for buying. 'My pleasure,' he said in a low, thick voice. 'My penance.' He raised his mug, winked and drank, and wiped his mouth with the back of a liver-spotted hand. 'Sins of our fathers,' he mumbled.

'You're a seafarer?' Abe asked.

'Fair and foul. A seafarer. Yes, indeed. That's me,

Captain Frank, old salt. Me and my father before me.'
He leaned forward and stared with bleary eyes at Tyler.
'God forgive him, he brought it here.'

Tyler, unsettled by his gaze, looked down at her beer.

'Brought what?' Nora asked.

'The beast.'

'The Beast House beast?' Jack asked.

'Aye, the filthy spawn of hell.'

'You're saying that your father brought it to Malcasa Point?'

'That he did, and I'm here to tell you the curse of it's a heavy burden to bear. Heavy indeed.' He took another drink.

Nora and Jack exchanged a glance as if they thought the man a lunatic. Abe was frowning.

'The guilt.' Captain Frank held up his thick, calloused hands. 'Do you see the blood? I do. I see the blood of its victims, and God alone knows how many. They don't tell it all on the tour. No indeed. Is my father there in wax? Is my sister Loreen, slain by the fiend seven years before I came wailing into this dreary world? No. You won't find them on the tour. You won't hear their names. How many others? Ten? Fifty? A hundred and fifty? Only God knows. God and the beast. People vanish. See their blood?' he asked, slowly turning his hands.

'You think it killed your father and sister?' Nora asked.

'Oh yes. Yes indeed. Little Loreen first. She was a child of three when he brought it home from some nameless forsaken island off the Australian coast. He was first mate, then, on the *Mary Jane* out of Sausalito. The summer of 1901, it was. They were becalmed, not a breath of wind, day after day, to fill the sails. The food went bad. The water casks emptied. They all thought surely they would die, and it's a shame they didn't. But on the thirteenth day of their travail, they spotted land. A volcanic island it was – all hills and jungle.

'A party went ashore. Fresh water was gathered from a spring. Fruit and berries were plentiful, but the men craved meat and found none. Now what kind of jungle is that that has no wildlife? It's none such as I have ever seen, or any of the men from the *Mary Jane*. It worked on their nerves, and many were anxious to return to the ship before nightfall. Even my father, as stout-hearted a fellow as ever walked a deck, confessed he greeted the sunset, that night, with unholy dread. But he wouldn't abandon the island, not until he was certain it bore no wildlife.'

Captain Frank swigged down some beer. He leaned forward, elbows on the table, and stared into Tyler's eyes as if she were alone with him. The noise of the bar – the talk and laughter, the clink of glasses, the clatter of pool balls, the pinging of the pinball machine, Willie Nelson's clear voice from the juke-box – all seemed strangely distant to Tyler.

'When darkness fell,' he continued, 'they surrounded the water hole. Men concealed themselves among the bushes and climbed into trees. Every last mother's son of them was armed, ready to slay any animal that might come to drink.

'The strategy worked. Near midnight, the creatures came. Twelve or fifteen of them wandered out of the jungle and waded into the pond to drink. My father admits he thought they were humans at first – some primitive tribe —but then he saw their faces in the moonlight. Their snouts. He knew they weren't human, but loathsome, unearthly beasts. He ordered the men to fire. Every last one of the creatures fell. Not a one of them got away. My father's face went ghastly pale when he told me of the slaughter, and what happened afterwards – how some of the men had their way with the female carcasses...'

'Frank,' Abe said.

The old man flinched as if startled from his dark reverie.

'I don't think we want to hear all this.'

'I do,' Nora protested. 'It's fascinating.'

'I don't mind,' Tyler said. She was trembling. She hated the story, but she had to hear the rest of it, and even resented Abe's interruption. She took a long drink of beer. Abe gave her a quizzical look, and refilled her glass from the pitcher.

'Go on,' Nora said.

Captain Frank looked to Abe for permission.

'Doesn't bother *me*,' he said.

'Then I'll ... the slaughter ... When it was done, my father found a survivor, an infant creature beneath one of the females – its mother, no doubt. Her body had shielded it from the storm of bullets. Father took this infant into his care.

'The others, the bodies, were...' He glanced uneasily at Abe. 'They provided sufficient nourishment to see the crew safely to Perth.'

'They ate them?' Nora asked.

'My father claimed they tasted rather like mutton.'

'Charming.'

'He named his creature Bobo, and though he was never fond of it he considered the filthy thing a great curiosity and kept it with him in a cage on the journey home. My mother, rest her soul, thought Bobo appalling. She begged him to get rid of it, but little Loreen found the creature delightful and spent hours behind our home, talking to it through the bars of its cage as if it were a playmate. At last, Mother prevailed upon him to dispose of it. He agreed to transport it to San Francisco, where he hoped to sell it for a good price to a circus or zoo. Alas, Loreen must have overheard the talk, for she opened the cage, the very next morning, and Bobo fell upon her. My folks heard her awful screams, but she was past helping when they reached her. The beast, small as it was, had torn her asunder, and was having...' Captain Frank glanced at Abe, and shook his head.

'My father beat it senseless with a spade. He thought he'd killed it. He put the remains in the flour bag, and dragged it up into the hills behind the Thorn house. The place was under construction, then. Lilly Thorn was just having it built. He buried the creature up there.'

'But it wasn't dead?' Nora asked.

'Not much more than a year went by, and there were three dead in the Thorn house: Lilly's two sons and her sister. Lilly escaped, but she was never right afterward and they carted her off to a sanitarium. The blame fell on a luckless chap name of Goucher, a handyman who'd stopped by, the day before, to chop wood. But my father'd seen the bodies. He had his suspicions, and spoke up for Goucher, claiming a wild animal must've got into the house, but he kept shut about Bobo, not wanting to bring blame on himself. Well, the crowd wouldn't listen. They lynched poor Goucher, strung him up from a porch beam.

'I wasn't born till six years later, that's 1909. I 'spect I'm what you'd call an accident, for I believe my folks were loath to have another child after what happened to Loreen. Oh, they treated me like royalty, but there was always a gloom in their eyes. The Thorn house, all the time I was growing up, stood deserted at the end of town. Nobody'd go near the place. It was said to be haunted. Every now and then, though, we'd have someone disappear. Then, in '31, the Kutch family moved in.

'They came from Seattle, and scoffed at warnings about the house, but they weren't settled in more than a couple of weeks before the husband and kids were slaughtered. Maggie was scratched up bad, but ... she'll tell you all about it if you take the tour. What she won't tell you – what maybe she doesn't know – is that my father, the night after the funeral, took his Winchester and went off to kill the beast.

'He was sixty-two at the time. He'd been living with the guilt for better than thirty years, and he told me that morning he couldn't abide it any longer. It was then I heard the whole story for the first time, and how he knew it must be Bobo, still alive, behind the murders. I begged him to let me come along, but he just wouldn't hear of it. He wanted me to stay behind, and look after Mother. It was as if he knew he would never come back, and he didn't. He was a good shot. I 'spect Bobo must've snuck up on him, caught him from the back.' Captain Frank raked the air, fingers hooked like claws, and knocked over his mug. Tyler flinched as it pounded onto the table. Beer flew out, splashing Abe, sliding in a sudsy spill across the wood. 'Oh, I'm...' The old man shook his head, mumbling, and swept at the puddle with his open hand. 'Oh. I'm ... I shouldn't of ... oh damn.'

The barmaid rushed up with a towel. 'We have a little accident here?' she asked, mopping the table.

'Nothing serious,' Abe said.

'If Frank's being a nuisance...'

'No. It's fine.'

'I should've warned you,' she said, casting a peeved glance at Captain Frank. 'Going at his Bobo story, I bet. He'll talk your ears off once he's soaked up a few. We've had folks get up and walk out. Haven't we, Captain?'

He stared down at his shirt. 'The tale must be told,' he muttered.

'Gives the place a bad name.'

'Pretty interesting stuff,' Nora said.

'Just don't believe a word of it,' the barmaid said. 'Come on, Frank. Why don't you go on back to the bar and leave these nice folks in peace.' She took his arm and helped him stand up.

'Hang on a second,' Abe said. He lifted a pitcher and filled the old man's mug to the brim.

'Thank you, matey. Let me tell you.' He met the eyes of everyone at the table. 'The hours of the beast are numbered. One night, Captain Frank shall stalk it to its lair and lay it low. The souls of the dead cry out for its blood. I am the avenger. Mark my words.'

'We'll be pulling for you,' Jack called after him.

'Jesus,' Nora said, and rolled her eyes.

Grinning, Jack shook his head. 'The old fart waits much longer, he'll be stalking it from a wheelchair.'

'He'll never do it,' Abe said. 'A guy talks it out that way, he doesn't act on it.'

'Did you believe it?' Tyler asked. 'About the beast?'

'He didn't *dis*believe it,' Jack put in.

'Hey,' Nora said. 'We've gotta tell Gorman Hardy about this guy. Maybe he'll put us in the Acknowledgment. "My gratitude to Nora Branson, Tyler Moran, Jack Wyatt, and Abe Clanton, whose valuable assistance led me to the true story of Bobo the beast." I ask you, would that not be terrif?'

'That,' Tyler said, 'would be almost *too* exciting.'

11

A sharp pounding on the door startled Gorman Hardy awake. He bolted upright and scanned the dark room, wondering where he was. Then he remembered.

It must, he thought, be Brian at the door. But why the frantic knocking?

Perhaps he had lost his key.

'I'm coming,' Gorman called.

The knocking continued.

He swung his legs to the floor and squinted against the brightness as he switched on a bedside lamp.

'I'm coming,' he called again.

The knocking didn't stop.

Something, he thought, must have gone wrong. More than a lost room key. Something bad enough to panic Brian.

He felt on the verge of panic, himself, as he stood up.

For the love of God, what had happened?

He was naked. He put on a satin robe, tied it shut, and opened the door.

Brian was not there.

On the dark stoop waited a man and a woman. The man was about forty and bald. He wore a blue windbreaker. His fists were clenched at his sides.

Gorman had never seen him before. The woman, an attractive blonde, looked familiar. She wore jeans and a checkered blouse and an open leather jacket. She looked like an older version of Janice. Gorman realized he had seen her at the Carriage House where she'd been performing hostess duties.

These people are Janice's parents.

He felt a little sick.

'Mr Hardy?' the man asked in a taut voice.

'Yes.'

'I'll try to be civilized about this, but it's two o'clock in the morning and our daughter is missing. Is she here?'

'No, of course not. Come in and see for yourselves.' He stepped away from the door to let them enter. The woman shut the door and backed against it as if to prevent Gorman from escaping.

The man, after a glance at the beds, stepped into the bathroom and turned on a light. He came out a moment later, and checked the closet. He looked at the connecting door, then at Gorman. 'What about Mr Blake?'

'I really can't answer for him.'

'You're together. You paid both rooms.'

'He is my associate, yes. But I have no idea why you suspect either of us might be harboring your daughter.' As he spoke, he walked past the man to the connecting door. He rapped it with his fist. 'Brian?' he called. He opened his side and tried the knob of Brian's door. Fortunately, it didn't turn. With any luck, if the girl was in the room, she would have time to get out. 'Brian?' he called again.

'Let's have a look,' the man said, striding forward.

'He drove her someplace,' the woman said, speaking for the first time.

'I'll take a look anyhow.'

Gorman stepped out of his way. He watched Janice's father insert a key and unlock the door. A lamp was on. Relieved, Gorman saw that both the beds were made. He waited while the man entered to search. Turning to the woman, he said, 'Is the car gone?'

She nodded. Her face was grim, lips pressed together in a tight line, eyes glaring at Gorman.

'I honestly don't know what to say,' he told her. 'You suspect that she and Brian went off together?'

'You wouldn't know anything about that,' she said, her voice bitter.

'I'm afraid not.'

The man came back into the room. 'Okay, buster, where'd they go?'

'I have no idea. I don't even *know* your daughter. Would she be the young lady who registered us?'

'She would be.'

'I haven't seen her since then.'

'Don't lie to us!' the woman suddenly blurted. She rushed to her husband's side. 'Show him, Marty. Show him!'

He pulled a folded sheet of paper from his back pocket. It shook in his trembling hands as he opened it. 'We found this in Janice's room,' he said, and held it out.

Gorman took the sheet. He stared at it. The bitch, he thought. Oh, the bitch! She was supposed to hide it! Brian's fault. Where is he? What could've possessed him to keep her out so late and allow this to happen? He's ruined it. He's ruined everything!

'What do you say to that, Mr Hardy?' the woman said, almost snarling.

He managed a smile as he handed back the contract. 'Janice planned to surprise you,' he said. 'If the proposed book is as successful as my previous one, this agreement will likely earn her in the neighborhood of a million dollars.'

The news had its desired effect. Janice's parents looked at each other, then at the contract. They seemed to soften, as if their pent-up rage was melting away.

'Is this on the level?' Marty asked. He sounded suspicious, but a hint of excitement glittered in his eyes.

'It most certainly is. The agreement gives Janice fifty percent of all earnings from the book. This includes the advance and all royalties. We're talking here about a hardbound sale, book club and paperback sales, foreign sales, probably a movie deal. So far, my previous book has brought in over three million dollars. I suspect the Beast House story will do as well, or better. And Janice will receive half of it all.'

And she will, he thought. Good Christ, she will. Now there was no chance of tricking her out of it. He felt sick.

The woman raised her eyes from the contract. She looked wary. 'What did Janice have to do for this?'

'The book was her idea. She initiated the contact with me. And she provided me with a resource that gives invaluable insight into the subject.'

'What's that?' Marty asked.

'Janice doesn't wish that known, but since you're her parents, I see no harm in telling you that she found a diary written by Elizabeth Thorn, the lady who...'

'Where is Janice now?' the mother asked. 'I realize this puts a somewhat different light on the subject, but where *is* she? Does it have something to do with this?' She nodded at the contract.

'I honestly don't know. When did you last see her?'

'Around nine,' Marty answered. 'She said she was going for a walk. This was right after she came back from delivering an ice bucket to Mr Blake – which, by the way, he didn't need in the first place. I saw two in there.'

'I can only suppose,' Gorman said, 'that Brian invited her to accompany him. Perhaps she lied to you, thinking you might disapprove of her traipsing off with one of the motel guests.'

Marty and his wife exchanged a glance.

'I take it she's done such things before.'

'Wherever they went,' Marty said, 'they should've been back long ago.'

The woman said, 'There's no excuse for this.'

'I quite agree,' Gorman told her.

'Where did he take her?' Marty asked.

'We have no proof that she went with Brian at all, but he left with the intention of exploring an area behind Beast House. He was hoping to locate and photograph a hole near the rear fence.'

'A *hole*?'

'It's mentioned in the Thorn diary. Allegedly, an underground tunnel leads from the hillside to the house's cellar. If Brian finds the opening, it lends a certain credence to the...'

'Janice wouldn't go anywhere near that place,' her mother said.

'Well, perhaps she didn't. I'm simply pointing out the purpose of Brian's search. That's where he intended to go.'

'She must've gone with him, Claire.'

Claire shook her head. She looked resigned, rather weary. 'I guess I wouldn't put it past her,' she admitted. 'This Brian, I saw him at the restaurant. He's a very attractive man.'

Marty put a hand on Claire's back. In a gentle voice, he said, 'I'll drive out and bring her home.'

'I'm sure she'll be right along,' Gorman said.

'We've been waiting up for hours, Mr Hardy. Have you got any idea what goes through a parent's mind when your kid's out at this time of night and you don't know where she is, what's happened to her? You tell yourself she'll walk through the door any minute, and all the time you're wondering if maybe some lunatic got hold of her, if maybe you'll never see her again.'

'I can assure you, Brian's no lunatic.'

'Why isn't she home?' Marty demanded. He sounded a little frantic.

Claire sighed. 'She probably got carried away and forgot the time.'

'I'll remind her of the time,' Marty snapped, 'when I get my hands on her.' He frowned at Gorman. 'Where, exactly, is this hole supposed to be?'

'If you'd like, I'll accompany you. I'm rather concerned, myself, at this point.'

'We'll all go,' Claire said.

'Just give me a minute to get dressed,' said Gorman.

They found the Mercedes just above the curve leading

into town from the south. Marty swung in behind it. He took a flashlight with him, and shone it through a side window. With a shake of his head, he came back down the road to Claire and Gorman. 'Nobody there,' he said.

'That young lady has a lot of explaining to do,' Claire muttered.

'So does Brian,' Gorman said. A million dollars worth, he thought.

They followed the road to the bottom of the hill, then crossed a ditch to the corner of the Beast House fence. Marty took the lead, trudging through the underbrush alongside the fence, playing his flashlight beam over the wooded slope on the right. 'Janice!' he yelled.

Claire tugged his shoulder. 'Don't,' she said.

'Janice!'

'I wish you wouldn't *do* that!'

'There's nobody to hear it but them.'

Gorman saw the woman look through the fence bars at the house. 'I just think we should be quiet about this.'

Now Gorman found himself looking at the house – at the darkness of the porch but especially at the windows. It seemed to have so many: a bay window directly across the yard from him, a casement farther along the side, three sets on the second story, a single high attic window just below the peak of the roof, a pair beneath the tower's cap. All were moonless and black. Malevolent eyes, he thought, recalling the words he'd spoken into his recorder that afternoon. He'd been waxing eloquent, then – spewing drivel. But now it was three o'clock in the morning and he suddenly wished he were back at the inn, snug in bed, because the windows did, in fact, seem to be watching him.

He forced himself to look away from them. He stared at the weeds ahead of his feet, at Claire's back, at the beam of Marty's flashlight sweeping over bushes and rocks and trees on the slope. And he felt like a man walking down a dark street, stalked by stealthy footsteps, afraid of what he might find sneaking up on him if he should dare to glance over his shoulder. He had to look. He searched the windows. Though nothing showed through their blackness, his skin went tight and crawly.

Tomorrow, if he took the tour, he would have to go inside. The thought of it chilled him. Perhaps he should forget about it, simply abandon the project. After all, tonight's disaster had diminished his and Brian's possible returns by half.

Half of a gold mine, he told himself, is considerably better than no gold mine at all. The book would be a winner, he had no doubt of that. After *Horror*, his reputation alone would insure tremendous sales. But the Beast House story had tremendous potential. It could easily surpass the success of *Horror*. He was a fool to consider giving it up. He would simply have to keep a stiff upper lip and take the tour.

In daylight, the house wouldn't seem quite so forbidding. Besides, Brian would be along. Probably several sightseers, as well. And certainly there couldn't be any danger involved.

'Marty!' Claire gasped.

The man had suddenly broken into a run. He raced around the corner of the fence. Claire took off, chasing him. 'Marty!' she called. 'What is it?'

He didn't answer.

Gorman hurried after them both, reaching the corner with a few strides, then slogging along the rear section of fence.

What craziness is *this*? he wondered.

But he certainly did not want to be left behind. As he tried to catch up, he felt a familiar but long-forgotten mingling of despair and humiliation. The residue of childhood 'games' in which he had too often been the victim. Hey, let's ditch him! Let's ditch Gory! C'mon, let's lose him! And off his pals would go, trying their best to leave him behind, lost and alone.

Gorman knew in this case that he was not being ditched. Marty had seen something. But the awful, desperate feelings remained and tears blurred his vision as he struggled to keep up with the runners. 'Wait up!' he gasped.

They didn't wait.

But suddenly they stopped.

Gorman grabbed a bar of the fence to halt himself. Gasping, he wiped the tears from his eyes.

'Jesus H. Christ,' Marty muttered.

Claire staggered away, bent over, and started to vomit. Marty was aiming his flashlight upward. Gorman followed its beam to the top of the fence.

Brian's legs hung down, one on each side. He was naked. He was on his back. The body looked as if it had been slammed down hard onto the pointed uprights. Gorman's sphincter went cold and tight as he saw where one of the spikes had penetrated. The other bars had entered in a straight line, the final one piercing the back of his skull. His left arm drooped strangely. Gorman realized it had been broken backwards at the elbow.

Marty's light skittered down the length of the fence. Gorman followed its quick course. There was not another impaled body. The man turned toward the hillside. 'Janice!' he yelled. His beam swept over the weeds and bushes, and stopped on something about thirty feet up.

A rumpled blanket. Scattered clothes.

Claire shrieked out her daughter's name and lunged toward the slope. She scrambled up it, falling to her knees, crawling, getting her feet under her and scurrying higher. Marty raced after her.

Gorman stayed where he was. He watched them for a moment, then turned his gaze to the body. He ached as if he could feel the spikes in himself. He wanted badly to run, but the thought of fleeing, all alone in the dark, filled him with dread. He was shaking. He clutched a bar of the fence to steady himself. The cold iron was wet and sticky. He jerked his hand away and stared at it. The smears looked black in the moonlight. He raised his eyes to Brian's body. Suddenly, he didn't feel so terrified.

With his clean right hand, he reached into a pocket and took out his cassette recorder. He switched it on. 'I am standing, as I speak, beneath the body of Brian Blake – my friend, my associate, the man who survived the horror at Black River Falls only to meet a hideous death at the hands of the Malcasa beast. He met his fate in the dead of night, while...'

'Hardy! Goddamn you, get up here!'

He nodded, and backed away from the fence. Before starting up the slope, he slipped the recorder into his pocket without turning it off. If only he'd had the presence of mind to record everything from the moment Marty and Claire entered his room! Of course, he'd had no way of knowing at the time that the encounter would lead to such a marvellous tragedy.

Brian slaughtered by the beast. And in such a grisly fashion. It was almost too good to believe. The book would skyrocket!

Not only that, but Brian wouldn't be around to collect his share of the proceeds.

Incredible!

Now, if only Janice's body is up here, nicely mutilated ... The parents will demand her half of the profits, but perhaps their claim wouldn't stand up in court.

'Look at this, you bastard!' Marty snapped, shining his light on the ground. Gorman recognized Brian's jacket and Hush Puppies. He saw garments all over the ground: a sweatshirt and brassière, cowboy boots, jeans, panties. The tangled blanket was dark with blood.

'Apparently,' Gorman said, 'they must have been ...'

'Shut up!'

Claire was a distance away, sobbing as she searched through bushes.

'I'm sorry,' Gorman said. 'Honestly, though, I had no idea they ...'

'You got her into this, goddamn you! I'll kill you if she ...'

'Perhaps she's all right. She might have fled.'

'You'd better pray she did.' Turning away, Marty shouted up the hillside. 'Janice! Jaaan – nice!'

Gorman crouched and picked up Brian's camera. The flash attachment was in place. He peeled off the lens cap, and raised the camera to his eye. Peering through the viewfinder, he aimed at the blanket. The girl's jeans and panties were also in frame. He snapped a shot. In the quick burst of light, he saw that the panties were pink, the blue jeans faded, the blue blanket splashed with crimson. The automatic film advance buzzed.

The *Horror* photos had been printed in black and white. For this book, Gorman would insist on color plates. At least a few for the hardcover edition.

He turned the camera toward Janice's boots. They were close together, one standing at a slant, propped up by the sole of the other.

Fabulous.

She died with her boots off.

As his fingertip sought the shutter release, Marty blocked the view and drove a fist into Gorman's belly. The blow smashed his wind out, knocked him backwards. The camera flew from his hands. His back hit the slope. He skidded downhill. His legs flipped high and he somersaulted. The earth pounded his knees, his belly. He clutched at weeds to stop his slide. Through his loud gasps for breath, he heard Claire shouting for Marty to stop.

The man came charging down.

'No!' Gorman cried.

Still in motion, Marty kicked at his head. Gorman shoved his face into the weeds. He felt the breeze of the passing shoe. Looking up, he saw that the momentum of the kick had thrown the man off balance. Marty flailed his arms and fell backwards. He landed on his rump. As he slid, the edge of a shoe scraped Gorman's ear.

Gorman grabbed the shoe and twisted it sharply. He heard a crackly sound of tearing cartilage. Marty

132

flinched with pain. His mouth sprang open and he let out a cry.

'Marty!' Claire yelled. She started down.

In seconds, Gorman would have her to contend with. Two against one. It's not fair!

He tugged Marty's foot. When the groaning man was close enough, Gorman punched him in the groin.

'Leave him alone!' Claire shouted. 'Don't touch him, you bastard!'

She was only a few yards away.

Gorman found a rock the size of a coconut, and slammed it down on Marty's forehead. He felt the skull crush under its impact.

A whiny sound came from Claire. She was climbing the slope backwards, shaking her head from side to side with tight little jerks, her arms batting the air for balance.

Gorman got to his knees. 'It's all right,' he told her. 'Don't be frightened. We'll get him to a doctor.'

Claire suddenly whirled around and bolted up the hillside.

Gorman went after her. 'Don't run!' he called. 'We can't help Marty if you run. Wait up!'

She kept going.

'Goddamn it, wait! I won't hurt you!'

Her foot landed on one of Janice's boots. She stumbled, but didn't fall.

Gorman hurled the rock. It caught her between the shoulder blades and bounced off. She went down, sprawling flat, and scurried to get up again. Gorman pounced on her back. His weight smashed her to the ground. Clutching her hair, he tugged her head toward him and stretched his right arm out past her shoulder and brought his fist back sharply to strike her face. The position was awkward. He couldn't get much power behind the punch. But he pounded her face again and again, very fast. She was crying and attempting to turn her face away. When she managed to grab his wrist, he yanked it free and drove his elbow down hard on her shoulder. That sent a shudder through her body, so he kept hammering down with his elbow, each blow making her cry out and squirm, until finally he somehow struck his crazy bone. His arm went tingly and numb.

Keeping his grip on her hair, he raised himself off her back. He sat on her rump. Her feeble writhing didn't worry him. He knew he'd taken the starch out of her. But he wasn't quite sure how to finish her off. As he shook his arm and waited for its weakness to pass, he scanned the moonlit ground. He saw no rocks close enough to reach.

She twisted under him.

'Stop it,' he snapped. He gave her hair a savage tug. 'And stop that sobbing.'

In a moment, his arm felt better. He raked his fingers through the weeds alongside Claire's body, and found a stick. It was slightly larger than a pencil, and neither end had much of a point. But perhaps it would do.

Clutching it like a knife, Gorman scooted up her back and rammed it at her neck, just below her right ear. The stick skidded down her skin, clawing a furrow. Screaming, Claire bucked and twisted in a frenzy. Gorman struck again. This time, a couple of inches broke off the stick, leaving a decent point. The third blow penetrated.

Her shriek leaped to a higher pitch. She thrashed wildly as he forced the stick deeper. Then he pulled it out and stabbed again. He kept plunging the stick into her neck long after the screams stopped and she lay motionless beneath him.

Then he climbed off her. The sleeve of his jacket was sheathed with blood. He wiped his hand on the seat of her jeans.

Patting his pockets, he made sure he hadn't lost his wallet or cassette recorder during the struggles.

The recorder. He took it out. Good God, it had been running throughout the killings. He would have to destroy the tape.

He would also have to get rid of his clothes. Every stitch. But that could wait.

Down the slope, he picked up Brian's pants. The underwear fluttered out. He dug into the pocket and removed the car keys. Wandering along the hillside, he found the camera. Finally, he knelt over Marty's body. The contract was in a pocket of the shirt. He took it out. Though he wasn't precisely sure why, at that moment, he also took Marty's keys.

Then he rushed down to the fence. With a final glance at Brian's impaled body, he ran.

12

The air felt chilly on Tyler's face, but the rest of her body was snug under the covers. Rolling over, she pushed her face into the soft warmth of the pillow.

The chirp and warble of birds sounded peaceful, stirred memories of distant summer mornings when she lay in bed, so comfortable she didn't want to get up, but was eager to get outside. Adventures beckoned: today the comic book stand (she'd make a fortune!), today the careers tournament with Sally and Huss and Loretta, today a picnic at the lake, today exploring.

Exploring was maybe the best – taking off, on bike or foot, to follow that road, that forest path, those train tracks, farther than she'd ever gone before.

Later came the mornings, almost painful with excitement, when she couldn't wait to get up and take the bus to the public pool where Skip Robinson would be practicing his backstroke and this time he might notice her. Finally, he did. And he was so shy. And he always smelled like Coppertone.

Abe smells like Brut. She squirmed against the bed, remembering the feel of his body as he embraced her last night. There on the stoop like a couple of teenagers while Nora led Jack into her room. If she'd asked Abe to come in, he would be next to her now. Instead, they'd gone alone to their rooms. Tyler had regretted it even then, feeling the loss like an empty ache.

I hardly know the man, she thought.

But Dan had been in her mind. She'd come here to find Dan, and it would've been some kind of vague betrayal to make love with Abe.

She wished she had.

She owed nothing to Dan. They'd made their choices five years ago and even if she found him today (in Beast House?) it was probably over for good. She shouldn't have let thoughts of Dan stop her.

More than that had stopped her. It was also wanting Abe so badly and knowing she might never see him again after today. He and Jack would head north; she and Nora would head south. And if she'd made love with Abe, the parting would be worse.

Thinking about it now, she felt the loss as if he were already gone.

We have today, she told herself.

They had agreed, last night, to meet for breakfast. And after that? The Beast House tour? Nora seemed determined to try it, and if Abe and Jack would go along . . . at least they'd be together that much longer.

Abe, I want you to meet my old friend, Dan Jenson. Dan, Abe Clanton.

Tyler? I can't believe it's really you. My God, let me look at you. You're beautiful! Lost a few pounds have you?

Jealous sparks from Abe's eyes as Dan sweeps her into his arms. Abe starts walking away. No, wait!

Too upset now to enjoy the luxury of the bed, Tyler got

up. She parted the curtains slightly and looked outside. Her heart jumped. Seated on the stoop directly across the courtyard, elbows resting on his knees, eyes down, was Abe. The morning breeze stirred his hair. He was frowning as if deep in thought. Thinking about me? she wondered.

Sure thing. You flatter yourself.

But he might be.

God, he looks so lonely and troubled.

Astonished by her boldness, Tyler stepped away from the window. She put on a robe over her nightgown and went to the door. As she opened it, Abe looked up. His frown melted into a smile. 'Morning,' Tyler called.

'Good morning.'

'Been up long?'

'Not long.'

'How about a cup of coffee?'

'How can I refuse?' He stood and brushed off the seat of his blue jeans. The jeans were old, worn pale at the knees, frayed a little at the cuffs. He wore new-looking boots. His white T-shirt hugged his torso, taking on the curves of his muscles.

Tyler was suddenly very aware that she was naked under her robe and nightgown.

That's hardly naked, she thought.

But she could feel the cool breeze curling up her legs, sliding between them. Her nipples pushed into the slick fabric of her nightgown. She was slightly breathless as she stepped back from the doorway to let Abe enter.

'So,' she said, trying to sound calm, 'did you sleep well? No nightmares about Bobo, I hope.'

He studied her face. 'I slept fine. How about you?'

'Like a log.' She broke from his gaze and turned away. Her knees were shaky as she crossed the room. She took the coffee pot down from the mounted hotplate, and carried it into the bathroom. She filled it and brought it back. As she plugged in the dangling cord, Abe walked up behind her. She turned to face him. 'It'll probably take a few . . .' Her voice fell away. She stared into his eyes.

His open hand caressed the side of her face. 'I missed you,' he whispered.

Tyler tried to speak but her throat was tight. She stepped into his arms, and kissed him.

Abe held her tightly, more tightly than last night, as if they'd been away from each other a very long time and he needed the feel of her body to know she was with him again. After a moment, his embrace loosened. His hands slid up and down her back.

Tyler wished he would hike up her robe and nightgown so she could feel his hands on her bare skin. But he patted her rump, and eased away.

Tyler untied her cloth belt. She parted her robe. She took him by the wrists and lifted his hands to her breasts. His hands were warm through the filmy nightgown. Her breath trembled as he caressed and gently squeezed. Then he shut the robe. Gripping its lapels, he pulled her forward and kissed her lightly on the mouth. He smiled. 'You trying to seduce me?' he asked.

'It crossed my mind.'

'Shameless hussy,' he said.

'That's me.'

'What about your friend, Dan?'

Her stomach tightened. 'What about him?'

'You came all this way to find him.'

'I know, but...'

'If I'm going to lose you to this guy, I'd rather not ... get in any deeper. I want you too much already. Don't make it any tougher on me.'

'Oh, Abe,' she whispered. His face blurred as tears filled her eyes. She stepped against him and held him tightly.

'There you go again,' he said, stroking her hair. 'Now why don't you get dressed, and I'll fix the coffee. You invited me in for coffee, remember?'

Tyler nodded. She wiped her eyes.

'Don't try undressing in front of me, either.'

She managed a smile. 'Darn, that was my plan.'

'I must be psychic.'

'Don't you want to see what you're missing?'

'That's it, rub my face in it.'

'You *must* be psychic. That would've been phase two.'

Abe laughed softly and shook his head.

Tyler stepped past him. He watched as she bent over the spare bed to search her suitcase. 'I thought you were going to fix the coffee.'

'Do you take anything in it?'

'Just black.'

But he didn't turn away. Tyler took out her corduroys, her yellow blouse, the filmy bra she'd worn last night, and a fresh pair of panties. She held up the garments for Abe to see. 'Do these meet with your approval?'

'Very nice.'

She gave him a coy smile. 'Dan never cared much for these,' she said, and let the bra flutter to the bed.

'You have a definite cruel streak,' Abe said.

'Do I?' She took the rest of the clothes into the bathroom. 'Ta ta,' she said, and shut the door. She leaned against it. Shutting her eyes, she could still feel his arms around her, the firm pressure of his body, his eager lips, the way he'd touched her breasts. *I want you too much already.* My God, had he really said that? He had, he had! She found herself smiling and weeping. *If I'm going to lose you to this guy ...*

No need to worry about that, Mr Abraham Clanton. Tyler Clanton.

She whispered the words.

Good Christ, don't get crazy.

But she felt crazy: joyous and guilty and confused. *He wants me, but how much? What's next?*

Breakfast is next. Take it one step at a time. Breakfast, then the tour of Beast House and confronting Dan (Jesus, what'll I say to him?), then what? Lunch, maybe. What happens when it's time to leave? Don't think about that. Not yet. Cross the bridges as you come to them. Maybe we can all stay one more night. Or two. Or ...

'The coffee's ready,' Abe called through the door.

'I'll be right out,' she said. Quickly, she shed her robe and nightgown. She used the toilet, washed, brushed her teeth, rolled deodorant under her arms, and dressed. It made her feel daring and sexy to wear the gauzy blouse without a bra. Luckily, there was a pocket over each breast. She tucked it in, leaned close to the mirror, and studied herself. 'Lookin' good,' she whispered. She unfastened another button to allow a glimpse of cleavage.

Nora would open still another.

She considered it for a moment, then shook her head.

Abe smiled when she stepped out. 'Lovely,' he said.

She glanced down at her blouse. 'Dan always liked me in yellow.'

Abe gave her a strange look. He must suspect. Wasn't her teasing a dead giveaway? Well, she would just let him wonder. At least for a while.

He gave her a plastic cup. Steam was still rolling off the coffee. 'Nora knocked while you were changing. They're just about ready to go.'

Tyler sipped the coffee, and wrinkled her nose.

'What can I say? It's instant.'

'At least it's hot.' She took her cup to the dressing table, sat down, and drank as she brushed her hair. Abe stood behind her, watching. 'Was Jack there?' she asked, and saw him nod in the mirror.

'Lucky Jack,' he said.

'Lucky Nora.'

Abe put down his cup. He rubbed her shoulders, and she moaned.

Then came a quiet knocking. He let go of her, crossed the room, and opened the connecting door.

'All set and rarin' to go?' Nora asked. She entered, followed by Jack. 'We thought it'd be fun to go in town for breakfast. That sound good to everyone?'

'Sure,' Tyler said, getting up.

Nora was wearing a tube-top that left her bare to the tops of her breasts. A faint red line marked her shoulder where the man, yesterday, had struck her with the radio antenna. Her skin had a rosy glow, and her hair looked damp. She must've recently taken a shower, Tyler

143

thought. Jack, too, was slightly flushed. Had they showered together? Made love under the hot spray?

Abe and I could've...

'Got your room key?' Abe asked her.

Nodding, she picked up her purse.

They went outside into the cool morning shadows, and Tyler slipped a hand around Abe's back.

'I think,' Nora said, 'I could go for pigs in a blanket.'

13

Gorman dreamed they were after him. He was running down a sunlit slope, laughing at first and waving the paper – the contract – overhead to taunt them. 'You can't catch mee,' he sang. He knew they couldn't. He was fleet of foot while Marty and Claire were staggering after him like sleep-walkers. No, like zombies. It suddenly struck Gorman that they were, indeed, zombies. That notion took away some of the fun: what if they *should* catch him? Zombies would likely treat him to a horror or two.

Though he knew they were after him, they were somewhat preoccupied. Marty was busy ripping to shreds a pair of pink panties while Claire was digging out one of her eyes with a blunt stick.

I never did *that*, he thought. You're doing *that* to yourself, sweety-pie.

Looking forward, he saw Brian wave at him from on top of the fence. Janice was up there, too, straddling the spike – one of them *in* her – writhing passionately on it while she sucked Brian's cock. She saw Gorman and sat up. 'Hey,' she shouted, 'that's *my* contract!'

'Finders keepers, losers weepers!' he yelled back, flapping it at her.

'Forget it,' Brian told her. 'You've got me.'

With a shrug, she leaned down again and took him into her mouth.

Gorman turned away and raced alongside the fence. Looking back, he saw Marty and Claire. They were close behind him, which didn't make much sense because he was running and they were shambling along slowly. Marty was stuffing bits of the shredded panties into his mouth. Claire, beside him, had one eyeball dangling over her cheek and was working on the other, trying to pry it out with her stick. Let her get that one, Gorman thought, and she won't be able to see worth shit.

Then he tripped over the end of a bathtub. He fell toward the water. The water was red. A naked woman, reclining in the tub, stretched out her arms to catch him. Her wrists were crossed-hatched with slashes. Martha! He fell toward her, and fell, and fell. 'Leave me alone!' he shrieked, and lurched awake.

The room was bright with daylight. Gasping for breath, he stared at the ceiling. He used the pillow to mop the sweat off his face.

Good Christ, he thought. What a nightmare.

He glanced at his travel clock. Nine twenty. He'd been in bed no more than three hours. But he'd had some sleep before Marty and Claire came knocking.

God, if only that had been nothing but a dream.

He crawled to the edge of the bed and sat up. The bruise on his stomach where Marty had punched him (*he* started it) looked like a smudge of dirt. There were a few minor scratches on the backs of his hands, but his knuckles weren't even skinned from rapping Claire's face. He walked to the mirror above the dressing table, and peered at his own face. Except for the bloodshot eyes, it looked fine.

He went into the bathroom. Kneeling beside the tub, he looked closely for traces of blood on the enamel, especially around the drain. The tub looked fine. It should – he'd bathed in the ocean before returning to the room and showering.

He turned on the shower, adjusted the temperature, and stepped beneath its hot spray. As he washed himself, his mind went over every detail. Had he overlooked anything?

The contracts. He had burned them both and flushed the ashes down the toilet.

The tape. He'd pried open the plastic cassette, stripped out the tape, and held it dangling over the toilet while it burned, making greasy black smoke.

The recorder. Since he'd touched its casing with his bloody hand, it had to go. It went into the ocean.

The camera. Same problem. Same solution.

His clothes. After tearing off the tags, he'd weighted each garment with a rock and hurled each into the surf. The shoes hadn't required rocks.

The cars. In Gorman's estimation, his solution to that problem had been brilliant and daring. At the time he'd taken Marty's keys, he hadn't known why he wanted them. But the scheme must, even then, have been brewing in his subconscious. Not until he reached the cars did the plan come fullblown to his mind.

Since he couldn't risk leaving even a minute trace of Claire's blood in the Mercedes, he left it untouched and drove Marty's car to the beach. He'd been very lucky finding the beach; the very first road leading west had taken him within a couple of hundred yards. He'd simply followed a moonlit path along a hillside and *voilà* – the ocean.

Farewell to the cassette player, the camera, and his clothes. The worst part was washing his body in the ocean. No, perhaps the worst part was the trek back to Marty's car, naked and wet and freezing, and frightened half to death that someone might see him. The area was desolate, though, and the only building with a view of the parking area appeared to have no windows.

He'd found a rag under the car's front seat. He'd used it to wipe the seat and steering wheel before climbing in, just in case some blood remained on them. Later, after parking behind the Mercedes, he'd used the same rag to wipe the car for fingerprints. When he'd finished, he wiped its outside handles and flung the keys far up the wooded slope. Then he had simply climbed into the Mercedes and driven it back to the motel. Stark naked. Right through the center of town. But he hadn't seen a living soul, thank God, and all the bungalows of the Welcome Inn were dark when he arrived.

Looking back on it now, he was amazed that he'd succeeded in carrying it off – amazed, indeed, that he hadn't allowed the panic of the situation to overwhelm and destroy him. For he would have been destroyed if he'd simply fled without taking elaborate precautions.

As matters now stood, even if suspicion should fall on Gorman, he was confident that he'd left no evidence connecting him to the crimes. And he had a marvelous bonus in his favor: investigators would naturally assume that the same perpetrator had dispatched

Brian, Marty and Claire. It would be obvious to anyone that Gorman was physically incapable of impaling Brian on a seven-foot fence.

Only one possibility worried him – that he may have been seen. Janice was unaccounted for. If she'd been alive on the hillside and witnessed the murders ... Possible, but highly unlikely since she neither appeared nor called out during the search. More than likely, she was dead. But Gorman had committed the murders within view of Beast House. Someone watching from a window could have watched it all. If that had been the case, however, and his crimes reported, certainly the police would have intercepted him at the cars. Since the police didn't show up, he could assume that either he wasn't seen or the witness had crimes of his own to hide – such as the murders of Brian and Janice.

The thought that he might have been watched by their killers sent a chill through Gorman. He suddenly felt squirmy. His scrotum tightened and his penis drew in as if to hide.

Who could have done such a thing to Brian? The strength it must've taken!

Perhaps, he thought, there is a beast.

He was no longer enjoying the hot spray of the shower. He finished rinsing the soap from his body, and climbed out. To perk himself up, he concentrated on his good fortune as he dried and got dressed.

The killer, whether man or beast, had done him a splendid service. Gorman may or may not be able to use the incident in his book, depending on the outcome of the investigation. Regardless, all the proceeds would now come to him. Every last cent. Even if Janice should miraculously reappear, the contracts were destroyed. The initial correspondence implied no commitment (perhaps he could find those letters and destroy them ... awfully risky ... why had he thrown away Marty's keys?) but basically Janice wouldn't have a leg to stand on without the contract itself.

Besides, she's dead.

Please, let her be dead.

As he finished buttoning his sport shirt, he heard a knocking on the door – a light, tentative rapping but it made his stomach lurch. It came from Brian's room. He took a deep breath, cautioned himself to remain calm, and stepped through the connecting doors. Both of Brian's beds were intact. He rushed silently to the closer bed, raked back its cover and sheet, and mashed the pillow. Then he opened the door.

'Good morning, Mr Hardy,' the woman said in a cheerful voice.

She was young and attractive, rather tall and nicely put together, looking fresh and altogether sexy in yellow shorts and a green tube-top that left her shoulders bare and hugged her sizable breasts. Gorman knew that he had met her before. Then he remembered where. The cocktail lounge. Yesterday evening. One of those librarians.

'Oh,' he said, smiling. 'Nina, is it?'

'Nora.'

'How are you this fine morning, Nora?'

'Just terrific. How about you?'

'Couldn't be better.' He took a deep breath. The warm air had a pine aroma. 'A gorgeous day to be alive,' he said.

'Every day's good for that,' Nora said. 'Anyway, the reason I dropped by, you mentioned you might be going on that tour today. Beast House?'

'Yes, I intend to.'

'Well, my friends and I are also going over there in a while. They've got a ten-thirty tour. We were wondering if you and Mr Blake might want to come along with us.'

Gorman glanced at his digital wristwatch. Nine fifty-two. It would be comforting, he thought, to take the tour with acquaintances. Far better than entering that awful house with a group of strangers. 'I would be delighted,' he answered, 'though I'm not certain about Brian. He seems to have wandered off, and I have no idea when he might be back.'

Nora glanced at the Mercedes. 'You think he went for a walk?'

'Apparently.' Gorman shrugged. 'Too bad for him. I'd be glad to...' He snicked his tongue. 'Oh, I do have an errand to run first. Suppose I meet you and your friends at the ticket booth?'

'Fine. Great.'

'At ten thirty, correct? I'd best get moving.'

Nora nodded, smiling. 'Okay, we'll see you there.'

She turned and started away. Gorman watched for a moment, enjoying the way her buttocks moved in the tight shorts.

Back in his own room, he uncapped his gin bottle and took a swallow. He found a telephone directory in a drawer of the night stand. Nursing the bottle, he searched the yellow pages. Under the heading PHOTO-GRAPHIC EQUIPMENT AND SUPPLIES – RETAIL were several listings. Most of the shops seemed to be located elsewhere; the book covered a county-wide area. Only Bob's Camera and Sound Center was in Malcasa Point. On the three-hundred block of Front Street. 'Marvelous,' Gorman muttered. He took a final swig of gin, and hurried out to the car.

Five minutes later, he drove past the store. He noted its location, and continued down Front Street, passing the dirt road he'd taken to the beach only a few hours earlier, then turning his eyes towards the grounds of Beast House. His gaze followed the rear fence until the building got in the way. On the other side, he picked it up again. He turned his head, watching the fence until the hillside rose up to block his view. From the two angles, he was almost certain he'd seen the entire length of the fence. Brian's body was gone. He hadn't noticed the other two, either, but of course their bodies wouldn't be easy to spot at this distance.

He'd half expected to find a gathering of police, but the region back there looked deserted.

Perhaps they had already completed their on-scene investigation and departed. That seemed unlikely, though. Surely there would still be officers scouring the area for evidence.

He continued up the road. Marty's old Plymouth, shrouded by morning shadows, was still parked on the shoulder where he'd left it. No police cars there. No coroner's van.

He rounded a bend, then made a U-turn. Coming back down the road, he kept his gaze on the wooded slope. The instant the rear fence appeared, he raced his eyes along it. From this vantage point, he could see almost to its far corner.

His doubts vanished.
The bodies had been removed.
But by the police? He didn't think so.

14

Janice rolled in her sleep and tumbled. Shards of pain tortured her awake. She lay motionless on her side, gasping, eyes squeezed shut.

Oh God, she thought, it hurts.

She whimpered from a searing rush of pain inside, and curled up. Her knees pushed against something soft and yielding.

What happened to me? her mind screamed.

Clutching her belly, she felt tape. She explored it with shaky fingers. It seemed to be holding a pad in place. A bandage? It ended just below her ribs. Moving her hands higher, she touched strips of tape on the underside of her left breast. The bandage started just above her nipple, covered the top of her breast and wrapped over her shoulder. The flesh beneath it felt burning. Her other shoulder was bandaged, too. Her right breast was bare, but tender as if bruised. Another bandage ran along her side to the hip. There, she found an elastic belt. She traced it to her groin and fingered the thick pad of a sanitary napkin.

What happened to me?

Raped. She must've been raped. The awful hurt inside. What did he use, for Christsake, a tree?

She started to sob, and the jolting spasms sent blasts of pain through her.

Who *did* this to me? God, why?

Brian? Did Brian? She remembered being with him, but . . . had he gone nuts or something?

Where am I, a hospital?

It didn't smell like a hospital, it smelled like a zoo. And she knew she wasn't on a bed. She was on the floor, a soft nap of carpet against her bare skin.

She opened her eyes. In the dim blue light, she saw a heap of pillows beside her. She must have been lying on that until she rolled off.

Blue light. Pillows.

Where am I?

Gingerly, gritting her teeth as pain ripped through her, Janice got to her hands and knees. She forced herself to stand. She swayed, and raised her arms for balance. Then she turned slowly.

Nobody here. Just me.

The room was slightly smaller than her own bedroom. Looking up, she saw that the ceiling was covered by mirrors. Except for the carpet and pillows, the room was bare. No furniture, no windows . . .

No windows!

The Kutch house?

'Oh God,' she whispered.

Flinching with each step, she staggered to the single door. She reached out an arm, slapped the jamb, and tried to brace herself. The arm folded. She fell against the door. But she grabbed the knob and held on tightly until the worst of the pain subsided. Then she tried to twist the knob. It wouldn't budge.

I'm locked in.

It came as no great surprise.

Still, she rattled the knob and yanked it, shaking the door in its frame.

Finally, she gave up.

She was out of breath, shuddering with pain.

She sank to her haunches. The bandage on her breast had pulled loose at the bottom. Blood was trickling from under it. She tried to press the tape down, but it wouldn't stick. Her skin was too slippery. Raising the bandage like a thick blue flap, she blinked sweat and tears from her eyes and stared at the wounds.

Her shoulder was torn and raw as if she had been gnawed by a dog. Below that, her flesh was ripped by four long scratches. Smoothing the bandage gently into place, she looked at her other breast. The skin was unbroken, but dark with bruises like a crescent of half a dozen dots. She lifted it and found a similar half-circle under the nipple.

Teeth marks?

But not from the teeth of a man.

Some kind of wild animal? A coyote, maybe?

Who are you trying to kid? she thought.

It was the beast.

Elizabeth Thorn's beast.

She couldn't remember any of it, but she knew it had to be so.

Oh God, the thing had raped her.

Quavering, she hugged her belly and leaned forward. She pressed her forehead against the door.

It had raped her. But it hadn't killed her. Someone

had bandaged her wounds. And now she was a prisoner in the windowless house of Maggie Kutch.

It'll be back, she thought.

It wants me again.

15

Hardy, a distance up the sidewalk, paused near the fence and took a photo of Beast House. As he lowered the camera, Nora waved. He nodded a greeting, and came forward. In spite of the mild breeze, Tyler thought he must be stifling inside his sport jacket. She was too warm, herself, and wished she'd worn shorts or a skirt instead of her corduroys.

'You remember Tyler,' Nora said.

'Of course. How could I forget such a lovely creature?'

Reluctantly, she shook his offered hand. 'This is Abe Clanton,' she said.

'Pleased to meet you, Mr Hardy. I've read your books.'

Hardy looked surprised as he took Abe's hand. 'In the plural?'

'Sure. There were some thirty before *Horror at Black River Falls?*'

'Forty-eight, in fact. More than a few under pseudonyms. I'm delighted to find a man who knows I existed before *Horror*. Delighted and stunned.'

'I especially liked your *Death Defiers* series. Always kept an eye out for them in the PX.'

'Ah, you're a military man. I should've guessed. That straight-shouldered bearing. A Marine, no doubt.'

Abe looked amused. 'That's right.'

'The author of *Death Defiers* is Matt Scott. May I ask how you saw through my nom de plume?'

'They had your name on the copyright page.'

'A singularly literate fellow,' he said, and turned to Jack. 'Another leatherneck?'

'Used to be. Jack Wyatt.' They shook hands. 'I saw your movie.'

'Ah.'

'I'm a singularly illiterate fellow.'

Nora laughed. 'Hey, we met a guy last night you'll want to interview. Captain Frank. He lives in a bus over there.' She pointed toward the woods along the far side of Beach Road.

'Interview?' Hardy asked.

'He claims his father found the beast on some island and brought it here.'

'The beast?'

She nodded toward the old house.

'That beast?' Hardy asked.

'Yeah. He's full of all kinds of disgusting details.'

'Why should I be interested?'

'For your book.'

He stared at her, looking as if he might decide to smile. 'I believe I explained, last evening, that I have no intention of writing about Beast House.'

'That's right!' Nora snapped her fingers and looked very annoyed with herself for forgetting. 'You did say that. I remember.' Suddenly grinning, she shook a finger at him. 'You'd better interview Captain Frank for the book you're *not* going to write.'

Hardy chuckled.

'Now don't worry about us. We won't breathe a word to a living soul that you're not doing a book on Beast House. Mum's the word, right, everyone? Your secret is safe with us.'

Tyler looked around and saw that the line was moving toward the ticket booth. A tight, sick feeling seized her stomach. Calm down, she told herself. It's nothing to get crazy about. Maybe Dan won't be here, after all.

But if he is?

She could wait outside, avoid him.

That wouldn't be right.

She fumbled with the catch of her purse.

'I'll get it,' Abe said.

'No, you've already . . .'

But he stepped ahead of her and purchased two tickets from the smiling blonde girl at the window. They stepped aside to wait for the others.

'Thank you,' she said.

'Are you all right?'

'Not very.'

'I'm sure Dan'll be glad to see you.'

'It'll be easier if he's not.'

Abe's eyes looked solemn. He rubbed her shoulder lightly, and let his hand fall away as Nora and Jack approached.

Nora frowned with concern. 'Are you sure you want to go ahead with this?' she asked.

'No. But I will.'

'Is there a problem?' Hardy asked.

'Tyler's old boyfriend is supposed to be . . .'

'Nothing's wrong,' Tyler said, annoyed with Nora for

161

broadcasting her private business to the man. She turned away quickly and stepped through the turnstile.

Abe joined her on the other side, and took hold of her hand. Tyler looked up at him. 'She's got a real mouth, sometimes.'

'I take it you don't care much for Gorman.'

'I think he's a sleaze.'

'I'd be inclined to agree with you.'

'I thought you were a big fan.'

'I've enjoyed some of his books. That's not the same as liking the guy who wrote them.'

They stopped behind the small group gathered in front of the porch. Nora and Jack came up next to them.

'What do we do, just walk in?' Nora asked.

'I'm sure there's a guide,' Abe said.

A guide. Dan? Tyler's heart gave a lurch. She squeezed Abe's hand more tightly, and stared at the shadowed door. She flinched as it swung open.

The person in the entryway wasn't Dan. She let out a deep, trembling breath as a gawky man stepped out. He looked about sixty, and walked with a stiffness as if he was in pain. Coming down the porch stairs, he held onto the railing. 'Tickets,' he said in a voice that sounded remarkably strong for a man of such frail appearance.

A couple of kids near the front backed out of his way.

Tyler heard a quiet click. She glanced sideways at Hardy, and was surprised not to find the camera at his eye. One hand was inside a pocket of his jacket. He gave her a quick smile, and took his hand out.

He's got a recorder in there, she thought. He's going to tape the tour.

Without asking permission? Of course, or he wouldn't be acting so sneaky. Illegal as hell, but that wouldn't bother Gorman Hardy.

It confirmed her opinion of the man.

Sleazy bastard, she thought.

Finished gathering the tickets, the bony man made his way up the porch stairs. He turned around and wiped his mouth with the back of a hand. 'Ladies and gents,' he proclaimed, 'it's now my honor to introduce you to the owner of Beast House, a gallant woman who passed through the purifyin' fire of tragedy and came out the stronger for it – Maggie Kutch, your personal guide for today's tour.' Like a tired ringmaster, he swept an arm toward the door and shuffled backwards to get out of the way.

An old woman waddled out of the house, bracing herself with an ebony cane. She looked old enough to be the man's mother but, in spite of the cane, she seemed to radiate strength. She was a big woman, broad-hipped, with a massive bosom swaying the entire front of her faded print dress as she limped to the edge of the porch. To Tyler, she looked like a rather stern grandmother. She wore tan support hose, and clunky black shoes with laces. As if to perk up her drab appearance, a bright red silken scarf wrapped her neck. Her face looked sour until she smiled. The smile wasn't particularly cheerful. It was almost a smirk.

'Welcome to Beast House,' she said. Her eyes roamed the group. Tyler felt a tingle of dread as the woman's gaze fell upon her. 'My name's Maggie Kutch, just like

Wick told you, and it's my house.' She paused as if challenging someone to disagree with her. Not a sound came from the audience. Several people were scanning the house front or staring at their feet, apparently reluctant to look at her.

'I started showing my house to visitors all the way back in '31, not long after the beast took the lives of my husband and three children. Yes, the beast. Not a knife-toting maniac like some folks'd want you to believe. If you don't think so, take a gander at this.' She plucked the scarf. As it slipped away from her neck, someone groaned. Maggie's fingers traced the puffy seams of scar tissue streaking her throat. 'No man did this to me. It was a beast with fangs and claws.' Her eyes gleamed as if she was proud of the marks. 'It was the same beast as killed ten people in this house, including my own husband and children.

'Now, you might be wondering why a gal'd want to take folks through her home that was a scene of such personal tragedy. It's an easy answer: M-O-N-E-Y.'

Tyler heard quiet laughter from Gorman.

The old woman swung up her cane and waved it toward a beam supporting the porch roof. 'Right here's where they lynched Gus Goucher. He was a lad of eighteen. He was passing through town, back in August of 1903, on his way to San Francisco where he aimed to work at the Sutro Baths, but he stopped here and asked to do some odd jobs in exchange for a meal. Lilly Thorn lived here back then with her two children. She was the widow of the famous bank robber, Lyle Thorn, and I always say she built this house with blood money. Blood comes of blood, I say. Anyway, Gus came along and she had him split up some firewood for her. He did his chore, took his meal for payment, and went on his way.

'That night, the beast came. It struck down Lilly's sister, who was visiting, and her children. Only just Lilly survived the attack, and they found her running down the road jabbering like a lunatic.

'Right off the bat, the house was searched from attic to cellar. They found no living creature inside, but only the torn, chewed bodies of the victims. A posse was got up. Over in the hills yonder, it came on Gus Goucher where he'd bedded down for the night. Him being a stranger, he was doomed from the start.

'He was given a proper trial. Some town folks had seen him at the Thorn place the day of the killings, and there weren't no witnesses to the slaughter with everyone dead but Lilly, and her raving. Quick as a flash, they judged him guilty. The night after the verdict came in, a mob busted him out of jail. They dragged the lad to this very spot, tossed the rope over this beam, and strung him up.

'Being amateurs, they done a poor job of it. Didn't think to tie him, but just hoisted him up. They say he hung here, flapping and kicking like a spastic for quite a good spell while he strangled.'

'Lovely,' Nora whispered.

'Poor Gus Goucher never killed nobody. It was the beast done it all.' She thumped her cane twice on the porch floor. 'Let's go in.'

As she turned away, Tyler looked up at Abe. He shook his head as if he found the situation grimly amusing.

'Barbie Doll was right,' Nora whispered. 'Tacky tacky.'

Climbing the porch stairs, Tyler released Abe's hand long enough to rub her sweaty palm on her corduroys. She had a leaden, sickish feeling in her stomach.

The group halted in the foyer. After the sunlight outside, the house seemed dark and cool. Tyler scanned the gloom, half expecting to spot Dan, in uniform, standing guard.

'Yuck,' said a girl near the front.

Smiling, Maggie pointed her cane at a stuffed monkey. It stood beside a wall, mouth frozen wide, teeth bared. 'Umbrella stand,' she said, and dropped her cane through the circle of its shaggy arms. 'Lilly was partial to monkeys.' She snatched up her cane and thumped the creature's head, bringing up a puff of dust.

'The first attack,' she said, 'came in the parlor. Right this way.'

Gorman jostled Tyler. 'Excuse me, dear,' he said, and made his way forward, pressing through the small group of people. He reached the door ahead of the rest, and followed Maggie through.

'A real go-getter,' Abe muttered.

'A creep,' Tyler said.

They entered the parlor. The group spread out along the length of a plush cordon. Just beyond the barrier bright red curtains hung from the ceiling to the floor, closed to conceal most of the room. Maggie, on the other side of the cordon, waited by a wall and caressed a fold of the velvety curtain. 'These are new,' she said. 'We just put 'em in. Gives a touch of class, don't you think?' She gripped a cord.

'Ethel Hughes, Lilly's sister, was in this room the night of August second, 1903. She'd come down for

Lilly's wedding, which would've been the next week if tragedy hadn't struck and put an end to it all. The beast come in through there.' She nodded toward the door behind Tyler. 'It took Ethel unawares.'

She gave the cord a yank. The curtains skidded open. Tyler heard a few gasps. A girl in front of her backed up quickly, stepping on her toes. A red-haired woman turned her face away. A boy in a cowboy suit leaned over the cordon for a closer look. Gorman raised his camera. Maggie bounced her cane off the floor. 'No pictures,' she warned. 'Anybody wants a memento of the tour, he can pick up one of our souvenir guidebooks in the gift shop for six ninety-five.' Gorman lowered the camera and shook his head as if disgusted.

'Sure did a number on that babe,' whispered a man to Tyler's left.

Reluctantly, Tyler lowered her eyes to the form of Ethel Hughes. The wax body was sprawled on the floor, one leg up and resting on the cushion of a couch. Its wide eyes gazed toward the ceiling. Its face was contorted with pain and horror. Its shredded gown, a white that had gone yellow like old paper, was blotched with rust-colored stains. The tatters covered little more than the breasts and pubic area. The exposed flesh, from neck to thighs, was punctured and striped with raw wounds. Bright crimson sheathed the body.

'The beast sprang over the back of the couch, taking Ethel by surprise while she was reading the *Saturday Evening Post*.' Maggie stepped past the body and pointed her cane at an open magazine spread out beyond the figure's outstretched right arm. 'This is the very issue she was reading when it got her.' She swept her cane around. 'Everything you see here is just the same as it was that night. Except for the body, of course.' She smiled. 'We couldn't have that, now could we? But we've got us the next best thing. I had this exact replica done up in wax by Monsieur Claude Dubois of Nice, France, way back in '36. Every detail is guaranteed, right down to each wound. Got my hands on the morgue photos.

'Like I say, it's all authentic. This is the very nightgown Ethel wore the night of the killing. Those brown spots are her actual blood.'

'Gross,' muttered the girl who'd stepped on Tyler's foot.

Maggie ignored her. 'When the beast finished with Ethel, it rampaged around the parlor. That bust of Caesar there on the mantel?' She indicated it with her cane. 'See how the nose is off? That's the work of the beast. It hurled that bust to the floor. It flung half a dozen porcelain figurines into the fireplace. It broke that chair. This beautiful rosewood table' – she tapped it with her cane –'was thrown through this window. All the ruckus, of course, woke up everyone in the house. Lilly's room was right up there.' She poked her cane toward the ceiling. 'The beast must've heard her up and about. It went for the stairs.'

Maggie closed the curtains. She limped around the cordon, and led the group out of the parlor. Gorman stayed close to her. In a loud voice he said, 'May I ask how you can be certain of the order of events? As you mentioned earlier, there were no witnesses.'

'Police reports and photos,' she explained, starting up the stairway. 'Newspaper stories. It was pretty clear the way it all happened. The cops just followed the blood.'

'Had the beast been injured?'

She cast Gorman an amused glance. 'Ethel's blood,' she said. 'It dripped off the beast all the way up here to Lilly's room.' At the top of the stairs, she turned to the left.

Tyler, reaching the top, looked to the right. Red curtains surrounded an area in the center of the corridor near its far end, leaving only a narrow passageway on either side. Another exhibit. How many are there? she wondered. And how many could she stomach?

Abe gave her hand a reassuring squeeze, and they entered the bedroom of Lilly Thorn. Again, the group spread out facing a cordon and a wall of red curtains. Maggie, at the far end, tugged the pullcord. The curtains flew apart. A wax figure in a pink nightgown was sitting upright on the bed, a hand to its open mouth, frightened eyes gazing past the brass scrollwork at her feet.

'We're right above the parlor, now,' Maggie said. 'When all the commotion woke Lilly up, she dragged that dressing table over to the door for a barricade, and climbed out her window. She dropped to the roof of the bay window just a ways down, and jumped from there to the ground.'

Gorman made a disdainful snort.

Maggie glanced at him sharply. 'Something wrong with you?'

'No, no.' He shook his head. 'My mind just wandered there for...' His voice trailed off. 'Please continue.'

'I've always found it curious,' she said, 'that Lilly didn't try to save her children.'

'Panic,' suggested a man beside the redhead.

'Maybe that's it.' Maggie shut the curtains. The group followed her into the corridor. 'When the beast couldn't get into Lilly's room, he went down the hall.'

He, Tyler thought. Suddenly the beast had become a he instead of an it.

They passed the top of the stairway. As they neared the curtained enclosure, the group formed a single file line. Tyler let go of Abe's hand. He gestured her forward, and she walked ahead of him into the gap between the curtains and the wall. Her forearm brushed one of the folds. She flinched away from its touch, and felt goosebumps scurry up her skin. Then the corridor was clear, bright from a window at its end.

'The beast,' Maggie said, 'found this door open.' She entered a room on the left. They followed her inside, and Tyler was careful not to stand behind the girl who'd stepped on her. 'This is where the children slept, though I 'spect they were awake when the beast came – maybe hiding under their covers, froze up with fear. Earl was ten, his brother Sam just eight.'

The curtains slid open.

The two wax bodies lay facedown between the brass beds. Their bloody nightshirts were ripped to shreds, and so was their skin. Tyler looked away. A rocking horse with faded paint rested beside a washstand. In one corner was an Indian tom-tom. A baseball bat was propped against the wall behind it. Suddenly, the boys seemed real to Tyler. She imagined them at play, laughing and chasing each other. She gnawed her lower lip and turned her gaze to the window. She heard Maggie's voice, but didn't listen. On the lawn below, she saw a weathered, lattice-work gazebo. Beyond it, the fence. Then the hillside, golden brown in the sunlight, with a few patches of green bush, clumps of rock here and there, a scattering of trees. It looked so peaceful. As she watched, a seagull swooped down, perched on the fence between a couple of the spikes, and pecked at something, apparently finding a snack. She wished she was outside, not trapped inside this mausoleum. Maybe Gorman felt the same way, for she saw that he, too, was staring out of the window.

Maggie finished, and they followed her into the corridor. This time, passing the curtained area, Tyler walked closer to the wall and kept her arms tight against her sides. As they approached the top of the stairs, Maggie said, 'Sixteen nights we lived in this house before the beast came. My husband, Joseph, he couldn't abide sleeping in one of the murder rooms, so we settled ourselves in the guest room. Our daughters, Cynthia and Diana, they weren't so squeamish and took the boys' room we just left.'

She led them through a doorway on the right, directly across the corridor from the entrance to Lilly's room. A cordon was stretched from wall to wall, but the room beyond it was open. Except for one corner. There, a set of red curtains hung from a curved bar, enclosing a wedge of floor.

Maggie pointed her cane at a canopy bed. 'On May seventh, 1931, Joseph and I were sleeping here. It was close to fifty years back, but I remember it all like it was last night. There'd been a good bit of rain that day, and it was still coming down when we retired. We had the windows open, and I laid there listening to the rainfall. The girls were tucked in down the hall and my baby,

Theodore, was snug in the nursery. I fell asleep, feeling peaceful and safe.

'Long about midnight, there come a sound of breaking glass from downstairs. Joseph got up quiet out of bed, and tiptoed over here.' She limped to a bureau, pulled open a drawer, and lifted out a pistol. 'He got this. It's an army model Colt .45 automatic.'

'Neat,' said the kid in the cowboy suit.

'Joseph cocked it, and I can still hear the noise of it.' Cane clamped under one arm, she clutched the black hood of the weapon and jerked it back and forward with a metallic snick-snack.

'Hope that's not loaded,' said the father of the girl.

'Couldn't hurt if it was,' Maggie told him. 'We plugged up the barrel with lead, this past year.' Aiming at the floor, she pulled the trigger. There was a clack. She returned the pistol to the drawer.

'Joseph took it with him,' she said, 'and left me alone in the room. I waited till I heard him on the stairs, then I crept out to the hall. I had to get to my children, you see.'

Leaving the curtains untouched, she stepped around the cordon. The group followed her into the corridor. She stopped at the head of the stairway. 'I was just here when I heard gunshots. Then come an awful scream from Joseph. I heard sounds of a scuffle, and I wanted to run, but I stood here frozen stiff, staring down through the darkness.'

She gazed down the stairs as if transfixed by the memory of it.

'Up the stairway come the beast,' she said in a low voice. 'I couldn't see too good, but his skin was white like a fish's belly, so white it seemed to almost glow. He

walked upright like a man, only hunched over some. I
knew I had to run and get to the children, but I couldn't
stir a muscle. I could only just stare. Then he made a soft
kind of laugh, and threw me to the floor. He tore at me
with claws and teeth. I tried my best to fight him off but
he was stronger than any ten men, and I was preparing
to meet the Lord when Theodore started up crying way
off in the nursery. Well, the beast heard it and climbed
off me and went scampering down the hall.

'I was hurt bad, but I went chasing after him. I
couldn't let him get my baby.'

She started hobbling down the corridor. Once again,
Tyler pressed herself close to the wall to avoid contact
with the curtains. There must be bodies inside, she
thought. Mutilated corpses of wax.

Just across from the boys' room, Maggie stopped. She
tapped her cane on a closed door to the right. 'This stood
open,' she said. 'I peered inside. There, in the dark . . .'

'Aren't we going in?' asked the redhead.

Maggie glared at her. 'I never show the nursery.'
Then she looked at the door as if she could see through
it. 'There, in the dark, I saw the pale beast lift my infant
from his cradle and tear him asunder. I was watching,
numb with horror, when something gave my nightdress
a yank. I found Cynthia and Diana behind me. Well, I
took a hand of each, and we rushed off. We went this
way.'

They followed Maggie through the gap on the other
side of the curtains. She stopped at a closed door across
the stairway. The group formed a half-circle around her.

'We got this far,' she said, 'before the beast leapt into
the hall and came after us.' She pulled the door open.

173

Peering into the dim recess, Tyler saw a staircase. The stairs led upward until the darkness consumed them. 'We ducked inside here, and I pulled the door shut. It was dark as a pit. I threw open the attic door at the top, and bolted it after us. Then we huddled in the musty blackness.

'We knew the beast was coming. We heard the creaking stairs, and he made quiet hissing sounds like he was laughing. Then he was sniffing at the door. We waited. The girls were sobbing. I can still feel how they both trembled in my arms. Suddenly, the door burst open and the beast fell upon us.'

Maggie eased the door shut. She leaned a shoulder against it, and let out a deep sigh.

'The screams,' she said. 'I'll never forget the screams, the snarls of the beast, the wet ripping sounds as he tore up my two little girls. I fought him until the screams stopped and he had me down. I don't know why he didn't kill me, and there's many a time I wished he had, but he just pinned me to the floor. I was too weak to fight him anymore, and I begged him to end it for me. After a minute, he scampered down the stairs leaving me alone up there with the bodies of my daughters. I never saw him again after that night. But others have.'

16

Janice lay motionless, staring at the mirrored ceiling. Sprawled on top of the pillows, she looked blue and dead like a corpse discarded on a rubbish pile. She was thinking about ways to commit suicide.

So far, she'd come up with a couple of possibilities. The light fixture in the center of the ceiling was about three feet beyond her reach. By stacking pillows, she could get to it. Unscrew the blue bulb. Stick in a finger. Electrocute herself. That would probably work. An easier method, the one she thought she might prefer, was to remove all her bandages and let herself bleed to death. Exploring her wounds, however, she'd found most of them to be superficial, little more than scratches and bites. They weren't bleeding much. She would have to work them open, or maybe take down that bulb and break it and use its glass like a knife to open her wrists or throat. She could do that.

There was one problem.

She didn't want to die.

They couldn't let her go, she was sure of that, but they had bandaged her wounds so they must want her to recover. Why? She could think of only one reason, and it sickened her: they wanted her alive as a plaything for the beast. Last time, she must have been unconscious. But if it came to her now, she would see it, feel its teeth and claws ripping her, its penis battering into her.

No, don't think about it. Maybe it won't happen.

It'll happen.

She pressed a hand tight against the pad between her legs.

I can't let it happen, she thought.

I've got to escape.

Sure. No sweat. Just break down the door and run like hell.

Little Joni, last summer, had escaped easily enough from that maniac who had them prisoners in the cabin. And Joni'd been tied to a bed. At least I'm not tied up, Janice thought. But the cabin door hadn't been locked from the outside, either.

They'll open the door, she realized. They'll have to. Someone, sooner or later, will come in to check on me, maybe to feed me, or – and the thought chilled her – to let in the beast.

When that door opened, she would get her chance.

But she had to be ready.

She rolled herself off the pillows, groaning as the movement awakened streaks and waves of pain. Crawling on her knees, she dragged several of the large pillows to the center of the room. She stacked them. As she pushed herself up to climb atop them, she realized that the bulb would be searing hot. She limped over to where she had been resting, and picked up another pillow. Its case felt like satin. She yanked, splitting one of the seams, and shook out the foam rubber stuffing. With her right hand wrapped in the slick fabric, she returned to the waist-high stack. She stepped onto the top. Her foot sank in, mashing deep. Arms out for balance, she leaned in, brought up her other foot, and straightened herself. The pillows wobbled under her. She teetered for a moment, then was steady.

With her covered hand, she reached up and gripped the blue bulb. She felt its warmth through the layers of satin. She twisted it. The bulb turned easily, and went out.

Not a shred of light entered the room to relieve the total blackness. Janice kept unscrewing the bulb, but the dark disoriented her. Though she tried to stand motionless, the pillows seemed to be shifting slowly under her feet. She swayed. Only her gentle hold on the bulb kept her from losing all sense of direction and falling.

It came loose in her hand.

Quickly, she took a blind leap forward. She seemed to drop for a very long time as if plunging into an abyss. Finally, the floor pounded her feet. Windmilling, she fell backwards. The floor slammed her rump. The back of her head and shoulders toppled the pillows. She writhed against them as pain surged through her body.

Good one, she thought. You probably opened up everything with that stunt.

But she felt proud. There was a ripple of excitement under the pain. *She'd done it!* She pressed the bulb to her chest, and flinched at its fiery touch.

Smart move.

Smart, all right. Now you've got a weapon.

She waited until the pain subsided a little, then crawled on her knees through the dark. After a long while, she bumped a wall. The door, she thought, should be over that way – somewhere to the left.

She didn't want broken glass where she would be waiting. Carefully, she unwrapped the bulb. It was still warm, but not too hot to handle. Gripping the base, she rapped its glass gently against the wall. Then harder. It burst with a pop that sounded very loud in the silence. Sliding her fingers up the neck, she felt a jagged rim.

She eased sideways. One hand on the wall, she made her way slowly through the darkness until she found the door. She sat down beside it. She leaned her back against the wall, drew up her knees, and waited.

From somewhere not far away came a sound like the cry of a baby. Maybe a cat, she thought. What does the beast sound like? No, it sounded too much like a human baby to be anything else. After a few moments, it stopped. The house returned to silence.

Janice frowned. A baby? Maggie Kutch was far too old to be its mother. Could it be, she wondered, that she was not the only prisoner in the house?

17

'Twenty years went by,' Maggie said, 'before the beast struck again.'

They were back inside the bedroom Maggie had shared with her husband. She was standing beside the red curtains that blocked one corner, a hand on the pullcord.

'This was 1951. Tom Bagley and Larry Maywood, a couple of youngsters twelve years old, broke into the house after dark. They should've known better, both of them. They'd come on the tour plenty of times, and heard me warn more than once that at night the beast prowls the house. I 'spect curiosity got the best of them. Curiosity killed the cat.'

'Satisfaction brought it back,' mumbled the girl who'd stepped on Tyler's foot.

Maggie heard the comment, and smirked. 'Didn't bring back Tom Bagley,' she said. The curtains slid apart.

The girl gasped and took a quick step away. Jack, behind her, protected himself with a raised forearm, gently nudging her to a stop.

The cowboy said, 'Oh, wow.'

The wax body on the floor was mangled, its clothes

torn open, a tatter of underpants draping its buttocks. The skin of its back was scored with scratches. Its neck was a pulpy stub. Its head lay nearby, eyes wide, mouth contorted in agony.

The other boy, about to raise the window, was peering over a shoulder at his dismembered friend. His face, oddly mashed and cracked, was somehow more unnerving to Tyler than the grisly remains on the floor.

'These two,' Maggie said, 'were in the house for a long spell, nosing around. They'd tried to pry open the nursery door. They'd gone up to the attic. But they were snooping here in this room when the beast found them. He struck down Tom, and Larry ran for the window. While the beast was tearing up his friend, Larry got away by jumping. 'Cept for me, Larry was the only soul ever to see the beast and live.'

Maggie smiled strangely. 'Now there's only just me. I hear Larry got himself killed in an accident last year.'

'What's wrong with his face?' Nora asked.

'Took a spill,' Maggie said. 'We tried as best we could to patch it up. Didn't do too well, did we? We got us a whole new head on order, but it ain't come in yet.'

She closed the curtains, and the group followed her out of the room. Hobbling past the top of the stairs, she stopped in front of the curtains that blocked the corridor. 'Here's our last exhibit of the tour,' she said. 'We just got it in this past spring. It's in a mighty inconvenient spot, but here's where it happened so here's where the display had to go or it just wouldn't be right.

'It happened just last year, back in the spring of '78. We had us a family name of Ziegler on the tour –

husband, wife, and their boy about ten. Well, the boy, he got spooked on the tour. Started crying and carrying on, so his folks took him off before we finished up. From what the mother said later, the father was mighty annoyed with the boy. Thought he hadn't acted manly. The last thing he wanted was a sissy for a son, so he dragged the youngster back here after dark.' A corner of Maggie's mouth curled up. 'Wanted to show him there weren't nothing to be afraid of. Only he was wrong and the boy was right. They broke in the back door, and they got just to here before the beast got them both.'

She yanked the pullcord. The front section of curtains flew open.

The boy was facedown, shirt torn from his back, his neck mauled.

The man sprawled beyond him was torn up, his severed arm lying across one thigh.

On the floor between them was a man in the shredded tan uniform of a police officer. His throat was torn out. Tyler stared at the grimacing face. She blinked as the corridor darkened. A stark blue aura flashed around the body. Through the ringing in her ears, she heard Maggie. 'A patrolman name of Dan Jenson, making his rounds . . .'

'Tyler? Tyler?' Abe's voice.

She opened her eyes. She was sitting on the floor, someone holding her from behind, her head down between her knees. She felt dizzy and nauseated. People were whispering. Raising her head, she saw Nora crouched at her side. Nora squeezed her hand. It was numb as if shot with Novocaine.

'You'll be okay,' Abe said from behind. That was him clutching her shoulders. 'Come on,' he said, 'let's get you out of here.' His hands slid under her armpits, and he lifted her. She glimpsed Dan's body again before Abe turned her away. No, not his body. A wax figure. But Dan.

Abe's firm hands guided her toward the stairs. 'I'm okay,' she muttered, shaking her head. He held her upright and loosened his grip, but stayed behind her as if prepared to stop another fall. 'I'm okay,' she said again. He came around to her side, and took hold of her upper arm.

'I'm sorry,' he said. His eyes looked sad and worried.

'I . . .' She looked back. Nora and Jack stood next to Abe. Down the corridor, several in the group were staring at her.

'We shouldn't have come,' Nora said. Her face was drawn with misery. 'Tyler, I'm sorry. I shouldn't have made you . . . Jesus, who would've thought . . . ?' Her chin started trembling, and tears filled her eyes.

Tyler squeezed her hand. Then she rubbed her own forehead. The skin felt cool and damp. 'I want to get out of here,' she mumbled.

She thought, I'm going to throw up.

She started down the stairs, Abe hanging onto her arm. 'Hurry,' she said. Four steps from the bottom, she lunged free of his grip and raced down. She dashed across the foyer, past the rabid-looking stuffed monkey, and yanked open the door. Glaring sunlight blinded her. The porch reeked of decayed wood. She hurled herself against the railing, leaned far over it, and vomited onto the brown grass.

* * *

'Some folks can't take it,' Maggie said. 'We get them every so often. Most'll just drop out of the tour along the way, but I've had maybe a score faint on me, one time or another. They ain't always women, neither. I've seen big, burly fellows keel over like they'd been poleaxed.' She grinned. 'Just figure you got a little extra excitement for your money.'

She closed the curtains. 'That'll conclude our tour for this morning, folks.' Gorman stepped aside to let her pass. He followed close behind her. Over her shoulder, she said, 'Now don't forget to visit our gift shop downstairs, where you can purchase your illustrated booklet on the history of Beast House and choose from our assortment of souvenirs.'

At the bottom of the stairs, she swung her cane to the left. 'Just down the hall there.'

Glancing that way, Gorman saw a wooden sign a short distance up the corridor. It read Souvenirs, and pointed to an open door. He hesitated while Maggie limped outside and several of the tourists stepped around him. He intended to visit the gift shop, but he didn't want to lose Tyler and the others.

An interview with Tyler would be marvelous. *Beast House is not for the squeamish. This young lady from our tour group actually passed out ...*

He stepped to the threshold. Tyler, along with her three friends, was already out near the ticket booth, heading away. Maybe he could catch up with her at the motel.

He went to the gift shop, and was vaguely relieved to find others inside. Behind the counter stood the gawky, grim-looking fellow who'd taken the tickets and introduced Maggie. As the man rang up a sale, Gorman reached into his pocket and switched off the cassette recorder.

He certainly hoped it had picked up all of Maggie's spiel. It should've worked fine, he assured himself. After all, it was brand new and identical to the one he'd discarded.

He should check the tape, however, as soon as possible. If, for some reason, it hadn't operated properly, he would have to repeat the tour. He hoped to avoid that.

For the others, the displays must have seemed like grotesque curiosities – the work of a disturbed imagination, a sham to draw tourists. Gorman, however, knew better. For him, the mutilated mannequins seemed no less real than Brian's body impaled on the fence.

Brian.

Pausing by a shelf of ashtrays and plates, he glanced around at the cashier.

That old geezer, certainly, would be incapable of sticking Brian up there. The same went double for Maggie. Only someone with extraordinary strength could have accomplished that feat, or taken him down again. These two might very well, however, be accomplices. According to the diary, the beast had lived with Elizabeth Thorn for a period of time before she allowed it to slaughter her family. Perhaps Maggie, now, was its mistress. Something to think about.

Wandering among the display tables and shelves, Gorman loaded his arms with souvenir items: a strip of six color slides showing the front of the house and several of the murder scenes; half a dozen picture postcards; the glossy eight-by-ten-inch booklet rich with text and photos; a shotglass with a gilt sketch of the house; a coffee mug sporting a color rendition of the house and the legend BEAST HOUSE – MALCASA POINT, CALIF; a plastic back-scratcher with the same legend along its shaft and a white hand with claws for raking the itch; finally, two bumper stickers – BEWARE OF THE BEAST with a hand at each end, claws dripping red blood – and I LOVE BEAST HOUSE with an illustration of the building. Gorman had grinned when he picked up that one.

He browsed the shop for a while longer, but found no more items relating specifically to Beast House. He carried his load to the cashier. Without a word or smile, the man started ringing up the items. He looked frail and oddly prim with his gray workshirt buttoned to the throat, but he'd obviously neglected to shave that morning. His chin was spiky with gray stubble. Gorman cleared his throat to conceal the sound of switching on his recorder. 'Have you worked here long?' he asked.

'Long enough.'

'Have you ever seen the beast?'

'Nope.'

'Do you believe it actually exists?'

'You took the tour,' the man said without looking up.

'Yes.'

'Them folks didn't die of the whooping cough.'

You wouldn't know, of course, what became of the three bodies I happened to notice behind the house last night? What, he wondered, might the fellow say to that?

'Comes to twenty-nine dollars sixty-eight cents.'

Gorman paid cash. He watched for a receipt, but the

tape was still curling out of the cash register when the man crinkled up the top of the loaded bag. 'May I have the receipt, please?'

'I got no use for it.' He tore it loose and slapped it down on the counter.

Gorman hurried out of the house. Squinting against the brightness, he looked for Tyler and her friends. They were nowhere in sight.

18

'Shall I take you back to the motel?' Abe asked.

Tyler, slumped in the passenger seat with her knees propped against the dash, shook her head and slowly unwrapped the stick of Doublemint Nora had given her. 'I don't think so,' she murmured. 'I don't think I want to be alone.'

Abe felt helpless, looking at her. He wished he could make her misery go away. He wanted to hold her gently and tell her it would be all right, but he knew that only time could blunt the shock and sorrow.

'Hey,' Nora said, 'why don't we head over to the beach? I always feel better at the beach when I'm low.'

Tyler folded the chewing gum and put it in her mouth. 'I'd like that.'

'My trunks are at the motel,' Jack said.

'We'll just walk on the sand.'

'I think I might like to swim,' Tyler said.

Her comment surprised Abe and pleased him. Many people in her place would want only to curl up alone with their loss. Her attitude seemed healthier than that. 'Swim we shall,' he said.

'We didn't even bring our suits,' Nora reminded her. 'I didn't, anyway, did you?'

'I want to buy a new one.'

'Sure. Okay. Me too.'

Abe pulled out and drove slowly up the road. 'Why don't we let you off at a store? You can buy your suits. Jack and I'll go on back to the motel for ours, and we'll pick you up in about fifteen minutes.'

'It may take longer,' Nora said.

On the next block, Abe spotted the sign for Will's Sporting Goods. White lettering on the display window announced guns, tackle, swimming and camping accessories. 'How about there?' he asked.

'We can give it a try,' Nora said.

He pulled to the curb. Tyler met his eyes. 'Hurry back,' she told him.

'I will. We'll meet you right here.'

She opened the door and climbed out. Nora pushed the seat-back forward. She looked at Abe as if about to say something, seemed to change her mind. She joined Tyler on the sidewalk. Abe waited for a car to pass, then swung onto the road.

'Christ,' Jack said. 'The poor kid.'

'She's holding up pretty well.'

'Gutsy.'

'Yeah.'

'Nora said she almost married the guy once. She finally figured she'd screwed up by turning him down, and came here to give him another shot.'

Abe nodded. He scanned the building fronts.

'Nora also said she was having second thoughts about it all. 'Cause of you.'

Abe said nothing, but he felt his heart speed up.

'She thinks Tyler's really fallen for you. No taste.'

Abe grinned. Then, down a sidestreet to the right, he spotted a pair of flag standards on the sidewalk. He turned. The gray stone building might be a post office, he realized, but it turned out to be the city hall.

'What are you doing?'

'You take the car. Get the trunks and some towels, and meet me back here. I want to do some checking.'

'On Jenson?'

'You got it.'

He eased in behind a pickup truck, left the keys in the ignition, and handed his room key to Jack. He left the car. He crossed the road at an angle away from the administrative offices' entrance, heading for a blue, five-pointed star suspended above a set of double glass doors. The doors read, Police Department Malcasa Point. Pushing one open, he entered a deserted waiting area. A partition of frosted glass ran the length of the counter top. He stepped up to one of its three windows.

'We'll want to impound it,' said the man. He was sitting on the corner of a nearby desk, his back to the window.

The female officer nodded. Her tan uniform was too tight across her broad chest and hips. She must be twenty-one, but she didn't look it. She wore her hair short, in a cut similar to Tyler. Her eyes were on the other cop, and she didn't notice Abe.

'Have Bix tow it in, but I want you supervising.'

'Oh, great. Bix is my favorite human.'

'Fortunes of war, Lucy. He's a jerk, that's why I want you out there. Give him half a chance, he'll screw up the works just to spite us. Soon as it's in the yard, let me know. I'll want to go over it myself.'

'Right.'

'Bix puts a grope on you, you have my permission to deck him.'

She had a nice smile. 'I'll run him in for nauseating a police officer.' She started to turn away, and spotted Abe. With a nod, she signaled that they had a visitor.

The man looked over his shoulder, smiled, and scooted off the desktop as Lucy headed for a side door. He was taller than Abe, with a lean, creased face. His gray hair was long at the sides as if to make up for what he lacked on top. His eyes were the same gray as his hair. Sniper eyes, Abe thought. But cop eyes, too – wary and somewhat bemused.

'Yessir,' he said. 'I'm Harry Purcell. What can I do for you?'

'I just finished a tour of Beast House.'

His smile slipped a bit. 'Yes?'

'They've got Dan Jenson on display over there.'

The smile vanished completely. 'I'm aware of that.'

'I was with a young lady who used to know him. Can you tell me what happened to him?'

Purcell's face pinched up as if he'd stubbed a toe. He said, 'Oooh. You mean she didn't know he was deceased?'

'That's what I mean. The first she knew was when she found his wax face staring up at her.'

'Oooh. That's raw, mighty raw. How's she bearing up?'

'She's managing.'

'The damn shit-house. Sometimes, I think I'd like to torch the place.'

'How was Jenson killed?'

'Went in without a backup. He was on routine patrol, noticed a light in one of the windows. Now, nobody goes in that place at night. Not even Kutch or Hapson. Claim they don't, anyway. So Jenson suspected prowlers. He radioed for backup, but we haven't got much personnel. Two-man shifts, and a watch commander on dispatch. Well, Sweeny'd picked that time to stop for a bite. Jenson said he'd wait for him, but then he went on in alone. And he didn't come out. When Sweeny got there, he found Jenson's radio car abandoned. He wouldn't go in the house alone, and I can't say I blame him. We rousted up the rest of the force, even got the volunteer fire department in on it, and went in. Found his body in the upstairs hallway. His, and the other two. Ziegler and his kid. Searched the place top to bottom, came up zilch.'

'What became of Jenson's body?'

'He had a sister come for it. Had it sent south. To Sacramento, I believe. It was a real shame. Dan was a fine young man.'

'There was a coroner's inquest?'

'Sure. Verdict was "death at the hands of another" on all three of them. Trouble was, we couldn't come up with "another". We carried out a full investigation, but it ran out of steam. Just wasn't much to go on. Couldn't even say for sure it was a man that did it. Might've been a wild animal, but we couldn't think what. We've got some coyotes in the hills, but they're too small. We considered maybe a dog – it'd have to be the size of a mastiff or Dane. We even had some talk of bobcats and bears, though I don't know where one could've come from. But all that's pretty much ruled out. Those are furry creatures, and the only hairs we picked up in the vacuum were human.'

'Could the wounds have been made by a human?' Abe asked.

The cop shrugged. 'If he was mighty strong and had a good set of fingernails.'

'They looked like claw marks on the wax.'

'We had a theory he might've used some kind of device, like a spading-fork or maybe a glove fixed up with spikes of some sort. Sounds a bit farfetched, but the whole situation was pretty curious.'

'Think the beast did it?'

'That's sure what Maggie wants the whole world to think. Her business picked up a hundred percent after the killings. Which gives her something of a motive, in my opinion. If I was to hazard a guess – and I haven't got a speck of evidence to back it up – I'd say Maggie was in back of it. I think her boy, Axel, is physically capable of ripping a man's arm out of its socket. Maybe Wick or Maggie were with him. They took care of Ziegler and his kid, killed Dan when he came up, then used something to claw them up to make it look like the work of their beast and hightailed it before we got the house surrounded. That'd be my best guess, but like I say, you can't take a guess into court.'

'What about the other killings?'

He leaned forward, elbows on the counter. 'I'll tell you what I think, and I'm not the only one in town who suspects the same. I say Maggie Kutch, maybe with Wick Hapson's help, murdered her husband and kids back in '31, mutilated the bodies and started up this story about a mysterious creature to tie it in with the old

Thorn killings and throw off suspicion. I was just a kid at the time, but I remember there was plenty of talk along those lines. Wick was in high school then and he used to do yard work at the Kutch place. There was talk about him and Maggie even before the killings. They came under plenty of suspicion, but it died down over the years. Started up again in the 'fifties, after the Bagley boy was murdered in there, but by then they'd been running the tour so long they half had people believing in that beast of theirs. And it didn't help any that the kid who survived – Maywood – claimed it was some kind of monster that did in his friend. Of course, he was hysterical. It was dark in there. He probably expected to see some kind of hellish creature and his eyes played tricks on him. Then again, maybe it was Wick in some kind of outfit. Who's to say?'

'You ever hear Captain Frank on the subject of the beast?'

'The old goat's got himself quite a yarn. What's he call it, Pogo?'

'Bobo.'

'If that guy told me I've got a nose on my face, I'd take a quick peek in the mirror before I'd believe him.'

Abe grinned. 'He's not too reliable?'

'Let's say he likes to be the center of attention, and he's figured out that just about everyone – but especially tourists – are as happy as pigs in shit to hear about the beast. He gives them what they want to hear, and he's center stage for half an hour or so.'

'He said the thing killed his sister.'

'I've checked it out. We've got files going back to 1853 when the town was founded. According to the reports, his sister was killed by a coyote. His father *had* been on a trade ship to Australia, but there's nothing to indicate he brought back an unusual animal. He could've, I suppose, but I think it's more likely Captain Frank just used his father's voyage to make the story sound good. If the old man had been a miner, he would've brought it up out of a shaft.'

'I see what you mean,' Abe said. 'I'd better get moving, I've got some people waiting for me.' He offered his hand, and the man shook it. 'I really appreciate your taking the time to tell me all this.'

'Sorry your friend had such a raw experience. You can tell her Dan died bravely in the line of duty, and we miss him around here.'

'I'll do that. Thanks again,' Abe said, and started to turn away.

'Say. One thing before you leave. You must've been in town last night, out at the Last Chance, or I don't suppose you would've heard the Bobo story.'

'That's right.'

'Stayed at the Welcome Inn?'

'From what I hear, it's the only motel in town.'

'Notice anything peculiar out there?'

'Peculiar? In what way?'

'Seems the Crogans, the family that runs the place, weren't anywhere around this morning. The cook phoned in around six to report it. The office was all locked up. We sent a man in, and it looks like nobody slept there last night. Just found their car abandoned down the road. No sign of them anywhere.'

'Odd.' Abe shook his head. 'No, I don't recall anything unusual.'

'We didn't think much of it till we found the car. That was about an hour ago. Seems like there might've been trouble.'

'I'll ask my friends if they noticed anything.'

'I'd appreciate it. We've got a man out at the Inn now to interview guests, but it seems most everyone's already taken off. Pay in advance, leave first thing in the morning. Folks on vacation, they always want an early start.'

'Well, I'll check.'

'Bring your friends around, if they saw or heard something. 'Course, all we've got now is a missing family. If it turns worse, we'll be in touch for sure.'

'Right. Well, I hope they show up.'

'You and me both.' He tipped a finger to his eyebrow. 'Have a good one.'

Outside, Abe scanned the roadside. The Mustang wasn't in sight so he walked to the corner. Looking down Front Street, he tried to spot Tyler and Nora. Apparently they were still shopping. After a car passed, he crossed and stood near the curb to wait for Jack.

Up the road a block, a blue and white patrol car swung out of the service station. That would be Lucy at the wheel, he thought, with Bix in the tow truck tailing her. As she drew near, she smiled at Abe and raised a hand. He returned her wave. Bix drove by with a finger deep in his mouth. The patrol car and tow truck moved slowly down the road, waited at a traffic light halfway through town, and moved on. They passed the ticket shack in front of Beast House, and soon disappeared where the road curved away into the wooded hills.

Abe turned his gaze to the sidewalk. A block down, a

woman pushed a baby stroller into a shop. When they were out of the way, he could see down to the sporting goods store. Still no sign of Tyler or Nora.

The Mustang pulled up beside him. Its passenger seat was piled with towels, his blue swimming trunks on top. He lifted the stack and sat down.

'Took me a while,' Jack said. 'I got waylaid by a cop.'

'The disappearing family?'

'You know about that. I'll tell you something you don't know.' He checked the side mirror, and eased into the deserted lane. 'They aren't the only ones missing. I was talking to the cop when up comes that Hardy fellow and says his friend, that Blake character, hasn't turned up all morning. Hardy hasn't seen him since last night.'

'The plot thickens,' Abe said.

'Yep. The cop was so intrigued by that little development he lost his interest in me, or I'd still be there.'

'Well, I don't think the ladies are finished shopping yet, anyway.'

Jack parked in front of Will's Sporting Goods. 'We'll probably have a long wait,' he said. 'You get a couple of gals trying to make up their minds on swimwear, it could take all day. So, what did you find out about Jenson?'

19

'Turn here,' Nora said.

Tyler, in the back seat, kept her eyes down as Jack swung the car onto Beach Lane. She didn't want to see the road she'd driven yesterday, but her mind dwelled on it: the windowless brick house across the field to the left, the woods to the right, the row of mailboxes, Dan's mailbox. She saw herself and Nora walking Seaside's shadowy ruts, the strange man staring out at them through the screen. She remembered the desolate, abandoned look of Dan's cabin with its empty porch, and how she'd felt anxious to get away from it. Without knowing, she'd somehow known her search for Dan would end badly. Dead more than a year. God, it was hard to believe. He lives in Beast House? I wouldn't say that, not exactly. That crazy old man, Captain Frank, had known all along. He'd toyed with her. Even last night, he'd kept it to himself. Maybe he just didn't have the guts to come out with it. Maybe he'd wanted to, but couldn't force himself to be the bearer of such news. Probably holds himself responsible, figures it was his father's Bobo that did it.

She wished he had told her. Nothing could've dragged

her into that awful place, if she'd known. Dan's body – no, not his body, just a wax dummy...

And she'd fainted. God, she'd fainted! Right in front of everyone. The memory made her skin go hot with embarrassment; just as it had every time she'd thought of it, even in the shop while trying to pick out a swimsuit.

Fainted. Barfed.

It would've been awful enough without all that, and she felt ashamed for letting the humiliation of it stand in the way of the grief she should feel over Dan's death. She should be mourning him, not blushing over the spectacle she'd made of herself.

But deep inside, where there should have been anguish, was only a hollow feeling that seemed distant from sorrow.

The car stopped.

'All out that's getting out,' Nora announced.

'You go on without me,' Abe said. 'I'll change in here.'

Tyler followed Nora out the driver's door.

'Too bad,' Nora said. 'I guess we won't have the beach to ourselves.'

Two other cars and a van were parked nearby, but Tyler saw no people about. They were probably already down at the ocean. 'I'll wait for Abe,' she said.

'No hurry,' Nora told her. 'We can all...'

Jack swatted her rump. 'Let's go,' he said.

The two of them started down a path along the low hillside, holding hands, Nora nodding as he spoke to her.

Tyler stepped to the front of the Mustang. She leaned against its hood, staring at the brown weeds and dusty path, very aware of Abe just behind her, probably watching her through the windshield as he changed into his trunks. She wondered why he hadn't put them on at the motel, as Jack must've done. She heard the quiet clink of his belt buckle. The car moved slightly against her rump, probably in response to Abe rising and settling in the seat as he took down his pants. Thinking about that, she felt a quick stir of excitement that made her guilt worse.

I'm not betraying Dan, she told herself. It was decided before I knew. I can't help how I feel. I can't. I'm sorry.

Her hands went quickly down the front of her blouse, flicking open its buttons. She slipped the sleeves down her arms, and draped the blouse across the hood. The sun's heat and the caressing breeze felt wonderful on her skin, and she could almost feel Abe gazing at her. She wondered if his trunks were on yet. Did the sight of her back, bare except for two thin cords, arouse him? She and Nora, after paying for their bikinis, had used the changing rooms to put them on. She almost wished, now, that she had left hers in its bag. She could've stripped naked here in the sunshine and the ocean breeze, with Abe watching in astonishment from the car. It seemed outlandish, but at the moment she felt capable of such actions. Giddy, maybe a little desperate. She could reach back, right now, and pluck the cords and let the top fall away and turn to face him.

He would think she'd gone mad.

Maybe I *have* gone mad.

Troubled by the urge to remove her top, she went ahead and opened her corduroys. She slid them down her legs, stepped out of them, placed them neatly on the hood without turning far enough to see Abe through the windshield. Then she leaned back again.

Abe was taking a very long time.

Maybe enjoying the show.

I ought to give him a *real* show.

My God, what's the matter with me?

Staring down at herself, she even wondered what had possessed her in the store. At home, she had a similar string bikini. She never wore it in public, only in the privacy of her enclosed sundeck. So why had she bought one just like it this morning? And why, even though it covered so little, did she have such a strong desire to pull it off and stand naked in front of Abe and . . . ?

I *must* be crazy, she thought.

And it must have something to do with finding Dan that way. Something to do with fear and loneliness. Maybe more to do with the feel of the sun and the sea air and the slick fabric on her nipples and the taut press of it on her groin and knowing she was so very much alive like an insult to death.

The sound of the door opening interrupted her thoughts. She turned around and watched Abe step out of the car. He looked sleek and tanned. His boxer trunks were pale blue. He had a bundle of towels clamped under one arm. 'That's quite an outfit,' he said.

'Thanks. I like yours, too.'

He laughed. 'Want to leave your clothes here?' He held out a hand. She gave him the blouse and pants. He put them in the car and locked up. He approached without looking at her. A troubled frown had replaced his smile. .

'What is it?' Tyler asked.

He shifted the bundle to his right arm, took hold of her hand, and led her toward the path. 'I didn't go back to the motel,' he said. 'I stopped in at the police department.'

'The police?'

'I wanted to get the story on Dan. I thought there were ... things we should know.'

The tight sick feeling seemed to swell inside Tyler. 'And?' she murmured.

'I didn't find out much. He was murdered there in the house. They don't know who did it. A sister from Sacramento claimed his body.'

'Roberta. She's an accountant. She had dinner with us once at Ben Jenson's. A very nice person.'

Abe let go of her hand. He put an arm around her and eased her close to his side. 'I'm awfully sorry about all this.'

'At least ... his parents aren't alive. It would've been terrible for them. He wasn't married?'

'I didn't ask. I assume he wasn't, since his sister ...'

'Probably not. God, it's funny. Yesterday, my biggest worry was that he might be married. Then, today, I was so worried that he wouldn't be. And all the time, he was dead in that house for everyone to gawk at.'

'It's not him, Tyler.'

'Yeah, I know. I keep telling myself. God, you wouldn't think they'd be allowed to put someone on display like that.'

'Madame Tussaud's been doing it for two hundred years.'

'Doesn't make it right.'

'No,' Abe said, 'it doesn't.'

'It'd probably take a court order to get it out of there.'

The path curved around the slope, and Tyler saw Nora and Jack down at the water's edge. Combers were rolling in. Off to the side, a woman stood in the surf holding the hand of a toddler. A man was jogging along the shoreline, a black retriever prancing ahead of him. Stretched out on a blanket near the foot of the slope was a young couple embracing. Tyler felt Abe's hand caressing her side. She took a deep breath of the fresh, tangy air.

'When are you leaving?' she asked.

'There's no rush.'

'Today? Are you leaving today?'

'That depends.'

'On what?'

'On you.'

She stopped walking. Turning to her, Abe let the towels fall. He looked into her eyes as his hands slid up her arms, cupped her shoulders. 'I'll stay another night,' she said, 'if you will.'

He smiled slightly. 'Do you think Nora would object?'

'Surely you jest?'

He eased Tyler against him. Gently. One hand stroking her hair, the other light on her back. She hugged him tightly. He was warm and smooth and solid, and she remembered embracing him that morning and the way his hands had felt on her breasts. It seemed like a very long time ago. Dan had been there in the room with them like a chaperon. If I'm going to lose you to this guy, Abe had said, I'd rather not get in any deeper. I want you too much already. The memory of his words made Tyler's heart pound fast. Guilt swept through her, and she hugged Abe more tightly to ward it off. Though he stroked her hair and back gently, as if intent only upon consoling her, Tyler felt his rising hardness.

Abe stepped back. His smile trembled. 'I guess I can stay one more night.'

Tyler nodded. She was a little breathless. 'I would like that,' she said.

He looked toward the water, and Tyler's eyes strayed down to his trunks. The bulge slanted upward, forcing the elastic band slightly away from his waist. 'There might be a problem,' he said, and crouched to pick up the towels.

'A problem?'

They walked down the path.

'The owners of the motel seem to be missing. Their car was found abandoned this morning. Nobody seems to know what happened to them.'

'Do you think the motel might close?'

'Maybe there's someone to keep it running, I don't know.'

'Oh, great. It's the only place in town, isn't it?'

'Far as I know. Brian Blake also appears to be among the missing.'

'What the hell's going on?'

'I don't know.'

'Oh, man. This town. I knew when we got here it was a creepy place. I wanted to get out of here last night. And I might've, too, except for you.'

'Except for me?'

'It's all your fault,' Tyler said, and squeezed his hand. 'I'm sorry.'

'Don't be. Besides, I don't think I could've pried Nora away.'

In the sand at the bottom of the hill, Tyler kicked off her sandals. She picked them up and hooked her arm through Abe's. The sand felt hot, almost burning. Nora and Jack were a distance up the beach, wading through the wash, but they'd left their clothes behind in a heap. Tyler dropped her sandals next to the pile. Abe put down the towels.

'Shall we go in?' Tyler asked.

'We both need to cool off.'

With a laugh, she dashed across the sand. Abe ran along easily beside her. Cold water splashed up her legs. She kicked through a knee-high wave, charged into one that chilled her to the hips, then dived. She went rigid with the cold blast, but moments later it no longer felt so bad. She swam out, the swells lifting her, easing her down. When something seized her foot, she thought *shark*! And then she thought, Abe.

She tugged free, came up for air, and whirled around. A moment later, Abe's head popped to the surface, hair matted down, face shiny and dripping. She swatted water at him. He ducked under the surface. She watched him glide forward, saw his arms reach out, felt his hands on her hips. He pulled her down. His body slid against her as if it were oiled. He nuzzled the side of her neck, kissed her mouth. They rolled under the water, embracing. One of his thighs pressed between her spread legs and she quivered and scissored her legs shut, trapping it there. She shoved a hand down the back of his trunks, fingered the crease of his rump, clenched a firm buttock and writhed against him. But

her lungs started to hurt. She pushed herself away from
Abe, clawed to the surface, and gasped for air. Abe came
up in front of her. Treading water, they panted for a
while.

'Trying to drown me?' Tyler finally asked.

'*You* trying to drown *me*?'

'What a way to go,' she said. The words reminded her
of Dan on the corridor floor, his throat torn out.

'What?' Abe asked.

'Nothing.'

'Nothing?'

'I keep ... forgetting about Dan. Then I keep
remembering.'

'Yeah.'

'Would you mind if we get out now?'

'Not if that's what you want.'

'We'd better.' She forced a smile. 'Before we lose our
suits.'

'As good a reason as any.'

Side by side, they swam closer to shore. Then they
waded out, the waves nudging their backs as if to hurry
them along. 'Let's just walk,' Tyler said.

'Towel?'

'The sun will dry us.' She took Abe's hand, and they
walked on the hard-packed sand, the wash of the ocean
sometimes swirling over their feet. The sun felt hot and
good. Gulls wheeled overhead, squealing. Jack and
Nora, a distance up the beach, were strolling slowly
toward them.

'There's something I want you to know,' Tyler said.

'Uh-oh.'

'Not really. It's just that ... I don't want you to think

... God, how can I say this? I felt the way I do about you before all this about Dan happened. You remember this morning in my room?'

'How could I forget?'

'That was before ... the tour. I'd already made up my mind not to ... get involved with him.'

Abe nodded as if he'd known that.

'I just don't want you to think the way I ... I mean, I'm not on some kind of bizarre rebound. It has nothing to do with him. Hell, I wanted you last night. But he was in the way, even though ... oh, God, doesn't that sound wonderful? He was in the way and now he's not.'

'I think I understand, Tyler.'

'You guys went in!' Nora said as she and Jack came near. 'Didn't you freeze your buns?'

'It wasn't too bad,' Tyler said. 'Give it a try.'

'No way. I'm gonna spread out one of those towels and catch some rays. We're gonna stay awhile, aren't we?'

'Sure,' Abe said. 'One thing, though. Is anyone opposed to staying over again tonight?'

'All *right*!' Nora wiggled her eyebrows at Jack. 'How about you, Tiger? Think you're up to it?'

'There might be a problem with the Inn,' he said to Abe.

'Weird, huh?' Nora asked. 'What do you suppose happened to those people?'

'I promised the cop I'd check about that,' Abe said. 'None of you noticed anything strange last night, did you?'

Nora said, 'Not a thing.' Jack shook his head.

'If the motel's going to close up,' Tyler said, 'we'd better find out. ' Her heart started racing. 'Why don't

Abe and I go on ahead and check it out? We can register, if everything's okay, and meet you back here.'

'Terrif.'

'That okay with you, Abe?' Tyler asked.

'Let's go.'

They left Nora and Jack spreading towels on the sand, and trudged up the slope. Tyler was eager and nervous. The parking area seemed very far away, as if the path had stretched itself simply to frustrate her. At last, they reached the car. Abe opened the passenger door. He rolled down its window, and tossed the towels into the back seat.

'Whoa,' Tyler said. 'I'd better put something on.'

'You look fine,' he said.

With a shrug, she climbed in. She jumped at the burning touch of the seat cover, then settled down and watched Abe wince as he sat behind the wheel. 'Hurt?' she asked.

'I can take it.'

'We should've put clothes on.'

'I like you this way.' Reaching over, he slid a hand up her leg. He patted her thigh, met her eyes for a moment, then started the car.

Tyler slumped down in her seat as they passed through the middle of town. Abe kept glancing at her, looking a bit amused. He drove in silence.

Nervous? she wondered.

'We'll check the office later,' he said finally.

Except for Gorman Hardy's Mercedes, the courtyard of the Welcome Inn was deserted.

'My room'll be fine,' Tyler whispered.

He parked in front of it. Tyler stepped out into the

shade. A mild breeze chilled the sweat on her skin. Leaning over the back seat, she gathered her handbag and all her clothes.

Her hands were trembling. She dropped the room key on the stoop. Abe picked it up and unlocked the door.

The room was dusky, the curtains drifting out from the open windows. The bed Tyler had slept in last night was still unmade. She stepped over to the dressing table, and emptied her arms.

In the mirror, she saw Abe come up behind her. Parting her hair, he kissed the nape of her neck. He caressed her sides, her belly. She watched his hands glide upward, and moaned as they cupped her breasts through the filmy bikini.

'Tyler,' he whispered.

'Huh?'

'It's a nice name.'

'It's a weird name.'

'I like it. I like everything about you.'

'Flatterer.'

'Yeah.'

'Do you like my sweat?'

'I like how it makes you slippery,' he said, sliding his hands down her belly.

'Soap will do that, too.'

'Mmm.'

'Let's take a shower.'

He fingered the ties at her hip. She lifted his hand away. 'Patience. We've got to rinse the salt water off our suits.'

He laughed softly and followed her into the bathroom. Leaning over the tub, Tyler turned on the hot water faucet. She kept a hand under the spout. The water, cold at first, slowly became warm. She flinched with surprise when Abe touched her rump. His hand was big and warm. It moved slowly lower. She gasped and felt her legs go weak when it stole between them. She gripped the edge of the tub to hold herself steady. Steam rose from the splashing water, hot against her face. She looked around. Abe gave her an innocent smile, and his hand went away.

Tyler turned on the cold water. She adjusted the faucet and touched the water. Still too hot. She reached again to the faucet, and felt Abe's fingers on her hip. Looking back, she saw him pluck open the knotted cords. He let the ends fall. The white triangle at her groin swung away like a hinged flap. She twisted the faucet. Abe untied the other side. She turned the faucet slightly more and felt a tingling brush of fabric as Abe drew the garment away. He tossed it over her head. It dropped into the tub.

'You're very helpful,' Tyler said.

'I try to be.'

She touched the water. It felt right. 'What about your trunks?' she asked as she twisted the shower handle.

'That's your job.'

The spray came down. Straightening up quickly, Tyler yanked the shower curtain almost shut. She reached through the gap to test the temperature. Abe, standing beside her, moved a hand down her back and rump. 'It's ready,' she said.

'Ladies first.'

Tyler climbed into the tub. She passed through the spray and backed up against a tile wall. Abe stepped in.

He closed the curtain and turned to face her, one eye squeezed shut against the pelting shower, a rather silly smile on his face.

Tyler eased into his arms. The water rained down on their faces as they kissed. His body was slick against her. His hands roamed down her back, caressed and plied her buttocks as if he was fascinated by the firm mounds. Then they slid up. They opened the ties behind her back, behind her neck. Holding onto the neck cords, he stepped away and peeled the bikini down. He let it fall to their feet. He gazed at her streaming breasts. He explored them with his hands, stroking and holding and squeezing, clasping the nipples between his thumb and forefingers, pinching them gently in a way that made Tyler catch her breath and squirm.

Crouching, he rubbed his face on them. She felt his nose, the tickle of an eyelash, the rasp of whiskers, kisses, the soft circling tip of his tongue, the firm pressure of his lips, the edges of his teeth. Tyler clenched his hair as he sucked. His mouth felt huge and powerful, drawing her in until it almost hurt, then going to her other breast and doing the same. As the mouth released her, she pulled his hair to make him stand. She latched her mouth against his, and writhed in his embrace.

Turning so the spray was on her back, she wiped the water from her eyes. She rubbed Abe's slippery shoulders and chest. She looked down at his bulging trunks. The narrow gap was there between the waist band and his belly, as she'd seen it on the path to the beach. Now she slipped her fingertips into the gap and drew the band toward her. Forehead resting on his chest, she stared down at him. His hands were motionless on her shoulders. She reached into the trunks, curled a hand around his thickness, and explored its hard length. Crouching, she pulled the trunks down his legs. He stepped out of them. Tyler's hands moved up his thighs. She gently squeezed the furry sac of his scrotum. She wrapped her fingers around his shaft, slid them lightly up and down, then kissed the slitted head. Her tongue swirled around the silken skin. Holding his buttocks, she licked down the underside, feeling the solid heat of him against her cheek. Then she took him in, lips stretching around his smooth flesh, tongue stroking. She drew him in deeply until her mouth could accept no more. He squirmed, clutching her hair, his rump flexed taut under her hands as she sucked.

'Better stop,' he warned in a husky voice.

She slid her mouth back, kissed the swollen knob, then sheathed him again.

'*Tyler.*' He pulled gently at her hair. She sucked hard as he eased her away. Then her mouth was empty and she rose and embraced him, feeling the hardness against her belly.

'I want you *now*,' she gasped into his mouth.

'Here?'

'Yes.' She lay down in the tub, pressing her knees to its walls, and Abe lowered himself onto her. The hot shower smacked her face. Then Abe's head blocked the spray. He was light on her, braced by his elbows and knees. As he kissed her, she felt a touch between her legs. He moved slowly, the head of his penis stroking her cleft. She flinched as it nudged her clitoris, squirmed and moaned as it stayed there, rubbing. Then it moved lower and very slowly slid in. She wanted it thrusting deep, but Abe held back as if to torture her. He withdrew completely, and she groaned. She dug her fingers into his rump. He pushed her opening. He entered. He suddenly shoved in fast and deep, spreading her, driving in farther and farther until she thought it impossible for there to be more – but there was more and it filled her.

They lay locked together, Abe deep in her body as if part of her. Neither of them moved. Tyler understood – and maybe so did Abe – how close they were to orgasms that would mean an ending, at least for now, to the terrible aching need for so deep a joining. She wanted to prolong the moment, to savor it.

The water was spraying down. It dripped off Abe's face onto Tyler's face as he kissed her lips, her nose, her eyes.

'Oh, Abe,' she whispered.

Behind the registration desk stood a portly, red-faced man in a white shirt and bow tie. Strands of hair crossed his head like streaks sketched on with a black pen. He made a lopsided smile. 'What can I do for you, folks?'

'We were guests last night,' Abe said. 'We'd like to extend our stay, if you'll be open.'

'Names?'

'Ours are under Branson,' Tyler said.

'Branson and Clanton,' Abe told him.

The man fingered through cards in a metal box. 'I'll be running the place for now,' he said as he searched.

'Have the police found out anything about the Crogans?' Abe asked.

'Looks bad. Blood in Marty's car. I'm his brother-in-law, you know. We've got a piece of this place, so I'll be seeing to matters. Hope my wife doesn't let the pharmacy go to hell.' He pulled out two cards. 'Here we go. How many nights will you be wanting to stay on?'

'One more,' Abe said. He tried to pay for all the rooms, but Tyler insisted on picking up the tab for hers and Nora's.

'Will the restaurant be open, too?' she asked.

The man nodded. 'We'll keep it running.'

'I hope everything turns out all right,' Abe said.

'I do, too, but I don't suppose it'll be that way. We've had folks disappear before in this town. It's not likely they'll show up again.'

'Take care, now,' Abe told him.

'I'll see your rooms are made up before long. I'll take care of it myself if I can't round up Lois. I think she knew I'd need her. That's why she hightailed it. Probably off at the beach with Haywood.'

'We're on our way to the beach,' Tyler said.

His eyebrows lifted. 'If you see Lois, you want to let her know her father needs her over here? I'd appreciate it. She's sixteen, long brown hair, wears this polka-dot bikini she ought to be ashamed of.'

'If we see her,' Tyler said, 'we'll tell her to come by.'

He thanked her, and they left.

'She wasn't the one we saw,' Abe said as they stepped down the porch stairs.

'No, but she might be there now. It's been a couple of hours.'

'Doesn't seem that long.'

She grinned, and Abe patted her rump. He opened the

passenger door. She climbed in. 'I hope Nora and Jack aren't burnt to a crisp,' she said.

'If they are, it was for a good cause.' Abe shut the door and walked around to his side of the car. As he sat down behind the wheel, Tyler leaned over. She kissed him.

She rode with her elbow out the window, the breeze tossing her hair and fluttering the front of her blouse. The two top buttons were open.

'Eyes on the road, buster.'

'It's not easy.'

She smiled and threw back her head. Abe glanced at her throat, the smooth tanned vee of skin below it, the pale slope of a breast as the breeze lifted a side of her blouse.

He turned away and watched the road. He felt very strange – pleasantly tired, happier than he could remember ever being before, yet troubled.

It couldn't be going better, he told himself

Maybe that's the problem.

Some problem

It's gone too well, too fast. It started less then twenty-four hours ago when he first saw her face – spattered by that lunatic's blood. When he first looked into her eyes, and felt as if he'd known her before. No, as if he *should* have known her before. As if she had always been out there, and he'd known it but not who she was or where to look. It was like finding a part of himself that had been lost.

From that time on, she'd been a constant presence in his mind. He'd wondered about her, worried and hoped. Yesterday afternoon had been very bad, especially when she went looking for Dan. During dinner and later, the threat from Dan had faded, but not completely, and he'd spent the night in a restless half-sleep, eager for the morning to come but dreading its arrival, afraid of losing her.

He nodded, realizing he'd discovered the source of his worry: he was *still* afraid of losing her.

The worry seemed unfounded. She'd apparently made up her mind in favor of Abe even before finding out about Dan's death. She wanted him – maybe as much as he wanted her. But their lovemaking had brought such a closeness, such a joining that he now had much more to lose than he'd ever thought possible.

It was amazing.

But frightening, too.

'You're looking mighty glum,' she said.

'Post-coital depression.'

She laughed. 'How long do you expect it to last?'

'Probably till we coit again.'

'Can it wait till after lunch?'

'If it must,' he said. He turned onto Beach Lane.

At the end of the dirt road, parked next to a pickup truck, was a long, gray Mercedes.

'That looks like Hardy's,' Tyler said. 'I wonder what Mr Wonderful's doing at the beach.'

20

'My father, he'd been living with the guilt more than thirty years, and he told me he couldn't abide it any longer.' Captain Frank raised the can of Bud to his mouth. He shut his eyes against the sun as he gulped.

Gorman took another can from the six-pack he'd brought along to lubricate the old man's tongue, and popped open its top. Captain Frank mashed his empty and tossed it. Gorman watched it drop a long way to the ground.

'It was then he told me, for the first time, all about Bobo and how Bobo must still be alive and murdering.'

'Have another,' Gorman said.

Captain Frank accepted the fresh can. 'Much obliged.' He settled back in his lawn chair and took a long drink. 'Well, I begged my father to let me go with him, but he'd have none of that. Wanted me to stay behind and look after Mother. It was as if he knew he'd never come back, and he didn't. He was a mighty fine shot with that Winchester of his. I 'spect Bobo must've snuck up on him, caught him from behind.' With his free hand, the old man savagely clawed the air. 'Just like that.'

'Was your father's body ever found?' Gorman asked.

'No, sir. I 'spect it's buried over yonder, more than likely in the cellar.'

'The cellar of Beast House?'

'That's what I figure.'

'If the beast actually killed him, as you believe, wouldn't the Kutch woman have put a replica of your father on display for the tour.'

'Could've, but she didn't. You ask me, the old bat's mighty careful who she exhibits. You look at who's in there. Take the Bagley kid, for instance. His friend, Maywood, got out alive and went running to the cops. Now how's she gonna deny the killing? She doesn't. She turned it to the good by having dummies made up. Same goes for the three last year. One's Danny Jenson, the cop. How's she gonna pretend it never happened? But let me tell you.' He squinted an eye at Gorman. 'There's plenty of folks just up and disappear. I figure Bobo got most of them. But old Maggie, she's not gonna put them on display when she's got a way to cover up. She'd have a whole house full, and how'd that look?' He took a long drink of beer.

'Four people disappeared last night,' Gorman said. 'The Crogans, who run the Welcome Inn...'

'Oh, dear Lord.'

'And a friend of mine.'

Captain Frank scowled at the top of his beer can.

'The Crogans' car was found abandoned this morning on the road to the highway.'

'Well, it got them. I was you, I wouldn't count on seeing my friend again. Or the Crogans, either. Their girl, she gone too?'

'Yes.'

218

He let out a long sigh. 'She was such a cute thing. Used to see her down at the beach. Always had a kind word. Goddamn, they should've known better. You just don't go near that house, not after dark, not unless you're looking to get yourself killed. They should've known that.'

'Does the beast actually leave the house?'

'Sure does. Unless Wick or Maggie are grabbing folks. One look at that pair, you know they'd be hard put to get away with it. Bobo's gotta be prowling around. In the hills back of the house. Down on the beach. Some twelve years back, we even had a gal disappear from the cabin next door.' He nodded to the right. 'Ry, that's her husband, he come home late from the Last Chance and she was gone. Folks all said she'd run off 'cause he was always whumping on her. But I knew different and told him so. He called me a screwy old fart and said to stay out of his business.'

He peered at Gorman and raised a thick white eyebrow. '*You* think I'm a screwy old fart?'

'Not at all,' Gorman assured him.

'Well, lots of folks do. They'll change their tune one of these days when I hand over Bobo's body.'

'You plan to kill it?'

'I'll get Bobo, or it'll get me.'

'Have you ever gone after it?'

'Why, sure. I've gone and laid ambush for it – oh, more times than I can count. But it's never showed up.'

'You've never seen it?'

'Not a once.'

'Have you ever gone into the house after it?'

'Now, that'd be trespassing.'

Gorman controlled his urge to smile. Obviously, the old man was afraid to enter Beast House. 'It seems,' he said, 'as if the house would be the best place to hunt it.'

Captain Frank squeezed his beer can and hurled it from the bus top. It hit a low-hanging tree branch and fell to the ground. 'Say, young man, how'd you like to take a look at my book?'

'What book?'

'I been keeping track. Yes, indeed. You'd be surprised.'

'I'd like very much to see it.'

The old man winked. 'Thought you might. You're a lot curiouser than most.' He pushed himself out of the lawn chair, and walked unsteadily along the top of the bus. 'Bring the beer along,' he said.

Gorman got to his knees and watched Captain Frank descend the wooden ladder. The moment the man was out of sight, he pulled out his pocket recorder. The tape was still running, but it must be near its end. The old geezer had talked for the better part of an hour – and what a story he'd told! Gorman couldn't have been more delighted. Everything was going his way. Everything! His fingers trembled with excitement as he ejected the tape's tiny cartridge, flipped it over, and slid it back into place. He returned the recorder to his jacket pocket. He grabbed an empty plastic ring of the six-pack. The two remaining cans clanked together at his side as he walked carefully toward the ladder.

He approached it with growing alarm. The ascent had been bad enough, but he suspected the descent would prove worse. The ladder was simply propped against the end of the bus, its highest rung level with his waist. What if it should tip over as he attempted to clamber on?

Gorman Hardy, noted author of *Horror at Black River Falls*, fell to his death . . .

Captain Frank was down below, gazing up at him. 'Would you mind holding the ladder for me?'

The old man shook his head as if he pitied Gorman, then stepped under the ladder and clutched its uprights.

If you're such a stalwart fellow, Gorman thought, why are you terrified of going after the beast? A screwy old fart, all right. And a coward. But his story was gold, and Gorman's fear subsided as he wondered about the man's book. Carefully, he mounted the ladder. It wobbled slightly. The rungs creaked under his weight. His legs felt weak and shaky, but finally he planted a foot on the solid ground.

'And you're still in one piece,' said Captain Frank.

Gorman forced a smile. He followed the man through a litter of beer cans alongside the painted bus. 'Did you paint this mural?'

'That I did.'

'I've never seen anything quite like it. Would you mind if I took a picture?'

'Help yourself. I'll just step inside and . . .'

'Stay here. I'd like you in the picture, too. The canvas and the artist.'

Captain Frank nodded. He moved to the open door of the bus as Gorman set down the beers and stepped away. In the viewfinder, the old man looked like a crazed tourist: Huckleberry Finn straw hat, red aloha shirt flapping in the breeze, plaid Bermuda shorts, spindly legs with drooping green socks and tattered blue tennis shoes. He held an arm out, a finger pointing at the mural.

Gorman took a few more backward steps to fit in the entire length of the bus, and triggered the shutter release. 'Marvelous! Now step over that way.' He waved the old man to the left. 'There. Right there. The ancient mariner and the albatross.'

'You know the poem?'

'Certainly. It's one of my favorites.' He moved in close and snapped the shot. 'Wonderful. Thank you.'

'Hope they turn out.'

'Shall we have a look at this book you mentioned?'

'Right this way.'

When the old man turned away to mount the steps, Gorman switched on his recorder. He retrieved the beers, and followed. He found Captain Frank in the driver's seat.

'Look here, matey.' With a sly wink, he whacked the sun visor. It flipped down. Secured to its back with duct tape was a sheathed knife. He tapped a fingernail against the staghorn handle. 'I'm ready for it, see? Just let old Bobo make a try for me.' He pushed up the visor, hunched over so his chin rested on the steering wheel, and reached under the seat. He came up with a western style revolver. 'My hogleg,' he announced. Thumbing back the hammer, he stared at the weapon as if it were a stunning woman. 'This darling's an Iver Johnson .44 magnum. She'll knock Bobo ass over tea kettle.'

'Is it loaded?' Gorman asked.

'Wouldn't do me much good empty.'

Gorman held his breath as Captain Frank lowered the hammer. When the revolver was safely stored away, the old man stood up. He stepped through the gap in the faded, split blanket draping the aisle. Gorman followed.

The rows of windows along both sides of the carriage had been painted over, tinting the dim light with hues of red, blue, green and yellow. A few, fortunately, were open to admit untarnished daylight and the fresh breeze. The original seats had been removed to make room for a strange assortment of furnishings: a cot with a rumpled quilt, a straight-backed wicker chair, a single lamp and several steamer trunks of various sizes, some standing on end, all cluttered with the odds and ends of Captain Frank's reclusive life. On the trunk nearest the cot, Gorman saw a copy of Peter Freuchen's *Book of the Seven Seas*, a Coleman lantern, a crushed beer can, and a revolver. He spotted three more weapons as the old man lowered himself onto the cot: a double-barreled shotgun suspended from an overhead luggage rack by a pair of misshapen wire hangers, a saber propped against a metal partition near the side exit doors, and the butt of a pistol protruding from the open face port of a deep-sea diving helmet atop one of the trunks.

'You've got quite an arsenal,' he said.

'Yessir. Just let Bobo come. I don't care where I'm at. Here?' He snatched the revolver off the trunk and jabbed the air with its barrel as if taking hasty aim at a host of intruders. 'In my galley?' He swept the gun toward the rear of the bus, where a second blanket draped the aisle just beyond the side exit. 'I've got a .38 Smith and Wesson by my stove. I've got a Luger in the head. I don't care where I am, I'm ready. Just let Bobo make a try.'

He put down the revolver on the floor by his feet. 'Have a seat, here, matey,' he said, and patted the cot.

Gorman peeled the plastic rings off the remaining beers. He gave one of the cans to Captain Frank, and sat down beside him. He popped open his can while the captain cleared off the trunk. The beer had lost its chill. He took a few swallows and wished he'd had the foresight to bring along a bottle of gin for himself.

The old man opened the trunk and lifted out a battered, leatherbound volume that looked like a family photo album. He closed the trunk, and set the book on its lid midway between himself and Gorman. Leaning forward, he flipped open the cover.

'Fabulous,' Gorman said.

'My father, he did that. He wasn't the artist I am, but he done the best he could.'

The pencil sketch, creased and smudged as if it had spent a lot of time folded in someone's pocket, showed a snarling, snouted head.

'That's Bobo,' Captain Frank said. 'My father, he drew it aboard the *Mary Jane* on the return voyage.'

Gorman stared at the head. It was a frontal view, not much more than an oval with slanted eyes, a half circle to indicate the snout, and an open mouth revealing rows of pointed teeth.

'Not a hair on it,' the captain said. 'Not even an eyebrow or a lash. And skin as white as the belly of a fish. Like an albino. Just no color at all, except for its eyes. My father, he told me its eyes were as blue as the sky.'

He turned the page. The next sketch, a side view, showed the creature's blunt snout. Except for the snout, the head looked almost human. Where the ear should be, there was a circle the size of a dime. 'Where is its ear?' Gorman asked.

'That's it. Nothing to it but a hole with a little flap of skin over it. That's to keep stuff from getting in. My father, he said Bobo could open up that flap like an eyelid and hear as good as a dog.'

'Incredible.'

Taped to the next page was a sketch of the beast standing upright. From waist to knees, its form had been obliterated by pencil marks as if someone had scratched over it in a fit of temper. The lead pencil point had even torn through the paper, rucking up an accordion wedge that had subsequently been smoothed down flat.

'What happened here?'

Captain Frank shook his head. He sighed. 'My mother did that. She was an awful prude, God rest her bones. I never got a chance, myself, to see the drawing before she ruined it.'

'That's a shame,' Gorman said. He studied what remained of the creature. Except for the claws on its fingers and toes, it appeared remarkably human. The shoulders and chest were broad, the limbs thick as if heavily muscled. One arm was longer than the other, but Gorman assumed that to be a fault of the artist. 'Do you know the size of it?'

Captain Frank took a drink of beer and rubbed his mouth. 'About three feet tall. That's what it was when my father got rid of it. 'Course, now, it wasn't much more than a year old, then. He said the full-grown ones they killed on the island were better than six feet.'

Gorman nodded, and Captain Frank turned the page. He expected another sketch, perhaps a rear view of the creature, but found instead a newspaper clipping. The handwritten scrawl at the top of the page read, '*Clarion*, July 21, 1902, Loreen'. The article's heading was printed in bold type.

MALCASA CHILD SLAIN BY COYOTE

Loreen Newton, three-year-old daughter of Frank and Mary, was savagely attacked and slain in the yard of her parents' Front Street home. Alarmed by the child's screams ...

Gorman shook his head as if dismayed, and turned to the next page without finishing the story. Taped to its center was the child's funeral notice. He didn't bother reading it. He flipped the leaf over, and unfolded the full front page of the *Clarion*'s August 3, 1903 edition. He stared at the stark headline:

THREE MURDERED AT THORN HOUSE!

'This is wonderful,' Gorman said.

'My father, he's the one saved these early articles. I'm the one added on, after he was gone, and put them all together here.'

After glancing at the four columns of small print, Gorman refolded the page. Subsequent articles described the capture, trial, and lynching of Gus Goucher. Then Gorman found another folded front page of the

Clarion, this one recounting the slaughter, nearly thirty years later, of Maggie Kutch's husband and children. After a few follow-up stories, Gorman came upon a clipping about the disappearance of Captain Frank's father.

'Here's where I started keeping them,' the old man said.

Gorman scanned a story about the opening of Beast House for tours. Then he flipped through page after page of articles detailing the disappearances of townspeople and visitors, two or three for each year. 'That's a lot of missing people,' he said.

'It's just the ones that got reported. I figure there's plenty more, folks nobody missed.'

'And you suspect the beast was responsible for all this?'

'Maybe not all,' Captain Frank admitted. 'Some of those folks maybe just run off, or got themselves lost in the hills, or drowned. There's no telling how many, but I'll wager Bobo got his share of them.'

'Why was nothing done about it? This must be fifty or sixty missing persons over a twenty-year period.'

'Well, sir, the police, they didn't see anything so strange about it. Lord knows, I told them time after time it was the beast making off with those folks. Did they listen? No, indeed. They seemed to think it was normal, losing a couple folks a year.'

'Acceptable losses,' Gorman muttered.

'And they made up their minds, way back, that I'm just a loony. I can't even get them to listen to me anymore.'

'Have you showed this to them?' he asked, tapping the scrapbook.

'Sure. Like I say, they think I'm loony.'

Gorman came upon another full front page of the newspaper. This one dealt with the attack in 1951 on Tom Bagley and Larry Maywood. After follow-up stories came more pages with clippings about disappearances. Finally, near the back of the book, he found articles about last year's slayings of the Ziegler father and son, and patrolman Dan Jenson.

He reached a blank page.

Captain Frank took a swig of beer. 'That's all, till tomorrow's *Clarion*. I'll be adding whatever they print on this business you told me about – the Crogans and your friend. They'll go in, sure enough.'

'You're pretty confident Bobo got them?'

'I'd wager on it, matey.'

Gorman nodded. He gently closed the book, and stared at it. 'This is a very impressive document, Frank.'

'I always felt it's been my duty to keep a record of all these goings-on.'

'How would you feel about making it public?'

'Public?' The old man raised a bushy white eyebrow.

'I'd like to write up your story. Are you familiar with *People* magazine?'

'Aye.'

'I'm a staff writer for *People*. Maybe you saw my piece on Jerry Brown?' There must've been a piece on Brown recently, he thought.

'No, I . . .'

'Well, that's all right. The point is: I find myself shocked and amazed by what you've told me this afternoon, by the information in your scrapbook, by the very existence of a monstrosity such as Beast House, by the seeming indifference of the local authorities to what appears to be a seventy-five-year string of disappearances and grisly murders. With your cooperation, I'd be willing to do a feature article that exposes the truth of the situation. With enough public awareness, the authorities will be forced to take action. The story, of course, will focus on you.'

Captain Frank frowned as if thinking it over.

'What do you say?'

He sighed. 'I've always planned to take care of Bobo myself.'

'So much the better. If you can do that before the story's printed, we'll include your account of the hunt and photos of you with the body.'

'I don't know, Mr . . .'

'Wilcox. Harold Wilcox.'

'I don't know, Mr Wilcox. It does sound like a fine idea. Mighty fine. What'll I have to do?'

'Nothing, really. Just leave it to me. You've already given me sufficient information. Of course, I would need to borrow your scrapbook, at least long enough to have its contents photocopied. I'd be more than glad to give you a receipt for it. There must be a copying machine somewhere in town . . .'

'Over at Lincoln's Stationery.'

'Fine. I could have it done this afternoon and get it back to you . . .' He paused. 'Would tomorrow morning be convenient for you?'

'I do hate to let it out of my hands.'

'You're welcome to come along, if you don't trust me.'

'Oh, it's not that I don't trust you, Mr Wilcox.'

229

'I could probably get it back to you this evening, if that's preferable.'

Captain Frank chewed his lower lip.

'I tell you what. Suppose I leave a deposit with you? Say a hundred dollars. You keep my money until I return the book to you.'

'Well, that sounds fair enough.'

Gorman removed a pair of fifty-dollar bills from his wallet. 'Do you have some spare paper so we can write out the receipts?'

'I don't guess we need to,' Captain Frank said, and picked up the money. 'You just take good care of this book for me, and I'll take good care of your money.'

They shook hands.

With the scrapbook clamped under one arm, Gorman left the bus.

On his way through town, he spotted Lincoln's Stationery. He grinned, and kept on driving.

21

Tyler, sitting on the edge of the bed, rolled a stocking up her leg. As she clipped it to the straps of her black garter belt, someone knocked on the door. 'Who is it?' she called.

'Me,' came Abe's voice.

'Just a minute,' she said, and quickly started to put on the other stocking. 'Are you alone?'

'Very.'

'Poor man.'

'That's me.'

She finished with the stocking, and rushed to the door. Staying out of view behind it, she pulled it open. Abe stepped into the room. 'That was quick,' she said as she shut the door.

In the ten minutes since he left he had changed into navy slacks and a powder blue polo shirt. Tyler had managed to blow-dry her hair and begin dressing.

'I just couldn't stand being away from you,' he said.

She stepped into his arms and kissed him. His hands roamed down her back, curled over her bare buttocks, pulled her closer against him. 'Nice outfit,' he said after a while. He fingered a strap of her garter belt.

231

'Glad you like it,' Tyler said, and hugged him hard as Dan forced his way into her mind. Dan, who had given her the first one, gift-wrapped, during cocktails at the White Whale restaurant on Fisherman's Wharf. It was red and frilly with lace. He'd added a pair of nylons to the box. Without his asking, she'd excused herself and put them on in the restroom. And now he was dead, his savaged body on display – not his body, she reminded herself. Just a wax dummy.

'What's wrong?' Abe whispered.

She shrugged. 'I don't know.'

He took hold of her shoulders and eased her away. He stared into her eyes. 'I know what's bothering *me*,' he said.

'What?'

'Tomorrow.'

She moaned.

'I don't want to leave you.'

'We could stay another day.'

'I'd like to, but that would only be putting it off.'

'Let's keep putting it off,' Tyler said through a tight throat. Her eyes felt hot. Then they filled with tears. She lowered her head as the tears started sliding down her cheeks.

'When do you have to get back for your job?'

She shrugged.

'*Do* you have to get back for your job?'

She looked up at him. 'Do you want me to starve?'

'No. I want you to come with me.'

'You do?'

'Of course. I . . . I think you and I . . . I guess the thing of it is, I love you.'

'Oh, Abe.' Sobbing, she threw her arms around him. 'I love you so much.'

For a long time, they held each other. When Tyler finished crying, she wiped her eyes on the shoulder of his shirt and kissed him.

'Well, now that's settled...' he said.

'What'll we do?'

'Join Jack and Nora at the Happy Hour.'

'About tomorrow.'

'Whatever we decide, we'll do it together.'

'I do have to get back to LA. Some time.'

'Can you postpone it a few days?'

'Sure. I guess so.'

'Why don't we check with Nora, then? If everybody agrees, we'll head on over to my place.'

'Your place? What place?'

'The Pine Cone Lodge. It's a resort hotel up at Shasta.'

'It's *yours*?' Tyler couldn't keep the astonishment out of her voice.

'Dad's and mine. He's been after me to take over running the place so he can work in some more fishing. I won't start right away, though. Hell, he's waited this long. We can spend a while just fooling around. It's pretty nice up there. You can see how you like it, see if it's the sort of place where you might like to settle down, raise some kids...'

'Kids?'

'You know, those tiny little human things.'

'My God, Abe.'

'If all that fresh air is too much for you, or you want to hang onto your job, I've had an offer from an old buddy

233

with the LA Sheriff's Department. He was pretty miffed when I turned him down. I'm sure he'd be more than happy, though, to...'

'No way,' Tyler said. 'I've never had anything against fresh air, and my job...' she shook her head, 'I can live without it. Besides.' She stared into his eyes. 'LA's no place to bring up kids.'

Grinning, he said, 'Well.'

'Well,' Tyler echoed. She kissed him again. 'I guess I'd better put some clothes on.'

'Don't do it on my account.'

Abe watched while she stepped into her pleated skirt and pulled her white cashmere sweater over her head. Sitting at the dressing table, she fastened a thin gold chain around her throat. Abe stood behind her, looking at her reflection as she brushed her hair and applied lipstick. Turning her head slightly, she studied a faint red blotch on the side of her neck. She wondered if she should try to cover it with makeup.

'How'd you get that?' Abe asked.

'You should know.'

He looked perplexed. 'Did *I* do that?'

'With your very own mouth, darling. I could show you five or six more, but since I'm already dressed...'

'It can wait till after dinner, I guess. It'll give me something to look forward to.'

She decided to leave it alone. After all, nobody would notice the blemish except perhaps Nora and Jack, and they were probably well aware that she and Abe had spent the afternoon making love. They had likely been busy with a similar pastime themselves.

She got up from the dressing table, slipped into her sandals, and picked up her purse.

'You've got your key?' Abe asked.

She nodded. He opened the door for her, and took her hand as they walked into the courtyard. In spite of the breeze, the late afternoon sun felt hot on Tyler's back. The air smelled sweet, an aroma of pine mixed with the fresh ocean scent. 'Is your Pine Cone Lodge like this?' she asked.

'It's a bit larger. You can see it for yourself tomorrow. Do you think Nora will mind the side trip?'

'I doubt that. She's always on the lookout for an adventure. Especially where there's a man involved. As long as Jack's going to be with us, I don't think she'll squawk.'

'We should change the driving arrangement so they can travel together.'

'So *they* can travel together?'

Abe squeezed her hand. 'Well, I wouldn't mind a new passenger. You're prettier than Jack.'

'Flatterer.'

They walked past the rear of Gorman Hardy's Mercedes, a reminder that Brian Blake had disappeared. Blake, the motel owners and their daughter. Though there'd been some speculation during lunch about the missing four, Tyler hadn't given them a thought all afternoon. She suddenly felt a little guilty about that, as if she'd selfishly ignored their plight, as if she'd neglected her duty to worry about them.

Whatever happened to them, she told herself, they won't be any better off with me worrying.

Besides, she didn't know the girl at all, had only

spoken briefly with the father when they checked in, had seen the mother just for a few moments last evening at the restaurant, and disliked Brian Blake.

That shouldn't matter, she thought. If something awful happened to them, you should be concerned.

Okay, I'm concerned. Right now, I'm dwelling on them instead of thinking about myself and Abe. That's concern. I hope they're all right. There.

What could've happened to them?

Her mind suddenly filled with a picture of Maggie Kutch grinning, opening a red curtain to expose a display of Blake and the others, their mutilated bodies sprawled on the bloody floor of a room, Blake's head torn from his neck, his open eyes staring at her.

'God,' she muttered.

Abe looked at her.

'I got thinking about Blake and the others,' she explained. 'I hardly even know them.'

'"Every man's death diminishes me because I am a member of mankind",' Abe quoted.

'Do you think they're dead?'

'I have no idea, really. But I'd guess it's a strong possibility.'

'Do you think the beast...?'

'If you asked Captain Frank, I'm sure he'd say Bobo's behind it. I don't know about that. But it's pretty obvious that a lot of people get themselves murdered in this town.'

'I can't believe there's actually some kind of monster.'

'It's been my experience that most monsters are human.' He opened one of the double wooden doors of the Carriage House, and followed Tyler inside.

They stepped toward the deserted hostess station. The gooseneck lamp over its reservations book was dark.

'Dinner?' called a teenaged girl rushing toward them from the dining area. Her blonde hair was gathered into a ponytail. She wore a black skirt. Her white blouse was primly buttoned at the throat. 'I'm Lois,' she said before Abe could respond. 'I'll be your hostess for tonight.'

'The missing Lois,' Abe said.

'No, I'm not the one who's missing. It's my cousin, Janice, and ...'

'Your father was looking for you earlier,' Abe told her. 'I see he found you.'

She rolled her eyes upward. 'Oh, that. He found me, all right. Boy. Now I know how the slaves felt. Too bad Lincoln didn't free me while he was at it. Anyway, you want a table for two?'

'We'll get back to you, Lois, after we've put away a couple of cocktails.'

'Oh, you're here for the Happy Hour.'

'Then dinner.'

'I could put you down now, if you'd like, and save you a nice table by a window.'

Tyler smiled. In spite of Lois's enslavement, she seemed eager to do the job well.

'Okay,' Abe said. 'How about two tables for two? We're with some friends.'

'I'd be glad to seat you together.'

Tyler said, 'Separate tables will be fine.'

Abe gave the girl his name, and she entered it in the reservations book. It was the only name on the page. 'Fine, Mr Clanton. Shall I call you in about an hour?'

'Perfect,' he said. 'You're very good at this. I thought your father planned to have you cleaning rooms?'

'He made me do some this afternoon. What a drag. This is much better. This is kind of fun, I guess.'

'Okay. Well, we'll see you later.'

They stepped around the partition and entered the cocktail lounge. Tyler looked immediately toward the corner booth they'd occupied yesterday. Nora and Jack were there.

So was Gorman Hardy.

'Damn,' she muttered.

'And you without panties.'

Tyler laughed. She felt herself blush, slightly embarrassed in spite of her pleasure that Abe was so aware of the fact. 'He'll never know,' she said. 'Besides, I don't think he'd be interested.'

Abe patted her rump. 'Any man would be interested.'

Nora spotted them and waved. Hardy, after a glance over his shoulder, slid his pair of drinks to the end of the table and scooted off the seat. He remained standing while they approached.

'Good evening, Tyler, Abe,' he said.

Tyler nodded but made no effort to smile. Abe shook the man's offered hand.

She sat down and pushed herself sideways. The leatherette upholstery felt cool through her skirt, then warm when she passed over the place, near the center, where Hardy had been sitting. She moved over until the seat was cool again. While Abe slid in beside her, Hardy took a chair from a nearby table and planted himself at the end.

'We were just talking about you,' Nora said.

Wonderful, Tyler thought.

'Yes,' Hardy told her. 'It must have been a terrible shock for you, coming upon your former lover that way.'

She narrowed her eyes at Nora, then turned to meet Hardy's eager gaze. 'It was not one of my better moments,' she said.

'Let me extend my sympathy to you.'

'Thanks.' With a feeling of relief, she saw the barmaid advancing toward their table.

'What would you like to drink?' Abe asked.

'A margarita, I think.'

Abe ordered margaritas for both of them.

'Be kind enough,' Hardy added, 'to refresh the drinks of my other friends. And my own, of course.'

A trifle premature, Tyler thought.

Nora was only halfway through her first Mai-Tai, with her free second drink untouched. Jack had just started working on his second stein of beer. Hardy, lifting a stemmed glass, polished off his first martini. He left the olive, and reached for the second glass. His eyes settled on Tyler.

'I am, as you've already surmised, writing a book about Beast House. I realize it would be painful to you, but if you're willing to discuss your relationship with Mr Jenson and your reactions to viewing his mannequin...'

'I would not,' Tyler said.

'If we could get together later for an interview...'

His persistence made her seeth. 'How's your hearing, Mr Hardy?'

Nora drew back her head and stared at Tyler wide-eyed as if amazed by the retort. Jack looked at his beer and seemed to be struggling against a laugh. Abe studied his folded hands.

'I would be more than willing,' Hardy said, 'to pay you for the trouble.'

Abe spoke without looking up from his hands. 'The lady said no.'

'Would five hundred dollars change the lady's mind?'

'Five hundred dollars,' Tyler said, 'would not.' She turned sideways, an elbow on the table, and stared at him. 'In my opinion, any book you write about Beast House would be just as exploitive as Maggie Kutch and her goddamn dummies. I'll have no part of it. In fact, since I'm not a public figure, my right to privacy is protected by law and if my name appears in your miserable book I'll sue your ass.'

Hardy smiled at the outburst. 'All right, Tyler. You drive a hard bargain. I'm willing to go as high as eight hundred.'

'No, thank you.'

'A thousand.'

Nora, looking distressed, said, 'That's your rent for three months.'

'I don't need it that badly.'

'How about throwing some of that money my way,' Jack said.

'I was coming to that,' Hardy told him.

'Well, all right.'

He shook his head at Tyler as if she were a stubborn child more to be pitied than condemned. 'Are you certain I can't persuade you to change your mind?'

'Positive,' she said.

The barmaid arrived with the drinks. Hardy took a bill from his wallet.

'I'll take care of ours,' Abe told him.

'There's really no . . .' Hardy started.

'I'll take care of ours,' Abe repeated in the same even tone.

They each paid. The barmaid cleared off the empty glasses and left.

Tyler's hand trembled as she picked up her margarita. Abe turned to her. His face was solemn, but he winked and clinked his glass against hers. A few crumbs of grainy salt fell from the rim, sprinkling the backs of her fingers.

'As I was saying,' Hardy's voice intruded, 'I have indeed been considering a proposition for you.'

'Fire away.'

Looking into Abe's eyes, Tyler sipped her frothy drink.

'As you know, my associate, Brian Blake, seems to have disappeared.'

Frowning, Abe turned away. 'Along with three other people,' he said.

'That's correct. And the police seem to have no clue as to their whereabouts. In fact, I was speaking to an officer only a short time ago. They've been conducting a search of the woods in the vicinity of the abandoned car, but so far they've come up with nothing at all. They suspect foul play, though I prefer to think that Brian and the girl simply ran off together and the parents went in pursuit.'

'Your theory doesn't hold much water,' Abe said. 'You've written enough mysteries to see it's full of holes.'

Hardy shrugged elaborately. 'Very true. If this were a plot, however, I'm certain I could devise a sequence of events to explain the apparent inconsistencies, to plug the "holes" as you put it. Let me put it before you, instead, that I've been a close acquaintance of Brian Blake for several years. To say that he is a womanizer would be a gross understatement. I have no idea what might have befallen Janice's parents, but the girl herself is probably, at this very moment, in a motel somewhere along the highway with Brian betwixt her thighs.'

'Betwixt?' Jack mumbled.

'Let's hope so,' Abe said.

'I suspect they'll return eventually, but Brian once vanished for three weeks after meeting a young lady at the MGM in Vegas. I've told all this to the police, of course. They're checking with motels along the coast. Unfortunately, I'm in no position to wait. I have commitments that require me to leave here first thing in the morning.'

He nodded at Jack. 'This is where you come in. Or you, Abe. Either of you men, I'm sure, would be more than capable of doing this little assignment. Brian's responsibility, you see, was to photograph the interior of Beast House. He'd planned to do it tonight, but since he's not here...'

'You want one of us to do it,' Jack finished for him.

'I'm prepared to pay a thousand dollars.'

'Cash?' Jack asked,

'Two hundred cash, the balance by check.'

'Since you're offering that kind of money,' Abe

said, 'I assume you don't have permission from the owner.'

'The Kutch woman won't allow photos of the displays.'

'So we're talking about an illegal entry,' Jack said.

'I shouldn't think that would present a problem to a man of your background.'

'A piece of cake.'

Abe looked at Hardy. 'This was supposed to be Blake's job. Was he trying to break in and get those photos last night.'

'No, no. In fact, he left the camera in his room. His disappearance, I'm sure, had nothing to do with our project.'

'If you want the pictures so badly,' Tyler said, 'why don't you break in and take them yourself?'

'I've considered that option, of course. The truth of the matter, quite simply, is that I would prefer not to. I admit the venture involves a certain amount of risk. I'm not as young as these men. For me, it would hardly be a "piece of cake". That's why I'm willing to pay such an exorbitant amount to have it done by one of them.'

In other words, Tyler thought, you're chicken.

He took a sip of his martini. Then, smiling as if quite pleased with himself, he reached into his back pocket and took out his wallet. He removed two bills. Tyler saw that they were hundreds. 'Do I have a volunteer?' he asked.

Jack and Abe looked at each other.

While they hesitated, Nora blurted, 'Shit, *I'll* do it.'

Hardy chuckled.

'You think I'm kidding? I can always use some extra . . .'

'I'll do it,' Jack said calmly. 'No sweat.' He reached out and Hardy placed the two hundred dollars in his hand.

'Are you sure you want to do that?' Abe asked him.

'Hey, a thousand bucks is a thousand bucks.' He grinned at Hardy. 'You've got the camera, film, flash equipment?'

'They're back in my room. I'll give you a check for the balance when you pick them up.'

'What is it you want, exactly? Just pictures of the dummies?'

'That's basically it. I'll require good coverage of each display, perhaps one long shot for the overview, and two or three from a closer range for details. I would also like the attic stairway and the attic itself, if possible. The nursery, if you're able to unlock its door. And the cellar. The cellar is extremely important. According to my sources, you should find a hole in its floor. A fairly large hole, perhaps two or three feet in diameter. I would like both a long shot and a close-up of that hole, if it exists.'

'Okay,' Jack said. 'You got it.'

'I'll go with you,' Nora said.

'No way, babe.'

'Oh, come on. You'll need a lookout, won't you?'

'I'll look out for myself,' he assured her.

'Please. I won't be in your way. I'd like to see what that place is like at night. Bet it's creepy as hell.'

'You just stay with Tyler and Abe.'

'Whether it's dangerous or not,' Abe told her, 'it is illegal. Better that you stay out of it.'

She frowned at her Mai-Tai, then at Jack. 'I don't think I like the idea of you going in there alone.'

'He won't be going in alone,' Abe said.

A chill crawled through the pit of Tyler's stomach. She stared at Abe. He put a hand on her thigh. 'Don't worry,' he said. 'We'll be back before you know it.'

'I can take care of it myself,' Jack told him.

'Sure you can. But you won't let your buddy miss out on the fun, will you?'

Tyler cut into her lamb chop. She forked a bite-sized piece and stared at it. Her mouth was dry. She didn't want to eat the lamb, or anything else.

'I'm sorry,' Abe said.

'I know. I'm sorry, too. That bastard.'

'Jack?'

'No, of course not. It's not his fault. It's that goddamn Gorman Hardy.'

'I can't let Jack go in alone.'

'I know you can't. I wouldn't ask you to. But don't you think there's any way you can talk him out of it?'

'A thousand dollars is a good piece of money. Besides, I've known Jack for a lot of years. He's a guy who likes to take chances. He gets a kick out of it. Don't let on to Hardy, but he could've got Jack to go in there for a six-pack of Dos Equiis.'

'What if I give him a thousand dollars not to? I'll let Hardy have his goddamn interview, and turn the money over to Jack.'

'You'd do that,' Abe asked, 'to stop him from going in?'

'To stop you.'

He looked down at his plate as if no longer able to bear her tormented eyes. 'I'll see if I can talk him out of it. I know he won't take your money, though, so forget about giving that interview.'

'Do you think he'll listen?'

'I could stop him, if I had to. But he's my friend. I know how eager he must be to get in there. Right now, he's probably hoping there *is* a beast just to make things more interesting.'

Tyler peered across the dimly lighted dining room at the corner table where Jack and Nora sat. Jack looked like an overgrown kid, grinning as he shoveled steak into his mouth.

'You think he really wants to do it that badly?'

'I know he does.'

'What about you?'

Abe raised his eyebrows. 'What do you mean?'

'Are you hoping there *is* a beast just to make things more interesting?'

He stared at her with solemn eyes. 'A lot of killing's gone on in that house. Whoever's behind it – or whatever – murdered Dan Jenson. I take that personally.'

'You didn't even know Dan.'

'You loved him once. If his killer's in that house and happens to come after me and Jack – well, it'll even things up a little. I don't expect that to happen, but if it does I'd be pretty damn happy about it.'

22

Janice's wait in the black room seemed endless. She regretted breaking the light bulb. She was glad to have a weapon, but the total darkness was bad. Some comfort came from the feel of the carpet under her rump and feet, the wall against her back. She even welcomed the pain of her wounds and the gurgling hunger growls of her stomach, for they helped confirm the reality of her body – a body she couldn't see and sometimes doubted.

Her hands roamed constantly over invisible, bare skin. Sometimes she stretched out flat to feel the carpet and the solid floor on the length of her. In that position the floating, disembodied sensations faded.

Her mind wandered restlessly.

What if nobody should come? What if they left her here to starve? She would die of thirst before starving. God, her mouth was dry. Her teeth felt like granite blocks.

She hadn't eaten since dinner last night. Breaded pork chops, white rice dripping with teriyaki sauce, iced tea. She wished she had a gallon of iced tea now. She would drink it straight from the pitcher, spilling some, letting it stream down her neck and chest.

They'll come, she told herself. Sooner or later. They wouldn't have brought me here and bandaged me just to let me die. They'll keep me alive for the beast.

Oh God, the beast.

But I'll fool them. They'll open that door and I'll be out like a flash and cut them up if I have to, they won't get me, they won't take me alive.

Or maybe the door will open and it'll be Dad or maybe the cops. They must be looking for me. But they wouldn't know where to look.

If only she had stayed home last night. It's a punishment. She'd had the hots for Brian and now she has to pay. What happened to Brian? He's probably dead. Maybe he's alive, though. Maybe in the house. A prisoner.

Somebody is. Somebody with a baby.

Maybe the house is full of prisoners.

That's why Kutch built it without windows. Not to keep out the beast, the way she sometimes claimed on the tours, but to keep her prisoners in.

Janice was sprawled flat on the floor, arms and legs stretched out, face pressing the carpet, her mind drifting from thought to thought when she suddenly heard footsteps. Her heart gave a lurch. She thrust herself up and crawled to the left, one hand raking the darkness in search of the wall. Her fingernails scraped against it. She slid her right hand sideways and felt the doorframe.

The footsteps sounded very close.

Patting the carpet, she tried to find the bulb. She'd left it near the door's edge, its jagged glass down so she wouldn't cut her fingers groping for it.

She heard the metallic scrape and snick of a key pushing into the lock.

Where is it?

Then the side of her right hand swept against the bulb. She clenched the grooved base, and started to rise as the door swung inward. The figure of a girl was silhouetted against the blue light from the corridor. She had a bag clamped under her chin, a can in one hand, a key in the other. Gasping, she took a quick step back as Janice lunged at her. The bag dropped to her feet.

Janice, surprised by the stranger's smaller size and apparent youth, couldn't bring herself to slash out. Instead, she grabbed a handful of the girl's T-shirt and yanked her forward. She hooked an arm around the girl's back, twisted, and slammed her against the doorframe. The girl grunted, but her left hand swung up, hammering the can against Janice's face. The blow stunned her. She staggered backwards, hanging onto the squirming body, and they both fell.

Janice was on the bottom. She rolled. She caught hold of the flailing arms, forced them to the carpet. As the girl bucked and writhed under her, she crawled up the body. She straddled the chest, used her knees to pin down the arms.

'Get *off* me,' the girl demanded. 'Get *off*!' Her legs flew up. A knee smashed against Janice's back. 'Bitch!'

Janice raised a fist. The girl's face, dim in the blue light from the corridor, looked fierce. But very young. She was probably thirteen or fourteen. She was part of this, though. She had to be taken care of. Janice shot her fist down. As it descended, the body jerked under her.

The light swept away. A moment after her fist smashed the sneering face, the door banged shut.

She was in blackness again.

She punched blindly in a rage, each blow hurting her knuckles sending pain up her wrists and forearms.

The girl was sobbing. 'No. Stop. Please!'

'Shut up. Don't move or I'll kill you. I swear I'll kill you.' To prove her point, she clutched the girl's throat.

'I promise.'

'Okay.' She relaxed the pressure, but kept her fingers around the throat. 'How do I get out of here?'

'You can't.'

'Just watch me.'

'You can't,' the girl sobbed. 'The door's locked.'

'You unlocked it.'

'Just to ... get in. When I kicked it shut, it locked again. Try it ... if you don't believe me.'

'Where's the key?'

'In the hall. I dropped it in the hall.'

'You mean we're both locked in?'

'Yeah, and you'd better not hurt me or you'll be sorry.'

Janice slapped her face. 'Who else is in the house?'

'You'll find out.'

She slapped her again. 'No more wise answers, you little shit. Who's here?'

The girl sniffled. 'Maggie,' she muttered. 'And Wick. And Agnes. And my mom and brother.'

'I heard a baby.'

'That's my brother, Jud. He's six months.'

'And the beast?'

She hesitated.

'Do they keep it here?'

'They don't *keep* it. This is its home.'

'It just wanders around loose?'

'Sure.'

'Great.'

'They'll come looking for me. When I don't come back...'

'That's just fine. I'll be ready.'

'You can't get out of here. It's impossible. You think my mom'd still be around if there was a way out? She's tried over and over but we always catch her.'

'*We*? You mean your own mother's a prisoner and you help the others?'

'We can't let her get away. She'd ruin everything.'

'What kind of a kid are you?'

She didn't answer.

'What's your name?'

'Sandy. Sandy Hayes.'

'Well, Sandy Hayes, *I'm* going to get out of here and ruin everything and you can fucking well count on it.'

'Fat chance.'

Janice squeezed her throat. 'Okay, lie still. Don't even think about moving.' She climbed off Sandy's body. Kneeling beside her in the darkness, she felt along the T-shirt to the waist of the pants. She fingered a belt. She opened its buckle and tugged it free. Draping it around her neck so she wouldn't lose it, she patted the pants' pockets. They seemed to be empty. She unfastened the waist button, slid the zipper down, and yanked the pants down Sandy's legs. The girl wore shoes. She pulled them off, set them nearby, and finished removing the pants.

She tried to put them on. They were much too small. After a short struggle, she gave up.

She slid her hands up Sandy's legs and hooked her fingers under the elastic of her panties.

'Hey!'

'Shut up.' She drew the panties down. She tried them on. The filmy material had enough stretch to allow a snug fit. She clutched Sandy's thigh. 'Okay, sit up and take off your T-shirt.'

She waited for it.

'Here.'

She swept out a hand and took the garment. Spreading it against herself, she could feel that it was far too small. A tight fit would hurt her wounds. She stretched its neck, yanked until it tore, then split the fabric all the way down. She put the shirt on easily, like a smock, the opening at her back.

Using the belt, she bound Sandy's feet together.

The hands were still free. A bra might be useful for binding them. She moved her hand up the girl's belly and paused at the feel of tape. 'You're bandaged?'

'I hurt myself.'

Her fingers glided over Sandy's skin, touching two more bandages: one on the side, one on a breast. The girl wore no bra.

'How'd you get hurt?' Janice asked.

'The same as you.'

'What?'

'You know.'

'The beast?'

'Yeah, the beast. He gets rough sometimes when we're getting it on.'

'You *let* him?'

Janice's wrists were suddenly clenched in the dark.

'You'll let him, too. Just wait and see if you don't. You'll get so you can't wait for him to come to you.'

Janice jerked free of the girl's grip. 'You're nuts,' she said.

'You'll see. Even Mom loves it. She won't admit it but she loves it.'

'That's why she tries to escape.'

'She just does that 'cause of the baby. She's afraid they might kill it, but they won't. See, they think she'd try to kill herself if they hurt Jud, and they don't want that. They want her alive.'

'What for?'

'Same reason they want you alive. They want you. *He* wants you. To make babies.'

Janice felt a cold tightness inside, 'Babies?' she murmured. 'Whose babies? Wick's?'

'Don't be silly. Wick isn't allowed to touch us. He tried to screw me once, and Maggie beat the crap out of him. Nobody touches us but Seth or Jason.'

'Who are they?'

'Sons of Maggie and Xanadu.'

'Xanadu?' A chill scurried up Janice's back as she recognized the name from Lily Thorn's diary.

'He was murdered last year. Mom's boyfriend killed him and Zarth and Achilles, but he paid for it. Maggie nailed him.'

'My God,' Janice muttered. 'Those were all . . . beasts?'

'Zarth was Maggie's, and Achilles was Agnes's. Xanadu was the father of both. Rucker killed all three, but Maggie nailed him before he got Seth or Jason.'

'So ... there are *two* beasts in the house? You said before there was just one.'

'*You* said there's one.'

'You didn't correct me.'

'Why should I?'

'You little shit.'

'Look, why don't you get off me? We can be friends. You're gonna be here a long time, and it'll be nicer for you if I like you. I can bring you up special stuff.'

'How do I get out of here?'

'I already told you, it's impossible.'

'Why?'

'They'll get you.'

'We're upstairs?'

'Yeah, but...'

'Which way's the staircase?'

'That's for me to know, you to find out.'

Janice straddled the girl again, and pinned her arms down. 'You said they'll be up here soon. They're gonna find you dead if you don't give me answers. Now which way are the stairs?'

'It doesn't matter. You can't get out anyway.'

'*Tell* me, damn it.'

'The door locks on the inside. Even if you...'

'Where's the key?'

'I'll never tell.'

Janice slapped her hard. The girl yelped with pain and twisted under her.

'Go ahead,' Sandy sobbed. 'Do whatever you want. I won't tell.'

Janice wondered where she'd lost the broken light bulb. Somewhere nearby probably. But she doubted she could force herself to cut up the girl anyway. She considered tearing off Sandy's bandages and digging into her wounds. The thought of it repulsed her.

'The key you used to get in here,' she said. 'Does it open the front door?'

'No,' Sandy murmured.

'Maggie must keep it with her.'

The girl sniffed, but didn't answer. Janice knew she must have guessed right. In that case, she would need to subdue Maggie to get the key – maybe take on the entire household. It seemed hopeless. 'The beasts,' she said. 'They're in the house?'

'Maybe.'

'If they're not here, where are they?'

'Sometimes . . .' she sobbed, 'sometimes they're in Beast House.'

'What do they do, wander back and forth?'

Sandy didn't answer.

'How do they get from here to there? They can't just go walking across the street?'

'Yes, they do.' She said it too quickly.

And Janice suddenly knew.

It seemed crazy, but so did the rest of this, and it appeared to be the only possibility. The original beast, Xanadu, had burrowed from the hillside and come up in Lilly Thorn's cellar. Why not another tunnel – one connecting the two houses? It would have to be a couple of hundred yards long, but why not? A tunnel leading from one cellar to the other. How else could the beasts move freely between the two houses? They certainly couldn't travel out in the open, walk across Front Street and through the gate without someone spotting them sooner or later. There had to be a tunnel.

And she would find it.

She didn't want Sandy to know what she had discovered.

'I guess I'll have to get that key from Maggie,' she said.

'You haven't got a chance.'

'We'll see.'

She climbed off Sandy, rolled her over, and sat on her rump. She slipped the T-shirt off, and fingered the three strips of tape used to hold the gauze pad to her left breast and shoulder. The ends on her breast had come unstuck, and dangled like small flaps. Gripping them, she peeled the bandage away from her torn flesh. She tugged the clinging strips off her back. When she tore away the pad, she had three strands of tape, each nearly a foot in length. She tugged on them. They seemed sturdy enough.

She pressed Sandy's wrists together and bound them tight with all three strips. She made sure the knots were secure. Then she rolled Sandy onto her back.

'Open your mouth.'

She felt the lips. They were pressed together. So she pinched Sandy's nostrils shut. The girl squirmed and moaned, but finally opened her mouth. Janice stuffed the bandage pad inside. She tore the center strip of tape off the bandage on her belly, stretched it across Sandy's open mouth, and pressed it firmly to her cheeks.

'No noise,' she warned. 'If I hear anything out of you, I'll come over and knock you senseless.'

The groaning stopped. The only sound was air hissing through Sandy's nose.

Janice put the T-shirt on again. She draped the girl's pants over her back, and crawled away slowly, one hand gliding over the carpet in search of the light bulb. She found it. Its jagged edge pricked her palm. Carefully, she picked it up. Near the door she came upon the can Sandy had dropped.

She left the pants and bulb and can against the wall where she could find them easily, then tried the door knob. It didn't move. The door had locked on shutting, just as Sandy had claimed. Though she was fairly sure the key had fallen in the corridor, she spent a long time searching for it.

Finally, she gave up. She sat beside the door, her back against the wall. She spread the pants across her lap and placed the bulb on them, base up. Then she picked up the can. It felt cold and heavy. It sloshed when she shook it.

Some kind of soda.

Her tongue rasped against the roof of her mouth, touched the dry blocks of her teeth.

Sandy had used the can as a weapon, bludgeoning her with it. Janice could use it that way, too, when the door opens.

But not if she drank its contents.

She licked the condensation off the can, and waited.

23

'Suppose we go along,' Nora said, 'and wait in the car?'

'Okay by me,' Jack said. He hitched up his sweatshirt and slid his Colt .45 semi-automatic under the waistband at the back of his jeans.

'I think it'd be better,' Abe said, 'if you and Tyler stayed behind. I don't know where we'll be leaving the car, but if a cop goes by and sees you two waiting, he might get suspicious.'

'Yeah,' Tyler agreed. 'That makes sense.'

'Why don't you wait at the Carriage House?' Jack suggested. 'Have a couple of drinks. We'll be back before you know it.'

Abe finished folding the thick blue blanket from his bed.

Jack slung the strap of Hardy's camera case over his shoulder.

'Go on out,' Abe told him. 'I'll be right with you.'

When they were alone, Tyler stepped into his arms. He held her gently against him. 'Just try not to think about it too much,' he said.

'Oh, sure.'

'Go over and have a couple of cocktails with Nora. Tell

259

her about our plans for tomorrow. If you don't gulp your drinks, we'll be on our way back by the time you finish your second.'

'You'd better be.'

'Count on it.' He kissed Tyler, and she pressed herself fiercely against him. Slipping his hands under her sweater, he caressed the warm smoothness of her back. 'I love you so much,' he whispered.

'I love you, Abe.' She looked up at him. Her eyes were glossy with tears.

'Don't let some guy pick you up while you're waiting, or I'll be really ticked.'

She almost smiled.

With a last, brief kiss, he eased out of her arms. He picked up the blanket and opened the door. Jack was standing by the Mustang, his hands on Nora's hips.

'Let's get,' Abe said. He opened the driver's door, dropped the blanket onto the back seat and turned to Tyler. 'See you in a while,' he said.

She nodded. With the back of one hand, she rubbed her nose. Nora went over to her. They stood side by side, silhouetted by the porch light behind them.

'If you're not back in an hour,' Nora said, 'we'll call in the Marines.'

'Dipshit,' Jack called. 'We *are* the Marines.'

She gave them a thumbs-up and Tyler waved as Abe backed the car away. He waved out the window, then turned on the headlights and steered up the center of the courtyard.

'This is gonna be good,' Jack said.

'I just wish we could've done it without the girls knowing.'

'No chance of that with Gory-babes popping the question in front of everyone.'

'He's such an asshole.'

'Gutless, too. Shit, if I was gonna write a book about that joint, I'd want to get in there at night and see what it's like. Catch the ambience, you know?'

'He'll probably want to interview us about that,' Abe said, and turned left onto the road.

'If he does, let's charge him for it. He throws around money like confetti.' Jack rolled down a window and stuck his elbow out. 'His check better be good.'

'He wouldn't dare stiff you.'

'I oughta hang onto him till I can get to a bank tomorrow.'

'I wouldn't worry about it.'

'You'd better. It's half yours, you know.'

'I'm just along for the ride.'

'Bullshit. It's fifty-fifty.'

'Just buy me a drink when we get back to the inn, and we'll call it even.'

'You're an easy guy to please.'

He slowed down as they entered the business area. The coffee shop where they'd eaten lunch was still open. So was a liquor store across the road from it, and a bar on the next block. Otherwise, the town seemed closed up for the night. The road was deserted except for a few cars and pickup trucks parked along its curbs.

'By the way,' Abe said, 'how do you feel about the girls coming along with us tomorrow?'

'To the lodge, you mean?'

'That's what I mean.'

'Well, all right!'

'No objections?'

'You kidding me?'

'Tyler'll check with Nora about it tonight.'

'Nora will come. She's hot for my bod. Who can blame her? It's magnificent. So's hers, by the way.'

'I've noticed.'

He laughed. 'Yeah? How'd you manage that? You haven't taken your eyes off Tyler since we got here. You two are really in it deep. Man, I've seen the way you look at each other. When's the wedding?'

'We haven't quite gone that far yet.'

'Really? That's a surprise.'

'I want to spend a few more days with her before...'

'That's it. Let her stew. Don't wait too long, though, or *she*'ll propose to *you*.'

'I might enjoy that. What about you and Nora?'

'That gal's a real kick in the ass, but I'm not gonna even think about getting tied down. Shit, I been married to the Corps for twelve years. I need to hang loose, you know? But I sure don't mind hanging loose with her for a while. I've never had it so good, I'll tell you that right now.'

Abe slowed down and turned his head to the left as they passed Beast House. The ticket booth was shuttered, the lawn beyond the fence dark. No light came from any of the windows. 'Looks deserted,' he said.

'Wonder if Bobo's in there.'

'I wouldn't get my hopes up.'

The road curved and slanted upward into the wooded hills. Abe eased off the gas pedal. He searched the road-sides for a place to pull off, soon found a wide shoulder and swung over. He killed the headlights and engine.

In the silence, Jack said, 'Do you think there is such a thing?'

'As Bobo?'

'Yeah.'

'Doesn't seem likely. But you never know.' He reached in front of Jack, opened the glove compartment, and took out his .44 caliber Ruger Blackhawk. He removed a box of cartridges and stuffed it into a pocket of his nylon windbreaker. On the floor under his seat, he found his flashlight.

They climbed from the car.

Abe lifted the blanket off the back seat and clamped it under one arm. He pushed the barrel of his revolver down the back of his jeans. He held onto the flashlight, but didn't turn it on.

They walked straight across the road, stepped through undergrowth on the far side, and leaped over a ditch. They made their way up the slope until Abe could no longer see the road through the trees. Then they traversed the hillside, following it downward. The foliage and dead pine needles crunched loudly under their shoes.

In a hushed voice, Jack said. 'You know me, I'm not your superstitious type.'

'Except you carried a rabbit's foot through three tours in Nam.'

'Well, that's different. What I'm saying is, I'm the last guy who's gonna believe in shit like ghosts and monsters, right?'

'So you say.'

'But, you know, this Bobo's supposed to come from that island near Australia. Look at Australia. They've got animals there that look like jokes: kangaroos, wallabies, wombats, platypuses. Who's to say Captain Frank's old man couldn't have run into some weirdo species and brought one back with him?'

'He could've.'

'We oughta keep an eye out for it.'

'I intend to.'

'We oughta try and bag the fucker.'

'We oughta try and get in, take the pictures as fast as we can, and get back to the girls. I don't know about Nora, but Tyler's so worried she can hardly keep herself together.'

'Gory's paying a thousand for a few snapshots of the place, figure what he'd pay for that thing's carcass.' Jack laughed quietly. 'He'd probably get the damn thing stuffed and take it on *Johnny* with him.'

'Why don't *we* get it stuffed and stand it up in the lobby of the lodge?' Abe suggested.

'Yeah! We can say it's Bigfoot.'

'On second thought, Tyler wouldn't go for that.'

'See? She's already got you by the short hairs, and you're not even married yet.'

Abe elbowed him. Then, through the trees ahead, he saw the side fence of Beast House. He pointed to the right. They started across the hillside, well above the fence and parallel to it.

'We'll just sell the thing to Gory,' Jack whispered. 'For a bundle. We'll buy a beauty of a Chriscraft for the lodge.'

'A deal,' Abe said. 'If it exists and if it shows up.'

'Just our luck, it won't.'

They followed the hillside in silence. Abe studied the house and its grounds as he walked. The yard looked deserted. The windows at the house's side and rear were dark. He was certain that lights would be on if anyone was inside either cleaning the rooms or standing guard.

'If we find it occupied,' he said, 'we'll abort.'

'Right,' Jack agreed.

'As of last summer, at least, they apparently didn't have an alarm system or guard...'

'Just the beast.'

'So unless they've tightened up security since then, we shouldn't have any trouble along those lines.' The slope eased downward into a ravine. At its bottom, Abe trudged through the low brush to the rear corner of the fence. He followed the fence, watching the distant road until the house blocked it from his view. Glancing over his shoulder at Jack, he said, 'Any cops show up, we ditch our weapons. If we can't pull a disappearing act, let them take us for breaking and entering. That's a minor charge next to resisting arrest or firearms possession.'

'We can always pick them up later,' Jack said.

Abe stopped near the center of the fence. He tossed his blanket over the spikes. It dropped silently to the grass on the other side.

'Watch out for those points,' Jack said. 'You'll be singing soprano.'

They both hit the fence at once, grabbing the crossbar, leaping, bracing themselves with stiff arms, planting a foot on the bar between the sharp uprights and springing down. Abe snatched the blanket from the ground and dashed across the yard, past a ghostly white gazebo, into the dark moon-shadow cast by the house. With Jack close behind him, he climbed the porch stairs.

The floor creaked under his weight as he stepped to the back door. He peered through one of its glass panes. Except for murky light from the windows, the interior looked dark. He moved aside. 'This is your game,' he whispered. 'You want to do the honors?'

Jack rammed an elbow through the lower right pane. A burst of shattering glass broke the stillness. Shards rained down on the other side of the door, clattering and tinkling as they smashed against the floor.

'Such finesse,' Abe said.

'Got the job done,' Jack told him, and started to reach through the opening.

'Wait. Let's give it a couple of minutes, see if anyone shows up.'

Abe watched the door windows. He listened carefully. No lights appeared inside the house, and he heard only the night sounds of the breeze and crickets and a few distant birds. He also heard his own heartbeat. It was loud and fast. He licked his lips. His stomach felt knotted and there was a slight tremor in his leg muscles. He didn't like waiting.

'Okay,' he said finally.

Jack put an arm through the broken pane. He felt around for a few seconds. Then Abe heard the dry snap of a clacking bolt. Jack withdrew his arm, turned the knob, and opened the door. Its lower edge pushed through fallen glass as it swung wide. Jack twisted his hand on the knob to smear his fingerprints, and let go.

Abe followed him into the room. Turning on his flashlight, he swept its beam over cupboards, a long counter and sink, an old wood-burning stove.

Jack whispered, 'Should I get a shot of the kitchen?'

'Let's start upstairs and work our way down. Grab one of here on the way out, if you feel like it.' Abe shut off the flashlight and led the way down a corridor between the staircase and wall. Stopping in the foyer, he glanced at the parlor, at the hall leading to the gift shop. Both were dark and silent.

Fighting an urge to hold the banister, he started up the stairs. No matter how softly he put his feet down, every riser creaked and groaned in the silence. If nobody heard the window break, he told himself, nobody will hear this. The thought stole into his mind that perhaps the smashing glass *had* been heard. Instead of coming to investigate, it had decided to lie in wait.

It.

This place is getting to you.

At the top of the stairs, he looked to the left. Moonlight from a casement window cast a pale glow into the corridor. He saw no movement. To the right, the hall was black. He remembered a window at its far end, but the curtains of the Jenson display blocked out any light from that direction.

'Let's do the kids' room first,' he said. 'Work our way toward the front.'

With a nod, Jack walked quickly up the hall. Abe followed, watching his friend shove the curtains aside as he passed close to the wall. The motion of the fabric forced an image into Abe's mind of something alive hidden within the enclosure. His skin prickled when the velvety folds swung against him. He rushed through the gap.

On the other side, he looked over his shoulder. The curtains still swayed as if stirred by a wind. He switched the flashlight to his left hand, reached behind his back, and drew out his revolver. The walnut grips were slippery with his sweat, but the weight of the weapon felt good. He held it at his side as he entered the bedroom.

With an elbow, he nudged the door. It swung almost shut. He pressed his rump against it until the latch snapped into place.

Jack found the drawcords and pulled. The curtains skidded apart.

'Make it quick,' Abe whispered. He shoved the flashlight into a pocket of his windbreaker and stuffed the barrel of the revolver into the front pocket of his jeans.

The room had two windows, one on the wall facing town, the other facing the backyard and hills. Stepping over the wax bodies of Lilly Thorn's murdered sons, he hurried to the far window. He looked out at the rooftops of the businesses along Front Street, at the lighted road. A single car was heading north. He shook open the blanket and covered the window. 'Okay,' he said, and shut his eyes to save his night vision.

Through his lids, he saw a quick blink of brightness. He heard the buzz of the automatic film advance.

Jack whispered, 'Say cheese, fellas,' and snapped another picture. Then one more. 'Done,' he said.

Abe swung the blanket over one shoulder. He pulled

out his revolver and returned to the door as Jack closed the curtains. Faced with the prospect of opening the door, he wished he hadn't shut it. His left hand hesitated on the knob.

Calm down, he warned himself.

He thumbed back the hammer of his .44 and yanked the door wide.

When nothing leapt at him, he let out a trembling breath. He kept his revolver cocked and stepped into the corridor.

'Fingerprints,' Jack said in a cheery voice that seemed too loud. 'I'll get 'em.'

Abe heard the knob rattle. Then Jack moved past him and crossed the hall to the nursery door. He tried the knob. 'How are you at picking locks?' he asked.

'Forget it,' Abe told him.

'I could kick it in.'

'Just grab a shot of the closed door. Hardy can run it with a mysterious caption. Hang on while I get the window.' He eased down the hammer and pushed the gun into his pocket as he rushed to the end of the corridor. Holding the blanket high to shield the window, he closed his eyes until Jack took the picture. Then he slung the blanket over his shoulder again, drew his revolver, and turned around.

Jack was gone.

The curtains surrounding the Jenson exhibit swayed a bit.

Abe's stomach tightened. 'Jack?' he asked.

No answer came.

He listened for sounds of a struggle, but heard only his own heartbeat.

He walked quickly toward the enclosure. Trying to keep the alarm out of his voice, he said, 'Jack, hold it in there.'

The bottom of the curtain flew up. He jerked back the hammer. A dim, bulky shape rose from a crouch. 'What's wrong?' Jack asked.

'You trying to spook me?'

Jack laughed. 'I didn't know you were spookable.' He held up the curtain while Abe ducked underneath.

'Let's just stay together, pal. I can't cover your ass if I can't see it.'

Jack let the curtain fall.

Abe took out his flashlight and turned it on. All around them, the red fabric hung from the ceiling to the floor. The air seemed heavy and warm, and he felt strangely vulnerable closed off from the rest of the corridor.

Jack stepped backwards, pushing out a side of the curtains, and raised the camera to his eye.

'Just a second.'

'What?'

Abe shone his beam on the wax figure of Dan Jenson. The body lay on its back near the forms of the Ziegler father and son, its throat torn open, its eyes glistening in the light. 'He's out of this,' Abe said.

Jack nodded. 'Yeah. I should've thought of that.'

Crouching, Abe grabbed its right ankle and dragged the mannequin through the split in the curtains. He switched off his light, stood up straight, and peered down the dark corridor. He breathed deeply. The cool air tasted fresh.

A thread of light flicked across the floor from behind

him. He heard the camera hum. A shuffle of feet as Jack changed position for another shot.

In his mind, he heard Tyler gasp, saw the color drain from her face, her eyes roll upward, her knees fold. He felt her weight against his chest as he caught her. He remembered the vacant look in her eyes afterward, and how she'd rushed out the door ahead of him and vomited.

He raised his foot. He shot it down hard on the dummy's face, feeling the wax features mash and crumble under the sole of his shoe.

Jack came up behind him. 'Jesus! What're you ... ?'

'Taking care of business,' Abe said, and stomped the head again. 'Let the goddamn sightseers gawk at someone else.'

When he finished, he shone his light on the floor. Nothing remained of the head but a mat of smashed wax and hair, and two shattered eyes of glass.

He turned off his light.

'Let's get on with it,' he said. 'The girls are waiting.'

24

Janice had lost her battle of wills with the soda can. She had gulped down half the cola, then sipped the rest of it slowly, savoring its cold sweet taste. She felt guilty as she drank. The full can might've made a good weapon. But she'd found reasons to justify drinking: she was mad with thirst, she figured the soda would give her energy needed for her escape, and she only had two hands anyway. She wanted one hand for striking with the bulb, the other for thrusting Sandy's pants into the face of whoever might open the door.

Or *what*ever.

Of course, she could use the full can instead of the pants. With the can, she might be able to stun the intruder with a good shot to the head. The pants seemed like more of a sure thing, though. They would give her momentary advantage by blinding and confusing her opponent.

As the final drop fell into her mouth, she wondered whether she'd made the right choice. Too late now for worrying about it.

She squeezed the center of the can. It made noisy popping sounds as it collapsed. Something jagged scraped her palm. She explored the area with her fingertips, and found that the aluminum had split open at a corner where the can had buckled, leaving sharp edges. She gripped the top and bottom of the can, and wobbled them back and forth, cringing at the noise, until the two halves parted. She pressed their edges against her bare thighs. They felt very sharp.

As she wondered how the new weapons might be used, she heard a quiet creaking sound from the corridor. Her heart thumped wildly. She wished she had time to check on Sandy, make sure the girl was still bound and gagged, but she had to be ready.

She stuffed the base of the light bulb between her lips. It tasted bitter. Getting to her knees, she swung the pants over her back, the legs across her right shoulder. She gripped each of the can halves, their crimped edges outward.

From the corridor came the sounds of slow footsteps. Shoes on the hardwood floor. Shoes.

So it's a human. Thank God.

She pressed herself against the wall. Her heart was thudding a fierce cadence. She sidestepped twice to get farther from the door.

The footsteps stopped. She heard a quiet, 'Hmm?' Then a sound of crinkling paper.

The food bag Sandy had dropped.

A key snicked into the lock. The knob rattled. The door eased open. In the blue light from the hallway, Janice saw a hand on the knob. A forearm. Then a heavyset woman leaned into the gap and peered through the darkness. 'Sandy?' she asked. It sounded like Thandy. The husky voice was unfamiliar to Janice. Whoever the woman might be, she wasn't Maggie

Kutch. Sandy had mentioned another woman, an Agnes.

'Thandy, why'th it dark?'

The door opened more. Agnes took a step into the room and bent over slightly as if to see better.

'Wha'th going on?' she asked. She sounded confused, but not alarmed. She bent over farther, and pressed one hand on her knee. Her other hand dangled in front of her, holding the paper bag.

Sandy started to make grunting noises.

Agnes jerked upright.

Rushing up silently behind her, Janice rammed both sides of her face with the cans. A bellow of pain tore the silence. Agnes clutched her face and turned around. Janice raked out with one can, slashing the back of her hand. Whining, Agnes reached out. She knocked the can away. She wrapped her arms around Janice. Her stench was sour and putrid. She felt hot, and her clothes were damp.

Her breath exploded out as Janice slammed a knee into her belly. Her arms loosened. Janice drove her knee again into the soft belly. Agnes doubled. Her face hit the light bulb, jarring the metal base against Janice's teeth. Squealing, she fell to her knees.

Janice staggered away from her.

The door was still open.

She ran to it. Glancing down the corridor, she saw no one. She pulled the door shut and tugged the key from its lock. She clenched the key. Sandy had said it wouldn't open the front door, but maybe Sandy had lied.

Just past her door, the corridor stopped at a blank wall. In the other direction, it led past several doors.

Most were shut. Near the far end was a banister. Janice took the bulb from her mouth and started toward the stairs, walking fast. She was fairly sure this level of the house must be deserted. Otherwise, someone probably would have responded to the commotion by now.

Deserted, maybe, except for Sandy's mother and the baby who must be locked in one of these rooms. As she hurried past the closed doors, she wondered about setting them free. Too dangerous. If she started opening doors, God only knew what she might run into. Once she was clear of the place, the cops could take care of the rest.

She came to the first open door. She glanced in as she stepped by it with two quick strides. The room was dark and silent.

One down, two to go.

She rushed by them both without incident. As she reached the banister, she flinched at a sudden knocking sound from behind. She had expected it, but it startled and unnerved her.

'He-e-elp!' Agnes yelled. Her voice was muffled. 'He-e-elp! Lemme out!'

Holding her breath, Janice started down the stairs. The area below was dim with blue light. She crouched to see under the ceiling. At the foot of the stairs was the foyer. And the front door!

The open area to the left was dark. To the right was the arched entryway to a room. That room was lighted blue. A dark curtain draped its wall. She saw a few scattered cushions covered with glossy fabric like satin, but no other furniture. She kept her eyes on its entry as she hurried to the bottom of the stairs.

The front door was no more than ten feet ahead. If she went to it, though, she would be in full view of anyone inside the room.

Sandy had claimed the key wouldn't fit.

Janice decided not to chance it. Eyes on the blue room, she eased around the newel post and tiptoed up a dark passage that ran between the staircase and wall. She followed it toward the back of the house and entered a room with a slick floor. This, she guessed, must be the kitchen. She closed the swinging door and felt along the wall for a switch. She found it. Blue light filled the room.

She stepped past the stove. Along the far wall was a sink, a long counter, cupboards above and below, but no door. Near the sink was a knife rack. She set down her bulb and key, her remaining half of the soda can. She selected a paring knife and a long knife with a serrated edge. She slid the paring knife into her panties. Its blade was cool against her hip. She clutched the long knife tightly in her right hand, and stepped to a closed door beside the refrigerator.

It wasn't locked. She pulled it open. Shadowy stairs led down to a blue lighted cellar. She pulled the door shut behind her. The air felt chilly. Shivering, she looked down at the blue carpet on the cellar floor. She saw a few scattered cushions.

Please, she thought, let it be empty.

Let there be a tunnel.

She took a deep shaky breath, and raced down.

The cellar was not empty.

With a gasp, Janice stopped abruptly. She squeezed the railing and stared through the dim light at the three figures.

They were against the wall. Two men and a woman. Naked and motionless. Their heads were drooped strangely. Janice took a step backwards up one stair before she noticed that their feet weren't touching the floor.

'My God,' she muttered.

She descended the rest of the stairs. Slowly, she approached the bodies.

Corpses, she thought. They're corpses.

One thigh of the woman was missing big chunks as if bites had been taken.

From the chest of each body protruded a steel point. *They're hung up on hooks.*

Janice felt sick and numb. She moved closer. Her legs were trembling.

All three bodies were badly torn, sheathed with dry blood that looked purple in the blue light.

She raised her eyes to a face, and slapped a hand against her mouth to hold in a scream.

One eye was shut. The other stared down at her. The tongue was lolling out. In spite of its contorted features, she recognized the face. It belonged to Brian Blake.

She looked at the face of the man suspended beside Brian.

NO!

Then at the woman.

IMPOSSIBLE! NO!!

Backing away, shaking her head, she stared at the faces of her parents. She fell to her knees. She covered her face.

From behind Janice came the metallic clack of a door

latch. She twisted around and looked at the top of the stairs. The door to the kitchen swung open.

Jack, standing in the doorway, snapped a photo of the stairs leading into the cellar of Beast House. 'Okay,' he whispered.

Abe turned on his flashlight. He stepped past Jack and started down. Halfway to the bottom, he stopped. He leaned over the railing and shone the beam into the space below the stairway. Nothing there. He leaned over the other side. A steamer trunk against the wall, but nothing else. Turning slowly, he raised his beam to the corner and swept it around the entire cellar. Along the walls, he saw a collection of old gardening tools: shovels, a rake and a hoe. Shelves, mostly empty but some lined with canning jars. Little else. The dirt floor was clear except for a few stacks of bushel baskets.

'Looks okay,' Jack said.

With a nod, Abe stepped down the rest of the stairs. He turned around and aimed his beam at the steamer trunk. Its latches were in place. 'Get whatever you need,' he said, 'and let's go.'

Jack, at the foot of the stairs, took three shots. Abe kept his eyes shut against the quick bursts of light from the flash.

'Let's go.'

'Hang on. I want a look around.'

Abe gave him the flashlight. As Jack started to wander the cellar, he gazed up the stairway at the door. He imagined it swinging shut. If someone came from above and locked it . . .

'Over here,' Jack said.

'What?'

'That hole Gory talked about.'

Abe hurried across the dirt floor and joined Jack beside a crooked stack of bushel baskets. The hole at his feet was roughly circular and almost a yard in diameter. It didn't go straight down, but dropped away at a steep angle in the direction of the cellar's rear wall.

Abe covered his eyes. Jack took a photo.

'That's it,' Abe said. 'Let's go.'

'Take this a minute.' Jack handed the camera to him.

'What am I supposed to do with it?'

'Hang onto it.'

Crouching, Jack aimed the flashlight into the hole. He lowered his face close to the edge and peered in.

'The girls are waiting,' Abe said.

'I know.'

'We're already late.'

'A couple more minutes won't make that much difference.' Lying down flat, Jack started squirming head first into the hole.

'You've got to be kidding,' Abe muttered.

'I won't go far.' Jack's voice came up muffled.

'The fun part,' Abe said, 'will be backing out.'

In the last glow before the light faded out, Abe fell to his knees and clutched a cuff of Jack's jeans. Then he was in darkness. Looking over his shoulder, he watched the dim patch of gray at the cellar door.

They could be up there, right now. They could be on their way out of the house.

He yanked Jack's cuff. 'Come on.'

Jack was no longer moving.

'Are you okay?'

'Yeah.' His voice sounded thick as if he were speaking with a pillow over his mouth. 'Goes on and on,' he said.

'Come out of there.'

'Oh, shit.'

'What?'

'Something up ahead. Looking at me.'

Abe felt the hair rise on the back of his neck. 'What is it?'

'Let me get closer.'

'What *is* it? Is something *coming*?'

'It's not coming. Huh-uh. It's . . . an owl head. No owl, just its head. Man, there's all kind of bones and shit down here.'

'Great. Time to leave.' He grabbed Jack's ankles and started to drag him out.

Moments later, light appeared in the hole – a glowing rim around Jack's shoulder. His head appeared. Abe kept pulling. Jack worked his way backward, elbows shoving at the clay.

Then he was out.

'Infuckingcredible,' he said. 'I could only see about twenty feet, but you oughta see all that shit. Bones all over the place down there.'

'Human?'

'Nothing that big. Maybe dogs, cats, squirrels, raccoons. Smaller stuff, too, like from mice or rats. Why don't you take a quick look?'

'Thanks anyway.'

'I wonder if I could get a picture of that stuff. Worth a try, huh?'

* * *

The quick, soft sounds of footsteps rushing down the stairs sounded more animal than human.

Janice pressed herself against the moist clay wall of the tunnel and stared into the blue light. Her heart felt as if it might smash through her ribs. Her breath came in harsh sobs. She clutched the knife with both hands, blade toward the cellar, and held her breath.

She only glimpsed the beast as it passed the tunnel entrance. Her knees sagged. She braced herself against the wall to keep from falling. Her stomach lurched. She swallowed the hot, bitter fluid that rose in her throat.

This – or one like it – was the thing that had raped her. Its claws had ripped her flesh, its snouted mouth had sucked and gnawed her breasts, its penis had been deep inside her and she could still feel the hurt from it.

This – or its brother – was the thing that had murdered her parents and . . .

She heard a wet, tearing sound.

Pushing herself from the wall, she stepped across the tunnel. Shoulder against the cool clay on the other side, she eased her head past the corner.

The beast, hunched over slightly, had its back to Janice as its claws tore flesh and muscle from her mother's thigh. She watched, too stunned to move, as it raised the dripping load to its mouth.

A corner of her mind whispered for her to flee, to make good her escape while the creature was busy eating.

No, she thought. I can't.

The sound of its chewing made her gag. She covered her mouth and ducked out of sight, but she could still hear it.

Jesus. It's Mom. It's Mom the thing is . . .

And then she ran.

She wasn't quiet about it. She knew she should sneak but she couldn't, she rushed across the carpet and a savage growl rumbled from her throat and the thing heard her and looked around with scraps of flesh hanging from its mouth and it looked at her with blank pale eyes as if it didn't give a damn and kept on chewing as it turned and swung a clawed hand at her face. She ducked and rammed the blade into its belly. It roared, spewing the food onto her hair and back. Staggering away, it smashed against her mother. The body's legs splayed out with the impact. The arms jumped. The head wobbled. The spike slipped out of sight as if sucked into the chest hole, and her mother dropped onto the beast, driving it to its knees.

Janice stepped back, staring at the tangled bodies, half convinced for a moment that her mother was somehow alive. Then the beast, down against the wall with the knife still embedded in its belly, grabbed her mother by the throat and groin and hurled her. The corpse flew at Janice, hit the carpet at her feet, and rolled toward her with flopping arms and legs.

Janice leaped out of its way, spun around, and raced back into the tunnel.

She should have kept on stabbing, damn it.

She cried out in agony as her shoulder slammed against the wall of the tunnel. She bounced off, collided with the other wall, and fell down sobbing. Quickly, she got to her feet. She stumbled onward, one arm out to feel her way, going slower now that she realized the tunnel had turns. Her right hip burned. She felt a warm trickle down her leg. The paring knife in her panties must have cut her during the fall. She pulled it out.

Except for her own sobbing and gasps for air and the slap of her feet on the hard earth of the tunnel floor, she heard nothing. If the beast was coming after her, it must be far back.

Maybe it was too badly hurt to follow.

It can see in the dark, that much she knew from the diary.

She wished she had burned the fucking diary.

None of this would've happened. She'd be safe in her bed at the inn and Mom and Dad would still be alive. How had it gotten to them, anyway? They must've come looking for her. God, she wished she'd stayed home. It was all her fault. She wished she'd never heard of Brian Blake or Gorman Hardy. They got her into this.

I got myself into this.

I got Mom and Dad killed.

But I can save myself. I can save that woman – Sandy's mother and the baby – if I can just get out of here. Get help.

Get to Beast House and out to the street. Get to the cops.

The wall went away from her knuckles. She felt blindly with both hands, discovered that the tunnel turned to the left, and hurried through the blackness.

What if there's a locked door at the other end?

There won't be. There can't be.

What if the other beast is waiting up ahead?

No.

What if Wick or Maggie or Agnes or Sandy or all of them reach Beast House first and cut me off?

I've still got a knife, she told herself. I'll rip them up.

And then her thoughts froze as she heard gasping, snarling noises from behind. She rushed on, driven by terror, heedless of the possible turns ahead. The sounds grew louder as she ran. She pumped her arms hard, stretched out her legs as far and fast as she could. Her lungs ached as she sucked breath. All her wounds burned as if their edges were splitting open from the strain. She winced as her right arm scraped a wall. Without slowing, she changed course toward the center.

Now the beast was very close. From the sound of its rattling growl, it could be no more than a yard or two back.

Her left side hit a wall. The blow twisted her. She slammed the moist surface, bounced off it, and fell. She landed on her back.

Staring up into the darkness, she couldn't see the beast. But she heard a dry hissing sound that was almost like laughter.

Something wet and slimy forced her legs apart. The T-shirt tugged at her, lifting her back from the ground for a moment before it came off her shoulders. She let its sleeves shoot down her limp arms. She felt the points of claws slide down her belly. Her panties were ripped away. Something warm splashed onto her belly, her chest. Its blood.

She felt its hot breath on her face.

'Bastard!' she shrieked, and drove the knife upward. It punched into the thing's flesh. She jerked it out and stabbed again as the beast wailed in pain. Then it batted her hand. The knife jumped from her numb fingers.

From just beyond her head came a scraping sound like wood sliding over dirt.

The beast clutched her shoulders, its claws digging in. Squirming, she rammed a knee into the thing. It kept its grip and knocked her leg aside. Its penis thrust against her thigh.

Its face, just above her own, was dead white and shiny like the flesh of a slug. Saliva spilled onto her from its wide mouth. She wondered why she could suddenly see its face and before she could figure it out the face jerked wildly upward.

The roar that blasted her ears sounded as if the world were exploding.

One of the creature's eyes was a shiny hole.

A side of its snout flew apart.

Its jaw disintegrated.

She turned her face away as what was left of the beast's head dropped onto her.

In the silence, Janice's ears rang.

A man's voice said, 'Holy shit.'

25

'How're you doing, ladies?' the barmaid asked.

'I could go for ...' Nora started.

'I think we should leave,' Tyler interrupted.

'They said we should wait here.'

'I don't care.' She got up from the table.

Nora shrugged at the barmaid. 'Guess that's all,' she said. She joined Tyler, and they hurried through the dimly lighted cocktail lounge. 'What's the rush, kiddo?'

'I can't stand waiting any longer. They said they'd be back in an hour.'

'So they're twenty minutes late. Maybe it took them longer to get in than they planned.' In spite of the reassuring words, Tyler heard tension in her friend's voice.

She pushed through one of the heavy wooden doors and held it wide while Nora followed her out. She took a deep breath of the chilly night air. Stopping by the antique carriage near the entrance, she gazed toward the road. No cars passed.

Nora wrapped her arm across her breasts, apparently cold in her filmy orange blouse. 'Why don't we go back in and have another drink? They'll be along pretty soon. I'm sure they're all right.'

'Are you?'

'Sure. Come on, it's better than standing out here freezing our tails.'

'I'll go crazy if I sit still any longer.'

'What do you want to do?'

'I don't know. Why don't they come?'

'They're probably on the way, right now.'

Tyler caught her breath as headlights brightened the road. She stared through the trees, and sighed when the vehicle sped past. Just a pickup truck.

'Let's take the car,' she said.

'Okay. At least it'll be warm.'

They followed the walkway to the courtyard.

'Have you got your keys?' Nora asked.

'Yes.'

'Do you want to change first?'

'No.'

She rushed to keep up with Tyler's quick pace. 'What's the big hurry? We'll probably just pass them on the road, anyway, and have to turn around.'

'At least we'll know they're all right.'

'We could miss them, you know. If they parked on a side road...'

'We'll turn around and come back if we don't spot the car.' She unlocked her Omni, dropped behind the steering wheel, and reached over to flip up the lock button for Nora. She keyed the ignition as Nora climbed in. When the door thumped, she shot the car backwards.

'For Christsake, calm down.'

'I can't.' She sped toward the road.

'There's no reason to panic.'

'They should've been back by now.'

'I know, I know.'

'Goddamn it.'

'It's all right.'

'No, it's not.' She eased off the accelerator only long enough to glance both ways, then swung onto the road with a whine of skidding tires, and floored it.

Nora buckled her safety harness. 'Come on, do you want the cops to stop you?'

Shaking her head, she let up on the gas pedal. The lights of town appeared as she rounded a bend. She passed the closed service station. On the next block, she slowed almost to a stop as a Volkswagon backed into her lane from a parking space in front of a tavern. Then she had to stop for the town's blinking red traffic signal. The intersection was clear. She gunned through it.

'Keep an eye out for the Mustang,' Nora said. 'I'll take the right, you take the left.'

Few cars were parked along this end of the street. Just ahead, the curb in front of Beast House's long fence was vacant. So was the shoulder across the road. Passing Beach Lane, however, the corner of her eye picked up a bright beam.

'Hold it,' Nora said.

She hit the brake. As the car jerked to a stop, she looked past Nora at the single approaching light. 'That can't be them,' she said.

'Maybe they lost a headlight.'

She waited. The steering wheel was slick under her hands. She rubbed them dry on her skirt. The wool made whispery sounds against her stockings. Then she heard the sputtery grumble of an engine. Twisting around, she peered out the backseat window.

A motorcycle came scooting up the lane, followed by a plume of exhaust and dust swirling red in its taillight. Hunched over its bars was a hatless Captain Frank, his white hair and beard streaming in the wind. The cycle tipped away as it made a quick turn behind the Omni and sped north.

'Look at that sucker go,' Nora muttered.

Tyler stepped on the gas. She drove slowly past Beast House, staring at the grounds behind its fence, at its dark front porch, its windows. It looked bleak and deserted. She could hardly imagine anyone actually entering such a place at night.

Abe and Jack could be in there right now, she thought. Sneaking through pitch-black rooms and corridors, knowing they're late and trying to hurry...

Or maybe lying torn and dead, two more victims of...

No!

They're okay. They're all right. They're fine. They have guns. They're trained soldiers. Marines. Leather-necks.

Beast House fell out of sight as she followed the road's curve up the wooded hillside, but her mind stayed inside the house. She spread open curtains and stared at maimed bodies, wondering which were wax, which flesh, which Abe.

'There it is!' Nora blurted.

Tyler's eyes fixed on the Mustang. It was parked off the road just ahead. Its lights were out. She gazed through its rear window as she swung behind it. Nobody seemed to be inside.

'Shit,' Nora said. She reached over and patted Tyler's

leg. 'Just sit back and try to relax. They'll be along any minute.'

Tyler killed the headlights and shut off the engine.

'I've got an idea,' Nora told her. She opened the glove compartment and pulled out the Automobile Club guidebook. 'This'll help pass the time. Turn on the overhead light.'

Tyler twisted the headlight knob. The ceiling light came on. Nora flipped through the pages. 'Let's see, now. Shasta. Here we go, Shasta Lake. It's here! The Pine Cone Lodge. My God, it's got five diamonds! The place must really be something, huh? Expensive, though. One person, fifty-five to sixty bucks a night. Two people, one bed, sixty-five bucks. Forty-five units. Twelve miles north of Redding, off Interstate-5. One and a half miles south of Bridge Bay Road turnoff. Overlooking Lake Shasta. Open all year. Spacious, beautifully decorated rooms with shower/baths, cable TV, fireplaces. Heated pool, whirlpools, free boats and motors. Fishing, water-skiing. It doesn't exactly sound like a dump.'

Tyler shook her head.

'You think you'll stay on there?'

'If he asks me to,' she muttered. 'Damn it, where *is* he?'

'Look, it probably took them ten or fifteen minutes just getting to the house from here.'

'Let's go over.'

'To the house? Are you nuts?'

'You can wait here if you want.'

'Christ, girl!'

Tyler turned off the light and opened her door. Before

she could shut it, she saw Nora crawling across the bucket seats. She waited beside the car until her friend climbed out, then hurried across the road.

'We're hardly dressed to go traipsing through the woods.'

'I don't care.'

'You'll get runs in your stockings.'

Tyler stepped down the steep bank of a ditch, her sandals sliding on the dewy undergrowth, tendrils clutching at her ankles.

Nora skidded, landed on her rump, and picked herself up. 'Shit. Have you flipped or something?'

Without a word, Tyler leaned into the opposite slope and started to climb.

'If you've got it into your head to go inside the house, forget it. For starters, we'd never make it over the fence.'

Reaching the top of the embankment, Tyler clasped Nora's hand and pulled her up. She stepped through dark spaces between the trees.

'Besides, we haven't got guns. They've got guns. Not that I'd go in there if we did have...' Nora's voice faltered.

From down on the road to their left and far ahead came the quick, slapping sounds of feet racing over the pavement. Tyler's heart lurched. She stared through the pines at the moon-spotted road.

'It's them,' Nora whispered.

As hard as she listened, Tyler only heard one set of footfalls. Fighting an urge to cry out, she darted back to the edge of the ditch. Poised above the drop-off, she gazed down the road and saw a single runner dashing up the center line. She groaned as she recognized Jack's blocky figure.

'Oh Jesus,' Nora muttered.

Tyler threw herself down the embankment, stumbled through the growth at its bottom, scurried up the other side and lunged onto the road.

'Jack!'

The man kept running closer with short, choppy steps. He flapped an arm at her. 'Get in your car,' he called.

'Where's Abe?'

'At the house. He's all right. I've gotta meet him in front.'

'What happened?' Tyler asked.

'Later.' He hunched over the Mustang's door, shoved a key into its lock, opened it and climbed in.

'He said Abe's all right,' Nora gasped, coming up behind her. 'Told you ... there was nothing to worry about.'

'Something happened,' Tyler said. Her near panic, she realized, had subsided into frustration.

They stood by the road while Jack swung the Mustang into a U-turn. As it shot off down the slope, Tyler raced to her car. 'Get in back,' she ordered. Jerking open her door, she flicked up the lock button for Nora.

The instant her friend was inside, she spun the steering wheel. The Omni made a tight circle, its headbeams sweeping the edge of the woods.

'Douse the lights,' Nora said.

She killed them, remembering that Jack had kept the Mustang dark as he sped down the slope.

'Geez, this is exciting.'

'Something must've gone wrong.'

'Stop worrying. Abe's all right.'

'I'll stop worrying when I see him.'

'You must really have it for that guy.'

'I do,' she said.

Hurtling around the curve at the bottom of the hill, she saw the Mustang's dark shape glide to the curb. It stopped in front of the ticket shack. She glanced at the grounds behind the fence, but saw no one.

Where's Abe? her mind screamed.

Jack leapt from the car. He left his door open, dashed around the front, and flung the passenger door wide.

Tyler steered in behind the Mustang. She hit the brakes. Her Omni skidded to a halt inches from the rear bumper. She jumped out, and took two quick steps before she saw, over the hood of her car, Abe come staggering from behind the ticket booth with a body slung over his shoulder in a fireman's carry.

Without room to step between the cars, Tyler crawled across the hood. She swung her legs down and rushed to Abe's side.

The girl he carried, wrapped in a blanket, was a blonde with hair hanging down over her face. Crouching, Abe lowered her feet to the sidewalk. Though she seemed conscious, her legs buckled. Jack grabbed her beneath the armpits, and the two men helped her into the Mustang's passenger-seat. Jack shut the door as Abe turned to Tyler.

'Are you okay?' she asked.

He nodded.

'What happened? Who's she?'

He shook his head. 'I'll go back in your car,' he said. 'Quick, let's get going.'

The sudden harsh knocking on Gorman's door sent a jolt through him, reminding him of last night when Marty and Claire had startled him from sleep. His calm returned when he realized it must be Jack and Abe. He checked his wristwatch. Eleven ten. They'd been gone for an hour and forty minutes, so they must've spent at least an hour inside Beast House shooting pictures.

'I'm coming,' he called. He closed Captain Frank's scrapbook, and slid it into a drawer of the lamp table. Before going to the door, he switched on his cassette recorder and pocketed it.

The man waiting under the porch light was neither Jack nor Abe.

'Captain Frank!' Gorman said, and forced a smile. 'I'm glad you're here. You must have come about your book.'

The old man looked angry.

'Come in, come in. I'm sorry I didn't manage to get it back to you this afternoon, but the copy machine at that shop was out of order. They told me they'd have it repaired before tomorrow morning, so...'

'Where is it?'

'Safe and sound,' Gorman said.

With a wary look in his eyes, Captain Frank followed him around the foot of the bed and watched as he removed the volume from the drawer. 'I'll take it now, Mr *Wilcox*,' he said.

'If you wish.'

'The fellow at the front desk, he says your name's Hardy.'

'It's true that's the name I registered under.'

'What's your real name?'

'Hardy. Wilcox, you see, is my pen name, my nom de plume. I use it for my by-line when I write for *People*.'

'Is that so?' He sounded skeptical. 'I think you aimed to steal my scrapbook off me.'

'Nonsense. I had every intention of returning it to you.'

'Aye. Maybe yes and maybe no.' Captain Frank pulled a scuffed leather wallet from a rear pocket of his Bermuda shorts, took out the pair of fifties, and held them toward Gorman.

Gorman stood motionless, the scrapbook in both hands. 'I take it, then, that you don't wish me to write the article.'

'Now I didn't say that, did I?'

'I can't write your story if you refuse to let me use this.' He shook the volume. 'It's a treasure, and I realize it must be priceless to you. I most certainly had no intention of purloining it. I would have returned it to you, this afternoon, if I'd had any inkling you might suspect me of such treachery. Is it my fault that the copy machine malfunctioned?'

'I don't 'spect so,' Captain Frank admitted. He looked almost contrite. 'All the same, I want you to take your money back and let me have the book. I just don't feel right, letting it out of my hands. I tell you what, I'll take it home with me and you come along tomorrow, if you're still of a mind to write this up. I'll drift on over with you, and we'll get us a copy made.'

Gorman made himself smile. 'That sounds perfectly reasonable,' he said. He handed the book to Captain

Frank, took the money and stuffed it into his shirt pocket. 'I do apologize,' he said, 'for inconveniencing you in this way. If I'd had any idea...'

'No, no. That's just fine.'

'Would you care to join me for a drink? I'm afraid I haven't any beer on hand, but does a martini sound agreeable?'

The old man's eyes gleamed. 'Why thanks.'

'Have a seat,' Gorman told him.

As Captain Frank lowered himself onto one of the twin beds, Gorman turned to the dressing table. He uncapped a fresh bottle of gin, and watched its clear liquid splash into the beaker from his travel bar. His hand trembled.

The bus is an arsenal, he thought. I could get myself shot, sneaking in there. With enough martini in his system, however, the old bastard ought to sleep like the dead.

Gorman added a dash of vermouth. He slowly stirred the mixture.

Like the dead.

He knows my name. He'll make trouble if I rob him of his precious scrapbook. Assuming, of course, he doesn't wake up and shoot me.

A pillow over his face while he's sleeping in a drunken stupor...

It seemed too risky.

Gorman wanted the scrapbook. Photocopies, however, would serve almost as well.

If he goes into the store with me, he might find out I lied about the machine breaking down. He might rebel, at that point, and refuse to cooperate.

He's an old man. The authorities in this podunk town might simply assume he died of natural causes. A pillow over the face in the wee hours...

Or he might commit suicide.

Gorman saw himself in the dark bus, taking the revolver from under the driver's seat, pressing it against the sleeping man's temple and firing.

No, no, no. Neighbors might hear the gunshot.

It was worth considering, though. If he could get away unobserved...

He filled two of the motel tumblers nearly to their brims, and turned to Captain Frank. 'Here you go,' he said.

'Thank you, matey.'

Gorman sat on the edge of the other bed. He sipped his martini. The old man took a hefty swallow, and sighed. 'Ah, that does hit the spot.'

'Drink up. There's plenty more where that came from.'

'Did I tell you of the time I took the tour?'

'The Beast House tour? No. When was this?'

'The very day Maggie Kutch opened it up for folks. I was just a lad. I shined shoes over at Hub's barber shop for better than two weeks, saving every penny and just waiting for Maggie to start the tours. Nobody in town talked about anything else, once it got out what she was up to – with the dummies and all. My mother, she said it was an abomination against God.' He took another long drink. 'I knew she'd throw a fit if she found out I aimed to visit the place, so I kept it to myself and went over to go in with the first bunch. You've never seen such a crowd. Half the folks in town was there, lined up to buy tickets. I knew right then word'd get back to her. I just about gave up on the idea, but I just had to go in. The thing of it was, you see, I half expected to find my father inside.'

'He was dead by this time?' Gorman asked.

'Aye. But I knew it was Bobo done him in, and I figured Maggie might have him in wax. I just had to see for myself, you know.' He swallowed a mouthful of martini. 'Well, my father wasn't there. I 'spect I should've been glad, but I wasn't. *Damnation*, he belonged in there! He deserved it. Bobo was his in the first place. He found it and brought it to town and it killed him. If anybody was gonna be on display like that, it should've been him. When the tour got done, I stepped myself right up to Maggie Kutch and said, "Where's my father?" She gave me a smile that made me want to smash her face, and said, "Why, son, I hear he run off with that tart from Wanda's."'

'Wanda's?'

'That was a local house of ill repute. Well, everybody on the tour laughed fit to bust. I ran off. It was all I could do to keep from crying, having me and my father shamed that way in front of everyone.'

'That must have been awful for you.'

'Aye.' He drank all but a shallow puddle, stared into the glass, and finished it off. 'If that weren't bad enough, I got a whipping for my trouble. Reverend Thompson, he saw me go in with the others and wasn't he quick to tell on me? Mother, she laid into me with a switch so I couldn't sit down for a fortnight.'

Shaking his head as if in sympathy, Gorman stood up. 'Let me freshen your drink for you, Captain.' He took the man's glass to the pitcher and filled it. Sitting down again, he said, 'Tell me about your seafaring days. You must have seen a lot of the watery part of the world.'

'Not all that much. I run a fishing boat off the dock in Brandner Bay. That's just up the coast about ten miles.' He took a drink. 'I always had a yearn to take a voyage. Fact is, I wanted to find me that island where my father come across Bobo. I figured I'd go in and see if there was more of them creatures. I had it in my head to wipe them out. But I never got around to it. Tell you the truth, I just couldn't force myself to leave. It was like I had to stay in Malcasa and keep an eye on Beast House. It's my destiny, you know, to stalk Bobo and lay it low.'

'Do you think there might be surviving...?' Gorman heard the sound of a car engine. 'Excuse me for a moment,' he said. Getting up, he stepped to the window. He pushed aside the curtain and peered out, cupping his hands beside his eyes to close off the reflection.

Two cars, a Mustang and a white Omni, drove through the courtyard. They turned toward the duplex of Abe and Jack. They stopped.

'Don't know whether there'd be survivors or not,' Captain Frank mumbled. 'I 'spect there might be.'

Gorman watched the car doors open. Tyler, Abe and Nora climbed out of the Omni.

'Curious thing,' Captain Frank went on, 'there being no wildlife on the island but those creatures, and them carnivorous. I given it a lot of thought.'

Abe opened the Mustang's passenger door. He and Jack helped someone out.

'I figure they polished off all the game, back somewhere along the line.'

In the light from Abe's porch, he saw that the passenger was a girl. Her hair was mussed. Her back was toward Gorman as they led her to the door. She wore a blanket that draped her body from shoulders to feet.

'So I 'spect, since they're meat-eaters, they must've kept going by eating each other.'

Though Gorman couldn't see the girl's face, he knew she must be Janice Crogan. He felt sick.

'You get that kind of thing happening a lot in your primitive cultures. Humans. They need their protein, you know. So they have wars with themselves, eat the ones killed in battle. Used to happen all the time.'

Gorman turned away from the window. Stunned, he dropped onto the edge of his bed.

Janice Crogan.

He'd sent those two bastards out to take photos, and they'd come back with Janice Crogan.

He lifted his glass off the floor and drank.

'So I figure,' Captain Frank said, 'that what my father and the crew of the *Mary Jane* ambushed was maybe just one tribe of the hellish beasts.'

Maybe it's not Janice, Gorman thought.

Who else *could* it be?

It certainly looked like her, but he couldn't be sure without seeing her face.

'If I'm not wrong, there's gonna be another tribe out there. Maybe two or three. Aye, who knows, the island might be...'

'I have to leave,' Gorman said. He stood up. 'I'd like to have you stay and talk, but some friends of mine just showed up.'

'Well, I want to thank you for . . .'

'Here.' Gorman capped the gin bottle. 'Why don't you take this along with you?'

'Oh, I couldn't take your bottle.'

'Please.' He thrust it toward the old man. 'Have yourself a nightcap when you get back to your bus. I'll be along in the morning and we'll have a copy made of your scrapbook.'

'A'right, matey. Thanks.'

Gorman picked up his room key and opened the door for Captain Frank. He stood beneath his porch light and stared across the courtyard at Abe's bungalow. His heart pounded furiously. In spite of the night's chill, sweat dripped down his face.

Captain Frank stowed the scrapbook and gin bottle in the saddlebags of his motorcycle. He mounted the bike. He stood on the starter, and the engine grumbled awake. With a wave he turned the bike, gunned it past the rear of Gorman's Mercedes, and sped toward the road.

26

Someone knocked on the door as Abe held the phone to his ear and listened to the faint ringing.

'Who is it?' Jack called.

'Gorman Hardy,' came the voice from outside.

Abe nodded. Jack pulled the door open and Gorman entered. The man, looking flushed and nervous, scanned the room. 'What happened?' he asked.

Jack put a finger to his lips.

'Where's everyone else?'

'The john.'

Gorman started for the bathroom, but Jack grabbed his arm. 'Just wait,' Jack told him.

'Malcasa Point Police Department,' said the voice on the phone. 'Officer Matthews speaking. May I help you?'

'I spoke to one of your people this morning.'

'Did you get the pictures?' Gorman asked Jack.

'Sure.'

'An Officer Purcell,' Abe went on. 'I realize he's probably off duty, but I'd like to speak with him. It's urgent.'

Gorman stared at Abe.

'I'll try to reach the chief at his home,' Matthews said.

'Give me your name and number, and I'll have him call you back right away.'

'Fine.' Abe gave his name. He read the Welcome Inn's number off the phone plate.

'Very good, Mr Clanton.'

'Tell him it's extremely important. If you can't get through to him, get back to me yourself.'

'I'll do that.'

Abe hung up.

'What's going on?' Gorman asked.

'We ran into your beast.'

'Wasted the sucker,' Jack added.

The man's mouth dropped open. 'You *killed* it?'

'Blew its fuckin' head off,' Jack told him, grinning.

'Who's the girl? I saw you come in with someone.'

'Janice Crogan,' Abe said. 'Apparently, she was out near Beast House last night with your friend Blake. She was pretty fuzzy about it all, but somehow she ended up a prisoner in the Kutch place. Blake's dead. So are the girl's parents.'

'Brian? Brian's dead? No!' He shook his head in disbelief. 'It can't be! He ... he's my best friend.'

'Janice says she found their bodies in the cellar of Kutch's house while she was getting away ...'

'With one of the beasts on her tail,' Jack added.

'*One* of the beasts?' Gorman asked.

'She said there's supposed to be a second one.'

'Incredible,' Gorman said.

'She's pretty beat up,' Abe told him. 'Mostly superficial scratches and bites apparently. Tyler and Nora are cleaning her up, checking her over.'

'Will she be all right?'

'Considering what she's been through, she seems to be in pretty good shape.'

The girl sat on the toilet seat, back resting against the tank, arms hanging at her sides, eyes staring ahead as if she were in a trance.

Tyler crouched in front of her, held her knees gently. 'It's all right, Janice. It's all right, now.'

Janice shook her head.

Nora turned on the shower.

'We'll help you get cleaned up now,' Tyler said. She spread the blanket open and moaned at the sight of Janice's torn, bruised skin – the blood and the filth.

'Jesus,' Nora muttered.

Tyler slipped the blanket off the girl's shoulders. 'Can you stand?'

Janice leaned forward. Nora and Tyler, on each side, helped her up. As Nora held the girl steady, Tyler stepped behind her. The girl's stringy hair was clotted with flecks of raw flesh. Bits of bloody matter clung to her back. Tyler gagged, eyes going wet. She took a deep breath and wiped her eyes. Both Janice's shoulders were raked and punctured. Lower down, her back was striped with claw marks. Her buttocks looked rubbed raw, as if she'd skinned them in a fall.

'The shower is going to hurt,' Tyler said.

'I've got it lukewarm.' Nora glanced at Janice's back and cringed. 'God Almighty.'

'One of us better get in with her.'

'Right.'

Nora quickly stripped while Tyler hung onto Janice's arm. When she was naked, she pushed aside the shower

curtain and stepped into the tub. Together, they helped
the girl climb over the side. Janice's mouth sprang open
and she cried out as the spray struck her back. The
water sliding toward the drain turned pink. Pieces of
flesh floated in it. Tyler turned away. The toilet seat
was smeared with blood. She shut her eyes and breathed
deeply, trying not to vomit. Through the hiss of the
shower, she heard the faint ring of a telephone.

'Abe Clanton.'

'Yes. This is Wallace Purcell from the police.'

'Thank you for calling. I'm the one who talked to
you this morning about Beast House. My friend had
been...'

'Oh yes. What seems to be the trouble?'

'We were out at the beach tonight,' Abe lied. 'On our
way back, we spotted a young lady who looked like she'd
been in some trouble. She was over near the front of
Beast House, just outside the fence. She was naked and
pretty beat up. We drove over to give her aid. It's Janice
Crogan.'

'You *found* her?' Purcell sounded amazed.

'She had just escaped from the Kutch house. She
said they took her there last night. Brian Blake and
both her parents are dead. Their bodies are in Kutch's
cellar.'

Purcell said nothing.

'The girl's with us. We're here at the Welcome Inn.'

'May I speak to her?'

'She's in the bathroom.'

'Did she describe her assailant?'

'Her assailant was the beast.'

'The *beast*?'

'It does exist. It apparently lives in the Kutch house. Maggie and the others keep it as a pet, or something.'

'And Janice claims this beast attacked her and killed her parents and Blake?'

'That's it. One more thing. Janice says she wasn't the only prisoner at the Kutch place. A woman is being kept there against her will, and she has an infant.'

Abe heard a sigh. 'Okay, Mr Clanton. Thank you for the information. We'll take care of the situation, and be in touch with you later.'

'Are you going out there?'

'You bet.'

'Okay. Very good. Be careful.'

'I always am. Later.' He hung up.

'What's the story?' Jack asked.

'The cavalry is going in.'

'Without us?' Jack asked.

'We weren't invited.'

'Let's invite ourselves.'

'I plan to.' Abe rushed past Gorman and knocked on the bathroom door.

Tyler opened it. Her face looked chalky.

'How's the girl?'

'A mess. But there doesn't seem to be much bleeding.' She glanced at Gorman. Looking back at Abe, she stepped out of the bathroom and shut the door. 'What's going on?'

'I just talked to the police. They're on the way to Kutch's. Jack and I are going to meet them there.'

Her mouth twisted. 'Don't go in.'

'We'll see if they need us.'

'Oh God, Abe.'

'I want you and Nora to stay here and look after the girl. Come out to the car with us. I've got a first-aid kit out there. Patch her up the best you can. When we get back, we'll see about getting her to a doctor or hospital.' He took Tyler's hand and led her to the door.

Jack and Gorman followed them out. 'Are you coming along?' Jack asked the man.

'Certainly. This may well be the climax of my story.' He slipped the camera strap over his head.

Abe opened the passenger door. Kneeling on the seat, he opened his glove compartment and took out a plastic box. He gave it to Tyler.

'Be careful,' she said.

'Don't worry.'

Jack, standing beside her, fed cartridges into the magazine of his .45.

'Do you have a gun for me?' Gorman asked.

'Sorry.'

Tyler wrapped her arms around Abe and held him tightly.

'I wonder if we might make a quick detour to Captain Frank's bus,' Gorman said. 'It's along the way. He has quite an arsenal, and I'm sure he wouldn't mind letting me use one of his guns.'

'No time,' Jack said.

Abe kissed Tyler hard on the lips. 'We'll be back before you know it.'

'That's what you said the last time.' Her voice sounded tight and shaky as if she might cry.

'And I did come back.'

'Took your time about it.'

'I'll be quick.' He patted her rump through the soft folds of her skirt. 'Get in there and take care of Janice.'

'Yes, sir.' Her chin trembled. She turned and rushed away.

'Let's haul ass,' Abe said.

Tyler shut the door and leaned back against it. Tears rolled down her face. Through her sobbing gasps, she heard the car speed off.

Damn it, how could he go and leave her again?

Because he's a man.

Because of his pride.

Because it's in his nature to help out even if it means putting himself on the line.

If he weren't that way, he wouldn't be Abe and maybe he would lack whatever it was that made her love him so desperately.

Damn it.

She wiped her face with a sleeve of her sweater. Then she pushed herself away from the door and walked across the deserted room.

From the bathroom came the steady rushing sound of the shower. She opened the door and stepped inside. Nora and Janice were dim shapes through the plastic curtain.

With a handful of toilet paper, she cleaned the blood off the seat. She flushed the paper.

'How's it going?' she asked, and skidded open the shower curtain enough to see inside.

Nora shook her head. Her lower lip was clamped

between her teeth. She was sobbing as she gently slid a bar of soap over Janice's back.

Janice stood under the nozzle, her hands flat against the wall, her forehead resting on the tiles. With the blood and grime washed away, her tan lines were visible – a pale strip across her back, a pale triangle on her buttocks. The sight of them made the girl seem more real, more vulnerable than before – a teenager who sunbathes and likes the beach and somehow got caught up in the horror.

The bruises and scrapes would fade away, in time. Tyler hoped the bite marks and claw scratches would leave no permanent scars. A shame on a girl so beautiful. But they looked shallow, as if the beast had been struggling with her, maybe trying to hold her still, not kill her. If she was lucky, they might go away, too.

Crouching, Nora soaped Janice's legs.

'I've got a first-aid kit,' Tyler said. 'Abe thinks we might take you to a hospital when he gets back.'

Nora looked up. 'Where'd he go?'

'Back to the house. The Kutch place.'

Janice turned her head sharply and stared over her shoulder at Tyler.

'Jack and Hardy went with him. They're planning to meet the police there.'

'Oh shit,' Nora said.

Janice frowned. Her eyes looked alert. 'Police? They're going in?'

'I guess so.'

The girl pushed herself away from the wall. She squinted as the spray struck her face, and turned around. Dropping the soap, Nora stood up. 'What...?'

310

'I'm going.' She bent over and rubbed the backs of her legs to get the suds off.

'I think you'd better stay with us,' Nora told her. 'You're in no shape to . . .'

'I've gotta be there.'

Tyler grabbed a wet arm as Janice climbed over the side of the tub.

'I'm all right.'

The girl seemed steady on her feet. Tyler let go, pulled a towel off a nearby rack, and gave it to her. Janice started rubbing her hair furiously.

'The police will take care of it,' Nora said. 'You ought to lie down in bed and wait.'

She shook her head. 'It's my parents. It's *me*. I've gotta be there.'

Nora shut off the water. 'You haven't got any clothes.'

She dried her face. She winced, her face going tight with pain as she blotted water from a torn shoulder. 'I've got clothes. In my room.'

'Or a car,' Nora said, climbing from the tub. 'The cops impounded your parents' car.'

'I'll drive her,' Tyler said.

'Oh shit,' Nora said.

'You guys get dry. I'll get Janice some clothes.'

She rushed from the bathroom. She grabbed her handbag off Abe's bed and ran out the door. The cool breeze felt good as she raced across the courtyard.

This time, she thought, there won't be any waiting, any stewing as she wondered if Abe was all right. In ten minutes, she would be with him. If he'd already gone into the house, she would go in, too. She would be at his side and know.

She shoved her key into the lock, twisted it, opened the door and swept a hand along the wall until she found the light switch. The lamp between the beds came on.

Her bed was still unmade from her afternoon with Abe, its coverlet on the floor where they'd kicked it down, the sheets rumpled. On the other bed was her open suitcase. Bending over it, she snatched out a neatly folded pair of blue jeans, the yellow blouse she'd worn on the tour, a pair of fresh pink panties and her sneakers. A bra? The straps might hurt Janice.

She considered changing herself. Not enough time. Clutching the clothes to her chest, she dashed from the room. The door smashed shut as she leapt off the stoop.

Except for Hardy's Mercedes and her own Omni, the courtyard was vacant. She saw no one wandering about. The windows of the other bungalows were dark.

Stopping at her car, she pulled open the driver's door. A shoe fell as she reached inside to flip up the lock button. She opened the back door, flung the clothes onto the back seat, and tossed the shoe in after them.

Then she rushed to Abe's bungalow. She twisted the knob.

Locked. Of course.

She pounded the door.

Nora opened it. Her hair looked dark and matted as if she hadn't taken time to dry it enough, but she was dressed except for her blouse. 'I thought you were getting Janice some...'

'They're in the car. She can dress on the way. Let's go.'

Holding the blouse to her breasts, Nora leaned out the doorway and glanced around.

'It's all right. Come on.'

Nora turned away. 'Come on,' she called into the room.

Janice didn't pause to question her. Nora stepped aside and let her pass. 'This car?' she asked, nodding toward the Omni. She fingered scratches at her side, but made no attempt to cover herself, as if unaware of her nakedness.

'I tossed some clothes in the back seat for you.'

With a nod, Janice started for the car. She moved stiffly, wincing as she climbed down the stairs, limping a bit as she stepped to the car. Nora, hurrying ahead of her, opened the rear door.

Tyler rushed to the driver's side and climbed in. The car wobbled as Nora dropped onto the passenger seat. Tyler twisted the ignition key.

'Let's take it easy,' Nora said. 'We've got an injured girl with us.'

'Hurry!' Janice blurted from the back seat.

Tyler rammed the shift into reverse and hit the gas pedal.

27

Abe eased off the accelerator as a pickup swung in from a sidestreet. It sped down Front ahead of them. It didn't stop for the blinking red traffic signal, and neither did Abe.

'Five'll get you ten that's the chief,' Jack said.

Just the other side of Beach Lane, it swerved onto the shoulder. Its tires kicked up dust as it lurched to a stop. Abe steered behind it.

'You lose,' Abe said as a stocky woman leapt from the pickup. Linda? No, Lucy, he recalled. She was out of uniform. She wore jeans and a flannel shirt. The shirt tail hung out, drawn in around her waist by her gunbelt. She glanced toward Abe's car, then turned and jogged past the front of her truck.

Abe, Jack, and Gorman climbed out. Gorman followed a few steps to the rear. Abe raised an open hand as their approach caught the attention of the others.

Four others. Lucy, Chief Purcell, and two officers in uniform. They stood near the open door of a police car. Another patrol car was parked just beyond them. The flashers were dark.

'Abe Clanton,' Abe said. 'This is Jack Wyatt, Gorman Hardy.'

Purcell nodded. 'You should've stayed at the Inn. But since you came, I want all of you to keep your distance. Stay here at the road unless we tell you otherwise. We don't want civilians getting mixed up with this.'

'Yes, sir,' Abe said. 'It's your ballgame. If you need a hand, though, give us a shout.'

'We'll take care of it,' Purcell said.

One of the patrolmen knelt on the car seat and came out, a moment later, with a shotgun. Abe recognized it as a .12 gauge Ithica semi-automatic.

'There's no rear exit to this place,' Purcell said.

'No windows, either,' Lucy added.

A quick flash of light made Lucy flinch. Purcell and the others frowned at Gorman.

Gorman snapped another photo. 'Thank you,' he said, and lowered the camera.

Purcell shook his head. 'Let's go.' He walked up the dirt driveway toward the house, Lucy at his side, the other two following.

'Are we simply going to stand here?' Gorman asked.

'We'll do as he said.'

Gorman took a step away, but Jack clamped a hand on the back of his neck. 'Stay,' he ordered. He looked at Abe. 'Do you think they am-scrayed?'

'Their pickup's in front of the garage.'

'They must know the girl got away. They've got three stiffs in the basement, that woman and baby prisoners, and a beast in there. How're they gonna cover up all that?'

'I'd say they can't,' Abe said.

'Hope those cops know what they're doing.'

'They asked us to stay out of it. We'll stay out of it.'

Near the dark front porch, Purcell pointed to each side. The two uniformed patrolmen spread out. They positioned themselves to the left and right of the porch stairs. Purcell and Lucy mounted the stairs. Lucy drew her revolver and flattened her back against the wall. Purcell stepped in front of the door.

'I can't *see*,' Gorman complained in a whiny voice.

'Shut up,' Abe muttered.

He stared at the distant door. He saw the shape of Purcell raise a hand to knock. He couldn't hear the knock. Purcell lowered the hand to his side.

Abe realized he was holding his breath. He let it out.

Then a dim blue swath of light silhouetted Purcell and someone standing in the doorway. Abe heard his heartbeat. Seconds were passing. Purcell must, he thought, be talking to the person. Who was it, Maggie Kutch? Probably denying...

A man's voice, faint with the distance, cried out, 'No!' Purcell suddenly hunched. A gunshot popped in Abe's ears. Purcell doubled over and staggered backwards. As he tumbled down the porch stairs, a blast from somewhere to the side sent the cop with the shotgun spinning. The other cop whirled around and aimed toward the pickup. Before he could fire, a shot kicked his head back.

Lucy froze against the wall as if crucified.

Abe dashed between the parked cars. He jerked the revolver from the back of his jeans as he raced in a crouch up the driveway. 'Hit the deck!' he yelled at Lucy.

The front door slammed shut, cutting off the blue glow.

Lucy crouched. An instant later came the flat bang of a rifle. She dropped to one knee and swung her revolver toward the pickup. She fired four quick rounds. A man cried out, came stumbling into Abe's view from the cover of the pickup's hood, fell to one knee and aimed his rifle at Lucy. He jerked and flopped to the thunder as bullets from Lucy and Abe and Jack socked his body.

Abe straightened up. He heard nothing but the ringing in his ears.

The sprawled man didn't move.

Lucy was still on one knee. Through the ringing, Abe heard shell casings clatter and roll on the wooden floor of the porch. He realized she was reloading.

He and Jack hurried forward. He crouched over Purcell. The man was on his back, clutching his belly and squirming. 'Take it easy,' Abe told him. 'We'll get help for you.'

He heard quick footsteps behind him. As he stood, a blink of light illuminated the chief's contorted face and bloody shirt. 'For Christsake, Hardy!'

Gorman sidestepped and took another photo of Purcell, then rushed toward the officer who'd fallen to the left of the porch stairs.

Jack, kneeling by the one to the right, called, 'This one's dead.'

Lucy backed down the stairs, her revolver aimed at the closed door.

Light flashed as Gorman shot two photos of the cop at his feet. Abe shoved him roughly aside and dropped down next to the motionless body. This one had a chest wound. He searched the neck for a pulse. 'Dead,' he called. He straightened up. 'Lucy, get back to your car and radio for an ambulance.'

With a nod, she took off running for the road.

Jack was standing above the man who'd ambushed the two officers. Abe went over to him. 'It's the old shit that took our tickets,' Jack said.

'Guess we cancelled his,' Abe said.

Gorman, panting, ran up beside them. His flash lit the skinny, grizzled old man. In the instant of brightness, Abe saw half a dozen bullet holes in the front of his sodden shirt and trousers: small entry holes from Lucy's .38, large exits from the slugs that had caught him in the back. Gorman stepped to his feet, crouched, and took another picture.

'We going in?' Jack asked. His voice was hushed and eager.

'Right.'

'She's gonna be ready.'

'She'll expect us to break through the front door. We'll go in the back.'

'There is no back door,' Gorman pointed out.

'There's the tunnel.'

'Where you killed the beast?'

'Want to see it?' Jack said.

'I must.'

'Better grab a weapon,' Abe told him.

With a nod, Gorman rushed over to the head-shot policeman. Abe and Jack reloaded while he took two photos of the dead man, knelt down, and lifted the revolver out of the grass.

'Do you know how to use it?' Jack asked.

'I've had some experience.'

'Just don't point it at anyone you don't plan to shoot.'

'I'm not a fool,' Gorman said.

Abe stepped over to Purcell. The chief still held his belly, but he was no longer squirming. 'We're going in to take care of business,' Abe told him. 'Hang on here. An ambulance is on the way.'

As they started for the road, Abe saw Lucy running toward them. Clamped under one arm was a first-aid kit. Abe rushed up to her. 'We're going in through a tunnel under the house.'

'Maybe I'd better...'

'Take care of Purcell. Keep an eye on the front door, but don't try to go in.'

She nodded.

'Who shot Purcell?'

'The Kutch woman. Maggie. She was just talking calmly and all of a sudden...'

'If she comes out, blow her down.'

'You're fucking-A right I will.'

Abe slapped her back, and ran for the road. Jack and Gorman followed. Abe stopped at one of the police cars long enough to find a long-barreled flashlight. Racing across Front Street, he glimpsed headlights far to the left. From somewhere in the distance came the sound of a siren. He dashed past the Beast House ticket booth, vaulted the turnstile and ran up the walkway.

'Wait up!' Gorman called.

He took the porch stairs two at a time, stopped in front

of the door, and rammed the heel of his shoe into it just below the handle. With a splintering crash, the door flew open.

He switched on the flashlight.

Jack came up behind him.

'Wait up,' Hardy called again. A moment later, he came huffing up the porch stairs.

The three men entered the house.

The beam of Abe's light caught the snarling face of a creature near the foyer wall. He turned his revolver on it, but held fire as he realized it was nothing but the old, stuffed monkey posed to hold umbrellas. He let out a deep breath.

'Let's take it cautious,' he whispered. 'There's one beast unaccounted for and three women.'

'Do you think they might be here?' Gorman asked.

'Anything's possible,' Jack told him.

'The tunnel's our way in,' Abe said, 'but it's their way out if they decide to retreat.'

'Do you think they had time to get here?'

'Yes,' Abe said. He started forward, the powerful beam of his flashlight pushing a stream of brightness into the dark.

Tyler swung off the road behind Abe's Mustang. The ambulance sped by. Near the porch of the Kutch house, a woman stood up and waved both arms. On the ground around her lay several motionless shapes. Tyler's throat constricted.

'My God,' Nora muttered.

The ambulance skidded onto the driveway, siren wailing, light flashing. It raced toward the woman.

'Follow it,' Janice said from the back seat.

Tyler stepped on the gas, swerved around Abe's car, and swung onto the driveway. The ambulance stopped. She slowed as she drew up behind it. Two attendants jumped down and ran to the back. As they opened the rear doors, she set the emergency brake.

'That guy down over there's a cop,' Nora said.

Tyler bolted from the car. She sprinted past the ambulance. In the glare of the whirling red lights, she saw a body to the left of the porch. It wore a uniform. A woman with a revolver in one hand was on her knees beside a man, gesturing to the attendants as they rushed forward with a stretcher. The man on the ground was a stranger.

'This is the guy from Beast House,' Nora called from the front of a pickup truck.

'Hey!' the woman shouted. 'Who are you people? Get out of here!'

'Were there three men here?' Tyler asked.

'Yes.'

'Where are they?'

She pointed. 'Said they're going through a tunnel.'

'Are they all right?'

'Yes! Get out of here!'

Tyler and Nora reached the Omni at the same moment. Janice was standing by the rear door. 'Get in,' Tyler snapped.

The three doors slammed shut.

'What're we doing?' Nora asked.

'Going after them.' Tyler rammed the shift into reverse and sped backwards toward the street.

'What good will that do?' Nora asked. 'We'll just be in their way.'

'We need guns,' Janice said.

Tyler mashed the brake. She shot the car forward, swung onto the grass beside the ambulance, and lurched to a stop. She and Nora leapt from the car.

'Hold it!' the woman cop yelled.

'We need their guns!' Tyler said. 'We want to help.'

'Help by getting out of here.'

The attendants lifted the fallen policeman onto the stretcher.

'Please!' Tyler said. 'We'll bring them back.'

The woman aimed her revolver at Tyler. 'Get!'

'For Christsake, lady!' Nora blurted.

She aimed at Nora.

'Stupid bitch!' Tyler cried. Whirling around, she climbed back into the car.

Nora dropped in and slammed her door.

'We're no good without guns,' Janice said.

Tyler steered the car around in a tight circle, then hit the brake. She stared past the tail of the pickup truck and across the treeless field at the woods beyond Beach Lane.

'Captain Frank,' she said.

'So what?'

'Hardy said he's got an arsenal.'

'Let's go!' Janice urged.

Tyler drove straight across the field, the car bouncing wildly over its bumpy earth, crunching through weeds and low bushes. Nora clung to the dashboard as jolts shook the car. Tyler struggled to keep her grip on the steering wheel. Soon, her headlights caught the row of mailboxes. She spotted the opening in the trees to the left as the car sprang over a small rise and dropped onto the dirt road.

'Oh shit!' Nora yelled.

Tyler yanked the wheel. She almost missed the tree. There was a jolt as she struck it. The right headlight smashed. But the car glanced off and kept moving, speeding down the narrow rutted lane of Seaside, its single beam thrusting into the dark.

'There it is,' Nora said.

Tyler shoved the brake pedal to the floor and steered for the bus. The car bounded off the road. Beer cans crunched under its tires. She blasted the horn.

Nora and Janice jumped out while she set the emergency brake. They were pounding the bus's door when she reached them.

'Wha's all this?'

Tyler spun around. Captain Frank's white-bearded face was at an open window halfway to the back of the bus. 'It's just us,' she said. 'Tyler and Nora. We talked at the bar last night, remember? We need your help.'

'Did I hear guns?' he asked. He sounded groggy.

'They're after the beast. Your Bobo. We want to help. Have you got guns?'

'Goin' after Bobo?'

'Hurry. You can come along if you want.'

'Uhhh.' His face left the window. A light came on inside the bus, illuminating its brightly colored panes. A few seconds later, the door wheezed open.

'My Lord, is that you, Janice Crogan?'

'It's me,' she said.

'Figured Bobo got you.'

'It did.'

'We've got to hurry,' Tyler said, stepping close to the door.

Captain Frank wore striped boxer shorts, and nothing else. His torso was matted with white hair. 'Grab some clothes,' Tyler said, 'and show us where you keep your guns.'

'Aye. Come on aboard, mateys.'

With the policeman's revolver clenched in his sweaty hand, Gorman followed Abe and Jack down the stairs to the cellar. He kept his other hand on the railing as he descended. Except for the bright path cast by the flashlight, all was black.

The risers creaked under their feet.

The dirt floor of the cellar below looked gray in the pale beam. Then the light swept from corner to corner. Shadows quivered and died as the light circled.

'There's your hole,' Abe whispered. He settled the beam on a patch of darkness near a pile of bushel baskets.

Gorman tried to speak. A choked sound came out. He cleared his throat and asked, 'Did you get pictures?'

'Sure,' Jack said. 'Then we heard Janice.'

In silence, Gorman followed them down to the cellar floor. They stood in a cluster at the foot of the stairs. Abe swung the light toward a wall beside the staircase. It stopped at a large steamer trunk. 'That's their door,' he said. Gorman noticed a short hank of rope nailed to a side of the trunk – apparently a handle for pulling it back against the wall.

The beam edged sideways. It lighted the tunnel entrance.

And the beast.

'Glad it didn't walk away,' Jack whispered.

They stepped closer.

The creature lay face down, just inside the tunnel, its shiny flesh so white it almost seemed to glow. Its back was splattered with gore. Gorman quickly looked away from the remains of its head.

'We didn't get any pictures of it,' Jack told him.

Gorman took a deep breath. 'Would you mind rolling it over?'

'We've got a job to do,' Abe said. 'You can stay here if you want.' He stepped over one of the outstretched arms and moved deeper into the tunnel.

'Wait. You can't leave me here.'

'Then come along,' Jack said, and went in after Abe.

The light faded to a dim glow as Abe disappeared around a bend. In another moment, Gorman would be left in darkness. Gritting his teeth, he started to edge past the beast. He stared at it, half expecting a clawed hand to dart for his ankle. Then the light was gone. He couldn't see the beast at all. Something nudged his shoe. With a yelp, he sprang away.

He rushed forward, bumped a moist wall, and felt his way along its turn until he spotted broken light ahead and the hurrying shapes of Jack and Abe.

'Wait for me!' he cried out.

Jack turned around. 'Quiet, damn it!'

Gorman quickly joined the two men. He stayed close to Jack. He couldn't free his mind from the beast at the tunnel's entrance. It must be dead. But had it stirred in the darkness, one of its sprawled legs knocking against his shoe? No, he must have simply kicked it in passing. It must be dead.

But what if it's not?

What if it's coming?

Ridiculous.

And yet, he could sense it creeping closer.

He stepped on the back of Jack's shoe.

'Damn it, watch where you're going.'

'Would you mind if I walk between you two?'

'Shit. Suit yourself. Step on Abe for a while.'

'Would you guys knock it off?' Abe whispered.

Jack pressed himself against a wall of the tunnel. Gorman moved past him. With the sound of Jack's footsteps behind him, he immediately felt better. But his heart continued to pound wildly. His mouth was dry and he felt vaguely nauseated. His legs trembled.

He wished he hadn't come along with these men. He wished he had stayed at the inn, out of harm's way.

Thinking of the inn reminded him of Janice.

So the girl wasn't dead. That was a blow. Apparently, at least, she had no suspicion that he'd murdered her parents. Thank God for that.

She would present a problem, however, even with the contracts destroyed. If she took the matter to court ... Of course, he might resolve the situation by giving her the agreed-upon amount.

Half of everything.

If *Black River* had been a blockbuster – a bunch of ghost nonsense with nothing but a single suicide (ah yes, suicide, Martha) to give it credibility and bolster sales – this one would skyrocket.

How many deaths? Four tonight. Three last night. Janice's imprisonment (I'll have to interview her about that), two captives in the Kutch house for God only knows how long. And the biggest bonus of all, the corpse of the beast.

National media coverage.

And me, Gorman Hardy, in the center of it all.

The potential was staggering.

Turning over half to Janice would be an outrage. If only the beast had killed her.

Without doubt, it had raped her.

And both her parents were killed.

Nobody would consider it unusual if a girl in such circumstances committed suicide.

He could hardly risk faking suicides for both Janice *and* Captain Frank.

There were other ways to handle Captain Frank.

Suicide was perfect for Janice. But what method? A girl would certainly be unlikely to blow out her brains. Slashing her wrists was out of the question: it would raise eyebrows if she died in the same manner as Brian's wife. An overdose? Perhaps. That might be difficult to arrange, but...

Following Abe around a bend in the tunnel, he saw a blue glow ahead. Abe switched off the flashlight. The glow, Gorman realized, must be coming from the cellar of the Kutch house. An icy tightness clutched his stomach. His heart thudded faster. His trembling legs felt leaden, as if they wanted to hold him back.

Jack nudged him from behind. 'Keep moving.'

He hadn't realized he'd stopped. He forced himself to take a step, another step.

Abe, a couple of yards ahead, crouched at the mouth of the tunnel. He inched his head forward and looked to both sides. Then he stood up and entered the cellar.

If there was any danger, Gorman told himself, Abe wouldn't walk in that way.

Clenching the revolver so hard his hand ached, he followed. His feet were silent on the blue carpet. As Abe strode toward the stairs, Gorman gazed to the right. On the far wall hung the bodies of two naked men – Marty Crogan and Brian. Their skin was blue in the strange light from the ceiling fixture. Their blood looked purple, almost black. Claire's body was sprawled on the carpet near one of the shiny cushions that littered the floor. He stared at the awful, gaping crater in her thigh. Panic choked him. He stood motionless, struggling for breath.

Jack, stepping in front of him, shook his shoulder. 'Hey,' the man whispered. 'Let's go.'

Gorman knocked the hand away, staggered backwards, twisted himself around and lurched for the tunnel. At its entrance, he glanced back. Abe and Jack, both standing at the foot of the stairs, watched him and said nothing. He flung himself into the darkness. He ran.

Let them think what they like.

Let them think I'm a coward.

With his left hand out, he felt the moist wall to keep his bearings and rushed away from the hideous blue light of the cellar.

Better the darkness. Better anything than to climb those stairs and enter that house. He dreaded coming to the end of the tunnel. The beast would be there. But it was dead (it *must* be dead), and a live beast was waiting for those two inside the Kutch house. Maggie with a gun, and maybe others, but most of all the beast – it *eats* people. Let it get those two fools.

It won't get me!

He ran until he collapsed. On hands and knees, he sucked in the dank air. He heard nothing except his noisy gasping and the pounding of his heart. He saw nothing but blackness.

How far had he come? Surely, he must be at least halfway. He wanted to rest, but he knew he wouldn't be safe until he was outside Beast House. He longed for the fresh night air, for the brightness of moonlight. He saw himself rushing across the lawn to Front Street, locking himself inside Abe's car ... If only he were there *now*.

Pushing himself to his feet, he reached out to the wall. He looked over his shoulder. Then he started forward again. After a few shuffling steps, he managed a slow jog.

You're all right now, he told himself. You're almost out. You'll be there soon.

Try not to step on the beast.

I'll fall on it, and it'll ...

If only he had a flashlight! Or even matches!

If only he knew how close it was!

It's dead. If you fall on it, you'll get messy but it's dead and can't hurt you and you'll know you made it to Beast House and you'll be outside in another minute.

Who says the living beast is in the Kutch house?

Who says it's not in Beast House?

That thought sent a shock of alarm through Gorman, but he kept on jogging. He shambled around a curve in the tunnel and saw dim light ahead.

There shouldn't be light.

It didn't make sense unless he'd somehow gotten turned around. But the light in the Kutch cellar was blue, not white like this.

He staggered around another bend, and stopped. He held his breath.

He squinted against the glare.

A gasoline lantern. It hissed in the silence.

A bearded man – Captain Frank – was crouching over the sprawled body of the beast. He had rolled it onto its back. Just behind him stood a girl in a yellow blouse. Janice! Nora and Tyler were there, too. They all held guns. They were all staring at the beast.

Raising his revolver, Gorman took careful aim at Janice and fired.

28

A blast roared in Tyler's ears. Janice spun and smashed against her. The girl's pistol bounced off Tyler's foot. Falling back against the tunnel wall, she flung an arm around Janice to hold her up. She staggered sideways with the weight, and fell to the cellar floor just outside the tunnel.

'Don't shoot! It's me!' Hardy's voice.

'Stupid fuckhead!' Nora cried out.

'Oh my God, I didn't mean to ... I thought ... My God, is she all right?'

As Tyler pulled her arm out from under Janice, Nora dropped to her knees beside them. Captain Frank rushed over with the lantern.

'Oh my God,' Hardy muttered, staring down at the girl. 'I'm sorry. I'm sorry. I was so frightened I didn't know what I was ...'

'Shut up!' Nora snapped.

Janice's eyes were open. Her face was contorted with agony. A bloom of red was quickly spreading over the front of her blouse. Nora ripped the blouse open. A button popped from it and flicked against Tyler's cheek. The blood was welling from a place just above the left breast, and close to the side. Nora slid fingers over the area, then pressed her palm tightly to the wound. Janice yelped and flinched.

Captain Frank, on his knees, slid the long blade of a knife up the girl's sleeve and sliced through the fabric. He rammed the knife into the dirt floor. 'Gotta turn her,' he muttered. 'See her back.'

'Yes,' Hardy said. 'There might be an exit wound.'

'Un...' Janice gasped. 'Under.' Her right arm lifted off the dirt and fell across her breasts. She pointed with a finger at her armpit.

Captain Frank eased her left arm away from her side. 'Here,' he said. 'Came out here. Nicked her arm, too.' He plucked a wadded red bandanna from a pocket of his Bermudas, pushed it against the wound, and drew her arm down to her side. 'That'll hold it.'

'We've gotta get her to a hospital,' Nora said. She looked over at Tyler. 'That policewoman. She can use one of the car radios. Have her call in for an ambulance.'

'But Abe.'

'He can take care of himself, damn it.'

'I'm going on over, mateys,' Captain Frank mumbled. 'You can keep my Coleman.' He yanked his knife from the ground and stood up.

'I'll stay with Janice,' Hardy offered. 'I'll tend to her wounds. Nora, why don't you go out and see to an ambulance?'

She nodded. 'Okay.'

Hardy knelt beside Janice. Nora took his hand and placed it against the entry wound. 'Keep a firm pressure,' she told him. With her clean hand, she stroked the girl's forehead. 'You'll be fine, kiddo. I'll be back in a few minutes, and we'll get you out of here.'

As she rushed toward the cellar steps, Tyler entered the tunnel. In the dim light from the lantern, she stepped around the body of the beast. She followed Captain Frank into the darkness.

Jack, his back to the front door, curled a hand around the knob and tried to turn it. 'Locked,' he whispered.

Abe nodded. So they wouldn't be opening the door to let Lucy in. She was good with a gun. She might've been helpful. He considered shooting out the lock, but the noise would give away their presence.

So far, they had checked out the kitchen, the corridor and the dining room. All were lighted blue like the cellar. Though they'd been constantly alert for an attack, so far they'd seen no one. The house seemed deserted.

Maybe everyone had fled. Abe doubted that Kutch and her group could have escaped through the tunnel to Beast House. There may, of course, be another way out — a tunnel at the back, perhaps leading toward the beach. That was possible, though Abe hadn't noticed any other exit in the cellar.

More likely, they were still in the house.

He gazed up the stairs.

Then, from the left, came a quiet sound like a girl sobbing.

Crouching, Jack edged sideways toward the arched entryway. Abe stayed close to him, stepping silently backward, keeping the rear covered.

The walls of the room were draped, from ceiling to floor, with blue curtains. A chill crawled up Abe's back. His eyes raced along the heavy folds, searching for bulges, for feet protruding beneath the lower edges. He saw nothing to indicate another presence, but kept scanning the curtains as he followed Jack.

The room was bare of furniture. Its carpet was cluttered with pillows and cushions of shiny blue fabric – some alone, others piled up.

He heard the sobbing again.

It seemed to come from behind a waist-high heap of pillows near the end of the room. Abe aimed his revolver at the center of the mound and sidestepped closer as Jack headed around the far side.

'Over here,' Jack whispered, and knelt out of sight.

Abe sprang past the pile to regain his view of Jack, and saw a girl lying face down on the floor. She was naked. One arm was bent close to her head, the other out of sight beneath her body.

Jack, on one knee near her head, had his .45 aimed down at her. 'Don't move,' he whispered.

The girl sniffed.

Abe kicked into the mounded pillows, sending them flying until he could see the floor.

The girl lifted her face off the carpet. 'Help,' she said in a choked voice. 'Please. I'm hurt.'

'Get your other hand where I can see it,' Jack said. 'It better be empty.'

'Can't. I . . . my arm's broken.'

Abe pivoted for another quick scan of the room, then dropped a knee onto the girl's spine. Her back arched. Her head jerked back. He slammed the barrel of his revolver against her upper arm, jumped aside as she cried out, and used his left hand to tug the arm out from under her. She held a small caliber semi-automatic.

He rapped her knuckles with his barrel. The pistol fell.

Now she was crying for real.

'Bastards!' she gasped. 'Stinking bastards!'

'Watch our tails,' Abe said.

Jack straightened up.

Abe shoved his revolver into his pocket. He twisted the girl's arm up behind her back.

'Let go! Asshole! You're gonna die!'

He yanked the belt from his trouser loops, forced her other arm up her back, and lashed them together.

'Where are the others?' he asked.

'You'll find out!'

'Upstairs?'

'Fuck you!'

He tugged the revolver from his pocket and picked up the girl's pistol.

'That belt won't hold her long,' Jack said.

'If she gives us any more grief, we'll kill her.' Abe stood up. He planted a foot on her back and shoved. 'Did you catch that, Tiger?'

'Fuck you!'

'Let's go,' Abe said.

'Upstairs?' Jack asked.

'You got it.'

Janice felt the hand go away from her chest. She pushed the palm of her right hand against the wound, and opened her eyes. Gorman Hardy was kneeling over her. 'Wha...'

'We've got to get out of here, Janice. We're in danger if we stay.'

'Huh?'

'The beast, I saw it move.'

She turned her head and looked toward the tunnel entrance. All she could see of the creature were its clawed feet. They looked motionless.

A cry leaped from her as Gorman tugged her arms, raising her back off the dirt. She stiffened her neck to stop her head from swaying. The wound burned as if a white-hot poker had been driven through her body and was still there. The sodden rag dropped from under her arm. Warm blood trickled down her breast and side.

She slumped forward, head between her knees. Gorman let go and stepped behind her.

'Try to stand up,' he said.

She felt him against her back. His hands clutched her sides, and she writhed as one of them pressed against claw scratches. He moved his hands lower. 'Is this better?' he asked.

She nodded.

She drew her knees up and shoved her sneakers against the dirt as he lifted.

As she straightened, her balance shifted backwards and they both staggered. Gorman gasped behind her. One of his hands flew up and clenched her breast.

'Sorry,' he said, and moved the hand down.

He turned her toward the stairs.

Her legs felt warm and weak, but they held her up as Gorman guided her along. She looked up the steep stairway. 'Can't,' she murmured.

'It's all right. I'll hold you. We'll be up at the top in a jiffy and out of here.'

In a jiffy. He sounded almost cheerful.

With her right hand, she gripped the wooden banister. She placed a foot on the first riser. Gorman clutched her hips, and lifted. She struggled up the first stair, the second. Then a wave of dizziness hit her. Her legs folded. She fell against the railing and hugged it.

'Goddamn it,' Gorman muttered.

'I can't,' she gasped. 'I can't. Let me . . . wait for Nora.'

'Do you want me to leave you here alone with the beast? I tell you, it's not dead!'

'Don't leave me.'

She tried to push herself away from the banister. Gorman pulled at her shoulders, and she cried out. He eased her forward onto the stairs. Slowly, bracing herself with her good right arm, she crawled higher.

'That's good,' Gorman said. 'That's a lot better.' He stepped around Janice and climbed above her. 'Almost there,' he said.

Three stairs from the top, another dizzy spell hit her. Her stomach convulsed. She lunged forward, pressing her head between the planks, and vomited through the gap behind them. When she finished, she lay there gasping and sobbing.

'Quick!' Gorman said. 'My God, it's sitting up!'

She jerked her head free and looked down at the tunnel entrance. From this angle, she couldn't see the beast at all.

Neither, she realized, could Gorman.

She raised her face, blinking tears from her eyes. 'You can't . . .'

'Damn you!' he bellowed. 'Come *on*!'

She raised her arm toward a higher step. He grabbed

its wrist with both hands and tugged, jerking her up and forward. Her cheek hit the edge of the landing. He dragged her. She scraped and bumped over the remaining stairs. With a final yank he threw her onto the landing.

'Okay,' he said. 'Up.'

She couldn't force herself to move.

Gorman stepped over her. He planted a foot beside each hip, and clutched her sides. A finger dug into the bullet hole under her arm, stunning her with a bolt of pain. He lifted her. First to her knees. Then to her feet. As she tried to lock her knees, he swung her around and pushed.

She plunged head first. She seemed to fall forever, a scream swelling in her chest as the stairs below drifted up at her. She flung an arm across her face. The arm went numb. The plank it hit burst apart. The top of her head skidded across the next one as her legs flew high and swung down. The edges of planks slammed her back and buttocks and legs. They scraped her back, bumped her head as she slid. Then she came to a stop, her rump on the cellar floor, her back against the stairs.

'My goodness,' said a voice above her. 'You fell.'

She brought her head forward, feeling a dim sense of relief that she could move it. Her legs were stretched out across the dirt. They seemed to belong to someone else. A sneaker had been lost in the fall. She wiggled her bare toes.

'But you're still alive.' She heard footfalls on the stairs. 'You must be part cat. Are you part cat, Janice? You're harder to kill than your mother was. A regular Rasputin.'

Across the cellar, near a stack of bushel baskets, a hand reached out of the ground.

Out of a hole in the cellar floor.

A dead-white hand, smudged with dirt but glistening in the lantern light. A hand with long, hooked claws.

Janice tumbled forward as something – Gorman's foot? – thrust against her back. Grunting, she sprawled face down.

Gorman rolled her over.

He straddled her, sat on her belly, smiled down at her. 'Unfortunately,' he said, 'you broke your head in the fall.' He gripped both sides of her head. 'I'm not sure I'm strong enough for this, but we'll give it the old college try.'

She drove a fist into his side. He grunted and his face twisted.

'Oh, you're a tough one.' He started to smile again, but then he looked up and his mouth sprang open. A shadow fell across Janice. The beast stood above her, reaching for Gorman. He sucked in a loud breath and flung out an arm to ward the thing off. His other hand went to his hip. Lifting her head, Janice saw him try to tug a revolver from his front pocket. He jerked the gun free as the beast's hands clamped the sides of his head. With strength she didn't know she possessed, Janice flung her right arm across her body, grabbed the rising barrel, and tore the gun from Gorman's hand.

The beast lifted him by the head. His feet swept past Janice's face. His shrieks hurt her ears.

She rolled over. Braced on her elbows, she turned the revolver around and cocked it.

The beast still had Gorman by his head. He waved his

arms and kicked and screamed as it shook him. Then it flung him against a section of shelves. Wood splintered. He fell sprawling to the floor under an avalanche of jars. 'Shoot it!' he cried in a choked voice. He staggered to his feet. He stumbled backwards as the crouching beast lurched closer.

Janice fired.

The slug knocked a leg out from under Gorman.

He flopped onto his back. The beast sprang onto him. He let out a piercing scream as its snout thrust into his groin, snapping and ripping. Soon, he was only whimpering. The beast raised its head and seemed to stare at him for a few moments. Then it scurried up his body, opened its mouth wide, and bit into his face.

Janice watched.

She watched until Gorman no longer groaned and whimpered, until the convulsions stopped shaking him and he lay motionless.

The beast climbed off him. Its body was smeared with Gorman's blood. It turned toward Janice and stared at her.

Its penis thickened and grew and stood upright.

She fired.

The bullet whined off the stone wall beyond its head. Hunched over, the beast hesitated. Janice aimed at its chest. As she squeezed the trigger, the creature lurched aside. It sprang across the cellar floor toward the tunnel where the other beast lay dead. Janice swung the pistol, fired again and again. Then the hammer fell with a dry clack. The beast vanished into the tunnel.

29

Tyler stopped abruptly when she heard the sound – a single *pop* that surged down the tunnel from behind. 'A gunshot?' she whispered.

'Aye,' said Captain Frank.

She stood motionless in the dark, hanging onto the old man's hand, and wondered what it might mean. Nora had a pistol, but had left the house and probably wouldn't be back yet. That left Gorman. Who – or what – had he fired at?

'Trouble back there,' Captain Frank said.

'Yes.'

'Let's not poke.'

With a nod that he wouldn't see in the blackness, Tyler pulled his hand and led the way forward. Her shoulder bumped a wall. She stepped to the right, and kept going.

Another gunshot resounded through the tunnel, followed soon by a quick flurry that all ran together and might have been three shots or four.

What's going on back there?

'Lord,' muttered Captain Frank.

Tyler stood still. She listened for more gunfire, but heard only the thump of her heartbeat and the old man's quick breathing.

'Strange business,' she said.

His hand was hot and slippery in her grip. She kept hold of it, and started walking again. She swept the pistol from side to side ahead of her, feeling for walls. Her knuckles brushed moist clay. She turned slightly away.

She wished they hadn't left the Coleman lantern behind.

With light, they would be out of this tunnel by now, not staggering blindly along its twists and curves.

They must be nearing its end.

But the tunnel seemed to stretch on forever.

With Abe in the lead and Jack covering the rear, they had walked the length of the upstairs corridor. Every door was shut. At each of them, Abe pressed himself to the wall and tried the knob. Every door was locked.

At the end of the corridor, he whispered to Jack, 'Let's start by the stairs and smash them open.'

They were halfway back when a door swung open twenty feet ahead. They crouched and took aim.

'We're comin' out.' Abe recognized the husky voice of Maggie Kutch. 'Don't shoot us.'

'Come out slowly,' Abe said. 'Keep your hands in sight, and they'd better be empty.'

Through the doorway sidestepped a young woman. Maggie, behind her, had a hand around her neck and held a revolver to her head. The woman cradled a baby in her arms. It was silent, but awake and fingering a strap of her nightgown.

'Drop your guns,' Maggie said.

'You drop yours,' Abe said, 'and place your hands on top of your head.'

'I'll shoot her brains out.'

The possibility sickened Abe. Without their weapons, however, they would be at Kutch's mercy. He had little doubt that she would fire on them the instant they were disarmed.

'You'll be dead,' Jack said, 'before she hits the floor.'

'Let's not have any shooting,' Abe said. 'Leave the woman here with her baby, and you can walk out. We won't make any moves to stop you.'

'Think I'm a fool?' Kutch asked. 'You drop your guns before I count three, or else. One.'

'Don't do it,' Abe warned.

'No, please,' the woman begged. She clutched the baby to her chest.

'Two,' said Kutch. Her voice sounded calm, as if she knew they would give up their guns to save the woman.

Tyler stepped into the dim blue light of the cellar. She stood motionless, gazing at the two bodies that hung from the far wall, thinking for a terrible moment that they were Abe and Jack.

Captain Frank bumped her side. 'Lord,' he whispered.

Her eyes lowered to the torn body of a woman sprawled on the floor. She pulled her hand from Captain Frank's grip, covered her mouth and turned to the stairway, and flinched as she heard gunshots from somewhere above. She raced across the carpet. She grabbed the railing. She started up, taking two stairs at a time.

With a look over her shoulder, she saw Captain Frank running in a drunken weave to catch up. She couldn't wait for him. But as she started to turn away, a pale shape sprang from the tunnel's darkness.

'Behind you!' she yelled.

The old man was too drunk or too slow. Even as he started to turn, the lunging beast rammed clawed hands down on his shoulders. He cried out. His legs folded. The beast batted the side of his head. Growling, it bared its teeth. Its snout darted toward the back of his neck.

Tyler fired. The blast stunned her ears. The revolver jumped.

She had aimed high, afraid of hitting Captain Frank. Her bullet plowed up a tuft of carpet near the wall.

The beast stared up at her. Its slanted eyes didn't blink. Its snout was smeared red, but not with Captain Frank's blood. Tyler remembered the gunshots she'd heard in the tunnel. They had been fired at *this* thing. Whose blood . . . ?

It scurried off the back of Captain Frank and rushed forward in a low crouch with its knuckles on the carpet like a gorilla. It was almost to the foot of the stairs when Tyler squeezed off another shot. Splinters exploded off the banister. The creature jerked its head aside as flying needles of wood jabbed its face. Its right eye spat fluid. It slapped a hand to its face. Screeching, it staggered backwards.

Tyler aimed at its head and fired and missed. She aimed at its chest and fired. Her bullet slashed a red streak across the top of its shoulder.

She tried to think.

How many bullets had she fired?

The beast was standing upright with its head back, roaring with pain or rage. It should be an easy target, but the angle was bad, shooting down like this.

If she tried to finish it off, she would empty her gun. Then what good would she be to Abe?

Captain Frank's gun!

It lay on the carpet near his body.

Unfired. Full.

If she could get to it ...

Holding her revolver with both hands, she aimed at the chest of the beast and squeezed the trigger.

The gun bucked. The creature grabbed its side, just above the hip. Spinning, it fell to one knee.

With the noise of the blast still ringing in her ears, she raced down the stairs. She rushed at the beast. She stabbed the muzzle against its head above an open hole where its ear should have been. Its elbow rammed into her thigh, knocking her leg back, twisting her. The front sight carved a gash across the side of its head as she started to fall. She jerked the trigger and wished she could call back the bullet because she knew, even as the gunshot crashed in her ears, that she had missed.

When Kutch said, 'Two,' the corridor roared.

Abe and Jack both fired at the same instant.

Abe had chosen, as his target, the area to the right of the young woman's ear. Maggie's gun was there. Half of her face was there, too, visible behind the woman's head.

Jack must have picked the same target.

Maggie's pistol leaped from her hand as if kicked, and bounced off her forehead. Her cheek blew open with a spray of blood. She flopped backwards. The woman with the baby hurled herself aside, hit the wall with her shoulder and sank to her knees. The baby cried wildly.

Maggie lay on her back. She didn't move.

Side by side, Abe and Jack ran forward. Abe stopped in front of the young woman. Jack went on ahead to check on Maggie.

'Are you all right?' Abe asked.

She nodded. She stroked the head of her baby, and looked up at Abe. 'Don't let...' She slipped a knuckle into the crying baby's mouth. Its wailing stopped. It sobbed and gummed her fingers. 'Don't let them get you,' she said. 'They're...' A muffled boom interrupted her. A gunshot from somewhere in the house.

'Jack, take these two outside.'

'Maggie's alive.'

'Leave her. Get these two...'

Jack's head jerked sideways. He swung his weapon. Abe pivoted, but before he could bring up his revolver a beast leaped onto him. It was half the size of the creature they had killed in the tunnel, but its weight caught him off balance. He fell onto the woman and baby, rolled off them, and let his gun fall so he could grab the throat of the beast as its mouth thrust toward his neck.

'Drop that knife!' Jack yelled.

Abe heard more far-off gunshots.

Then he glimpsed a fat woman in the doorway with a butcher knife. Her face was wrapped in bandages. He cried out in pain as claws raked his back. Then he was on top of the beast. It twisted and thrashed under him, and gurgled as his thumbs dug into its throat. Its claws tore at his sides and arms. Letting go with one hand, he smashed a fist against the side of its head. He struck it again. Then its teeth snapped shut on his fist. Pain shot up his arm. His left hand released its throat. He grabbed the top of its snout, forced his trapped hand down, and yanked the jaws wide. A gristly, cracking sound. The beast flinched rigid. Abe pulled his bloody hand from its mouth. The jaw hung slack, the tongue drooping out one side.

He ducked as it swung at him. Claws dug into his scalp, forcing his face down against the slick flesh of its chest. He drove fists into both its sides. The claws eased up. He shoved himself backwards, shaking his head free. Its penis rubbed his cheek. He jerked away from it, lunged farther back, and grabbed the beast's ankles.

It sat up, swatting at him, missing. On his knees, he dragged it. He lurched to his feet, pulling it along the carpet as it flailed the air and kicked its trapped legs.

'Hold still!' Jack yelled. 'I've got it.'

'Mine,' Abe grunted. He lifted the squirming beast. It flapped its arms. Its head slid across the carpet, then left the carpet. Abe swung the creature upward, turning, and slammed it against the corridor wall. Its head thudded on the wood. He released its ankles. It dropped to the floor.

As it tried to get up, Abe stomped on its head. He lost his balance, stumbled across the corridor and hit the wall. The fat woman in the doorway was staring at the beast, shaking her head and mumbling. Jack held his pistol on her. The butcher knife lay at her feet.

Breathless, Abe staggered over to her. He picked up the knife. He knelt over the writhing beast, flipped it onto its back, and slashed its throat. A hot splatter of blood blinded him, sprayed into his open mouth.

Tyler landed on her back in front of the kneeling beast. She started to bring up the gun. The beast knocked it from her hand. She flung up her other arm to block a blow to her face, but not in time. The impact dazed her. Her arm fell to the floor. She wanted to struggle, but her body seemed too weary. She felt as if she were outside herself, observing.

The beast straddled her.

Its claws hooked into the front of her sweater and ripped.

Its hands felt slimy on her breasts. Did they leave trails like a snail? Its claws scraped slightly, almost tickling. Its head moved down. Its tongue rasped over one of her nipples. Fluid from its punctured eye dribbled onto her chest. Its nose was cold like a dog's. Then she felt teeth on her breast, on the underside and top, and she knew it had her whole breast inside its mouth. Its tongue swirled and thrust.

The mouth went away. The cool air of the cellar chilled her wet flesh. The mouth took in her other breast. It was not so gentle, this time. Its teeth squeezed. She tried to lie still, but her muscles tensed. The jaws clamped tighter. The pain cleared her mind. She was no longer distant and observing, but she didn't dare to struggle. Not now. Not with her breast in its teeth. The creature squirmed, pulling on her. Then it let go.

Claws scratched her belly. They dug under the waistband of her skirt and pulled with such force that her rump lifted off the floor. Raising her head, she saw the beast on its knees between her legs, ripping away her skirt. It gave a final yank, and flung the garment aside.

She saw its huge, erect penis.

No!

Jerking her knees high, she rolled. Her foot brushed the creature. Then her legs were clear and she kept rolling, kept flipping herself over. She didn't look back.

Facedown, she shoved herself off the carpet. She staggered forward. The stairway was far to her left. She ran for it, and heard a rumbling growl behind her.

Claws pierced her shoulders. Weight pressed down, collapsing her legs. She fell. The floor hammered her knees and palms. With the beast on her back, she crawled closer to the stairs.

It reached under her. It gripped her breasts. Pulled. Her hands left the carpet. She was squeezed against its slick chest, lifted off her knees. Its teeth caught the side of her neck as if to hold her still. She felt its penis between her legs, shoving her higher as it carried her toward the stairs.

Kicking and squirming, Tyler clutched the creature's hands and tried to tear them away from her breasts. They squeezed more tightly. The claws dug in, piercing her skin.

The beast slammed her down against the stairs. The edges of the risers pounded her body. She felt the hands go away from her breasts. Claws scraped along her ribs and sides. They dug into her hips. The shaft began to slide backwards.

Tyler clamped her legs shut. She couldn't stop it, but the beast licked her neck and pushed forward again as if it liked the feel of her hugging thighs. Twisting, she darted a hand down between her body and the stairs. She gagged as she clutched the slimy flesh. Gripping it with all her strength, she snapped her hand sideways. It didn't break, or even bend. It moved forward and back, using her hand, while the panting beast lapped her neck.

She tugged. Her hand flew off the slick penis and struck one of the risers.

The beast clutched her thighs, pulled, lifted. Tyler's knees left the stairs. Clinging to the plank at her shoulders, she bucked and thrashed. 'No!' she shrieked.

Her right hand let go of the stair.

She slapped it down between her legs.

The beast thrust. Pounded the back of her hand with such force that her forehead bumped the edge of the higher step.

The penis didn't go away. It rubbed over her knuckles, moved down to her fingers, tried to nudge between them. Tyler shoved her hand lower.

The beast made a low, gurgling growl, its breath hot against her neck.

Then it bit.

Tyler whimpered as teeth sank into the back of her hand, tore the skin away, nibbled the raw wound, bit deeper. Her hand was on fire, but she kept it tight against her body.

Her mind was numb.

It can't have teeth. Not *there*!

But it did.

They burrowed into her hand and ripped like the teeth of a mad rat trying to eat its way through.

My God.

Oh my God.

The growls of the beast sounded almost like laughter as it chewed her hand.

It's enjoying this.

If it wanted, it could knock my hand out of the way. It doesn't have to do this.

Tyler heard blood pattering one of the steps.

She wished her hand would go numb. It seemed to grow more tender, instead. The teeth felt like white-hot needles as they nipped and tore. Her whole arm burned and trembled.

The teeth went away.

The growls of the beast no longer sounded amused. Suddenly, it roared. Claws stabbed her thighs as it jerked her backwards. It rammed. Tyler's hand exploded with pain. She shrieked as two of her fingers snapped.

A thunderous blast pounded her ears.

The claws jumped, raked her thighs, released her.

She fell sprawling onto the stairs.

Another explosion. She pushed herself up. Stared at her right hand. The back of it was bloody pulp. The two broken fingers had already begun to swell. Weeping, she turned herself over and saw Captain Frank standing above the beast.

It lay on its back, writhing. It had a hole through one side of its head, another through its chest. Tyler's eyes moved down to its huge penis. Sheathed with blood. Her blood. Shreds of skin clung to the blunt end. The teeth parted, snapped shut.

Captain Frank fired into its head until his gun was empty. He gave Tyler a crooked, slightly drunken smile.

'Didn't I tell you?' he asked. He winked at her. He fiddled with his Luger. Its magazine dropped to the carpet. From the pocket of his baggy Bermuda shorts he took a full magazine. He slid it up the handle, and pulled at a mechanism on top of the pistol. 'Didn't I tell you I'd lay it low?' he asked, and started shooting again.

Tyler watched the dead beast jerk as bullets punched through it. Then she shut her eyes.

As the firing went on, she felt the stairway tremble under her.

'Ahoy there!' Captain Frank yelled.

The shooting stopped.

Tyler opened her eyes. Abe's face, upside down, was close above her. 'My God,' he said.

He stepped down the stairs and sat beside Tyler. She turned, and raised her arms to him.

30

Tyler held him fiercely. He stroked the back of her head. 'It's okay, it's all over,' he whispered. 'Are you hurt badly?'

'Just ... my hand.'

Abe looked at it, pain in his eyes. 'Jesus,' he muttered. He started to take off his shirt.

'I blasted it to smithereens,' said Captain Frank. He sounded gleeful.

'Is Jack all right?' Tyler asked, as Abe began to wrap the shirt around her torn, broken hand.

'Jack's fine. We took care of business. Where's Nora?' he asked.

'I don't know. Outside, I guess.'

'That Hardy fella plugged Janice,' Captain Frank said. 'We left them back at the other house, and Nora ran off to get help.'

'Hardy *shot* her?'

'Took her for the beast.'

'Did he get her bad?'

'I guess she lived through that, but we heard some shots back there. This creature must've popped in on them before it come for us. Gave me a nasty wallop, but I'm okay. Come to my senses in time to blast it up.'

Abe finished wrapping Tyler's hand. 'Let's get out of this place. Get you to a hospital.' Gently, he pulled the tattered front of the sweater across her breasts.

She groaned as she sat up straight.

Captain Frank picked up the remains of her skirt. He looked away as he handed the garment to Abe.

Abe helped her stand. He wrapped the skirt around her. Captain Frank provided his belt to hold it up, then searched for her sandals. He found one half hidden under the first stair, the other near the head of the beast. Abe held her steady while she stepped into them.

The old man picked up the revolver he had let Tyler borrow, shoved it into a front pocket of his Bermudas, and slid his Luger into the other pocket. 'Guess we're all set,' he said.

He started up the stairs. Abe put an arm around Tyler's back, and together they climbed out of the cellar.

They entered the kitchen of the Kutch house. They walked down a narrow, blue-lighted corridor. A group of people was standing in the foyer. Jack had his gun aimed at a fat woman with a bandaged face who looked a lot like Maggie Kutch. A thin, pale woman in a nightgown stood with her back to the door. She held a baby to her chest.

Jack frowned. 'Holy shit,' he said. 'What are *you* doing here? Tyler? What happened?'

'They ran into another beast,' Abe said.

'Holy shit.'

'I laid it low,' said Captain Frank. 'Blew it to kingdom come, matey.'

'Where's Nora?'

'She's okay,' Tyler said. 'I think.'

'Where's that girl?' Abe asked. 'The one who tried to shoot us?'

'She's my daughter, Sandy,' said the woman with the baby.

'We looked for her.' Jack shrugged. 'Don't know where she went.'

'Okay. Well, let's get out of here.'

'The door's still locked,' Jack said.

'Let's shoot the lock.'

'I know where the key is,' said the woman with the baby. 'I'll get it. It'll only take a second.'

'Okay,' Abe said.

She held out the baby to Jack. 'Would you hold him? I'll be right back.'

'Sure.'

'He's Jud. Judgement Rucker Hayes.' Her voice trembled slightly as she spoke the name.

Jack took the baby and smiled down at it.

The woman started up the stairs.

'The key's up there?' Abe asked. He sounded worried.

'No sweat,' Jack said. 'Maggie's out cold. She'll be lucky if she makes it.'

'Okay. But don't go close to her.'

The woman hurried up the stairs. At the top, she turned left and disappeared down the corridor.

'We'll be out of here in a minute,' Abe said, and patted Tyler's back.

The baby in Jack's arms made gurgling sounds.

'He's a cute little fellow, isn't he?' Jack said.

Smiling, the baby reached up and clenched his cheek. 'You're a toughie,' he said, and tickled Jud's belly.

The mother appeared at the head of the stairs.

'Get the key?' Abe asked.

She nodded. She started down.

The front of her nightgown was dark and matted to her breasts. Her face was spattered and dripping.

'My God,' Abe muttered. He rushed up the stairs. Her arm stretched down to him. From her fingers dangled a thin chain.

'The key,' she said.

'What happened? Are you hurt?'

'No. I'm just fine. Just fine. She ... Maggie ... she murdered Jud. Jud. My ... the father of my child.'

Abe stepped onto the stair beside her. He put an arm around her back.

'I used the knife.'

He led her down.

'Maggie used a knife on Jud, and I used a knife on her.'

'It's all right,' Abe said.

'It felt right.'

'Maggie came to and attacked you when you went to get the key.'

'No. No, she...'

'That's the story.'

'Oh.'

Abe unlocked the front door and opened it slowly. 'We're coming out,' he called to the policewoman on the lawn. 'It's all over.'

The woman holstered her weapon.

Tyler followed Abe onto the porch, and took a deep breath of the night air. The ocean smelled good. The moon was high.

31

Sandy, huddled in the darkness of the storage area beneath the staircase, waited.

Hugging her knees to her breasts, she had listened to the gunshots and wanted to help. But she had already tried helping: the two men with the guns were too smart, too quick. And so she stayed hidden.

There were more gunshots.

Feet racing down the stairs, pounding down them so hard that dry flecks sprinkled her shoulder.

Then more footsteps making the planks squeak and groan over her head.

Then the voice of her mother calling out to her: Sandy, where are you? Please. Are you here? I still love you, honey. Everything will be all right, now.

She didn't move. She hardly dared to breath. Someone walked very close to the staircase panel but didn't open it — probably didn't realize it could be opened.

Soon afterwards, she heard other voices. She couldn't make out the words. Someone went upstairs. Someone else went part way up.

Then everyone was gone.

Still Sandy waited. She wondered what had happened:

who had been shot and who survived? The thoughts made her feel sick.

Wick was probably dead. He was a creep, anyway. And Maggie and Agnes wouldn't be any great loss, either. But Seth and Jason and little Rune – if they'd been killed... She sniffled quietly in the darkness as tears trickled down her cheeks.

Later, more people came into the house. Sandy stretched out on her back, listening and waiting. The people stayed and stayed. She thought they might never go away. She was very tired, but her mind swirled, unsettling thoughts keeping her tense and awake.

What if they found her? No, they won't.

What had happened to Seth and Jason and Rune?

What would become of her? She was only fourteen. Wick was probably dead. Maggie had shot that cop and murdered Jud last year with Mom as a witness, so even if she had been taken alive she would never come back.

Agnes might come back. If they couldn't pin anything on her. If they didn't send her to the loony bin. Agnes was slow in the head, but not crazy so they might let her go. She would inherit the house – and Beast House.

Yes.

If Agnes came back, it wouldn't be so bad. Sandy could run things herself. She could start up the tours again.

And Agnes knew about babies. She'd helped in Mom's delivery.

She'll help me.

Sandy slid her hands over her belly. The turmoil in her mind subsided.

The voices outside her hiding place went on. Footsteps moved up and down the stairs.

She wondered, for a while, what name she should give the child? Seth? Jason? She didn't know which was the father. Besides, those were old-fashioned names. Nerdy. Maybe Rich or Clint or ...

Then she fell asleep.

Epilogue

Tyler twisted her finger free of the baby's tight grip, and knocked on the cottage door.

'Who is it?'

'Me,' she said.

'Just a sec, hon. I ain't decent.'

'When has that ever stopped you?'

A moment later, Nora opened the door. She wore a yellow bikini that looked brand new and covered very little.

'You aren't losing any time,' Tyler said.

'I spotted Jack down at the dock. He didn't see me. I'm gonna surprise him. Hand over the kid.'

Laughing, Tyler held out the baby. He flung out his arms and legs as if afraid of being dropped, and grabbed a strap of Nora's bikini. Wrapping her arms around him, she held him close. 'I think I'd like to keep you, Scotty.'

'Get your own. I'm sure Jack would accommodate you.'

'I'm sure he would.' She sat on a side of the king-sized bed. 'So, how's life in the boondocks?'

'Couldn't be better. How's life in the urban sprawl?'

'It's getting to me. I spent the whole year thinking

365

about this place. I guess it sort of grew on me. So did Jack.'

'He must've. You haven't unpacked yet.'

'I don't plan to stay.'

'But...'

'I'm gonna cajole Jack into letting me stay with him. Smart, huh? You can rent out this room to a paying customer. I saw the no vacancy sign out front.'

'He's got an A-frame just down the...'

'I know, I know. I haven't been exactly out of touch with him.' She flopped backwards across the bed and hoisted Scotty high. He gasped and started to cry. She lowered him quickly. 'Oh shit, now I did it.' Sitting up, she handed him back to Tyler.

He wrapped an arm around her neck and held on tight. 'Did big bad Nora scare you?'

'That's it, turn the kid against me. If it wasn't for me, he wouldn't be here. If I hadn't flipped the bird at that jerk on the highway...'

'That's right. Say thank you, Scotty.'

Scotty sobbed.

'Which reminds me,' Nora said. 'Guess where I spent last night? The Welcome Inn. They were full up, just like you guys, but Janice let me stay in her parents' room.'

'How is she doing?'

'You mean you don't know?'

'Well, I've seen her on television a few times and I know the book has been on the bestseller list for the past six weeks.'

'She got – good Christ – over a million for the

paperback rights. The film's all set to go into production in about two weeks. They'll be shooting on location.'

'But how's she doing?'

The brightness left Nora's face. 'She woke me up last night, screaming. A nightmare. We stayed up till morning, talking. She has these nightmares but they used to be every night and now they're not so frequent. She said it helped, writing the book – got a lot of it out of her system. It also helped because she got involved with this guy, Steve Saunders. Hardy's agent sent him out to help her with the thing. He ghosted it for her, and then did the screenplay. I guess the two are thick as thieves, but he's back in LA till the shooting starts. I talked her into phoning him at about seven this morning, and that cheered her up. I guess she's doing okay.' Nora's smile returned. 'Hey, we went over to the Last Chance after dinner last night. Good old Captain Frank was in rare form. He's one hell of a local celebrity.'

'Bet he loves it.'

'The man's in his glory. You should've heard him. "Aye, I laid the beast low, mateys." Everybody in the place buying him drinks. He said to give you his regards, and I'm supposed to tell you that you're welcome to keep his belt.'

'I've been meaning to send it back.'

'You can save your postage.' She pushed herself off the bed. 'Well, kiddo, I'd love to stay here and chat all afternoon, but I have this pressing engagement. You know how it is.'

'I know.'

Nora stepped past her and opened the door.

'Wait,' Tyler said. 'Did you take the tour?'

'You've got to be kidding. For one thing, the line was about half a mile long. And they've raised the ticket price to twelve fifty. Must be making a mint.'

'Who?'

Nora shrugged. 'Kutch's daughter owns the place. I don't know who's guiding the tours. I caught a look at her. Some kid, can't be older than fourteen or fifteen.'

'The place should've been closed down.'

'Shit, it should've been burnt to the ground. But at least it hasn't got Dan anymore. I checked with somebody coming out, and he's not part of the Ziegler exhibit. I guess they haven't bothered to have him replaced.'

'I'm glad.'

'Hey, I almost forgot your book.' She stepped over to her open suitcase. From under the gown on top, she pulled out a book with the familiar dust jacket: *The Horror at Malcasa Point* by Janice Crogan. The cover showed a crude, childish sketch of a beast, pencil scratches obliterating its anatomy from hips to knees. 'Have you already got a copy?'

Tyler nodded.

'Well, I bet yours isn't autographed. Let me make sure this isn't Jack's.' She opened the book. 'Yep, this is the one.'

Tyler sat on the bed, rested Scotty on her lap, and accepted the book.

'See you later,' Nora said.

'The cocktail lounge at six,' Tyler reminded her.

'Right. We'll be there.'

Then Nora left.

Tyler turned to the title page. In blue ink just below

the author's name was scrawled: To my good friend, Tyler and to Abe who saved my life – my thanks and best wishes. The things that go bump in the night are dead. Long live us. Love, Janice Crogan, August 3, 1980.

Island

Richard Laymon

'This author knows how to sock it to the reader'
The Times

When eight people go on a cruise in the Bahamas, they plan to swim, sunbathe and relax. Getting ship-wrecked is definitely not in the script. But after the yacht blows up they're stranded on a deserted island. Luckily for them, their beach camp location has fresh water and fire wood, and there's enough food to last them out.

Just one problem remains as they wait to be rescued – they are not alone. In the jungle behind the beach there's a maniac on the loose with murder in his heart. And he's plotting to kill them all, one by one . . .

'A brilliant writer' *Sunday Express*

'In Laymon's books, blood doesn't so much drip, drip as explode, splatter and coagulate' *Independent*

'One of the best, and most underrated, writers working in the genre today' *Cemetery Dance*

0 7472 5099 5

headline

Among the Missing

Richard Laymon

At 2:32 a.m. a Jaguar roars along a lonely road high in the California mountains. Behind the wheel sits the beautiful wife of Professor Grant Parkington. In spite of the night's chill, she wears only a skimpy night-gown. She has left Grant behind. She's after a different kind of man – someone as wild, daring and passionate as herself.

The man she wants is waiting for her near the road. Mrs Parkington stops for him. 'Where to?' she says. He suggests the Bend, where the Silver River widens and there's a soft, sandy beach. With the stars overhead and moonlight on the water, it's an ideal place for love.

But no love will take place there tonight. In the morning a naked body will be found – a body missing more than its clothes . . .

'If you've missed Laymon you've missed a treat' Stephen King

'No one writes like Laymon and you're going to have a good time with anything he writes' Dean Koontz

'A brilliant writer' *Sunday Express*

0 7472 6072 9

headline

The Midnight Tour

Richard Laymon

'The Beast House – legendary site of ghastly murder! See with your own eyes where the bloody butchery took place!'

The sales pitch hasn't changed much over the years – except now you can listen to it on earphones. But the audio tour of the house only gives a sanitized version of the horrific events that made the Beast House infamous. If you want the full story, you'll have to take the Midnight Tour. Saturday nights only. Limited to thirteen courageous tourists. It begins on the stroke of midnight.

You'll be lucky to get out alive . . .

'If you've missed Laymon, you've missed a treat' Stephen King

'No one writes like Laymon and you're going to have a good time with anything he writes' Dean Koontz

'In Laymon's books, blood doesn't so much drip drip as explode, splatter and coagulate' *Independent*

'A gut-crunching writer' *Time Out*

0 7472 5827 9

headline

Dreadful Tales

Richard Laymon

On a hot summer night in West LA, Shane Malone sits sweltering in front of the computer, thinking how easy it should be to write a contribution for an anthology; an anthology in which every chilling tale must end in the death of a twenty-two-year-old woman in her apartment.

Ideas swirl, but it has to be a grabber – Shane doesn't want to look like a slouch. And the deafening music blaring from next door is not helping. Shane furiously bangs on the neighbour's door, ready to let rip. But Francine just happens to be a twenty-two-year-old woman who will not be argued with . . . and Shane is about to find out that life really can imitate art.

So begins the first tale in this terrifying collection of short stories – a delicious cornucopia of homicidal maniacs, vampires and lust-crazed teenagers – that showcase the macabre genius of Richard Laymon, 'one of the best writers working in the genre today'– *Cemetery Dance*.

'A brilliant writer' *Sunday Express*

'Laymon offers unexpected, well-rounded characters blown about in a narrative that moves like the wind' *Publishers Weekly*

0 7472 6463 5

headline

Now you can buy any of these other bestselling
Feature titles from your bookshop or
direct from the publisher.

FREE P&P AND UK DELIVERY
(Overseas and Ireland £3.50 per book)